BY ORDER OF THE PRESIDENT

BY ORDER OF THE PRESIDENT

MICHAEL KILIAN

ST. MARTIN'S PRESS • NEW YORK

I should like to emphasize that this is a novel and that
the characters, except where stated, are fictional and
created to serve the purposes of the story. Certainly
nothing in here is intended as a reflection on anyone in
the United States Government, past or present, or any
government.

Design by Janet Tingey

Library of Congress Cataloging-in-Publication Data

Kilian, Michael, 1939-
By order of the president.

I. Title.
PS3561.I368B9   1986   813'.54   86-13804
ISBN 0-312-11116-9

First Edition

10 9 8 7 6 5 4 3 2 1

For Annie,
for Darla,
and for David

All that we see or seem
Is but a dream within a dream.

—EDGAR ALLAN POE

ACKNOWLEDGMENTS

Television is a major theme of this book. I am very grateful to Jim Michael of NBC News in Washington and my very good friend David Elliott, editor of the "Today Show," for augmenting my family and professional experience in television with their excellent tutorials on modern-day television technology and technique.

I am also very grateful for the help and advice I received from some other valued friends—James O. Jackson, Moscow bureau chief for *Time* magazine; Ray Coffey and George de Lama, veteran correspondents for the *Chicago Tribune*; Col. Robert Brown, publisher of *Soldier of Fortune* magazine; and Tex Harris of the U.S. State Department. My thanks go also to Nigel Sheinwald and Andrew Burns of the British Embassy.

Tom Dunne and Pamela Hoenig are editors without peer and I'm extremely glad for their superior skills and friendship. Margaret Schwarzer, also of St. Martin's, was a wonderful help too. The same is very true of a New York literary gentleman named Dominick Abel.

I am indebted to my wife, Pamela, and sons, Eric and Colin, as only they can know.

Acknowledgments

1

Moving carefully in the narrow confines of the tower's pitch-dark crawl space, Manuel Lopez Angel Huerta slid the M-16 rifle from its sheepskin case and set it gently on the metal floor beside him.

He had been two nights and a long day in this cold, painful place, with only a penlight for illumination. This second day would be a much shorter wait. He had eaten the last of his food and stowed the remnant garbage in the same self-sealing plastic bag that held the human waste he had produced in his confinement. His only sustenance now would be the cocoa beans he methodically chewed. They and the drive of his hatred would suffice, would warm him, clear his eyes, steady his fingers. Hatred and vengeance, debt and honor, these alone drove him now.

Hatred was his only remaining possession. His house had been burned; his wife and three children had been found in a row of bodies lying alongside the ditch in which they had been shot. It had been only a few months before. Huerta had not expected an opportunity for revenge to come so soon, nor that it would come in this country, but it was welcome.

He had hidden the money they had given him here on the battlefield, with some papers, but he had no illusions that he would live to recover it. He had no wish to. He wondered if they had realized this when they gave it to him; if they had followed him to see where he had put it. But it did not matter. He had no survivors to whom he could leave anything. The cause he served would receive from him a gift much greater than money.

Inching along on his back, he shifted himself until he was under the removable plate that led to the tower platform above. He had jammed it closed with a wedge when he heard the men begin their careful examination of the tall structure, and they had left satisfied, without disturbing him.

Only one of them now remained, and he seemed relaxed. Huerta heard only an occasional shifting of feet above him.

Slowly, slowly, he removed the wedge. A push now and the plate would fly open and he could rise rifle-first.

But not yet.

He must wait for the band music. The second playing of the song they had made him listen to over and over. "Hail to the Chief."

It would be an hour or more. He would pray. He had abandoned the church long ago, but in recent weeks had returned to its road. In a whisper, he would speak now, to God, to Jesus, to the Holy Virgin, to all the saints he could remember. He would thank them for this, for his manhood, for his death to come. Fifteen of his relatives and friends had been killed, most of them dumped like rubbish. Manuel would soon join them, but he would die more a man than anyone in his country.

He slipped another bean between his teeth, the acrid juice sliding into his throat as he mashed it. He stroked the stock of the rifle and pressed the cold barrel against his cheek. He closed his eyes, and waited patiently for the music.

The presidential motorcade, eleven vehicles shepherded by three marine helicopters, hastened along U.S. Route 15 toward Gettysburg at well above the speed limit, splashing with fits of spray through the flat highway puddles left by a now dissipating November storm. The first vehicle was a Maryland state police car. After that came the first of the Secret Service cars, carrying five agents, four of them armed with Uzi submachine guns. The three identical armored Lincoln limousines in which the presidential party rode were next, followed by the Secret Service communications station wagon, which contained among other things the air force colonel who carried the "football," a briefcase full of the computer-coded missile-launching plans the president needed to fight a nuclear war. In its rear-facing seat, another Secret Service agent with an Uzi sat scanning the moist gray skies through an open back window.

Immediately behind were the two cars carrying the press pool. Then came the "war wagon," a black recreational vehicle converted for use as a heavy weapons carrier, its ordnance including machine guns, gas grenades, shoulder-fired rockets, and even a small anti-aircraft missile launcher. It had been a regular component of presidential motorcades ever since the suicide car bomb attacks against American embassies and other installations back in the Reagan administration. Following that were another Secret Service sedan, and, at the end of the motorcade, an additional state police car.

President Henry Hampton rode in the middle Lincoln with Irving Ambrose, his White House chief of staff, and his driver, Peter Schlessler. Albert Berger, the head of the Secret Service Presidential Protection Division, better known as the White House detail, was supposed to accompany him as well. But, as often occurred, Hampton had dismissed him because he wanted to talk with Ambrose about confidential political matters.

Schlessler had been Hampton's driver and aide when the president had been governor of Colorado. When the Secret Service had insisted that the presidential limousine be driven by an actual Secret Service man, Hampton had simply sent Schlessler through a Secret Service training course and then had him accredited as an agent.

He was a good driver, Schlessler. He'd been a good scout car and jeep driver in Vietnam, but tended to oversteer the heavy limousine in rainy weather and was continually sideslipping on the sharper curves. Hampton, busy with his speech, paid no mind. Had he used a helicopter to make this trip, as all of his recent predecessors would have done, he would have been at his destination by now. But he intensely disliked those noisy, precarious machines. He was fond of saying it was because helicopters were designed to want to fall, while fixed-wing aircraft wanted to fly, even with engines off, but some in the press more accurately attributed his phobia to his experiences as an infantry captain in the Vietnam war.

In any case, the Gettysburg battlefield was just seventy-five miles from the White House. After his speech, Hampton was going no farther than Camp David, a scant twenty miles to the south. It was not pleasant flying weather in any event, the lowering clouds and drizzle interspersed with passing thunderstorms and only an occasional vague glimpse of sunlight to the west.

"Did you know that there were three drafts of the Gettysburg Address?" Hampton asked Ambrose. "No mention of God in the first or second. We didn't get 'this nation, under God' until the final one."

Hampton was perusing a small notebook he had taken from the open black leather briefcase on the seat beside him. He was an inordinately Anglo-Saxon-looking man, his long-jawed face as ruddy as a drunkard's, his eyes the sea blue-gray of the Vikings who had raped and pillaged his Briton ancestors a millennium before. He wore his sandy gray hair long enough to comb over his ears, which were unusually large, but had it trimmed carefully every few days. He was a fastidiously elegant man, wearing sometimes as many as four different shirts in a day, having the dark, pin-striped suits he favored meticulously tailored to fit his tall, long-boned frame perfectly, his long wrists covered by suit jacket and shirt cuffs reaching to just the proper place. The press marveled at how well his Kevlar bulletproof vest fitted under his suit jacket. But as only a very few knew, he refused to wear even the thinnest such protective garment. None of his aides had ever seen him with his tie loosened, and certainly not with his shoes off, except in a long-ago campaign television commercial in which he was filmed wading in a cold Colorado stream.

"I thought Lincoln just scribbled the whole thing on the back of an envelope," Ambrose said.

"Lincoln never scribbled anything," said Hampton. "He never put a word to paper he hadn't considered carefully."

"If you can't believe the envelope story, what can you believe about him?"

"You can believe he was the smartest and most effective president in the history of the United States. He didn't just preserve the Union; he created it. Before the Civil War, you know, people used to say, 'The United States are.' After the war, it was 'The United States is.' Lincoln did that. He may have suspended habeus corpus and jailed his political enemies to do it, but it was the greatest accomplishment in the history of the presidency. I really envy him."

Ambrose fell silent. Though history was Hampton's mania, Ambrose knew relatively little about it, having studied and remembered only that which bolstered his prejudices. He sincerely believed the nation would have been better served if Lincoln had left well enough alone. The South, Ambrose felt, would have freed the slaves in its own time—in its own way.

He didn't particularly like the nickname Bushy, which was owed to the luxuriant thickness of his now gray, close-cropped hair, but he preferred it to Irving, which he had all his life feared made him sound Jewish. Ambrose came from a working-class Colorado family whose lowest esteem had always been reserved for Jews, Mexicans, Chinese, blacks, Italians, and Indians. A short man who had sought to compensate for his size with an inordinate muscle development that only emphasized his small stature, he had been Hampton's battalion commander in Vietnam. Retiring only a colonel, though he was a West Point man, Ambrose had taken a job managing an amusement park outside Denver until a newly elected Governor Hampton offered him a job on his staff. He had quickly risen to the top and stayed there. Hampton called him and Schlessler the most loyal subordinates he had. "If you can trust a man in combat," Hampton liked to say, "you can trust him the rest of your life."

The press tended to ignore Ambrose's military record and concentrate on the amusement park. The White House had quickly become known as the "fun house," and Ambrose's unfocused briefings as "merry-go-rounds" or "thrill rides." Hampton was pleased with this. He had been fearful the media would instead have dwelled upon the many former military men around him. A *Time* magazine writer had floated the term "Hampton's khaki mafia," but no one had picked up on it. Ambrose the Ferris-wheel operator made for better jokes.

The visual distortion of the thick, bulletproof glass of the side window made Ambrose slightly ill. He shifted his gaze to look straight out the less disconcerting windshield, staring at the twirling red Mars lights atop the roofs of the security cars preceding them. Ambrose had been in the White House nearly two years, but those bright bursts of heralding color still thrilled him with a sense of his own power, a sense never before satisfactorily provided, even by the experience of command in Vietnam.

Yet there were limits to this power that no bystander, or even White House correspondent, could ever know. President Hampton was a man who acted on sudden whim, secret fears, and private, sometimes bizarre perceptions. Ambrose, who issued orders from his big White House office dozens of times a day, never did so without the nagging apprehension that he might be abruptly countermanded.

Ambrose had a serious problem now. An army friend he had proposed as ambassador to Ireland, a brigadier general with an Irish name and father, was being opposed by the vice president's allies in the Senate, including the chairman of the Foreign Relations Committee. There were some painfully effective measures Ambrose could take to shove these people out of his way, but he was unsure of the president's response.

"Damn!" said Hampton, staring hard at the last page of his speech. "Sometimes I think Barnes's brain is solid brick. This won't do."

"What's wrong?" asked Ambrose. He had hired speechwriter Barnes from a conservative newspaper in Indiana.

"We have to have something from the Gettysburg Address. But this is so damned wrong: 'That government of the people, by the people, for the people, shall not perish from the earth.' What the hell does that have to do with the V.A. bill?"

Ambrose reached for the radio telephone at his right elbow. "I'll have him fix that right up."

"No," said Hampton. "I'll take care of it. I think I have a better line." He studied his notebook. "Here we go. 'The brave men, living and dead, who struggled here.' The brave men, living and dead. Perfect." He scratched the offending phrase from the speech with a gold pencil and scrawled in the new-found replacement.

"Perfect," Ambrose said. He wiped his forehead with his handkerchief. He would wait to bring up the Irish ambassadorial appointment until they were in the more relaxed atmosphere and circumstance of Camp David.

It was November 19, the anniversary of Lincoln's Gettysburg Address. Hampton was going to give his own speech in exactly the same place—at the edge of the National Cemetery just behind what had been the Union lines in the great battle, near the point where Pickett's charge, and the Confederate cause, had reached and faltered. As Lincoln's had not immediately, Hampton's speech would make news. He would be signing a bill to make the Veterans Administration a full-fledged cabinet department. Its sponsor was a member of the liberal opposition who was running for president in the next election and wanted to soften his antimilitary image. The president would in return receive a freer hand in his conduct of the expanding war in Central America.

Hampton, known as "the great compromisor" as Reagan had been called "the great communicator," had triumphed again. It had become a cliché response among the White House press corps to seize upon his every act and pronouncement as further evidence of his moderation and flexibility.

He often played on Civil War themes. A graduate of the University of Virginia and Harvard Law, he had grown up in rural, if wealthy, Loudon County, Virginia. His father was a Virginian, but his mother represented seven generations of Pennsylvanians. In this Gettysburg speech, he would name those of his ancestors who had fallen on both sides. He had recently done the same thing in a speech at the Antietam Battlefield in Maryland, standing on the old stone bridge where General Burnside had ordered one of them forward to die.

The president returned his speech to its protective plastic case, put that in his briefcase, snapped it shut, and slid it toward Ambrose, who lifted it off the president's side of the leather seat and set it on the floor.

"We'll have some whiskey and a good movie tonight," Hampton said, leaning back and putting his hands behind his head, with a care to avoid creasing his suit coat. "Jerry Greene got us an advance copy of *Fragments*. They say it's the best movie ever made about Vietnam."

"The heroine's a slope," Ambrose said.

"We all had such heroines." The president looked to the distorted glass of the thick side window, then closed his eyes.

"Bushy," he said, finally, without opening his eyes. "I want you to withdraw the Donlon nomination."

"It's only ambassador to Ireland."

"Bushy. Half the committee chairmen in the House are Irish. They do not like Donlon. They think he's a flag-waving fool. They're afraid he'll get mixed up with the Sinn Fein on the Ulster thing. Our people on Senate Foreign Relations feel the same way."

"You mean the vice president's people."

"Irving. I want him pulled. I said it in the beginning. I've said it a thousand times since. I'll say it again. We'll get what we want. But we can't afford to put anything in the way. Donlon is in the way."

"Yes, Mr. President."

"I'm pleased to hear you say that, Colonel."

With that, Hampton touched upon Ambrose's most sensitive vulnerability. For all of his twenty-five years in the service, he had with desperate hope looked to retiring as a general officer, if only to make up for his having graduated from the Point next to last in his class. But they had passed him over too many times and shoved him into retirement with nothing more than the colonelcy that itself had been too long in coming. Now, Hampton, the secretary of defense, and Senator Andrew Rollins of Tennessee, the president's best friend in the Congress, were working discreetly to get Ambrose promoted to brigadier general in the reserves. It meant everything to him.

They were taking a very long time with this promotion. There were times when Ambrose despaired of getting it before Hampton's term expired.

As Hampton said, Ambrose would put nothing in the way.

The motorcade crossed the Pennsylvania line, speeding through a wide shaft of inadvertent sunlight. Far ahead, a Pennsylvania state police car roared from the shoulder onto the highway and quickly gathered speed. As the Maryland car pulled off, the Pennsylvania cruiser eased slowly back until it became an integral part of the motorcade. The president appeared now to be sleeping, or at least in deep and private thought. Ambrose folded his arms and yawned. At length they reached Highway 97, following it northwest toward Gettysburg under skies that had again turned to gloom. Soon, Day-Glo colored billboards began to appear, advertising some of the glut of commercial tourist attractions in the town. Ambrose revered the battlefield as passionately as Hampton did, and had no tolerance whatsoever for the glitz that had grown up around it.

In the limousine behind, C. D. Bragg, the president's young and ruthlessly effective chief political adviser, sat with Jerry Greene, White House communications director, going over the television campaign videotape footage they hoped to acquire at Gettysburg. The Marine Band would be there, and a costumed ceremonial unit of Union infantry. Greene, a genius at such work, had ordered three White House video units to the ceremonial grounds. In the front seat of their car, next to the driver, was Albert Berger, the head of the Secret Service's one-hundred-fifty-man Presidential Protection Division. As was always the case now when he was exiled from the president's car, he sat with a radio microphone in one hand and his unholstered .357 Magnum revolver in the other, his face a grim weaving of numberless anxieties.

In the first of the press pool cars, there was laughter, much of it coming from a bountiful, blond young woman named Bonnie Greer, White House correspondent for the nation's largest satellite news network. Her laughter, among other amiable responses, was provoked by the irreverent banter coming from the man seated beside her, a celebrated news magazine correspondent with whom she had slept on past campaign trips. When the ceremonies were concluded and the president safely within the secure confines of the Camp David compound, they planned to meet for dinner and renew the relationship. In the car with them was a middle-aged newspaper columnist who had once gotten very drunk at a campaign stop in Philadelphia with Bonnie Greer and kissed her in an elevator in the Barclay Hotel. He was secretly ecstatic to be assigned to the pool with her, and secretly devastated when it became obvious she had forgotten his name.

In the communications station wagon, the air force colonel with the "football" stared ahead as he always did, bored almost to the point of trance. If he had, as they said, the most important job in the American military, it was also the one with the least to do. Some liberal academic theoreticians had proposed that the key to the "football" and its computer codes be imbedded in the chests of the colonel and his colleagues so that the president would have to cut them open before waging nuclear war, and thus be reminded of the human price that would have to be paid. Thoughts of that, at least, kept the colonel awake.

In the rear-facing seat of the station wagon, the Secret Service agent with the Uzi cradled in his lap kept looking to the low hills in the west. He was from southwestern Wisconsin, and the distant blue ridges rising from the yellow-brown November meadows reminded him much of home. Having worked without break the last full three weeks of the congressional election campaign that had just ended, he, too, was tired. But he didn't need gory thoughts of chest incisions to stay alert. It was his sworn and sacred duty. He kept reminding himself of that. Still, the radio voice in his earpiece caught him by surprise. It was the agent in the lead car.

"Arrive, arrive," he said. "Arrive, arrive."

Before the president's limousine had pulled to a stop, Special Agent Berger was out of his own car and running to the president's door.

The ceremonies surpassed all the hopes and plans of young Greene, C. D. Bragg, and Bushy Ambrose, not to speak of the president. Though a misty haze remained in the air, the rain had ceased. The speaking platform had been carefully placed so that the cemetery grave markers appeared just over Hampton's shoulder. The array of television cameras before him included those from the big three networks, the largest cable and satellite networks, and two Philadelphia stations. Because of the looming and detracting presence of the huge battlefield observation tower, the best cutaway shot was a view of the battlefield that incorporated the president's profile. Color material abounded—the somber martial music, old flags, marching men in Union blue, barking cannons and billowing smoke, sad-eyed veterans old and young, small boys in souvenir foraging caps. The audience was made up of equal parts of townspeople, tourists, schoolchildren, and veterans groups. They cheered and applauded at every opportunity and joined with great enthusiasm when Hampton led them in a singing of the "Battle Hymn of the Republic." The middle-aged newspaper columnist, glad for material wherever it came from, spotted a black veteran with tears in his eyes among the spectators and exclaimed to a colleague that Hampton was at last making inroads with black voters. Bonnie Greer succumbed to tears. They came welling forth in a great flood at the very end, when a golden shaft of dying afternoon sunlight slanted through the lower limbs of the trees to crown the president's head. From his place near the parked limousines, Jerry Greene thought it almost enough to make him religious.

Then the glorious moment ended, shattered by the Marine Band's striking up "Hail to the Chief" once more. Shaking hands, Hampton followed Berger and his pushing agents back to the motorcade, pausing a few final steps from his limousine to wave to the crowd. Then, as Berger snapped open the door, President Hampton turned and spoke a few words to Ambrose.

The first two shots came in quick snaps, followed by a cacophonous, continuing blare of gunfire. Ambrose, frantic, looked right and left, his peripheral vision catching finally the bursts of gunfire from the observation tower. The president was being pushed into the limousine by Berger, who then stood up and took one or more splashing bullets in his back. Ambrose snatched up Berger's big revolver with its short, three-inch barrel, and pointlessly began to return fire. Many others were doing the same.

Ambrose had a more compelling duty, an all-consuming duty. He lunged, pulling Berger's body off the president, then heaved and shoved Hampton all the way inside the car. Clambering in after him, he slammed shut the heavy door with such surprising force it rattled. Schlessler, dutifully, was behind the wheel, looking more terrified than he had ever been in Vietnam.

"Get out of here!" Ambrose yelled. "Go, go, go!"

Schlessler jammed the limousine into drive and, with tires churning angrily through the dirt and gravel, spun onto the road. He hit the switch that simultaneously locked all four doors, and then the one that turned on the shrill, warbling siren. Within twenty seconds, he had the big car up to sixty and climbing.

In the communications station wagon parked near the speaking platform, the agent in the rear-facing seat had snapped awake from his reverie of the autumn colors of Mineral Point, Wisconsin. Half rising, he brought his Uzi up to bear, not at the tower, but toward the equestrian statue above the cemetery grave markers where he had seen two quick flashes of gunfire almost the instant the shooting had begun, gunfire aimed at the motorcade, at the president. Lacking a clear field of fire, the agent slammed down the station wagon's tailgate and stepped out on it, rising for a better view. Unfortunately, his foot slipped on the rain-damp surface. More unfortunately, his finger was on the Uzi's trigger. As he fell, an arc of bullets stuttered out of his weapon and whipped into the press section.

The CBS White House correspondent, keeping her wits about her enough to begin describing the macabre scene into a microphone, was standing too far to the right to be hit. The NBC reporter was in the line of fire, but he dropped to the ground at the first shots and so escaped a spinning round that would have caught him in the clavicle. Bonnie Greer, still standing, was struck in the breast and then the chin, the latter bullet carving an enormous mouth in her face and erupting from the back of her falling head in a fountain burst of blood. The newspaper columnist, standing just behind her, caught her flung body full in the chest, along with the second bullet to strike her. He died with her lying on top of him, her blood flowing over his face.

People were dropping, rising, running, screaming, falling. They ran in panicked little mobs, stumbling into one another and shrieking, hurling themselves on and away in all directions, their cries and wails sweeping back and forth as though blown by vicious and capricious winds. In all, eighteen people were struck by bullets, six of them dead. There was now gunfire from every quarter, as Secret Service men blazed away in an increasing concentration at the tower, a blizzard of sparks scattering from the struck metal, the human figure there surely dead but kept in a frantic, spastic dance hanging over the rail by the converging torrents of bullets. There were no more flashes from the statue. Finally, there was no more gunfire toward it.

One of the White House helicopters circled tightly, madly, over the clearing, the Secret Service man in the right-hand seat recording the savage, surreal ballet below with a videotape camera that was among his equipment. There was a gunport in the Plexiglas and he had an Uzi, but he was fearful of hitting people in the fleeing crowd. Besides, the sniper was more than dead. The streams of bullets had nearly cut his body in two.

In the president's limousine, Schlessler kept the accelerator to the floor. "Where?" he said. "Where do we go?"

"Anywhere!" Ambrose shouted. "Just get the hell out of here. Go south. Yes. South. Go back the way we came!"

The speedometer reached seventy-five, then eighty, then eighty-five. A helicopter roared over them, then slipped away to take up moving station in pace with them to their left. In the distance behind them, twin sets of tiny, twirling red lights popped onto the highway and began an accelerating approach. Schlessler kept snatching quick looks back at Ambrose.

"The president," he said. "How is the president?"

Ambrose looked down at the sandy-gray head he cradled so tightly against his lap.

"The president is fine," he said. "He's fine. It's OK. Everything's OK. Everything's going to be all right."

"Is he alive?"

"I said he's fine, damn it! He's hit. He's out. He caught it in the side of his neck. We've got all hell breaking loose, Pete!"

"Where do we go? Where's a hospital?"

The speedometer was pegged, functionally useless. The red lights behind them were closing rapidly. The helicopter pilot, talking into a microphone, was edging closer and closer to them. Schlessler turned on the security radio and it exploded in voices. Ambrose hugged the president's head.

"No hospital," he said. "We'll go to Camp David. Get us to Camp David. We don't know who did this, Pete! We don't know who we can trust! Camp David will be secure. Get there. Never mind anything else."

"It's twenty-five minutes to Camp David, even if I howl all the way!"

"Howl. Keep it to the floor. Keep going! We need friends, Pete. We need military." He lifted his hand from the president's head to pick up the radio telephone. "I'm going to call in marines from the chopper squadron at Bolling. I'm going to call in a battalion of the Eighty-second Airborne from Bragg. I'm going to call in the Special Function Force."

Unlike Ambrose, Schlessler was paying attention to the loud tangle of voices on the Secret Service radio.

"They want me to pull over!" he said. "They've got a paramedic for the president!"

"Fuck 'em, Pete! The fucking Secret Service let this happen! Keep going! Just get us to Camp David! Go!"

2

Vice President Laurence Davis Atherton lay on his bed in his underwear and expensive black Brooks Brothers socks, contending with a rare moment of complete inactivity. He let his mind wander where it would, from the volume of the steady rainfall outside his window to the girls he had dated here in New York—and taken to this hotel—during his years at Princeton. But his thoughts all came back to the White House again, and his wretched role as presidential front man and alter ego. According to the schedule, Henry Hampton was to meet with the Honduran ambassador that night, doubtless to discuss another turn in the war. Atherton, who knew ten times more about Central America than Hampton or anyone in his entourage, was relegated to addressing a Catholic political dinner at the Waldorf. That was one of Atherton's political advantages for Hampton: Atherton was Catholic. As a congressman, he had had a fairly liberal voting record on domestic issues, if not foreign affairs. The party had taken a thoroughgoing pasting in the fall congressional elections in the Northeast, and Atherton was being sent in to help repair the damage.

He looked at his watch. Even if they adhered strictly to the schedule, he wouldn't be home until at least one A.M. He kept the face of the gold Rolex before his eyes, following the resolute sweep of the second hand. He had an impulse to fly back to Washington that very moment.

He hadn't slept with his wife for three weeks. He'd not slept with any woman for five days. The following afternoon he was supposed to fly up to Cape Cod and defend the administration there, attempting to make the locals happier about Hampton's leases for off-shore oil drilling in Nantucket Sound. Atherton's unsuccessful campaign for the presidency had taken two years, three months. After becoming Henry Hampton's running mate, he had campaigned hard for their ticket for another four months. He might as well have been on a campaign ever since he took his oath of office as vice president. That fall, he'd performed at more than twenty-five fund-raisers on the East Coast alone.

He'd come to look forward to the funerals that were the other major function of his office. He could do with one now—one for a dead Italian. A few days in Rome would be a restorative for his nerves; a long afternoon spent pondering the Etruscan wall paintings in the Villa Albani, an evening with dry wine and the pollo alla Nerone at the Cecilia Metella.

But not that night. The welfare of the Republic, as construed by his party, came first.

He stretched out his long legs until the muscles were taut. The newspapers had called him the handsomest man ever to run for the presidency. He had small, soft, almost feminine features—the newspapers called them "Ivy League"—but a dark complexion, with dark hair and eyes and an incandescent smile. It was his greatest political attribute. In college, twenty years before, it had kept his bed warm with sweet young things. It still did. His wife had come to hate it.

Atherton had money, more money than all of Hampton's Coloradans put together. On his Italian-Mexican mother's side, his family was one of the oldest and richest in California. His WASP father, a San Francisco entrepreneur who was said to have invented the term "venture capitalist," had merely trebled the fortune, growing hugely wealthy on everything there was money to be made from in California—cotton farms, ranches, wineries, banking, shipping, and, most particularly, real estate.

His father had been deeply disappointed when Atherton chose to go east for college instead of to Stanford, and furiously angry when his son abandoned the family interests for a career in politics. He'd been won over only when Atherton eventually persuaded him that a family business that had become an international conglomerate needed one of its own in Congress.

Atherton was thinking of the presidency even then. It was something his father could never attain, something Atherton could achieve largely on his own. He'd made a good run for it. After he'd won the New York primary, the political writers began calling him the man to beat—for about a month. But the shrewd Hampton once again positioned himself in the exact center of the mainstream, playing the moderate against the backdrop of Atherton's "liberalism" and the fiery right-wing radicalism of the party's conservative champion, Senator Davis.

Atherton's primary victories and delegate strength had been enough to compel Hampton to enter into a complicated deal at the convention, but now he was free to dump him and was giving every indication he intended to do so. He'd told a number of political writers he was thinking of letting his party choose his ticket mate when he ran for reelection—leaving Atherton with the prospect of becoming a vice presidential has-been at the age of forty-three. Few vice presidents ever became president. None had who'd been dropped from the ticket after a single term.

He heard the muffled sound of a telephone ringing, and then loud voices. Soon they were quite near, inside the sitting room of his suite just beyond the door. His own telephone began to ring. He'd been scheduled for two hours' sleep. He looked again at his watch.

Aside from his wife, Sally, and the president of the United States, only three people were permitted to walk in on Vice President Laurence Atherton unannounced: Richard Shawcross, his chief of staff; Neil Howard, his longtime press secretary; and Mrs. Hildebrand, his chief secretary and dragon lady. It was Howard who entered, not speaking until he had closed the door against the din outside.

In public, he called his boss "Mr. Vice President." Alone, it was as it had been when Howard had gone to work for Atherton in his first term in Congress.

"Larry," he said, his voice subdued, his eyes stricken with more than his usual hangover. "There's been an assassination attempt on the president."

Atherton abruptly sat up, swinging his legs over the side of the bed. He rubbed his eyes. It was raining so hard outside, the windows were opaque with sheets of water. For the longest time, he said nothing.

"My God."

His voice was so quiet he could barely hear it himself. He stood up, feeling absurd in his underwear. To his amazement, his hands were shaking. He was trembling all over, and suddenly perspiring.

"Larry?"

"Is he all right?"

"That's not clear," Howard said. "Bushy Ambrose took him off in the limousine. To Camp David, not a hospital. Agent Berger's dead. There's no Secret Service with the president, except Schlessler. There were a lot of people hit."

"Camp David? Where did this happen? I thought the president was going to Gettysburg today."

"He did. He was hit just after his speech. It's not very far from there to Camp David."

"God." Atherton stared at the window. He clenched his fists to stop the trembling, and took a deep breath. "It's finally happened."

"Larry."

"What?"

"Larry, we have to get going. We have to get back. At once."

Atherton sighed, glancing down at his stocking feet, then over at his suit coat draped on the chair. There were five people who carried the plastic laminated "Gold Codes" card with the number sequences needed to authorize the Pentagon war room to launch a nuclear strike—the president, vice president, secretary of defense, deputy secretary of defense, and the chairman of the Joint Chiefs of Staff. Atherton had always worried about Hampton's. His own was in his wallet, just as though it were another credit card.

The "Gold Codes" card could only authorize an all-out nuclear assault. For anything more selective, the array of "Emergency War Orders" in the thick briefcase that constantly accompanied the president was needed.

There was a war on in Central America. There were some Americans fighting in it.

"Where's the colonel with the 'football'?" Atherton asked. "Who's in charge at the White House situation room?"

"That's not clear either. Larry, it's going to be a slow go to the airport with this weather. The police aren't in place. We can't use a chopper with this visibility."

Atherton stood thinking.

"Larry? Do you want a drink? You look like you need a drink."

Atherton was not much for alcohol, except for wine in the course of a meal, but Howard was very much correct.

"Yes, scotch. And be generous. Get someone in contact with the White House and the Joint Chiefs, if you can. See if you can contact Ambrose. And I'd like to talk to Mrs. Hampton."

"Yes, sir."

"Don't let Mrs. Hildebrand in here. Not until I'm dressed."

"Sure, Larry."

But when Howard returned with a bathroom glass brim full of Johnnie Walker Black, the vice president was still in his underwear, his eyes fixed on the now illuminated television screen where Tom Brokaw was talking about an unconfirmed Central American terrorist plot to kill the president.

Atherton took the glass. "What in hell went wrong with the Secret Service?"

"Beats me. Berger's the best. When he and the president were hit, the others must have gone bananas. There are a couple dozen people down."

On the screen, Brokaw began a recapitulation, starting with a report that Hampton apparently had not been injured. Atherton drank.

"Here I am in New York," he said.

"We've got to go, Larry. They're almost down to minimums, but there's sufficient visibility for a takeoff. We should be able to have wheels up in an hour. If you get going."

"Any word on who did this? This TV talk about Central Americans?"

"Nothing reliable. Not yet. The colonel with the 'football' is still at Gettysburg, incidentally."

Atherton drank again. On the screen, they were showing long-shot footage of the president being pushed toward his limousine by Special Agent Berger, whose own body then slipped from view.

Then came the scene of the crowd being cut down by the Secret Service man's errant burst of bullets. Atherton looked away, and then drained his glass in a single nauseating, burning, stiffening gulp.

The news came to Secret Service Director Walter Kreski from all directions all at once. He had been sitting quietly in his office in the imposing building at 18th and G streets, reading through field reports with his mind more on the Mahler on the FM radio than bureaucratic detail. As the books and chess sets indicated, Kreski was a very intellectual cop.

From habit, he had turned on his two-way radio monitor, following the dull blur of official conversation with that part of his mind not absorbed by his reading and the symphony. When it came alive with shouting voices he snapped around in his leather chair. Before he could quite determine what the sudden urgency was about, one and then the other of his telephones began to ring. Just as he picked up one, his deputy director burst through the door with all the violence of a surprise raid.

"Walt, we've had an action! Up at Gettysburg! The president's hit!"

Kreski, a tall man with a graying, reddish-blond beard, rose from his chair so fast it fell over. "Hit? How serious?"

"I don't know. Ambrose has him in the car. He's gone nuts. He's heading back toward Maryland."

Kreski stared at the radio monitor with a stupefaction arising from utter helplessness. Then he bolted toward it, snatching up the microphone.

"Berger's dead," said the deputy. "We've got a lot of casualties. A lot of civilians."

The director ordered everyone off the air, then asked for the agent nearest the presidential limousine. It was Hammond, one of his best.

"I'm in . . . I have to call it pursuit, sir. Mr. Ambrose and the president are proceeding to Camp David. We have two chase cars and a helicopter accompanying."

"Are you in contact with the president's car?"

"Affirmative. They're not talking much. Agent Schlessler responded only once."

Agent Schlessler. Kreski grimaced.

"What is the president's condition?"

"Apparently good, sir."

"Have you talked to him?"

"Negative. Only to Schlessler."

The telephones were clamorous. Kreski's office was filling up with people. His secretary was at his desk, holding one of the phones.

"It's the FBI director, Mr. Kreski."

He told Hammond to stand by. His deputy had turned on the television set.

"Walt, what have you got?" said the FBI man, Steven Copley, an old friend.

"President's hit. I guess it's minor. Bushy Ambrose is taking him to Camp David. I have many dead. I lost Berger."

"Any ID on the assailant?"

"Not yet. Male Hispanic."

"Right. I think we have a conspiracy, Walt. We took in two male

Hispanics in New York a few minutes ago. I was just going to call you. They were in a building overlooking the vice president's motorcade route. They had Mauser automatic rifles."

"What kind of Hispanics?"

"Honduran. Illegals."

"Bloody damn."

"It gets worse, Walt. There's a bombing in Chicago, and National Park Service police report another at the OAS building. Did you hear it?"

"Negative. Ambrose is calling in military," Kreski said, listening to Dan Rather on the television.

"I don't blame him."

"I'm not sure he knows what he's doing."

"It's a mess, Walt. You want some help up at Gettysburg?"

"Yes."

"I'll send an evidence team up by chopper. Walt?"

"Yes?"

"We just picked up three more Hispanics in Chicago. I'll get right back to you."

"Okay."

Kreski set down the phone, ignoring the other one and its shrill ringing. On the television screen, Bonnie Greer was dying, arms flung upward, body arched back.

"Bloody damn," he said.

"It was Special Agent Schultz who did that," Kreski's deputy said. "They have him in custody. He tried to shoot himself."

Kreski's secretary was holding the other phone.

"It's your wife, director."

"Tell her I'll call her later. Tell her I don't know any more than what's on television."

He looked to the screen. CBS's Bill Plante was doing a standup in front of the White House. Kreski studied the faces of his subordinates as they followed the television coverage. It was disquieting. There was something ghoulish and eager about their expressions. His deputy was profoundly serious, but rapt.

Kreski gripped the man's shoulder. "Get back to Hammond on the two-way. I want a minute-by-minute report."

"Yes, sir."

There were sirens outside the window on Pennsylvania Avenue. Why in hell were there so many sirens?

"The secretary of defense has put the military on Def Con Two," someone said.

Defense Condition Two. It meant scrambled B-52 bombers and open doors on Minuteman silos. Soldiers all over the globe would be issued live ammunition. There would be hard staring at the horizon. If the soldiers were nervous enough, some more people could be killed.

A red-haired girl from Kreski's press office came in. She glanced at the director, gave a quick, nervous smile, and then stared at the TV screen where an armed guard was pushing Bill Plante to the side.

"What the hell is that about?" Kreski asked.

"Not our guys," said someone. "He's one of the White House marines."

"The press have been ordered off the White House grounds and into the EOB," someone else said.

"Who the hell ordered that?" Kreski demanded.

The man shrugged.

Kreski looked at his secretary, who had been with him for eleven years. "Get me the White House. Whoever's in charge."

"Hammond says Ambrose has ordered the Special Function Force up to Camp David," said Kreski's deputy. "The man's lost his mind."

"I'd be a little panicky myself in his situation," Kreski said.

"He used to be a combat commander in Vietnam."

"He's behaving like one."

Kreski's secretary stuck her head back in the door. "They've closed the White House switchboard."

Kreski swore, to himself. "I'm going over there," he said.

"I'll call you a car."

"It's two blocks. I'll run."

It was raining again, hard enough to soak his head and shoulders by the time he reached 17th Street. Without slowing his stride, he crossed through the traffic, splashing into a deep puddle on the opposite side, startling pedestrians at the curb. There was a long official car pulling into the White House North Gate, two military jeeps behind it. The concrete barricades that had been emplaced after the terrorist bombings in the Reagan administration required a ninety degree turn executed from a complete stop.

Slowing to a walk at the pedestrian entrance, Kreski continued past the guardhouse window, presuming, as always, he would be recognized and admitted. But there was no welcoming buzz. The iron gate remained locked.

The white-shirted guard, a burly, dark-haired man with a bushy mustache whom Kreski knew well, shrugged abjectly and gestured to a marine sergeant standing next to him. The White House marines were supposed to be decorations, ceremonial symbols to add a little color to the presidential decor. Now they were running the place.

The sergeant stepped outside. "Sorry, sir. No access."

Kreski pulled out his security badge, feeling as ridiculous as he was angry. "Do you know who I am? What my job is around here?"

"Yes, sir. You're Director Kreski. Sorry, sir, no access. Only cabinet officers."

"You goddamned idiot! I'm the head of the Secret Service! The president's been shot!"

"Orders, sir."

"From whom?"

"My CO, Captain Tomlinson."

"Call him."

"Sir, I've no . . ."

"Call him before I have you arrested for obstruction of justice!"

The young sergeant stepped back into the guardhouse, letting the heavy, bulletproof glass door slide shut behind him, but he picked up the phone.

A reporter Kreski recognized, a white-haired man with his White House press credentials hanging uselessly from a chain around his neck, was leaning against the wrought-iron fence beneath an umbrella.

"I left my tape recorder in the press room," he said. "They won't let me go back for it."

"Go buy another," Kreski said. He turned away. Folding his arms, he stood staring hard at the front portico of the Executive Mansion.

It was easily ten minutes before a figure came running down the drive from the West Wing lobby. It was Dick Shawcross, the vice president's chief of staff.

"Now you know how it feels," said the reporter, when Kreski was finally admitted through the gate.

Kreski paused, then laughed, not a little bitterly.

"Who declared all this martial law?" he said to Shawcross as they headed up the drive.

"The president."

"In person?"

"Through Ambrose. *Colonel* Ambrose."

Shawcross had been Vice President Atherton's roommate at

Princeton and, later, his law partner. He had a neat, upper-class smile.

"The president's favorite colonel."

They hurried down the carpeted stairs to the White House situation room. It was crowded with high-ranking aides and military brass, though only a few cabinet officers were present; Kreski went to the attorney general first.

"Steve Copley's arresting Hispanics, Hondurans, it looks like," Kreski said. "There was a bombing at the OAS Building?"

The attorney general frowned. "That's right. A bomb blew up a trash basket. We just had one at the Rayburn Building that took out six cars."

"It's still an active situation then?"

Attorney General Allen Wilson was a bald-headed man, with close-cropped white hair at the sides, but still quite youngish-looking. He had been a million-dollar-a-year bond lawyer on Wall Street. He looked very vague and uncertain.

"I don't know," he said.

Treasury Secretary Robert Heinke grasped Kreski's arm. "What do you have, Walt?"

"Damned little. Ambrose and the president are heading for Camp David. By car."

The secretary nodded, encouraging Kreski to go on. The commerce secretary, an attractive if somewhat plump woman of fifty-one, came up beside him.

"I have my best man in a car behind them," Kreski said, after a brief pause. "And everyone else who can get into a car is trying to catch up. But my people don't seem to be in much demand. I feel like I've been put on hold."

"That's how we all feel," said the attorney general.

"What's the point of all this military?" Kreski said.

"I haven't the foggiest. I wasn't consulted. It all came from the president via Ambrose and Jim Malcom."

James Creek Malcom, the Colorado mining magnate Hampton had first made ambassador to Canada and then his national security adviser and head of the National Security Council, was not in the room. Kreski could see a navy officer busy on a computer terminal near the end of the conference table. It connected with the computer-teletype terminal of the Moscow "hotline" in the Pentagon war room.

"Why the Def Con Two?" Kreski asked.

"They told the JCS it was precautionary," said the attorney general. "If they are Hondurans, then Nicaragua and Cuba may be involved. If they're involved, then the Soviets are probably involved."

L. Merriman Crosby, the secretary of state, an inordinately patrician-looking old gentleman with four decades in Washington, joined them.

"What do you know, Mr. Kreski?" he said.

"Mr. Secretary, I came here to find out what was going on."

"Well, it's an awful state of affairs, don't you know, but we've largely learned only what they're telling us on television. We've been sitting in this room with very little to do."

"Where's the secretary of defense?" Kreski said.

"He's just left the Pentagon. In a helicopter, don't you know. We presume he's coming here. The rest of the cabinet, indeed, all of the president's closest associates, appear to be en route to Camp David."

It had been more than idle rumor that the agreement reached between Hampton and Atherton at the convention had included more than a gift of the vice presidential nomination. Atherton had also been awarded five cabinet posts. Hampton had kept all the others, plus national security adviser. None of his people were present.

"Walt, are you going up to Camp David?" said the treasury secretary.

"Not yet. As soon as the weather breaks, I'm going to go to Gettysburg. I'm afraid my agency is responsible for the deaths of at least four people."

"More than that, I'm afraid," said the attorney general. "We're told six, probably more."

"Ghastly," said Crosby. He glanced at the pointless confusion in the crowded, windowless room, then looked back to Kreski.

"If you can spare ten minutes, Walter, there's something we'd appreciate your doing for us," he said. "It's rather important. Someone has to go over to the Executive Office Building and say something to the news media."

"I'm not the president's press secretary. I'm the last person who should do that."

"The White House spokesman has locked himself in his office," said the treasury secretary. "I think he's trying to get through to Ambrose."

"If one of us in the cabinet goes before them we could give the same unfortunate impression Haig did in 1981—'I'm in control here, here in the White House.' There's already been entirely too much talk of a coup as it is. We need to get a calming message out to the nation. It's vital."

"They trust you, Walt. And you're nonpolitical."

"But I've no handle on what's going on."

"Just throw some of the television coverage back at them. Call it 'tentative field reports.' Unconfirmed."

They all turned to the bank of television monitors against one wall. On one screen, ABC's Sam Donaldson was standing in front of a belligerent-looking White House military guard at the gates. Donaldson was saying the marines had seized control of the White House.

"Good God," Kreski said.

"We need you, Walter. Now. Please."

"I've never done this."

"They'll believe you, Walt."

"I won't believe me."

There were only two kinds of people in the Congress at that moment, those running pointlessly and madly through the halls as though they could accomplish something toward dealing with the crisis, and those staring at television sets. In an expansive suite in the Russell Senate Office Building, the staff of Senator Maitland "Meathead" Dubarry of Louisiana were captives of the television. In his huge private office, Dubarry had his set on, but paid it little attention. As often happened when floor votes were called, the assassination attempt had caught Dubarry with too many drinks in him.

His glass was again empty. He waved it at the woman in the office with him, a cotton-candy blond secretary whose principal office skill was fellatio. She took it to a cabinet by the street windows and filled it precisely halfway with vodka—a patriotic American brand distilled in Virginia—and topped it with Tab. The senator had a weight problem that was rapidly becoming a cardiovascular problem.

As she added ice and stirred, the tall, rumpled, middle-aged man sitting on the edge of Dubarry's desk cleared his throat noisily. Reuben Jackson was the senator's administrative assistant, the functioning chief authority in the office, and he did this whenever Dubarry was doing something wrong.

"There's probably going to be a leadership meeting before we're done with this today," he said. "Maybe you ought to go easy for a while."

Dubarry had the third highest seniority of his party in the Senate, and, owing to the system that honored it, had become chairman of the Armed Services Committee as well as the chairman of his party's Senate conference. There was talk that he might end up being elected president pro tempore when the new Congress sat the following January. The incumbent, a man even older than Dubarry, had been defeated in his bid for reelection.

Dubarry was not inclined to try for it, however, as it would mean giving up his Armed Services post, worth billions to Louisiana and possibly reelection to him.

"Our president has survived," Dubarry said, as the secretary handed him his brimming glass. "Damn good reason to celebrate. You oughta celebrate, too, Reuben. Make him a drink, Lillian."

Jackson shook his head at her. On the television screen, Bonnie Greer was falling to the ground.

"Lillian, honey," said Dubarry. "Go out and tell someone to get all this on videotape next time they run it. We're going to want to see this again."

"I just hope they're keeping their cool in the White House," Jackson said.

"The angel of death is passing among us," said Dubarry. The television screen faded to black, and then a slide appeared with a picture of Bonnie Greer smiling, the dates of her birth and death just beneath. After that, the network went to a commercial.

3

"He's dead," said Charley Dresden, watching the television screen over the rim of the large glass that held his second lunchtime Manhattan. The drink was an indulgence for him. He had signed a contract that morning to produce some television commercials for a seaside amusement park. The money would pay the rent for his one-man advertising agency for two or three months, and he had been feeling celebratory. But no longer. He had known Bonnie Greer a few years before, during one of his incarnations as a television station news director.

The restaurant was crowded, and many of the customers had come into the bar to follow the television reports. No one paid Dresden much attention.

"If he was dead they'd say so," said the bartender, putting Dresden's newly totalled check on the bartop. "The TV guys were there and they say he isn't."

"Lou, the TV guys don't know," said Dresden, unsmiling. He looked solemn enough for the tragedy on the screen, but it was his ordinary expression. At thirty-five, he was a handsome man in a drawn, weary way, with a few odd scars on his face, he looked a little too German for an American, especially a Californian. The dark

Prussian blue of his eyes was a stark, cold color against his tan and graying blond hair. He almost never smiled anymore, except when he was with women.

On the screen, President Hampton was again being pushed at his limousine by Agent Berger, who then doubled backward as though in sudden pain and fell down, his shirtfront crimson. When they cut again to the footage of Bonnie Greer's head exploding, Dresden looked away. She had been a gushy young reporter just out of Santa Linda State when he knew her. He had given her a glowing reference for a good job with a network station in San Francisco. Now she was butcher's meat.

"Look at his face next time they run the tape, which will probably be in about three minutes," Dresden said. "Mortality writ large."

The bartender, a longtime friend, normally deferred to Dresden in all matters concerning television, but not now.

"Charley. It's official. He's alive. Until someone comes on the tube there and says he's dead, I'm going to have to say you're nuts."

"What if I came on the tube and said he was dead?"

"What?"

"What if I walked over to the TV station and sat down on the news set and announced in authoritative tones that the president was dead? Then you'd believe me, right? Anything I'd say."

"You're nuts, Charley."

"I'll bet you fifty dollars."

"You've got too big a tab here to make bets."

"I'll bet you my tab, double or nothing."

"Forget it, Charley."

He moved away to take care of another customer, leaving Dresden to his drink. Antoine's was the most expensive restaurant in Santa Linda, California. Despite the French name—the proprietor was actually an Anthony Ciardi—the cuisine ran more to steaks and prime rib than continental fare, and the decor was that of a California interior decorator's vision of an English club: vinyl, wallboard, and Formica doing for genuine leather and walnut.

Dresden had been a regular customer since he had first come to Santa Linda from New York some fifteen years before. Channel Three, the television station where he had risen to the high position of program director, was two blocks up the street. The city's major advertising agencies and its sole newspaper, the Santa Linda *Press-Journal*, were not much farther. Dresden and most of the restaurant's patrons knew each other well, which is why Dresden sometimes found himself alone at the bar.

He would finish this second Manhattan and then return to his office via a Burger King or a taco stand. That would be lunch. Dresden worked very hard, and so stayed in business, as few California hip-pocket ad agencies ever managed to do for long. But his former television colleagues in Santa Linda considered him very much the has-been. When he could, he economized.

On the television, Tom Brokaw and Roger Mudd of NBC were looking at a map of the Gettysburg battlefield. Brokaw noted that the assassination scene was not far from the stone marking the high-water mark of the Confederacy at the farthest reach of Pickett's charge, and that Hampton was born a Virginian. He and Mudd started filling the time with a discourse on Henry Hampton's fascination with the Civil War.

A man and a woman came up behind Dresden. She took the empty seat next to him and the man stood just behind her. They appeared to be waiting for a table. She looked expensive, a trifle over thirty, a trifle flashy, more likely from Southern California than the Bay Area. The man was older, well into his forties. Dresden nodded to them. The woman gave him a quick, disinterested smile and the man ignored him, waving to the bartender. He ordered two daquiris.

"The president's dead," Dresden said.

"What?" said the woman. "Did they announce that?"

"No," said Dresden. "But it's obvious from the tapes. He's a dead man."

The man gave Dresden a belligerent look. Charley was not a man to pick fights, but he did not like this stranger.

"Ease up, Charley," said the bartender.

"Just trying to serve the cause of truth. 'I shall tell you a great secret, my friend. Do not wait for the last judgment. It takes place every day.'"

"What are you talking about?"

"Albert Camus. He wrote in *La Chute*. He also said, 'The absurd is the essential concept and the first truth.' Only Hampton's death is not absurd. It follows logically."

The woman's companion had ceased to ignore Charley. "What do you mean, 'logically'?"

"I mean the war," Dresden said, pleased with the woman's interested gaze. "Hondurans, El Salvadorans, Guatemalans, Nicaraguans,

Cubans, Russians, Libyans, Iranians. He became a marked man the minute he sent in the first combat unit."

The other man's voice lowered with menace. "You're talking about the president of the United States. He's been shot. He could be dying."

"He's already dead."

The woman kept glancing from Dresden to her companion, gauging, guessing what each would do. The man seemed unsure.

"I think you'd better shut your mouth," he said finally.

"I'll say what I damn well please in this bar."

"I think you better take it back about the president asking to get shot."

The man appeared as muscular as he was richly dressed. His deeply tanned face had mean lines in it, but his eyes were weak. He seemed the sort who would fend off competition with raised hackles and growls, not by going for the throat of the first challenger; the sort to establish his territory with expensive suits and women, and no doubt a very expensive car outside. He was not the sort to piss in the dirt upwind. When necessary, Dresden was.

"A hundred dollars says he's dead," said Charley. "Surely you have a hundred dollars on you."

"I'm not going to bet on the life of the president of the United States."

"Two hundred dollars then. We'll make it worth your while."

"Five hundred dollars!"

It was not the woman's companion who spoke but another voice, one Dresden knew too well. He turned in his seat to see James Xavier Ireland hulking over him, one hand on the back of Dresden's chair, the other clutching hundred-dollar bills. Ireland had once been his boss and friend. He had long since ceased being either.

"Put up or shut up, Charley. Five hundred dollars. You've been ruining my lunch. If you can't put up the money, then for God's sake, shut up!"

Ireland was now owner and president of Channel Three. A one-time protégé of Dresden's television pioneer father, he had given Charley his first real job. Most station owners would have been back in their news rooms at such a time, grandly interfering with the news director's efforts to respond locally to the assassination attempt. But Jim Ireland always prided himself on being a man who knew how to delegate authority, which was to say, he hated having anything to interrupt his lunch.

"I'll write you a check," Dresden said, reaching into his coat pocket. Ireland, a big man, stayed his hand.

"No you don't, Charley. But I'll tell you what. If you don't have the money, we'll go for different stakes. If the president turns out to be dead, and you win, I'll stop having lunch at Antoine's. But if you lose, if it turns out he's alive, as seems to be the case. If he comes on the screen and smiles and waves. Then, Charley, you stay out of Antoine's and you never come in here again! Is it a bet?"

The bartender leaned forward. "I'll take care of this, Mr. Ireland. Charley, why don't you take off for a while? Just go somewhere and cool off. It's a bad time. Here, I'll take care of this." He picked up Dresden's check and began tearing it into pieces.

The woman turned away completely. Dresden stood up and drank the last of his Manhattan.

"It's a bet," he said to Ireland. Then, pushing past him, he walked slowly out into the brilliant sunshine.

It was four blocks back to Dresden's office—six, if he didn't want to walk past the Channel Three studios. Still feeling the humiliation of his long ago firing from there, he seldom did. Today he would. Today he felt bold.

Dresden passed up the Burger King for the taco stand. Cheeseburgers were cheeseburgers, but a satisfactory Mexican meal required wine, even a meal of tacos. He had most of a half gallon bottle of Almaden burgundy in his office. It was a day for drink.

His advertising agency, as he grandiosely called it, was in an old, two-story stucco building, with a cracked and faded red-tile roof and a long balcony that ran across the front of the second story, where Dresden's office was. He did much of his thinking on that balcony, which was sheltered by a large old palm tree and had a pleasant view of the street. There was a beauty shop on the first floor, and Charley enjoyed dragging his swivel chair out and watching the customers come and go, especially in hot weather.

The sign on his door said THE DRESDEN ORGANIZATION. He still laughed to himself at the pretentiousness of that, but he had never thought of changing it. His father had used that name for one of his unsuccessful companies, his last.

There was some mail on the floor. He sorted through it quickly with his foot, kicking those envelopes that looked to contain bills apart from those that might contain checks, except that, ultimately, none looked to contain checks. His secretary, Isabel Torrijos, was not yet back from lunch. Perhaps she had taken them to the bank. Isabel was religious. She prayed for checks.

Shoving the mail aside, he went through the reception area into his own office, a large room with rear windows overlooking the alley. All was a little dusty, but the furniture had originally been expensive. Among the Mexican prints on the wall were a few framed advertising awards. Prominent on the long shelves that lined one wall were the four Emmys he had won, three at Channel Three and another at a station in San Francisco. They and the dusty office were all that was left to him of his career, the definitive summation of his professional life.

He set the bag of tacos on his desk, filled a coffee cup with wine, and eased himself into his chair. His life. He sipped from the cup. "There is no wealth but life." John Ruskin had written that. Dresden's father had often lectured him with that quotation.

Dresden's dead father. This room and its contents were the definitive summation of that man's life as well. Charley sipped again. The wine was good, but the aftertaste was the slightest bit off. He had left the jug on the shelf too long. He would have to drink this up soon.

His phone rang, a briefly startling intrusion. He stared at the instrument a moment, forcing himself to put aside optimistic thoughts of another client, preparing himself for someone to whom he still owed money. There weren't many. Seared by the havoc caused by his father's huge debts and crushing bankruptcy, Dresden always paid off his creditors as soon as possible. Inhaling deeply as he stiffened his posture, he picked up the receiver.

It was only Cooper, the owner of the principal saloon in Tiburcio, the old mining town in the mountains west of Santa Linda where Dresden had lived for nearly all his fifteen years in California. Cooper, a retired Coast Guard officer, was calling to ask if Dresden knew anything more about the assassination attempt on the president. Charley started to say he was sure the president was dead, but caught himself in time, realizing that line of discourse would be better saved for when he was once again in Cooper's saloon. Instead, he said, "It's just what you see on television."

"Was it the KGB?"

"They haven't told me, Coop. I'll see you tonight."

He hung up. Even if he were still with Channel Three, he wouldn't be able to say anything more certifiably factual than that.

Cooper often acted as though Charley were a regular guest at the White House, simply because he had been in television.

A glint of reflected sunlight caught the wings of one of the Emmys on the shelf, rendering it instantly glorious. "If you want to win awards, Charley Dresden's the best," his advertising colleagues were fond of saying. "But his commercials just don't sell." Father unto son.

Dresden's father Max had been one of the founding geniuses of American television, reigning as such for ten years in the 1940s and 1950s, until his network was bought by investors interested solely in money and having few scruples about what went onto the screen to fetch it. Max Dresden had resigned in high anger, shortly before he would have been fired, and then went through a succession of lesser television and advertising jobs, and finally his own unsuccessful firms. Ultimately bankrupt, he had shot himself, leaving no insurance.

Charley had been about to enter his sophomore year at New York University when his father had fired that shot into his head, making a grotesquerie of the front seat of his mother's expensive and unpaid for Mercedes. When the big house in Westchester was sold and the debts settled, his mother took a job in a local village shop. His sister, Augusta, went slightly insane and married the first wealthy man who would have her. Charley supported himself in New York City as best he could, attending night school. Then Jim Ireland had "saved" him.

Once a network protégé of Dresden's father, Ireland had bought into Santa Linda's Channel Three when it had been a small and failing concern and had turned it into one of the most profitable television stations in California. He was happy to offer his old benefactor's son a job.

As Santa Linda grew, rivaling the sprawl of nearby San Jose, just across the mountains, Charley Dresden prospered, too, for a time. Originally hired as a writer of commercials, he became production chief, assistant program director, and program director in quick succession.

But Ireland insisted upon running the station as an efficient business, not a stage for the creative indulgences of a self-styled genius with sometimes terrifying social habits. Dresden occasionally came to work drunk, and sometimes with girlfriends. He had Wagner, Eric Satie, and other favorite composers booming from a phonograph in his office throughout the day.

One morning when a sound effects record on Dresden's office phonograph accidentally entertained nearby staff with the sound of speeding railroad trains, Ireland could take no more and fired Dresden without further discussion. He gave Charley a particularly generous severance, a year's salary, in part out of his loyalty to Charley's father but mostly because he hoped Charley would use it to travel far—with luck, all the way back to New York. But Charley stubbornly stayed on in California.

Familiar noises announced the office door opening and Isabel's return. She looked in, her dark, pretty face brightening at seeing actual work on his desk in addition to the wine and tacos. She helped support a family that included six children besides herself, and was engaged to a pharmacist at the drugstore down the street.

"There was a check from Frank's Used Cars," she said. "Three hundred ten dollars."

"They owe me twenty-one hundred dollars."

"That's why I thought a three-hundred-ten-dollar one might actually be good. I got it into the bank as fast as I could."

"If it clears, give yourself a hundred of it. A bonus."

"Charley . . ."

"If through some miracle it actually does clear, we should both consider it a bonus. That bastard keeps trying to pay me off with one of his used cars."

She smiled again. "You'd be better off with a bounced check."

He finished the cold taco and dropped the bag into his wastebasket, returning to his work. It did not proceed well. His gaze kept shifting to his office television set. Finally, pouring more wine, he turned it on. A tall, bearded man identified on the screen as Walter Kreski, director of the Secret Service, was speaking to a crowd of noisy, shouting reporters. As best as Dresden could determine, the man was saying that a Hispanic illegal alien had been identified as the gunman in the assassination attempt.

"Jesus," said Dresden, half aloud. "Every Latino in the country is going to be rousted tonight."

The bearded man stopped speaking and stepped away. He was followed on the screen by Brokaw, who announced the network was going to replay the tape of the shooting and warned that, as it was after school hours, parents might want to keep their children away from the television set. Dresden leaped forward, slapped a cassette into his creaky old video recorder and, as President Hampton's figure appeared on the screen, pushed down the record button.

Now he would have his own tape, which he could examine minutely and professionally in the slowest possible motion. He would prove his point yet. He would win his bet. Dresden knew better than most what a man's face looks like when he dies from a gunshot. He had been with his father in that Mercedes.

The network footage ended with a shot of one of the correspondents picking himself up from the ground, his face all dirt and fear and horror. Charley hit the stop button, and then the rewind, and then play. A flickering moment later, President Hampton was visible again, but in vibrating, multiple images. Warped rainbows tracked across the screen. The damned tape recorder wasn't working properly. He had meant to get it fixed but had put it off. He kicked the recorder hard. The screen went blank.

The foul weather delayed the vice president's return from New York for nearly two hours.

By the time he reached Andrews Air Force Base in the Maryland suburbs southeast of Washington, the weather had changed, not to something better, but to something strange—remnant cumulus clouds dragging in shreds and tangles across a clearing yet darkening sky, their edges glowing with the last pink tinge of sunlight. From the east, the night seemed to follow Atherton's helicopter up the river.

As always, the city appeared before them abruptly, a stage setting revealed as though by a suddenly drawn curtain, its entirety contained within the view from Atherton's window—the Capitol building at the far stretch of the Mall at the right, the Washington Monument and Jefferson Memorial in odd juxtaposition in the foreground, the curving sweep of the Ellipse leading to the distant focal point that was the White House, President Henry Hampton's home.

Atherton remembered March 1981, and Vice President Bush's tactful gesture. He would do the same. He would not come swooping down upon the South Lawn as though seizing command. He would go first to the Vice President's House on Observatory Hill, and then arrive at the White House by car, discreetly.

He pulled at Neil Howard's arm and told him to pass on the instruction to the pilot.

"Larry, we're overdue as it is."

"I want to go home. We'll get to the White House soon enough."

His wife, Sally, dressed as though she were still at Stanford in a beige cashmere sweater, plaid skirt, and loafers, came running out of the Victorian mansion known simply as the Vice President's House at his approach, long dark hair flying behind her. She hugged him very tightly, trembling.

"Larry, my God. Thank God."

He held her a long moment, stiffly, saying nothing. Her body was the first warm thing he had touched that day, but he still felt cold.

"I didn't know what to think, Larry. They wouldn't tell me where you were. They're saying on television it's some kind of Latin American plot. God, what's happening?"

"I'm all right, baby. Everything is all right."

"Is the president okay? The television reports are so confusing."

"They say his wound isn't very serious," Atherton said with uncertainty. "He went to Camp David." He put his arm around her shoulders, and started walking with her back to the house. His daughter was not in evidence. "Where's Cindy?"

"She went riding out in Middleburg. I think she had trouble getting back. There've been a lot of police going up and down Massachusetts Avenue. Did you know they sent marines here to guard the house?"

"I saw them."

"They put a machine gun by the garage. They have it aimed down the driveway at the gate."

"Don't be frightened. It's there to protect us."

"Everything scares me. Especially when you're gone."

"Have a drink with me, Sally," the vice president said. "In the library."

It was his favorite room in this gloomy old house. His wife had ordered a fire to be lighted, making the room cheerier, though Atherton still felt the numbness that had struck him with the first news of the assassination attempt and the heavy civilian casualties.

The television set was on. Walter Kreski, the Secret Service director, was standing before reporters, attempting to explain that preliminary reports indicated a possible conspiracy and that a number of suspects had been arrested. Yes, they were Hispanic. No, he had no more details to give out, except that the worst appeared to be over and that everything was under control. No, he would not discuss the shooting of bystanders at Gettysburg, except to say that it had been a terrible, terrible accident and that the agent involved had been taken into custody. When the reporter asked about the need for so much security at the White House, ninety miles from the assassination site, Kreski replied that it had been a presidential decision about which he could not comment. He excused himself and walked away, a tall man moving calmly.

The butler brought the drinks and Atherton took his to the couch, settling back wearily. He allowed himself a large, anxious sip of the nearly straight whiskey, but it did nothing for the coldness within him.

He would at least have Kreski to turn to. There was no one more reliable in the White House. No one more competent. No one more apolitical. No one more willing to follow instructions, discreetly. No one better placed to determine the president's actual condition, and what was going on up at Camp David.

His wife huddled close. Her eyes were red. Except for servants and armed men, she had been alone all afternoon. He put his arm around her once more, just as Tom Brokaw explained from the television screen that the briefing from Kreski had been taped earlier and that the Secret Service director had since left Washington for Gettysburg. Brokaw then interrupted himself to say he had just been informed that the vice-president had returned to Washington but was in an undisclosed location—possibly the Pentagon.

"You know, when I heard the news, my first thought was, now Larry is president. I was horrified to be thinking that, but for all the wrong reasons. I suddenly realized how much I'd hate it if you were president. I hate it that you're vice president. I wish you had never run. I wish we could go back to California."

He rubbed her shoulder. "It'll all be over soon, baby. Things will get back to normal."

"I don't want that either."

On the screen, the network was returning them to the battlefield once more, to the huge clown's mouth exploding in Bonnie Greer's face and the crimson plume sprouting from her blond hair. Atherton closed his eyes and leaned back his head. It would be just like 1981, the shooting and falling and screaming; like the small, awful circle in Jim Brady's head, Bonnie Greer's mouth turned to maw, over and over and over again, tormentingly, every time he looked at a television set.

Atherton's head snapped forward. It occurred to him he had not yet seen any of the footage of Hampton actually getting shot. But he was too late. Brokaw was back on the screen, with great seriousness announcing a commercial. Atherton stood up.

"I can't sit here like this, Sally. I have to get to the White House. I just need a couple of minutes to think. Call our Secret Service detail, will you? See if they know where Cindy is."

"They didn't before. I'll try again." She took her drink with her, something she seldom did.

He turned off the television set rather harshly. With his own cold glass in hand, he stepped outside onto the curving wooden porch. The night was fully upon them, but the sky still seemed odd, the wraithlike remnants of cloud now aglow with the reflected light of the city. He began to walk, a sea captain on his deck. Reaching the side of the house facing Massachusetts Avenue, he paused to peer down through the leafless trees of the hillside at the heavy traffic. In the near lanes, moving toward the city center with surprising speed, was a large canvas-topped truck. Atherton could see the white stars on the side. U.S. Army. Would there be convoys of them next? Bushy Ambrose was a colonel.

The truck hurried on, passing by the British Embassy and disappearing into the general blur of distant taillights. Atherton stared after it. He wasn't aware of his wife's presence until she touched his back.

"You're shaking," she said.

He drank from his glass, steadying himself. "I'm cold," he said.

"Cindy was held up at a roadblock in Virginia. The CIA blocked off Georgetown Pike, Chain Bridge Road, and the Parkway. She had to make a detour down Highway 7 and got caught in the traffic at Tyson's Corner. She'll be home soon, though. Agent Leonardi said they were crossing Key Bridge."

He didn't speak until they were once again in the library. His impulse—no, his longing—was to return to the couch and the fire and hear nothing more about this day until he could at last sleep. But they would come for him. He could already hear telephones ringing elsewhere in the house.

Atherton held his wife's hand. "You stay here with Cindy when she gets back. Have something to eat. I'll be back as soon as I can, but it will be late. Don't go anywhere. Don't talk to anyone on the phone unless you're sure it's me, Shawcross, or Neil Howard."

"I thought you said everything was going to return to normal."

"Soon enough, baby. But not tonight."

Atherton's small motorcade entered the White House grounds via West Executive Drive and pulled to a stop opposite a side entrance to the West Wing. He hesitated, rubbing his cheek distractedly as a marine guard yanked open the door. He had been dreading this moment since he had first received the news of the attempted assassination in New York. He feared to enter this place. He was trembling again.

He stepped out of the car, jamming his hands into his coat pockets and nodding to the guard's brisk "Good evening, Mr. Vice President." Moving quickly with his small entourage along the crowded, thickly carpeted corridor, he reached his office and shut the door behind him. He had sent Neil Howard to the White House ahead of him. Howard was standing by the fireplace with Shawcross. They had pulled loose their ties, but, contrary to habit, kept their suit coats on. Assassination attempts were formal occasions.

"First things first," said Atherton, taking off his own coat and dropping it over a chair as he crossed to his desk. "What is the president's condition?"

"We don't know."

"It's the most important question being asked in the entire world at this moment and the White House can't answer it?"

"Not this White House," said Shawcross.

"In the United States of America that question has to be answered. At all times," Atherton said.

"They put out a two-line statement from Camp David," said Howard. "'The president has been wounded but is well. He is receiving medical treatment.' It covers everything but is perfectly meaningless."

"Sounds like Jerry Greene," Shawcross said. "Vintage Greene. The president's communications director is a regular Dr. Goebbels."

Someone had lighted the fire. Atherton went to it, standing for a moment, then dropping into an adjacent chair. The numbing coldness had been replaced by fatigue.

"All right," he said. "What's next?"

"That's up to you," Shawcross said. He looked as nonchalant as always. Only his profuse sweating betrayed his anxiety. "In the EOB auditorium you have several hundred members of the press who think there's been a coup. In the White House situation room you have five members of the cabinet doing their best to give the impression that no one's in control, here in the White House."

"Who?"

"Our guys. I think their guys are probably on their way to Camp David. The secretary of defense has come and gone."

"There are none of Hampton's people in the White House?" Atherton said.

"The budget director is believed to be holed up in a back booth at Mel Krupin's. Except for Weigle, and more about him later, the Hampton contingent here is fairly low echelon."

Weigle was Hampton's press secretary. It was typical of his relationship with the president that he had been left behind at the White House while Hampton had gone to Gettysburg to make a speech.

"Let's have more about Weigle now," said Atherton.

"Walt Kreski tried to go over to the EOB to calm down the press corps. It was the consensus in the situation room that he should. Weigle tried to stop him. He said only he was authorized to make statements. But the esteemed secretary of state overruled him."

"Has Weigle gotten through to Camp David?"

Howard shrugged. "He hasn't made any statements."

"Here in the federal city," Shawcross continued, "we have a number of military units milling about, all apparently under the radio-telephone command of Colonel Irving Ambrose. And, at the Pentagon and wherever our servicemen and -women so proudly serve, there is a condition of alert known as Def Con Three. For a while they had it up to Def Con Two. I don't know if they're genuinely paranoid or what, but they're playing this terrorist conspiracy thing for all it's worth."

"They have every right to be paranoid. Did Ambrose order the alert?"

"No, the esteemed national security adviser, from his home, with the subsequent approval of the esteemed secretary of defense. It's the first thing he did when he heard the news. He told the JCS he thought it wise."

"It is unwise. The SAC missile people'll have all their console keys out, waiting for the phone to ring. Get to the JCS and see if they can't step down to Def Con Four. I'm still the crisis manager here. What else?"

"Every member of Congress and half the uncrowned heads of Europe have called asking for a fill, and the hotline teletype with our Russian brothers has been humming rather briskly. Eighth Army command in Seoul reports some sporadic firing up on the DMZ."

"And Honduras?"

"All quiet."

"You're sure?"

"Yes, sir."

"What else?"

"Aside from the stock market digging itself a new cellar and some rioting here and there, we have the matter of Daisy Hampton. She's still in the East Wing, in the family quarters."

"Has she talked to the president?"

"I don't think so. I don't know."

"Has anyone? Is there anyone in the White House who has talked to the president of the United States?"

"The secretary of state got through to Peter Schlessler up at Camp David. He said the national security adviser would get back to him directly. He said the president's personal physician had arrived and was administering emergency treatment to the patient. Some military medical staff from Fort Bragg are en route. A big team."

"We've made contact with the president's chauffeur," Atherton said. "How marvelous."

His nerve was coming back. Perhaps it was because he at last had something to do, that he could take action, affect matters.

"All right," he said. "Disperse the group in the situation room. Tell the esteemed secretary of state to get back to his office and to summon the Soviet ambassador there at once. Inform everyone there will be a cabinet meeting at eight A.M. tomorrow and a meeting of the National Security Council, such as we can find of it, along with my staff, at nine P.M. tonight."

"Can you do that, Larry? What about the president?"

"An excellent question, isn't it? If they want to countermand me, fine. Keep Camp David informed of everything. In the meantime, I'm going to do the best I can to restore a little order to this situation."

He was completely in control of himself now, in command.

"What are you going to do now?" Howard said. "Go over to the EOB? Want me to work up a little statement?"

"No. First things first. I'm going to see Mrs. Hampton."

"You'd better bring some bourbon. She's probably out by now."

✲   ✲   ✲

The First Lady was alone in her private sitting room. She sat in the dark by the odd half circle window, the light from the streetlamps illuminating her face. The view was of the Treasury building, one of the bleaker prospects from the mansion. Her face was bleak as well. She had been one of the great beauties of Virginia when Hampton had carried her off to Colorado. As with many Virginia women, she had not survived transplantation well.

"Daisy?" He closed the door quietly behind him, shutting out, among others, the First Lady's press secretary and her chief of staff, a pudgy young man with fluttery hands.

She said nothing. He approached and touched her shoulder, leaning over to look into her face.

"Daisy?"

She looked away, to the table beside her, picking up a glass unsteadily. She sipped from it twice, then turned her sodden eyes to him.

"Have you come to take me up there, Larry? I don't want to go up there."

"Daisy, I'm just here to see you." He gently squeezed her shoulder. She seemed so frail.

"Sit down, Larry."

He did so obediently, taking a chair opposite. There were sirens in some distant street.

"I knew this would happen," she said finally. Her speech was slurred, and he had to listen with care. "I told him this would happen. Told him. When he stirred up that damned war, I told him."

"Daisy . . ."

"It's finally happened, Larry, and you know what? I'm almost glad. Mr. Vice President Laurence Atherton, sir, the First Lady is almost relieved that her husband's finally been shot. Not dead. I don't want Henry dead, Larry. I love him, Larry. I still do love him. But since he's going to live, I'm glad they shot him. Maybe now he'll change. Maybe he'll give it a rest now."

"Have you talked to him, Daisy?"

She stared out the window. He wondered how many nights she had sat there like this. In normal times.

"Daisy?"

"No, I haven't," she said, with a slight sniffle. "Talked to Bushy. He called to tell me Henry's all right and that Dr. Potter is there. He wants me to come up. I don't want to, Larry. I want to stay here."

"Would you like Sally to come over?"

"No. Thank you, but no."

He rose. He started to turn on a nearby lamp, but caught himself. "I have to go now, Daisy. I have to deal with the press."

"I know. You must carry on."

"Can I get you anything?"

"Have them bring me some more bourbon. And make sure they do."

He touched her shoulder again. She brought her own hand to his for a moment, then it fell limply away.

"Take care of yourself, Daisy. I'll look in on you as soon as I can."

"Don't bother. They'll be coming for me, Larry."

In the corridor outside, Atherton drew the First Lady's chief of staff aside, and then close.

"Mrs. Hampton is going through a very difficult time," he said. The smaller man nodded vigorously. "She's to have whatever she wants, and that includes some more Jack Daniels Black."

"But . . ."

"I'm going to check on that."

"Yes, Mr. Vice President."

Shawcross, Neil Howard, four Secret Service agents, and two marines with carbines accompanied him on the short walk from the West Wing across West Executive Drive to the EOB. Howard had written up a brief statement, but Atherton just slipped it into his suitjacket pocket. He was not a brilliant public speaker, but he always did better on his own.

Stepping into the bright lights and noise of the EOB auditorium, he thought of martyrs entering the arena of the Colosseum of Rome. His entourage moved with him to the podium, a praetorian guard. Still, the mob of reporters surged around him. A storm of questions assaulted him. His ear could make sense of only a few: "Are we going to war, Mr. Vice President?" "Why are you treating us like prisoners, Mr. Vice President?" "Will the president live?" "Are you arresting Hispanics on sight?"

Finally, Neil Howard jumped up on a chair and began to shout them down. "Let the vice president speak! If you want to hear him, you'll have to be quiet! Shut up, everyone! Shut up! Let him speak!"

Howard's unexpected and uncharacteristic rudeness served its purpose. The din subsided. In a minute or so there was relative quiet, but the tension was explosive.

"I, I have a brief statement to make," Atherton said, sticking his hands in his pockets. "I've just come from the First Lady. As you may know, the president is at Camp David. He's been wounded, but apparently not badly. The surgeon general, who is also President Hampton's personal physician, is attending to him. Mrs. Hampton is doing well, under the circumstances. She'll be joining her husband shortly, I imagine."

The heat from the lights was unbearable.

"There's still a lot of confusion over what's happened," he continued, trying to avoid looking long at any one reporter. "The assassin, the would-be assassin, was killed in an exchange of gunfire. There were arrests made in New York, where I was, and in Chicago, where the secretary of housing and urban development was. There were some arrests here. I believe the situation is now well in hand.

"I think I speak for President Hampton in saying that the horrible accident up at Gettysburg, in which so many innocent people were killed and injured, friends of yours, friends of mine, was one of the saddest things, one of the worst tragedies that could befall any administration. We're all just terribly, terribly sad and sorry. Our hearts go out to everyone who's suffered. We're going over everything and will make a full report as soon as possible, as soon as we know just what occurred."

One of the younger reporters began to interrupt with a question but was silenced by the fierce glares of those around him.

"As is necessary in an emergency like this, our armed forces around the world were placed on a high state of alert," Atherton continued. "We now see no immediate threat of hostilities, and the alert's being relaxed. Everything is under control. We're doing everything we can to bring things back to normal.

"Now I'm sure you'll understand that I have an awful lot to attend to. If you could just hold your questions until next time . . ."

The silence was broken by a detonation of shouted words. As Atherton withdrew behind his phalanx of aides and security men, he heard himself called Bonnie Greer's murderer. And there was someone shouting, "What about the coup?"

Allen Wilson, the attorney general, was waiting outside. "Back to normal, eh? Not anytime soon."

"What do you mean?"

"Colonel Ambrose—I mean, the president of the United States—has federalized the National Guard."

"Here? In D.C.?"

"Here? Everywhere! Every military unit in the continental United States is now technically under the direct command of the president—and Colonel Ambrose."

Autopsies were not Walter Kreski's forte. He had served a few brief years as a policeman while completing law school, but little violence had come his way. In all his career, he had seen the body of someone shot to death only twice. Now, in the crowded Adams County Morgue, he was making up for that with a vengeance.

He had looked first at the body of the suspect Huerta, what there was of it. They had all but shoveled the man's remains into the body bag. His right hand seemed to be the only part of him untouched by bullets. There were ink stains on the fingertips. Copley had had the fingerprint check done immediately. The FBI director was the better cop.

He had gone next to Al Berger's remains, and wished he hadn't. The purpose of this ghoulish perusal was to examine wounds, to imprint their images firmly on his mind for when he would be able to read the autopsy reports, which otherwise might be perfectly meaningless to him. But when they rolled Berger over on his stomach to expose the holes in his back, Kreski knew he had asked too much of himself. Berger had long been his friend. Kreski had fought hard to secure the man the post of head of the White House detail and had every hope Berger would succeed him as director when he retired, as he intended to do when he made thirty years the following summer. Berger's son was dating Kreski's daughter. It would fall to him to talk to that son, but here he was looking at the boy's father as though at some laboratory specimen.

Kreski turned away, inhaling deeply, trying to ignore the gaze of the Pennsylvania state trooper standing opposite him. Then he forced himself to the sight of Berger's back, glancing over it quickly to get the grim business done. There was the red stripe of a cut or burn across the left shoulder that might have come from a bullet. In the left lower back was a large, jagged hole from a bullet that had taken out much of the man's chest in exiting. That was all.

He stepped back, nodding. He wanted to light his pipe, but feared he might gag. There were more bodies to see. The next one he went to proved to be Bonnie Greer's. They had left her eyes open, still staring in pain and wonder. Her lower jaw was gone. Clenching his fists, his nails digging into the flesh of his palms, he held himself in place as the attendant continued to pull down the sheet to reveal her chest and the second navel that had been created in the side of her breast—a neat, round hole, unlike the rougher one in Berger's back.

"That's enough," Kreski said.

He had made a point of attempting to interview Agent Schultz as soon as he had arrived at Gettysburg—a useless undertaking, for the man was nearly catatonic, muttering something about a horse. It was well Kreski had done that first. If he were left alone with Schultz now, he would probably kill him.

"Seen enough, Walt?"

He had been joined by a man wearing a Burberry raincoat, blue blazer, gray flannels, black loafers with tassels, a white button-down shirt, and a striped college tie. Steven Copley never let you forget he had gone to Princeton.

"Yeah, I surely have."

The FBI director had a very youthful face. Some said he had dyed his hair its snowy white so he would look sufficiently mature for his job.

"Let's take a walk, Steve. I can't stand the smell in here any longer."

The air outside was cold, but clear and clean. Kreski filled his lungs with it, then, exhaling as they started down the walk, reached for his pipe and tobacco pouch.

"I'm going to have to arrest your man Schultz," Copley said.

"I know." In the cold, crisp, oxygen-rich air, Kreski soon had his pipe glowing red.

"If we don't, the Pennsylvania authorities will lock him up here. He hit a twelve-year-old boy with one of those rounds."

"Yeah. He did do that."

"Walt, can you survive this all right, politically?"

"You tell me."

Copley said nothing. As they walked along past the old nineteenth-century houses, his leather heels rang out sharply against the pavement, echoing. It was as though the little town was again its quiet self, asleep on an autumn night—not crowded with police and government agents going about a grim business.

"The Congress will want public hearings," Copley said. "The White House will be looking for a scapegoat. You're going to have a rotten Thanksgiving."

"I'll probably have to resign. I was going to do it this afternoon."

"But you only have a few months to go before you qualify for early retirement."

"The Secret Service has never before disgraced itself like this."

"Walt, the president's alive. Your guys did their job. So did you."

"A lot of people aren't alive."

"Al Berger. But that was his job. The others were an accident. You're not to blame."

There was an odd, distant sound. Kreski listened to it a moment, then recognized it as a faraway trailer rig, speeding somewhere through the night, the driver busy with his own problems, knowing little of theirs.

"Walt, what kept you from resigning this afternoon?"

Kreski puffed on his pipe before speaking. "Because, if they'll let me, I want to help find who did this."

"Agent Schultz . . ."

"Not just that. This whole thing. I want to find out who made it *happen.*"

"Well, the pieces are certainly falling together, but your participation in the investigation is something I'd hate to do without. I'll do whatever I can for you, Walt. I've made some friends here and there."

It was an understatement, and Copley wasn't noted for them. He was one of the few people in Washington with close ties to both the president's and vice president's factions.

They reached a large, white, turreted house on a corner, and, in unspoken decision, turned and began to head back.

"Steve. Al Berger had a funny wound. Huerta was shooting from above. The bullet that hit Al struck low and exited high. And it wasn't fired from the direction of the tower."

"Yes. That's right."

"What do you make of it?"

"I wouldn't be surprised if there was another shooter there, firing at the president. This is turning out to be a pretty large conspiracy."

"You've made a lot of arrests."

"We could well end up making more than a hundred. We'll have to let a lot of them go. Except for the illegals. But I think we have most of the principals. I can't think of a case where we've had so many informants."

"You didn't get whoever it was who fired that second shot at Berger."

"No. All we have here in Gettysburg is the remains of that bastard Huerta."

"Whoever it was, that second shooter wasn't anywhere near the tower."

"We don't know where he might have been. And we won't until we can determine all the trajectories. That won't be easy. What we really need is the prime piece of evidence, but that's at Camp David."

"What's that?"

"The president's limousine. From the tapes, I gather it took a number of rounds. We could string trajectories all over the battlefield if we had that car."

They walked on, Kreski staring down at the darkened sidewalk ahead of him. A local police car drove by, slowing as it passed them, then hastening on.

"You made that fingerprint ID on Huerta very quickly," Kreski said.

"First thing I had done. As soon as I heard 'male Hispanic,' I had them run the prints not only through our computer files but through Immigration's. Got them back first bounce. The man was arrested earlier this year in Florida and sent back to Honduras."

They were nearing the morgue.

"Steve, I've not much taste for going back in there."

"I don't blame you. I'm going to be seeing what's left of Bonnie Greer's face the rest of my days."

Kreski took a last puff, then knocked his pipe against the heel of his shoe, red coals scattering into the shadows.

"I'm going to go to Camp David now, Steve. I want to see the president."

"I was going to do the same thing when we're cleaned up here. I might as well go now. We can ride together."

"I don't have room for you in the chopper. It's one of those three-place Bells and I have to keep a communications man with me."

"I wouldn't take a helicopter down there in any case. They just issued a NOTAM. Because of the emergency, any aircraft flying within a nautical mile of the Camp David perimeter will be fired upon. They have all kinds of surface-to-air stuff on that mountain. Bushy's back in his element."

"I want to go to Camp David."

"Then drive. Just like they did."

"Ambrose has ordered the Special Function Force in," Kreski said. "They might blow us off the road before we can identify ourselves."

Copley tightened the belt of his raincoat against the increasing cold. "Walt. You're the director of the Secret Service. I'm the director of the Federal Bureau of Investigation. This is the United States of America."

It was late afternoon, the time of day when Charley Dresden could escape the taco stands, shopping centers, bowling alleys, and cheek-by-jowl housing developments of Santa Linda, and transform his life, however temporarily, by turning his car down a side street off Morelos Boulevard and heading west through an old section of the city into the hills. When he reached the top of the high ridge separating the crowded Santa Linda valley from the still wild and open Heather River valley and the Santa Cruz mountains beyond, the transformation was complete. In some sunsets, it was as close as he came anymore to a religious experience.

The state and county were talking again of building a four-lane expressway through this valley from Santa Linda, to connect with another to run south from Almaden and San Jose. That dreadful prospect made him press harder on the accelerator, as though to escape it.

Dresden owned two cars, the old black MG roadster he was driving and an ancient Armstrong-Siddeley saloon that now spent most of its time immobile in his garage, waiting for parts or the wherewithal for extraordinarily expensive repairs. He had bought the old British sedan on impulse years before, to impress a Santa Linda State College girl he was then dating, a rich, blond sorority girl—Kappa Alpha Theta.

Her name was Madeleine Anderson. Her family was socially prominent for the very California reason that her father had been the largest Cadillac dealer in the Santa Linda valley. She had done some modeling in college, and they had used her in some commercials filmed at the television station. She was the blondest girl Charley Dresden had ever met—a Scandinavian princess.

Maddy read poetry, and had written a considerable lot of it, some to him. She knew Russian, and fancied Aubrey Beardsley prints. Altogether, not a girl for Santa Linda. She had moved to San Francisco after graduating, and there, in an airy old balconied apartment near Twin Peaks, had provided Dresden with, among other savored memories, the finest morning of his life.

He had been thinking of Maddy that afternoon—because of her husband. The man she had married instead of him was now the junior United States senator from California.

He turned on the car radio and searched for music, but found only continuing news accounts of the assassination attempt and snapped it off. Someday he would find a place to live where no one cared who was president or what happened to him. He thought he had found such a place when he moved to Tiburcio.

Approaching a crossroads marked only by a stop sign and a shack of a Mexican beer bar, he slowed and then swerved to the left, following a blacktop highway that climbed along the skirts of a steep, tree-covered mountain for a few miles, then fell abruptly into what was called the Tiburcio canyon, a narrow valley containing Malchiste Creek and the village of Tiburcio. The town had just two roads, running along either side of the creek.

Dresden's house was on a back road, but he drove first to Cooper's Tiburcio Saloon and Grocery, which was also the town post office, an adobe brick building with bars on the back windows that had been built in 1848. He picked up his mail in the grocery and then crossed through a curtained doorway to the saloon. He didn't need to order the bourbon and water that Cooper set on the bar for him. It was ritual.

Cooper—no one ever used his first name except his sister, Belinda, when she was angry—had been a Coast Guard patrol boat skipper until he'd tired of it and taken an early retirement. A weathered, muscular man with some ten years more of life than Dresden, he had a face as worn as an old rug, a gruff and simple friendliness caught up in its folds and lines and grizzle. Normally, they would have shared recountings of each other's day, but this evening Cooper was absorbed by the bar's television set, usually the least used appliance in the establishment.

The local news was on—Santa Linda's Channel Three. Jack Laine, a failed nightclub singer before he turned to television, was still the anchor.

Dresden began to hurry through his drink, glancing over the mail. The large, bulky envelope would be a screenplay he had sent to an agent in Los Angeles, doubtless rejected. It was a script for a police melodrama in which no one was killed, injured, or beaten, and no automobiles sailed through the air.

"They sure did kill a lot of people when they missed the president," Cooper said.

"They didn't miss him, Coop."

"Well, they didn't kill him."

"Yes, they did."

"What'd you say, Charley?" The saloonkeeper turned. He looked as though he were going to bring his beer down to where Dresden sat.

"Nothing, Coop. See you later."

"Tonight?"

Charley had brought the unfinished commercial for the amusement park home, having convinced himself of the lie that he was actually going to work on it.

"Sure. Tonight."

Dresden's small house was on the mountain side of the back road, set well back against the slope and adjoining an old cemetery, long since filled. He parked the roadster haphazardly on the grass of the front yard, leaving the top down. Inside, he went first to the long living room that took up the rear half of the house, dropping his briefcase, pouring himself more whiskey at his old mahogany bar, and then going to the old red velvet Victorian chair in the corner. It was by a picture window that overlooked the cemetery, and was his favorite sitting place in a house filled with them.

Charley slumped down in the chair, stretching his long legs to prop his heels upon the old miner's trunk he kept beneath the window. The view was of the road and creek and some of the town buildings beyond, as seen through the hanging vines that drooped from the old oaks of the cemetery. The grave markers were wooden, and only a few remained, none of them fully upright. Most of those buried there were children, victims of the myriad plagues and diseases that wandered the West in the mid-nineteenth century. A last shaft of sunlight caught one of the markers now, slanting in through a defile in the opposite ridge line. In Santa Linda, it would not be sunset for another hour. Here, it would come soon.

He went out the back door and up the path that led through the flower garden behind the house. He managed to keep it presentable with the help of a woman friend fond of flowers. Set into the mountainside just above the garden was a creaky old latticed, brick lanai, equipped with a brick grill and a refrigerator that no longer worked, furnished with a few old rusting lawn chairs and a long porch swing. He settled into that, pushing it into motion with his feet as he let his gaze travel up and down the valley. He had brought many women up to this swing to be in love with over so many—too many—years. Never Maddy Anderson, though. Hers was a place in his life not in keeping with this house. He brought his glass to his lips and set to imagining her lying with him among the pines and mesquite of the mountain behind him, drinking rough wine and watching stars, sometimes shooting stars, as he had done with other women. Too soft, her skin; too gentle, her soul, for Tiburcio.

His mind, impatient, was interested in something else. The unanswered question that had itched at him all afternoon returned. Not whether the president was truly dead. He still had no doubt of that. But what possible reason there could be for not saying so. Of what use to anyone was a dead president?

The sun went down before he wished. After his simple meal he returned to the living room, but found he could not listen to music with much contentment. He stood and moved about the long room, ultimately pacing it. He opened his old trunk, rummaging through a thick packet of old photographs in the untidy memorabilia there until he found, as though miraculously, his favorite of Maddy Anderson. He stared at it a long while. She was lovely in it, but his memories of her physical presence, of the touch of her slender hand at the back of his head, of the loveliness of her scent, were better.

He put on his suit coat again and hurried out to his car. Dresden still dressed with the formality of his native East, an idiosyncrasy that had gained him the undeserved reputation as Tiburcio's only gentleman. He had even been elected mayor once, an honor he had hastily resigned upon discovering it tended to involve him in the settlement of often violent domestic disputes, especially in the Tiburcio Saloon and Grocery, which served in lieu of a town hall.

There were no disputes underway when Dresden entered. There was no one there but Coop and the tiny figures on the television screen. The saloonkeeper quickly made clear his interest in Dresden's presence there that night. He wanted to go into Santa Linda and needed someone to watch the store and tend bar until his sister Belinda returned. Obviously, Coop wanted to be well on the way to Santa Linda before she did. Coop had a new girlfriend, a widow who ran a taco stand.

Charley had no objection. He had done this many times before.

After Cooper left, his lurching pickup truck moving off with a clattering roar, Dresden set about reordering the place more to his liking—turning off and unplugging the television set, turning on the gas log in the huge fireplace, closing the always gaping doors to the rest rooms, and depositing a couple of quarters from Coop's back bar change in the jukebox. He chose mostly from a few selections that the Coopers had kept on the machine for years, in part for his benefit—Ray Charles's "I Can't Stop Loving You," Ramsey Lewis's

"Memphis in June," Michel LeGrand's "A Man and a Woman"— old songs, scratchy echoes of old times.

He made himself a large, carefully mixed Manhattan, brought it to a chair by the fireplace, and relaxed, tilting back against the wall. The huge old room was full of ghosts, bizarre specters of gloriously bizarre times.

Dresden had become the blood brother to a Yaqui Indian in this room, had danced Greek dances and picked up full bottles of beer from the floor with his teeth, had won and lost thousands of dollars at poker, had shot a man, had seduced sweet girls and knowing older women.

Time had run all together now. The young girls, wherever they were, were well on the way to middle age, but in Charley's memory-filled mind they were still fresh and tender. He could be holding Maddy Anderson's hand at this moment, if he closed his eyes, as he had so often at odd, gentle times, quiet times like this.

Maddy Anderson was now thirty-two. Dresden nearly thirty-six. The happy-forever he had found in Tiburcio was turning out to be merely his lifetime, and it was slipping away. If he persisted here, he would soon be old Charley Dresden, just another peculiar character at the bar, drinking in private sadness amidst an ever-increasing crowd of strangers.

Poe had written:

> Lo! Death has reared himself a throne
> In a strange city lying alone
> Far down within the dim West,
> Where the good and the bad and the worst
> and the best
> Have gone to their eternal rest.
> There shrines and palaces and towers
> (Time-eaten towers that tremble not!)
> Resemble nothing that is ours.
> Around, by lifting winds forgot,
> Resignedly beneath the sky
> The melancholy waters lie.

Poe had died at forty.

Dresden finished his drink and rose from the chair, gladdened by the sound of a car approaching. It went by, but another shortly after slowed and turned with a flare of headlights into a parking space near the saloon's front door. It was Danny Hill, an aerospace engineer who lived in a small cabin next to the firehouse and dressed like a sourdough. He had been hired back from his company's last recession furlough, but his money still went mostly for alimony payments and the upkeep of his Porsche, the one expensive possession he permitted himself.

Dresden bought him a beer. Hill had worked on Dresden's Armstrong-Siddeley the previous weekend—without pay and without success, but with considerable effort.

Hill glanced at the darkened television screen. He wore the kind of haircut that pilots did in the early 1960s and smoked a pipe. He was a man who listened to opera on his phonograph, sometimes all through the night, and threw rocks at his neighbor's cats. He was Dresden's best friend, in Tiburcio.

"Anything new on the president?"

Dresden shook his head.

"He's a lucky stiff, ain't he?"

Dresden paused. As was usually the case when he was broke, Hill had been depressed and irritable for several days. Charley didn't want to provoke an argument or fight—not with a friend.

"You don't think they might have killed him?"

As the words came out, he found himself beginning to tire of them.

"Charley, old mate, if he were killed he'd be dead. And they'd be playing Bach fugues on the radio. Last thing I heard on the way home was Willie Nelson." He put down fifty cents on the bar. "Give me one of those boneless chicken dinners, will you? I skipped lunch."

Dresden reached to the basket behind him and set a hard-boiled egg and a napkin in front of his friend. It was likely all the man might eat that night.

He picked up the half dollar, but opened another beer for Hill and paid for it himself.

Another flare of headlights announced additions to their evening— old Ed Farber and his wife stopping in for a beer on their way home, en route from other bars where they had stopped for a beer on their way home. A short while later, the Amadeo sisters arrived—Audrey, who was still considered one of the most attractive women in the canyon, and her twin sister, Annette, who at two hundred-forty-some pounds was not. Audrey ordered a Southern Comfort and Coca-

Cola, as always. Annette merely sat, waiting for the time when someone would get drunk enough to buy her a drink or ask her to dance.
Whenever someone did Cooper usually cut him off from further
drinks shortly afterward. It was one of the mysteries of Tiburcio how
Audrey could stay so slim on Southern Comfort and Coke and Annette could maintain her bulk on nothing.

Curly Lewes came in, a technician at the aerospace firm where
Hill worked, a woman-hungry man with troubled, sometimes mur-
derous eyes and a bad leg from a free-fall parachuting accident. He
asked if he could drink on his tab, and Dresden nodded. Lewes was
the man Dresden had shot. They had been arguing, but the gun had
discharged by accident, wounding Lewes glancingly in a hard roll of
belly muscle. Lewes had sworn to kill him after that, but now loved
to show off the scar to women.

Belinda, Cooper's sister, entered with a wide swing of the door.
Though it happened a half dozen times a day, her arrival was always
an event. She was a large, blowsy, but majestic red-haired woman,
this night wearing a somewhat ratty mink stole over a somewhat
dated black cocktail dress. In her tow was another imposing character, Roy Larson, her lover and the county sheriff. Their affair was a
long-standing one, but tended to wane in the periods when he was
out of office. Some said Belinda had simply found an inexpensive
way to deal with Tiburcio's lack of a police force. Belinda said there
were too many evil minds and nasty tongues in Tiburcio. Dresden
always sided with Belinda.

Charley came out from behind the bar and unplugged the
jukebox, to much angry consternation. "Police business," he said.
The television picture came on slowly, revealing an automobile flying through the air. The networks had returned to entertainment programming, as had the San Jose and Salinas stations, but Channel
Three was running a special on the assassination attempt, a tearfully
blinking Jack Laine interviewing Senator George Calendiari, a bald
yet very handsome man with dark eyes and a bandit's mustache. His
family owned one of the largest wineries in California, and additional
fortunes in real estate.

Dresden stared unhappily. Calendiari was Maddy's husband.

Calendiari expressed his shock and concern and then sat back,
waiting for Laine to ask something intelligent. The director would be
running the tape footage soon.

"Roy," said Charley to the sheriff. "They're going to put on the
tape of the president getting shot. I'd like you to look at it."

"Already saw it, Charley."

"Take another look, a close look."

On the screen, Bonnie Greer died yet again.

"You've seen a lot of people get shot, Roy. You've seen every kind of corpse. Look at him, Roy, and tell me if our president isn't a dead man."

Except for the television, the bar had become eerily quiet. Everyone but a pawing couple in one of the back booths was listening to them, watching the screen. The regulars wondered if they might be on the brink of another Tiburcio entertainment—an argument leading, with luck, to a brawl, and with the sheriff.

The footage of the president came and went in a virtual instant.

"All right," said Dresden. "Dead or alive?"

"Alive," said Larson.

"Roy, did you see his face? That expression? He wasn't just wincing!"

"Charley, I could spin you around and jab you a good one in a kidney. Your expression would be ten times worse than his was."

Belinda snapped off the set, marched to the jukebox, restored it to operation and full volume, and marched back. "Come on, Charley. Happy times."

Dresden shook his head in resignation. The raucous frivolity returned. He let himself succumb to the general contagion. By the time he drove home shortly after two A.M., he actually was happy, if quite thoroughly drunk.

His mood improved still further. In his front yard was a white Triumph TR-6. Gloom there might be in Washington and all the land, but in Tiburcio, California, in the glorious domain of Charles A. Dresden, there would be jubilation and celebration. Zack was back.

Charlene Zack was doubtlessly the most attractive woman who had ever set foot in Tiburcio. Much of Dresden's local status derived simply from her. Tall and sandy-haired, she had legs that might have earned her a considerable income as a model, if she had any inclination to rent herself out in that fashion, which she did not. The daughter of a low-ranking navy officer, her childhood spent at a variety of grubby naval bases around the country, she had graduated from high school in Vallejo and married almost immediately thereafter, as though finally to anchor herself. Yet she had divorced almost immediately after that. Though under age at the time, she had been able to lie with enough skill to gain a job as a cocktail waitress, a California tradition for young women in her predicament. It led to another marriage—and another divorce, happily for Dresden.

She had been working for a local public relations agency when Dresden had met her, though in two bouts of hard times since she had been compelled to take up the waitress tray again. He had met her not through his work but at a beach down the coast from Santa Cruz, on a warm, sunny winter's day. He'd been walking along the line of surf without another human in view when he glanced up and saw her in the doorway of a public cabana, her naked torso exposed as she changed clothes. The door had blown open but she didn't close it; just stood there, returning his gaze, challenging him to move on, or stay. Finally, he turned away, hurrying to his car. He followed her Triumph to a noisy bar down the coast road, and that night he saw her naked torso again.

Charlene was now a fairly well-paid blackjack dealer in Lake Tahoe, where she'd been working for several weeks. A highly intelligent but badly educated person, she was driven by a curiosity that others mistook for restlessness. She'd become the same kind of migratory creature she'd been as a child, but a voluntary one. At intervals of a year or two, she'd slip away from the Bay Area to Southern California, and then drift back again. Occasionally, she might find reason to live for a time up in Portland or Tahoe—even Honolulu once. Dresden's house in Tiburcio was her one permanent place. They had a very firm understanding about their separate lives and wide-ranging freedom, but this was Charlene's home. It was she who had kept up the garden behind the house. It was because of her that Dresden now took other women who came into his life elsewhere, even if that meant the back storeroom of Cooper's saloon.

She was asleep, lying facedown in the large Victorian bed that mostly filled the small bedroom. Charley removed all his clothes and slipped in beside her, running his hand along her back.

"So," he said, "there's a Zack in my sack."

She grumbled happily, stirring beneath his touch.

"Get your own Zack," she said. "This one's taken."

"By whom?"

"By the sandman. I need some Zs, you oversexed Kraut bastard. I've been hours and hours on the road. There was snow in the mountains."

"What brings you back? Looking for clean underwear?"

"Don't wear any."

"I know."

"I made my stake, Charley. I had some bloody good luck at the casino across from ours. I called you, but you were out, or drunk. I've got more than six thousand in cash in that purse over there. I'm going to be around awhile."

"Do you want to try public relations again? You can work out of my office if you like."

"Not tonight. Private relations tonight."

She turned over and looked at him, appreciatively. His happiness passed all quantifying. He had Tiburcio and he had Zack back. Now it truly didn't matter who the president was, or what happened to him.

Copley and Walt Kreski had put together a motorcade of five cars, racing them from Gettysburg down through Maryland with sirens shrieking and all lights flashing. The soldiers at Camp David would at least have some fair idea that they were not the Russians, if that still mattered.

It was not the army who stopped them when they at last entered Catoctin Mountain Park on the road from Thurmont, however. The uniforms were those of the Maryland State Police. The men in the raincoats with them were Kreski's Secret Service.

"The president's people put us under military orders, sir," said Agent Hammond, after he'd come to the open window of Kreski's car.

"I heard your radio transmission," Kreski said. "At least they're using us."

"It's a job these state troopers could handle on their own, director. Our mission is to stop all vehicular traffic at this point. I guess yours, too, sir."

"Has anyone been allowed through?" Copley asked.

"Just one car—with escorts. It was Mrs. Hampton. In a limo. Agent Coates recognized her."

"No one else?"

"No one they'd let come up. A lot of press. We let them camp out here, but some MPs came by and ordered them all back to Thurmont. There's been a lot of helicopter traffic, director. For a while it was almost constant."

"Are you the only checkpoint?"

"Oh no, sir. They've got a perimeter intersecting the road about halfway up. There's another position at the guardhouse and a lot of heavy weapons stuff up at the compound gate. I wouldn't mess with them, sir. They're kinda overweaponed."

Kreski sat staring at the forested mountainside beyond the reach of the headlights. All was blackness.

"Do you have communications with them?" Kreski said finally.

The agent nodded and pointed to a man with a handheld radio.

Kreski took a deep breath. "All right. Inform them of who we are and that we're coming up, to meet with the presidential party as per instructions. Get those sawhorses out of the way." He gently put the gear-shift lever into the drive position.

"Instructions?" said Copley, when Hammond had moved away.

"I'm sure it's covered somewhere in the procedure book." Kreski picked up the microphone of his car radio, waiting. When the barricades were pulled back he still hesitated. He didn't need to be doing this. He had a wife and a daughter in college. He was going to retire in a few months. He'd already been offered a good job with one of the biggest security firms in the country and two banks had asked if he would serve on their boards of directors. "All right. All units. Proceed."

On orders, they took the climbing road as fast as possible, the sirens screaming, the whirling Mars lights and side-mounted searchlights flashing wildly as they bounced and roared along the twisting course. The soldiers at the first line did nothing. Though holding weapons at the ready, they stepped aside in time for Kreski's motorcade to sweep by without much slowing. At the next position, the guardhouse that normally would have been manned by Kreski's people, the troops were unyielding, remaining positioned across the roadway with weapons leveled. At Kreski's orders, the cars ground and slid to a halt, two almost colliding. Kreski turned off the engine as an officer came toward them. He was a first lieutenant, exceedingly young, and wore the special pale green medal that Hampton had had created for those who had served in Central America.

"Are you Kreski? Sir?" he asked, in a gruff manner that suggested he would just as soon kill them both. Kreski nodded. "And you're Copley? Sir?"

"Director Copley," Copley said. "The Federal Bureau of Investigation."

"Yes, sir. May I see some identification?"

Both handed over their IDs, Copley with much irritation. The lieutenant examined them on both sides, and ran his thumb along the edge of the lamination.

"We're finished for the night at Gettysburg," Kreski said. "I'm required to report to the president's staff."

"Me too," said Copley, joining in the lie.

"I don't know anything about that, sir," said the officer, finally returning the identification cards. "My orders are to allow you to proceed to the compound gate. On foot. Someone will meet you there."

"Both of us?" Copley asked.

"Yes. Sir."

As they trudged up the grade, their shoes scuffing slightly on the blacktop, the wind came at them fiercely from spaces between the trees, stinging their flesh. Copley pulled on gloves.

"I begin to wonder why I was so anxious to come up here," he said.

"I'm wondering why we don't have an escort."

"Well, I'm not going to go running off into the bushes, Walter. I wouldn't be surprised if they had claymore mines set up."

"I suspect they do."

"Maybe they're hoping we'll trip one."

"You were reminding me this is the United States of America."

Another officer at the gate brought them inside, with some reluctance. Kreski felt akin to a prisoner of war being led through his own surrendered fortifications. He had been to Camp David hundreds of times in his career, the last hundred times as the man in charge. The security of this place had been among his most important responsibilities, and now he was being treated as a threat to it.

They were taken up a short, paved walk to the cabin nearest the gate and ushered inside. It was empty. There was no heat, not even a fire. Left alone, they seated themselves but did not speak. In a very short time, they were joined by two men they knew only slightly— Peter Schlessler, Hampton's driver, and C. D. Bragg, who was on the White House payroll as a presidential assistant but who served Hampton almost entirely as a political adviser. In a field noted for conviviality, Bragg was a cold, serious practitioner of his profession, a scientist among glad-handers and consensus-makers, a specialist who excelled at assessing the weaknesses of others.

"How is the president?" Copley asked.

Bragg studied him, as though trying to measure the degree of the

FBI director's sincerity. "He's doing fine." Bragg turned to Kreski. "What have you learned?"

"We've made multiple arrests," Copley said. "Nearly all Hispanic. There's a provable conspiracy, apparently Honduran, with apparently provable links to Nicaragua and Cuba."

Copley hadn't told Kreski that.

Bragg was still looking at Kreski. "What have you learned at Gettysburg? Were there other gunmen involved? Other snipers?"

"Probably. We don't have everything put together yet."

"Can you document the connection to Honduran terrorists? Do you have enough to justify a press conference statement? A U.N. resolution condemning the governments of Cuba and Nicaragua for responsibility in this?"

"Yes," Copley said.

"Not yet," Kreski said.

"We're meeting now in the president's lodge," Bragg said. "The president has asked Colonel Ambrose to take charge of things for the time being. Colonel Ambrose would like to meet with you at ten A.M. tomorrow."

"Here?"

"At the Rustic Motel in Thurmont. During this emergency, that will be our public contact point. The park here is going to be sealed off. We want to isolate the president as much as possible until the situation is secure."

"But the Rustic will be full of press!" Copley said. Kreski wondered if the man was beginning to lose control.

"We're having it cleared," said Bragg, rising. "You're to bring everything. Autopsy reports. Diagrams. Evidence technician reports. Arrest records. Colonel Ambrose wants to know everything you know."

"By ten A.M.?"

"What about the White House? The vice president? My other responsibilities?" Kreski asked.

"You're to carry out your other duties as always," Bragg said. "To the best of your ability. Our concern here is for the president's safety and for the most thorough possible investigation of the assassination attempt."

"I'm not a homicide investigator," Kreski said. "That's Director Copley's expertise."

Bragg continued to ignore Copley, whose exasperation was becoming very obvious. "Colonel Ambrose, and the president, have great confidence in your professionalism."

Kreski started to leave.

"You're to interrogate every one of your agents who was on duty at Gettysburg and instruct them not to leave the Washington metropolitan area."

"I'll deal with my men."

"Just do what you're goddamn told, director."

Bragg and Schlessler waited until the sound of Kreski's and Copley's motorcade had disappeared far down the hill, then hurried back to the presidential lodge. A huge fire was blazing on the hearth and the living room was fairly crowded, with people sitting in large, comfortable armchairs and drinking, some in sadness, some to deal with stress, some to calm themselves in the general air of excitement in the room. Schlessler went immediately to attend to those who desired refills. Bragg went to the fireside, where Ambrose sat looking at a yellow legal pad. "They'll be at Thurmont tomorrow," Bragg said.

"Do you think they'll tell us what they know?"

"Kreski will."

Ambrose nodded. Bragg returned to the seat he'd occupied earlier on the couch against the wall. Next to him was Jerry Greene, the president's advertising expert and media adviser. Next to him was Dr. Jerome Potter, the president's physician. In chairs nearby were the national security adviser, the secretary of defense, the army chief of staff, Senator Andrew Rollins of Tennessee, Hampton's principal man in the Congress, and David Callister, the conservative newspaper columnist and television commentator who had written of Hampton as a presidential possibility long before Hampton had given it any truly serious thought. Hampton had returned the favor with a genuine and most useful friendship.

Ambrose brought all talk to an abrupt halt by standing. He glanced at almost everyone, as a company commander might do, looking for demerits. He waited still longer, until the mood in the room was as somber as it had been when the meeting had begun. Then he held up the legal pad that had made the rounds of the room. "Everyone has read this now?" There were noddings. "There is complete understanding? There is complete agreement?" The noddings increased. Ambrose put the pad carefully into the flames, onto the top of the brightly burning logs. He drank, almost in some ritual toast, then set down his glass on the mantel with great care. His face was very flushed.

"Gentlemen. This has probably been the worst day of our lives. It could also be the most important day of our lives. Now, I think it would be . . . I think that, before we retire for the night, I think that we should all go in now and see the president."

5

Dresden awoke restless at the first glimmer of light, a barely perceptible predawn glow faintly outlining the smoothness of Charlene's bare shoulder and a few corners of furniture. He sat up slowly, quietly, reminding himself that he had had only a few hours sleep, and not caring. His mind was fully active, thoughts racing. Awful, bloody, remembered televised scenes from Gettysburg had chewed at the cozy bliss that had followed his making love to Charlene, but the alcohol had dealt with them. Now they had returned.

Moving quietly, he slipped from his bed and went into the living room, sitting restlessly on one of the velvet chairs for a moment, then fetching a nearly full gallon jug of wine from behind the mahogany bar. With it in hand, he went out the double doors into the shadows of the garden, and climbed on up the slope to where a crude dirt road had been cut across the face of the ridge, a favorite sitting place of his. Lowering himself gently to the cool earth and dangling his long legs over the edge of the road, he took another sip and put back his head, closing his eyes.

When he opened them again, it was to an entire world, his world. The broad vista before him encompassed much of the Heather River valley. Directly below him was all of Tiburcio, town, creek, and valley. To the southwest was the draw in the mountains that led, eventually, to Santa Cruz and the sea. No one who had ever sat in this place could possibly wonder why he had stayed here and would never leave.

The view was as intoxicating as the wine, even in the gloom of dawn, and too distracting. He looked down at his hands.

Why would they try to keep a dead man alive? They had a vice president, a cabinet—a Congress. Of what use was a dead president? What lunacy was running rampant in the national government? How was one to fathom lunacy, especially with mere logic?

There had been a forest fire in these mountains ten years before, a wild, mad aberration of nature that had consumed twenty-five thousand acres before it was done. The fire had spared the village of Tiburcio, but only just, leaping the creek a few miles upstream from the town and sweeping up and over the ridge. Dresden had driven into the burning mountains, using a station wagon news unit from Channel Three, bringing with him a photographer and a girl named Tracy Bakersfield, who had then been a freshly hired young videotape editor in the newsroom. Charley had almost gotten them killed, taking them onto a mountaintop clearing ringed by burning trees and failing to heed the hissing sound of a nearby oak wrapped in flame just before its superheated sap ignited and the tree exploded before their eyes, stunning them with its rush of heat. He had taken Tracy's hand and run. They had reached the station wagon in time, but nearly lost it and their lives backing down from the summit through a narrow defile where the swiftly moving fire had enveloped both sides of the road. Only their reckless speed in reverse—the slightest error in steering could have spun them into the flames—brought them through this gauntlet with no more harm than a few scorched patches on car paint and clothing.

He had fallen desperately in love with Tracy Bakersfield that night, though ultimately to no avail. After taking her home he had come back to this place in Tiburcio and watched the fire burn on through the night and into the dawning morning. The sun had risen through layers of smoke and haze over a bizarre and barren landscape that might as well have been another planet's.

The trees had all grown back now. At the ridgeline opposite, over which the flames had come marching like one of the vast armies of antiquity, the sun would shortly shine on stands of pine and oak and patches of gentle yellow meadow. If he'd keep quiet, if he'd forgotten about the president, he could continue his life as serenely as before. Nothing would disturb this.

Dresden rose, stretching. He had decided what to do next.

Tracy Bakersfield was now teaching a television course at Santa Linda State and living in Villa Beach over on the ocean. Dresden still saw her occasionally, though she was married. The gentleman had changed her name to Tracy Kluggerman. She remained a genius at videotape editing. She was the finest editor of tape or film Charley had ever encountered in all his career. That she had become nothing more than a teacher at a second-echelon state university was not illogical. She was very happy and living where she wished, just as he was content and fulfilled living in Tiburcio. California was like that.

He would seek her out, as soon as possible. But first he would need an assassination tape of his own.

Still puzzling over his unanswered questions, he started down the slope toward his darkened house.

Vice President Atherton had put on one of his darkest suits, one usually worn at foreign funerals. To preclude too great an aspect of mourning, he had added the touch of a light blue shirt and crimson silk tie. These were television clothes. He would likely spend a sizable part of this long day on television.

Two extra Secret Service cars had been added to his motorcade and a new route to the White House was being taken. Normally, the Secret Service rarely varied from three routes—as Atherton knew them: the ten-minute, fifteen-minute, and twenty-minute routes. It was nearly impossible to get directly downtown from Observatory Hill any other way. But this morning they were taking a circuitous one that had already consumed fifteen minutes, driving north up Rock Creek Parkway and then doubling back south again all the way to the Potomac River.

He was briefly enticed by the notion of a catnap, but thought better of it. A Ronald Reagan might have been able to get away with sleeping through a crisis, but not a young vice president. And certainly not this crisis. He had another compelling reason for wakefulness. Laurence Atherton now believed in the possibility of himself being assassinated even more than the Secret Service did.

Atherton had slept badly and little the previous night. The National Security Council meeting he had called had been delayed for more than an hour for lack of sufficient principals, and he'd finally been compelled to proceed with the emergency conference without the absentees. Lacking the secretary of defense and the national security adviser, the meeting was without much purpose. Merriman Crosby, the secretary of state, reported that the governments of Nicaragua and El Salvador had vehemently denied any complicity in the shootings and had charged the United States with rigging the assassination attempt to discredit their revolution. The chairman of the Joint Chiefs said that military activity had virtually ceased in the combat sectors of Guatemala, Honduras, and Costa Rica. He reported that the National Security Agency, which operated a supersecret global electronic eavesdropping network chiefly for the military, had picked up increased communications traffic between Moscow and Havana, as well as between Washington embassies and a great many home foreign ministries. It otherwise had found little out of the ordinary.

Old Admiral Elmore, the director of Central Intelligence, had attended the meeting in a rare appearance. For most NSC sessions, he customarily sent a deputy. A grim, cold-faced professional appointed by President Hampton's predecessor, the retired flag officer and former National Security Agency chief had been steadfastly neutral in the rivalry between Hampton and Atherton forces in the White House. He had remained silent for most of the meeting and expressionless throughout all of it. In response to a question at the beginning, he had said none of the nation's intelligence agencies had received any indication that an internationally organized assassination plot had been in progress. At the conclusion of the session, he informed them that all intelligence assets in Central America had been ordered to determine the extent of any foreign involvement in the plot, if any, though none now could be proved beyond the arrests of Honduran nationals by the FBI. There were times when Atherton wondered which government the old admiral was working for. Probably his own.

The motorcade swept around a curve and along a stone embankment bordering the Potomac, its waters now glittering in the early morning sunshine. The cars in the opposite lanes had been slowed to a standstill by the heavy traffic, and each motorist's eyes seemed to meet Atherton's as they went past. The vice president eased back against the seat and out of their sight. There was a late edition of the *Washington Post* on the seat beside him, but he ignored it. The paper would be full of important information, but not that which he needed most to know. What was going on up at Camp David? What madness had enveloped the most powerful office in the free world?

After the National Security Council meeting Atherton had joined with Shawcross, Howard, Secretary of State Crosby, and the attorney general, his closest allies in the cabinet, for a private conference of their own. Not daring to use the vice presidential mansion, knowing the extent of listening devices throughout the government buildings of Washington, he chose instead a back private dining room of his club, which he had seldom visited since becoming vice president.

In that discreet surrounding they had talked over their next course of action, finding little opportunity for any. Camp David had given them no instructions whatsoever. Camp David had been informed of Atherton's call of NSC and cabinet meetings, and had not responded, unless the rude silence could itself be considered a pointed response. It had been decided to proceed in similar fashion. They would go to their offices and attend to the daily routine of their governmental responsibilities, but nothing beyond that.

With one exception. The news media were behaving almost hysterically about the lack of information and presidential presence, and shortly much of the public would be doing the same. Atherton would take it upon himself to calm the nation, or at least make clear that there had been no coup, that the White House was in safe hands, and that the government was functioning normally. He would stay off "Today," "Good Morning America," and "CBS Morning News"—for the time being—but he would grant enough interviews to satisfy all three networks' evening news programs and the major wire services. If Bushy Ambrose objected, well enough. Let him come forward, and bring President Hampton with him.

With a whoop of sirens, the motorcade again turned, crossing the oncoming lanes onto a road that led north past the Lincoln Memorial. Atherton turned to look at the huge columns and the darkness behind them, his mind filling with the image of the great, staring statue within. Atherton was no worshiper of Lincoln, but he felt in awe of the man's extraordinary place in history. It was awe compounded by a sense of his own inadequacy, and despair that the reference to him in the history books would be a footnote in the account of a failed and mediocre administration in the service of a vain and ineffectual man. Hampton styled himself the great compromiser. Atherton saw him as weak and equivocating, a dodger of opportunity, an evader of the historical main chance. Lincoln was the greatest war president America had ever had. Hampton kept his dirty little war in a closet. When John Wilkes Booth's bullet crashed into Lincoln's skull, it destroyed a monumental intellect. What had the bullet that struck Hampton destroyed, if anything?

The thought of bullets brought the remembered sound of them—snaps and poppings as heard on the television news, shattering explosions in Atherton's mental ear. He shivered, putting his head down and folding his arms tight against his chest. He would concentrate on the approaching cabinet meeting. The Hampton men would doubtless stay away. His own remnant force would be going through the motions largely for the benefit of the public.

The only meeting of consequence that day was likely to be the one ordered by Colonel Ambrose at Camp David, to be attended by Walt Kreski and Steve Copley of the FBI. Both Copley and Kreski had promised to give Atherton a full briefing after they returned—if they returned.

At yet another turning, the White House swept distantly into view across the Ellipse, looking not at all the place of dread and menace it had the previous night. Quite the contrary. As long as Hampton, Ambrose & Co. remained in hiding in their Maryland mountain fortress, the White House would be Atherton's domain.

He began to rehearse answers to questions he could expect from the television interviewers. They would most certainly not be the right questions, but then, he hadn't the right answers.

Summoning his courage, for he feared humiliation as much as anything that had threatened him in his life, Charley Dresden spun his old MG into the Channel Three parking lot with a nonchalance that required a great deal of acting. His old parking place four spaces from the main door was, of course, occupied, as all of them on the paved portion proved to be. He was compelled to park in a gravel side lot, next to a rusting van that had the name of an obscure country and western band on the side. There were a number of cars he recognized, but none he recalled belonging to Jim Ireland. Stepping out of the roadster, he snatched up his briefcase as he might a weapon before going into battle.

The receptionist was new, which helped, as he was going to play this very straight. He asked for Bert Novak, a salesman he occasionally drank with in Antoine's when Jim Ireland wasn't around. The wholesome, sweet-faced brunette motioned him to a chair, where he remained ignored for nearly twenty minutes. At last Novak appeared in the doorway, but the man hung back, holding onto the door, looking impatient.

"I'm kinda busy, Charley," he said. "What's up?"

"I got the amusement park account," Dresden said, rising. "I want to buy some air time."

It was a lie. His contract with the advertiser was merely to produce the commercial, not to buy time for it on television stations. What Dresden was doing was extremely unethical and probably illegal.

Novak stared at him a moment, frowning and blinking. "Doesn't he want to wait until after the rainy season?"

"He thinks he can attract some business during the Christmas holidays."

"Santa's coming on a roller coaster?"

"It's only money, Novak." Ed Stanley, the station's sales manager, kept a sign on the back of the sales office door: REMEMBER . . . IT'S ONLY MONEY. It was intended for the benefit of station executives squeamish about running commercials for aluminum siding sales outfits and furniture stores that catered mostly to poor Mexicans.

"How many spots?" Novak asked.

"Two."

Novak frowned again.

"Two a night," Charley said. "For two weeks." The amusement park man had actually mentioned such a possible schedule.

As Novak wrote up the contract in his small cubicle of an office, Dresden kept as calm as possible. He was fraudulently committing himself to an obligation of several thousand dollars.

"Charley, I'll need some money up front. I'm afraid you're still on the bad list."

"You mean before the spots run."

"Before they get on the schedule."

"I'll drop a check by tomorrow." Dresden signed the contract, then sat back. "As a certified client, I'd like to ask a favor. I've got some footage of his thrill rides I have to preview, and my recorder's on the bum."

"Charley. You can't mess with our equipment unless we produce the spots. You know the rules."

"I'm not asking to do any editing now. I just want to look at some tape."

Novak sighed. "The client is always right. Even you, I guess."

"Don't tell Ireland that. He would differ."

Dresden actually did have some amusement park footage—an old commercial the park operator had used years before and had given to Charley as an example of what he didn't want. It was very bad. Charley ran it through three times, pretending to study it. The consumption of time was making him nervous. This particular editing and previewing room was just off the main corridor and a fairly public place. Novak had kept the door open because of the heat generated by the equipment.

"I've another favor to ask," Dresden said. "I need a tape of the shooting of the president."

"For a commercial?"

"For history. I tried to record from the networks, but my machine screwed it up. It won't cost you anything. I just want to record from your stuff. I brought along an empty cassette." He took it from his briefcase and held it up.

"Charley. I'm really busy."

"Look, Bert. I just did you a favor. My client wanted to put the whole schedule on Channel Eleven in San Jose."

"All right. I'll go over to the newsroom. Wait here. Don't go wandering into the control room and get yourself in trouble."

"I won't budge." He didn't. He sat motionless, as though that would keep people in the corridor from noticing him.

"They need this right back," Novak said, returning. "So hurry. It's good quality. It was taken right off the network feed."

The taped gunfire had only just commenced when Dresden sensed the hulking figure in the doorway behind him. He had no need to turn to confirm that it was Ireland. He knew his luck.

"What the hell do you think you're doing, Bert?" Ireland thundered.

"Charley's a client."

Ireland swore. "Like hell he is. The son of a bitch is just trying to use our equipment, to try to win a goddamn bet with me!"

Before Ireland could speak further, Dresden leaped up, hit the "stop" and "eject" buttons, snapped out both tape cassettes, and slapped them down on the console. "Say no more. I'm leaving."

"Now!"

Dresden retrieved two of the tapes and dropped them into his briefcase, handing the third to Novak. He waited for Ireland to step aside—if he brushed against the man, he feared there'd be violence—and hurried down the hall, pausing on the way out only to smile at the receptionist and say, "Thank you, sunshine."

He smiled again as he roared the MG out into the street. The tape he had handed Novak was of the old amusement park commercial. The network assassination tape was safe in his briefcase.

"You're a crazy man, Charles Dresden," he said to himself, to the world. "But you're smart. And you're right. You're right, and the whole world is wrong."

Bushy Ambrose had taken a two-room "suite" at the Rustic Motel in Thurmont, and had had the desk pulled away from the wall so he could sit behind it and deal with his visitors as though he were in his White House office. Both Walt Kreski and Steven Copley had arrived with aides, but Ambrose had insisted on meeting with them alone, himself joined only by Peter Schlessler. He went wherever Ambrose did now, or where Ambrose sent him. Some said Schlessler was actually more loyal to Ambrose than to the president, and it was probably true. Schlessler had served the colonel in Vietnam. After getting out of the army he had gone on the bum and gotten into more than occasional trouble. Ambrose had rescued him, giving him a job at the amusement park and eventually making him his top assistant. He had come along when Ambrose had joined Hampton's staff in the Colorado governor's office.

Ambrose spent more than an hour looking through the reports Kreski and Copley had brought with them, asking periodic questions in the manner of an inquisitor. Kreski felt almost as though he were under arrest. Finally, Ambrose slapped the folders shut, folded his hands, and glared at them as might an army CO having to deal with two GIs returning AWOL.

"There's a lot of paper there but what there's most of is bullshit," he said.

"Colonel?" Copley said. Ambrose did not like being called colonel.

"You've got it all tied up, except you only seem to have one real fact. That the president was shot at by a now deceased wetback named Manuel Lopez Angel Huerta."

"We might learn more if we could retrieve the bullet or bullets that hit the president for ballistics," Copley said.

"There was one," Ambrose said. "It passed through."

"They could be imbedded in the limousine."

"How can you tell them from all the other bullets? Anyway, the limo stays up here, for the time being." Ambrose's eyes fixed on Kreski. "Your Agent Schultz. I want him charged with everything in the books, including war crimes and violation of the Hatch Act, if need be."

"He has been," Copley said.

"He's become a psycho case," said Kreski, softly. "We have him in St. Elizabeth's."

"Great. Where they put John Hinckley," Ambrose said. "I want Schultz in jail, instanter. I want his supervisor suspended. The networks are screaming about Bonnie Greer."

"His supervisor was Al Berger," said Kreski.

"That reminds me," Ambrose said, reaching for one of the file folders. "The only other fact in here is that you've established that Berger was struck by a bullet different from those fired by the wetback, one fired by a party unknown. All the Secret Service and police on the scene say they were firing away from Berger. Party unknown is another assassin?"

"Apparently so."

"Why didn't you come out and say so clearly? There's no other evidence of this party unknown, no footprint, no shell casings?"

"No shell casings," Copley said.

"There were a thousand footprints," Kreski said. "People ran in every direction."

"And all these arrests," Ambrose said. "These Hispanics in New York sound like drug dealers."

"As the report notes, weapons were recovered from the rooftop," Copley said. He looked exasperated, and was sweating slightly.

"And this revolutionary group in Chicago, La Puño. Admiral Elmore says no one in Central Intelligence has ever heard of it before. The Defense Intelligence Agency says La Puño has no connection with the Honduran Army of the People's Liberation or any of the other guerrilla groups."

"If we had learned about it beforehand we would have stopped this from happening," Kreski said.

"These people in Chicago," Ambrose continued, "aside from their being associated with La Puño, all you can really charge them with is being illegals."

"For now," said Copley.

"You've made no arrests in Washington? Three bombs were exploded. They blew up some parked cars in the Rayburn and a wastebasket at the OAS building."

"No arrests," Copley said. "Yet."

"Have you made any arrests he hasn't, Kreski? Do you have any new suspects?"

Kreski shook his head. "We're doing our best. My principal concern has been protecting the senior members of the government."

"Damn straight," said Ambrose. "But you sure fucked up that mission in Gettysburg. That's why we're staying up here. If that embarrasses you, too bad. The president's life comes first." He shoved the reports across the desk in their direction. "I want to hear from both of you twice a day, and sooner if you should learn a new fact."

Schlessler stood up. It was the first time he had moved during the entire interview. Kreski started to rise, but Copley remained seated.

"If you don't mind, Colonel," he said. "We'd appreciate a little assistance. It would certainly help if we could interview the president."

"Impossible. Certainly not now. I was with him all the time. There's nothing he could add."

"If we could at least have the president's clothing—as evidence."

"Not now."

"There's something called obstruction of justice."

"There's something called endangering the life of the president."

"By taking his clothes? His suit jacket and flak vest?"

"Enough of this, Copley. You are an employee of the Justice Department. Kreski, you work for the Department of the Treasury. The attorney general and the treasury secretary serve at the pleasure of the president. Do you read me?"

"At the moment, the attorney general and the treasury secretary have no way of knowing the president's pleasure."

"Yes, they do! Through me and the White House staff! We don't know what's going on out there, damn it! All we have is a pile of hamburger that used to be a wetback and a bunch of innocent dead people. The president of the United States was almost one of them, and neither of your agencies knew the first goddamn thing about it. Your job isn't to write another Warren Commission report. It's to find out who tried to kill the president and whether they're going to try to do it again and what we can do to stop it!"

"Will you at least tell us the president's condition?"

Ambrose glanced at Schlessler. "The president's condition is good." He stood up and folded his hands behind his back. "He took a bad round, gentlemen. A through-and-through wound in the muscle where the neck joins the shoulder. But he's coming along fine. Dr. Potter will be making a statement later."

"Why wait? The public ought to know," said Copley. "The networks have been screaming about that too."

"We've kept the public informed. We issued a statement last night. We don't need to grant Barbara Walters an interview."

"The public would like to see the president, if that's possible."

"It's not. This is a serious goddamn security situation! This is damn near a military situation! You're the country's top cops, aren't you? Now go out and do your goddamn jobs!"

Copley, who had gone to Harvard Law as well as Princeton, never liked being called a cop, or even a policeman.

"It's time to go, sir," Schlessler said.

Copley at last arose.

"Well, Bushy," he said, as he should not have. "The American people at least ought to know who's running the government while the president is, uh, recovering."

But instead of becoming angrier, Ambrose suddenly calmed.

"The president will decide that shortly," he said, and walked out. Schlessler waited until Kreski and Copley had left the room, then closed the door and followed his superior.

As they returned to their cars, Copley said, "I think we've just seen who's running the government."

"Maybe the networks will start screaming about that," said Kreski.

Tracy Bakersfield had no class to teach that day and was at her home by the sea. Dresden had not talked to her in three or four months, but as always she sounded delighted to receive his call, though she never made any to him. After he made his strange request, she paused, but then agreed. She had always indulged him in sisterly fashion.

Her car was being repaired and her husband had the other one, so it was necessary for Dresden to drive out for her. There would be no work that day on the new commercial. He didn't mind. He would meet the deadline somehow, in a flash of brilliance and an hour or so of concentrated effort, as had served him in such situations before. Were he to fail and miss the deadline, well, there were other clients, somewhere.

He found her asleep, reclining in a lounge chair on the scrubby lawn behind her house. It sloped down to the brink of the cliff and overlooked a wide expanse of ocean. Hidden from view was the little village of Villa Beach that was crowded against the base of the cliff below. Only a glimpse of the town's long wooden fishing pier, a concrete breakwater, and a lone palm tree was visible. But Tracy's small house and lawn possessed as full a sweeping prospect of sea and embracing coastline as there was in California. At night the lights of Monterey could be seen far to the south.

She slept in quiet repose, dressed in a pale blue blouse, khaki shorts, and well-weathered boating shoes, her slim, tanned legs crossed at the ankles. She was nearly Charley's age, and her skin had bathed in too much sea and sun, but her face was still as gentle and childlike as when he had first met her. She had the most perfect and innocent eyes, now all the more innocent closed in slumber.

His ardor for her had once been all-consuming, manifest in much foolishness. He recalled wading fully clothed out into the waves in the midst of an afternoon's storm to raise a glass of wine to pounding sea and glowering sky to proclaim his love for her. If she had been impressed, it had done him little good.

Tracy awoke as he stood looking at her. He adjusted his expression, then smiled. As she sat up, she looked at the sparkling ocean, and said, "You're going to take me away from a lovely day."

"I really appreciate your doing this for me. I was afraid you would think I was crazy."

"You're not crazy. You just never grew up. I'm very fond of little boys," she said, but kindly, indulgently.

"Tracy, this tape is important to me."

"To win a bet with Jim Ireland?"

"To win a bet with television."

She gazed at him a long moment, her eyes less childlike, full of the bond between them. "Sometimes I don't understand you, Charley."

"You're the only one who ever does."

She smiled, but shook her head, then got nimbly to her feet. "At least it will be a pretty drive over the mountains." The remark was very like her. She would indeed enjoy the drive, though it was one she took almost every day.

It was an anomaly of television that the facilities in Santa Linda State's School of Broadcast Journalism were much more elaborate and expensive than those of Channel Three, or any other commercial station in the Bay Area, including San Francisco's. Commercial stations were in the business of making money. State colleges were in the business of spending it. The videotape editing machine Tracy went to was a top of the line Sony 800.

Charley hesitated slightly before handing her the tape cassette. She had a deep-seated psychological aversion to any manifestation of death, dying, wounds, pain, injury, or any kind of suffering. Years before, while he was driving her home late one night, they had come upon a horrible accident involving two cars and a horse trailer. One horse was dead. The other, missing most of its two front legs, was thrashing and screaming. A policeman emptied his pistol at the poor animal but succeeded only in wounding it further, increasing its fury. Finally, another policeman managed to shoot it through the head, and it collapsed dead, but there was still screaming. It came from Tracy.

She had spent all that night lying face up on her living room floor, fully awake and staring at the ceiling. There had been nothing at all gentle or childlike about her eyes then.

"I've seen the tape, Charley," she said, quietly. "Everyone in America has."

"Not the way they should have."

She turned to the console, inserted the tape, and, with the sureness of a cathedral organist, moved her fingers over the lighted buttons. In a moment President Hampton was on the screen, speaking, Gettysburg's grave markers in the background. No words could be heard, however. Her finger flicked at a button marked "Audio, Ch. 1." A network correspondent's voice filled the room.

Unlike film, videotape has two sound tracks. With another flick, she hit "Audio, Ch. 2." The correspondent's clipped, precise tones were replaced by the president's practiced, sonorous ones.

"Go forward to the first gunshots," Dresden said.

She did, the squeaky jabberwocky of accelerated speech produced by the racing tape on fast forward suddenly replaced by snapping pops. In an instant she had the tape reversed to the president standing by his car, then she let it run forward again at normal speed, and quickly froze it. The president had a quizzical look on his face, but neither of the two men with him seemed concerned.

"Okay," Charley said.

Tracy switched to the slowest of forward speeds, the distorted sounds expanding and falling in groans. The first shot came as an audible mushroom. All three men on the screen reacted glacially, their facial muscles slowly contracting, the president's in particular. He was by then about to get into his car, but no wound appeared on him.

The second mushroom of sound produced a more pronounced facial contraction.

"Stop."

There is a third track on videotape, carrying neither picture nor sound. Known as the control track, it consists of numbered editing pulses, one per frame. With film, because of the distance between the lens and sound drum of projectors, the sound track is eight frames ahead of the picture. With videotape, audio is in exact line with video, and both sound tracks and picture are edited at the same peak of each pulse.

"Wait," she said.

Frame by frame, she moved the tape backward and forward, the slow groans of sound dragging in and out of new audible shapes. On the downside of one, she stopped the tape. She peered at the screen, studying the image carefully, then said, very quietly, "There's your wound."

For a moment he couldn't see it. He'd be needing glasses soon. Wiping his eyes, then blinking, he looked again. She pointed to a small spot on the president's back, just to the right of the left shoulder joint, where the muscle climbs to the neck.

"You're sure it's not an imperfection?"

"I'll punch it up on a larger unit. It's the highest resolution monitor we have."

Her fingers moved to another section of the console, then, hitting the "Standby" button, she rose from her chair. She took him down a short hall to a viewing room with a large television screen inset in the wall. There was a female student with an obvious weight problem seated in one of the chairs, eating a cheeseburger as she read through some technical manual.

"Please pardon us," Tracy said. The student nodded.

Tracy turned on the monitor. The president was now giant-sized and the spot was a well-defined circle, with puffs of cloth bits and other material visible in a vaguer circle around it. Tracy paused, swallowed, then pointed to a place on the screen in front of the president.

"You see?" she said.

He squinted. "No."

"Wait." She adjusted the controls of the monitor, deliberately exaggerating the brightness and color tones. What had struck him as specks of dust on the screen turned to incandescent pink and grew threefold in size, glowing.

She coughed. "That's from the exit wound. That's blood." She turned away while he stared. Finally, he looked back to the woman student, whose widened eyes were fixed upon the screen.

"Could you excuse us, please?" he said.

"Please," said Tracy.

Uncertain, suspicious, obviously fascinated, and perhaps a trifle frightened, the student did as she was asked, hesitating at the door, then hurrying on.

"Can you do all this again?" Dresden said when the student had gone. "With the next shot?"

"From now on, track two is nothing but shots."

"The next one that hits him," Charley said. "If one does."

She coughed and swallowed again. "All right. Sit down and wait. It may take awhile to get it right."

He did as bidden. The screen went blank. In less than five minutes it filled with video again. The president was being pushed into the limousine by a man who'd been identified as one of his Secret Service agents. With the monitor's color tint control still set at maximum, a small but shimmering circle showed on the agent's back. Three dots of exaggerated pink appeared in the air in front of the president. The agent looked to be directly behind the president's body. The flying drops of blood were just inside the limousine. They could not have come from the agent. The bullet that produced them had quite definitely traveled through the bodies of both men, apparently emerging from just above the president's stomach. It could not be a wound to enjoy for long.

Dresden leaned forward, staring, hand cradling jaw. When the screen faded to black and she rejoined him he said: "I am right. Absolutely right."

She put her hand on his arm, lightly. "Yes, Charley. Once again you're right."

"Is there a way you can get me a print of all this?"

"I'll make you up a tape. Freeze frames. Both of the wounds. The full sequences."

"I love you, Tracy Bakersfield."

Her hand dropped. "I won't be long. Then we can go home."

As they were walking out to his car she asked an obvious question. "Surely other people will be going over the tapes like this—the police, the FBI, the networks?"

"Maybe. They certainly ought to be."

"Then why are you?"

"Because they might not. Because someone should, if only me."

"But why wouldn't they?"

"People like to believe what they're told. They really didn't get into the Kennedy assassination like this until months after the fact."

"I don't remember that."

He opened the door for her. "I really appreciate your helping me. Everybody else has been treating me like a fool."

She sat staring forward, saying nothing. She remained silent all the way out of Santa Linda and over the mountains and down the coast road. He wondered whether she had become traumatized by the so minutely examined violence and gore on the tape or if she was just not in a mood to speak as loudly as riding in his open car required. He let her be. When they pulled up at her house he put the gearshift in neutral and left the engine running.

She didn't move, but continued to gaze ahead, to a view of sea beyond the end of the drive. It was now a darker, bluer hue. He took her hand.

"I'm sorry. I shouldn't have asked you to do that. All that bloodshed."

"That's not what's bothering me, Charley. I'm worried about what you're going to do with this tape. I don't like it that people think you're a fool. You're not a fool, Charley. You're the most intelligent man I've ever known. I don't want them to laugh at you, to try to laugh you out of Santa Linda."

"They won't. They can't."

"Yes they can, Charley."

"Santa Linda, maybe. But not Tiburcio. I'll go to work tending bar for Cooper, and write TV scripts on the side. No one's going to make me leave."

"What are you going to do with the tape, Charley?" Her voice was very low, a monotone.

"Bring it to the attention of the American people."

"And how are you going to do that?"

"I'll find a way. You once told me I could do anything I wanted to do."

"I wish I hadn't. And anyway, I said you could, not that you should."

"Now you tell me."

She was herself again, even a hint of smile at the corners of her mouth, though there was still sadness in her eyes. He squeezed her hand, and she squeezed his.

"*Muchas gracias, mi hermana.*"

At the Spanish word for sister, her smile became sunshine. "Please take care of yourself, Charley. We love you. Don't wait so long to call. Or come by."

And then she was gone. He was left with only a darkening sea and fading sun, and an old but well-remembered loneliness. Dresden gunned the engine and backed with squealing tires out of the drive. In a moment, he was flying along the coast road at seventy miles an hour. He had triumphed, had he not? He was right. He had proved beyond any doubt that he was absolutely, utterly, and supremely right, and that the whole world was wrong. The evidence was in the tape cassette that lay in the well behind his seat like a small chest of gold. But triumph was small remedy for this kind of loneliness. He wished to be in that small cliffside house, with that extraordinarily lovely person who had so charmed his life, to be with her for the full last of the sun upon the darkening water, and for more.

Tracy had once told him he always wished for the wrong things. He did not. He wished wrongly for the right things. He roared the old MG through a yellow light and up a curving incline to the highway that crossed the mountains, passing cars in a blur and moving the roadster up to its top speed. His mind shifted to an old, unwanted thought. What if that wish had been fulfilled? What if that small house and its wonderfully endearing occupant were his for the rest of his days? He had never married. Freedom was life. At the least, it had always been his life. He had never really asked for more.

He turned on the radio, hoping somehow for a song from the old days, "Memphis in June." There was only the news. The president was alive and well, it said.

The vice president had postponed their meeting until evening, leaving Walt Kreski with a block of time in which, if he chose, he had nothing to do. He so chose, using the time to drive about the crowded streets of Washington in the dark November rush hour, not a little cheered by the normality of automobile horns and slowly moving taillights. If the country was on the brink of governmental collapse, it had not yet been reflected in the car pool restrictions on Route 66 and other commuter highways.

Kreski used this time not to collect his thoughts but to evade them. They would lead inevitably to an oppressive guilt—for what he had allowed to happen to the president, to Al Berger, to the people slain by Agent Schultz, and to Agent Schultz. It was doubly frustrating, because, though he felt it painfully, he could not yet prove his guilt to himself. His self-blame would not stick.

He had dismissed his driver and taken the wheel of the unmarked black Oldsmobile himself. In a dereliction of duty he would not have countenanced in a subordinate, he turned off the two-way radio and the other radio monitors in the car and instead turned on the car's AM receiver, tuning it to a station that played continuous elevator music and broadcast news only on the hour. With that, even putting from his mind the holstered revolver beneath his suit coat, he plunged into the downtown traffic, comforted by the familiarity of it all—the high-priced lawyer and lobbyist influence peddlers becoming mere motorists as they pulled out of the parking garages along K Street, the streetwalkers beginning their workday in what remained of the honky-tonk district around H Street and 14th, the clusters of clerks and secretaries waiting for the buses that still chugged and rattled along Pennsylvania Avenue, keeping schedule despite the supposed national crisis. It had been that way after the attempted assassinations of President Ford in the 1970s and after the shooting of Ronald Reagan in 1981. Life went on. Government went on. That was perhaps its only virtue.

He proceeded south toward the Mall, which, in contrast to the crowded nearby avenues, was a place of dark and stillness, with only a few yellow squares of light visible in the facades of the giant museums that lined it. To the east, at the end of the Mall, the floodlit dome of the Capitol loomed over all, its marble and sandstone as chill as a gravemarker's but still astir within with life and business. Kreski drove toward it as though beckoned, turning right at the security barricades at the foot of the hill onto a short road that led obliquely to Independence Avenue and the huge House office buildings beyond.

This city was his beat. In his long tenure with the service, Kreski had walked alleys from Waterloo, Iowa, to Waterloo, Belgium; had prepared motorcade routes from Walla Walla to Singapore. But Washington, D.C., was Base One. Every major intersection and vantage point was a vivid image in his mind. He had memorized windows from the slums of northeast Washington to the top floor of the Metropolitan Club downtown. Like a beat cop, he had learned the rhythms of the city, knew instinctively what was normal and what was not. He had learned to itch when something not fully perceived by his senses was amiss.

As he drove up the hill on Independence Avenue, he knew precisely where units of the U.S. Capitol police and his own agents were positioned in the shadows behind the newly strung barbed wire, parked dump trucks, and concrete barriers. He sensed the presence of the sniper and shoulder-held Stinger antiaircraft missile teams on the rooftops of the office buildings and the two wings of the Capitol. Passing the blockaded drive leading to the East Portico, he could imagine the radio conversations between those in the new command post established beneath the Capitol's central stairs and the men out on the perimeter.

He had produced this, working most of the night and for all of the day left after his morning meeting in Maryland with Bushy Ambrose. He had secured Capitol Hill, the White House, and a dozen other government buildings—excepting only the Pentagon, State Department, Justice Department, and FBI buildings, which insisted on providing their own security. In the manner of some bureaucratic god, he had drawn up a list of government officials and relatives who in his judgment merited protection and had pulled in agents from all over the country to provide it.

He was exhausted, troubled that he had been able to devote so little time to the investigation of the assassination attempt itself, but otherwise he felt very satisfied. His praetorian guard might have failed the president at Gettysburg, but it would not fail again. The windows of the congressional office buildings he passed were mostly lighted. With the midterm election over, the staffs had returned to their labors, preparing battle plans for controversial legislation deferred because of the campaign, preparing as well for the even nastier fights over leadership positions and committee assignments that would come in a few days.

He turned onto the street that led past the Capitol's east face, passing also the Supreme Court building, which he had transformed into a fortress as well. Reaching Constitution Avenue, he found the Senate office buildings also well lit. He had blood on his hands from Gettysburg, but he was doing his job.

Starting down the slope back toward Pennsylvania Avenue again, Kreski glanced along the Mall to the floodlit obelisk that was the Washington Monument, red aviation warning lights twinkling on the top. Armed National Park Police had cordoned it off. No one was going to blow up the Washington Monument, either.

The marines were still in place at the White House but, on belated orders from Bushy Ambrose, Secret Service personnel were now on station with them and overall charge of the security for the Executive

Mansion had been placed in the hands of Kreski and the man he had tentatively named to fill Berger's post, Agent Hammond. As he drove through the main gates, Kreski felt as though he were passing through a border checkpoint, as though Camp David was the capital of one country and the White House that of another. The difference was that the leader now waiting for him in the White House was someone tangible he could talk to—must talk to, as commanded.

Kreski had expected to find a number of people in the vice president's office—the attorney general, the treasury secretary, the director of Central Intelligence, and other important officials and aides. Instead he found only Atherton and Steve Copley, who once again had arrived before him. Copley's report, now grown in size, was on the vice president's desk. Kreski placed his own next to it, then took a chair.

Atherton pulled the stack of paper toward him without speaking, and then began to read. He appeared somewhat agitated. Kreski remembered how cool, calm, and gracious George Bush had been on the occasion of Ronald Reagan's shooting. Atherton was no Bush. For all his studied manners, Atherton was not gracious. The Secret Service code word for him was "Suntan." Kreski could remember when these code words were almost poetic. The one for President Eisenhower had been "Providence." That for Jacqueline Kennedy was "Lace."

"Well, Walt," said Atherton, finally. "This is very disturbing. When I read Steve's report I came to one inescapable conclusion. Your report states it even more clearly. There was a second gun, a second assassin—or would-be assassin—and he got away clean without leaving any evidence. We have a great big loose end."

"Yes, Mr. Vice President."

"We're not even sure that this Manuel Huerta's shots even hit anybody."

"Just as I said, Mr. Vice President," said Copley.

"He might have hit the president," Kreski said. "But Dr. Potter's medical statement didn't make that clear. We've no idea, really."

"So we have a definite conspiracy, a conspiracy of at least two. At the same time, it appears we've arrested a lot of people we shouldn't have."

Copley looked down at the carpet. He'd been in the Maryland mountains and up at the crime scene for most of the day, but his shoes were perfectly clean and polished.

"We had to move fast, sir," he said. "This was an attempt on the life of the president of the United States. As Walt will tell you, there wasn't much time for Miranda and the rules of evidence. And we did recover those firearms from the motorcade route in New York. There were those simultaneous bombings here in Washington. If we can tie Huerta to La Puño in Chicago, we may not have to let anyone go."

"Walt, what do you think?" Atherton leaned far back in his chair. His agitation had subsided. His question was uttered almost as though he had asked about a new campaign slogan. His dark eyes were studying Kreski with great intensity.

"I have to defer to the ranking police authority," Kreski said with a nod to Copley, "but going by standard operating procedure, there's no grounds for much of a case yet. Border violations and illegal possession of firearms in New York; no reason at all to hold those people in Chicago, until someone can tell us more about La Puño. I don't doubt there's a conspiracy and a Hispanic one involving Central America, but we've got to prove it."

"I agree," said Atherton, letting his chair drop forward. "But you have to understand my problem—indeed, the president's problem, if we can ever get to talk to him about it. The war in Honduras already has a lot of people fired up, on both sides of the issue, now that we've got U.S. troops in combat. If the attack upon the president is related to the war, as it appears, there's going to be tremendous public pressure to do something about it. It won't do just to start letting people go."

"But if there's no evidence of their being involved in the crime," said Kreski, "or any crime . . ."

"The American Civil Liberties Union is already moving in the case of the Chicago arrests," Copley said. "Habeas corpus."

"The president has the constitutional right to suspend habeas corpus," Atherton said.

"Sir," said Kreski. "That's not been done since Lincoln and the Civil War."

"We don't know what we have on our hands here, Walt," Atherton said, rising. He walked over to his fireplace, which was crackling noisily. Like so many Californians, he did not bear well the damp cold of Washington winters. "In any event, I don't have that power. I don't know what power I do have. Steve said Ambrose indicated that would be decided soon."

"'Shortly,'" Kreski said. "I suppose that depends on how quickly the president recovers."

"If he recovers," Copley said.

"Don't talk that way," said Atherton, nervous again. He began to pace back and forth in front of the fire. "I'll have to continue as spokesman. No one up at Camp David seems interested in the job. The networks are howling, gentlemen. We've got to calm them down, calm the nation down. We need to give them some facts."

He settled into a chair next to the fireplace, hunched over with his chin on his fists.

"Walt," said Atherton. "I gather you've got the city pretty well secured."

"Yes, sir. I've had to pull in agents from all over the country. I'm afraid I've given counterfeiters a big window of opportunity. The other police agencies were very helpful. The military wasn't, but Ambrose finally got them off my back late this afternoon. . . . Sir. In my report. There's a list of those I've added for Secret Service protection."

"I looked at it. Seems fine."

"I had requests from nearly every member of the Senate and about half the House. We have no responsibility for the Congress, but I—I didn't want to leave security only to the Capitol Police. I did what I could."

"Don't worry, Walt. No assassin is going to want to waste a bullet on the likes of Meathead Dubarry." He stood up and resumed his pacing. "We've got to get more facts. More facts. Steve, I want your people to concentrate on this La Puño thing. Lean on the CIA for help. The old admiral's acting like a stone wall. Walt, pursue the second gun. Work it hard. Your men on the scene are our best bet."

"Yes, sir."

"All right, that's all for now. Keep me informed the way you do Bushy Ambrose. Steve, can you spare me another five minutes? There's another matter I want to talk to you about."

Kreski was glad to leave. He wanted fresh air and to put the White House out of sight and mind. He wanted sleep. He would embrace sleep as he would a woman, as he would his wife.

Reaching his car, he found someone else in the driver's seat, Agent Lockhart, a huge young man just three years out of Yale.

"Glad I caught up with you, Director," he said. "Mr. Hammond said you weren't to be left alone."

Kreski sighed and got into the front seat. "All right. I'm too tired to be driving anyway."

"Where to?"

"Home. Tell Hammond he's in charge until he hears from me.

I'm going up to Gettysburg, first thing in the morning. I want you at my house at six A.M."

"Are we going to drive, sir?"

"Negative. I'll want a chopper. I'm going to be in a hurry to get up there."

When they were certain Kreski had left the White House Atherton and Copley slipped from the vice president's office and took a corridor that led to a side door opening onto the gallery adjoining the Rose Garden. Wearing nothing warmer than their suit coats, they stepped out into the windy cold. No one was naïve enough to believe there was such a thing as an unrecorded conversation anywhere inside the White House anymore.

"Do you trust Kreski?" Atherton asked.

"He's about as reliable a man as you'll find in Washington."

"But where are his loyalties? Now, after what's happened."

Copley stuck his hands in his pockets and hunched his shoulders against a gust of wind. "I'm sure his loyalties are still to his job."

"I think Ambrose trusts Kreski," Atherton said. "I think Kreski can get close to him; can find out what's going on up there. But I don't think he'll do it. For us, I mean."

"I think he'll do whatever he's ordered."

"I want to penetrate Camp David, Steve. On our own. Do you have any agents working under military cover?"

"Yes. I've a special task force team in California working with the DEA on some military drug smuggling. And some at Fort Bragg on a civil rights case."

"Fort Bragg? Eighty-second Airborne?"

Copley nodded.

"That's a godsend, Steve. Work out some way to get a guy or two sent up to Camp David, the lower ranking the better. The only pass an enlisted man needs to go anywhere is a mop and a bucket."

"All the men on that detail are outfitted as privates."

"Good. We've got to get in there, Steve. We've *got* to find out just exactly what in hell has happened to the president of the United States. *I* could be president of the United States at this very moment, and not know it!"

When Copley had gone Atherton returned to his office and summoned Press Secretary Neil Howard and Chief of Staff Richard Shawcross, who'd been told not to go home until Atherton released them.

The day had been taken up by a seemingly endless succession of conversations, both public and private, in meetings, in interviews, in corridors, even in the bathroom. He'd met with his contingent of the cabinet, with all manner of security officials, with his staff, and with his allies from the House and Senate. He'd had a session with the head of the Business Roundtable, a discreet lobbying group consisting of many of the chief executive officers of the nation's Fortune 500 companies, as well as with the ambassador from Honduras. He'd granted interviews to five television networks, including cable and satellite, both wire services, all three news magazines, and five newspapers. He'd had little time for food and was on the point of being willing to kill for sleep.

There was one thing he had had no time for at all. He had failed to watch or listen to a single newscast. Howard was about to correct that failing.

"I made a tape of all three evening news shows," he said. "Do you want to start with the segments with your interviews in them?"

"No," said Atherton. "I was at the interviews. I want to see all the things that went on in other places. I want to see the entire newscasts."

"It'll take an hour and a half."

"That's all right. I want to see what the people of America have been seeing. Next time edit out the commercials."

As Howard went to the videotape machine, Atherton turned wearily to Shawcross, who was sweating again.

"Dick. In the morning, issue a directive that, starting tomorrow, there will be a National Security Council meeting every morning and a cabinet meeting every afternoon, until further notice."

"What are you going to talk about?"

"Plans for the Thanksgiving holidays, if need be. Maybe we can draw Ambrose out."

"All set," said Howard. Atherton nodded, a button was pushed, and in a moment, NBC's Tom Brokaw was on the screen.

"Tonight," he said, "the government of the United States is under siege. The president is in hiding in the Maryland mountains. The vice president is barricaded in a White House bristling with troops and weapons. The Capitol is a fortress and its members are escorted by armed guards. And in Central America, the war goes on. For more, we'll start with Chris Wallace in Thurmont, Maryland . . ."

"What you have to realize," Howard said, "is that Brokaw's piece is the most responsible and dispassionate of the lot."

Atherton put a hand over his eyes and slid down further in the cushions of the couch. He listened to every word the newscasters uttered, however.

Paul Bremmer was a creature of habit to the same excessive degree that Charley Dresden was one of compulsion. They had been friends for fifteen years and at one time neighbors in a pool and balcony apartment building on the east side of Santa Linda. Bremmer's apartment had been kept almost militarily neat while Charley's grew ripe with the accumulated aftermath of endless parties. Paul had driven a pristinely kept Jaguar XK-E that he had taken in for tuning and servicing exactly every one thousand miles. Dresden had run through a collection of cars as varied as his women friends, keeping, finally, only the Armstrong-Siddeley that he often had to push out into the street to solicit a starting push from passing motorists. It had been Paul's custom to retrieve his newspaper from his doorstep at exactly the same time every morning. He never knew what he might expect to find on Dresden's doorstep—sometimes empty whiskey bottles, occasionally a piece of furniture, once, a sleeping woman.

For all his fastidiousness, Paul was a newspaperman, and a very good one. He had been a reporter on the Santa Linda *Press-Journal* when he and Dresden had first met. By the time Dresden had been fired from Channel Three, Paul had risen to the rank of city editor. Now he was the *Press-Journal*'s lead columnist, appearing three times a week on the front page of the paper's second section.

As reporter and city editor, it had been Bremmer's habit to pause for two beers after work in the bar of the Santa Linda Hotel next to the newspaper's offices downtown. Now, though quitting time was more likely to be five in the afternoon instead of one A.M. and he had a wife and three children waiting for him in his big, rambling house in the mountains east of Santa Linda, Bremmer still stopped at the hotel bar for two beers. Dresden caught him just two inches from the bottom of the second.

"Paul, I need to talk to you."

Bremmer motioned to the empty stool next to him, glanced at his beer, then his watch.

"Have another," Charley said, "on me." He signaled to the bartender.

"I've got to get home, Charley."

"Of course you do. And you will. But I've got a good story for you. About the president. Indulge me and have another."

Bremmer nodded to the bartender. Dresden ordered a bourbon and water for himself. When they'd been served he sipped and waited for Paul to show more interest, to bite.

"All right, what's the story?"

"Simple enough. The president's dead."

"He's dead? It's on the wires?"

"No. I seem to be the only one aware of it. And Tracy Bakersfield."

"Charley, old buddy. The president is at Camp David and you're here, three thousand miles away. How did you come by this information?"

Dresden set the videotape cassette on the bartop. "It's all in there."

"You have a new tape? It shows the president dead?"

"It's the same footage everyone's been looking at for a day now, only no one's really looked at it."

Bremmer shook his head. "I've really got to get home, Charley."

"Just take a look at it, Paul. It won't take three minutes. Do you have access to a video recorder?"

"There's one in our conference room." He finished his beer and stood up, shaking his head once more. "You make life too interesting, Charley," he said, and picked up the tape.

The conference room was just off the news room, and the night city editor and a rewrite man joined them, the former much younger and the latter much older than Dresden. They all stood in front of the screen as the tape began to roll.

"There," said Charley, as the succession of long freeze frames Tracy had prepared went by. No one said anything. All faces, including his friend Bremmer's, were blank. Dresden rewound the tape a short distance, then played it again. "You see, no pink dots, the gun shot, and then pink dots, right in front of the president."

The city editor came close and peered at the screen. "I think you just have a bad tape," he said. He paused at the door, ignoring Charley. "Sorry, Paul."

The rewrite man shrugged and followed after. His eyes looked as though he saw pink dots most of the time.

Bremmer dropped into a chair. "Run it one more time, Charley."

When the tape had completed its third performance Dresden shut off the machine. Bremmer continued to stare at the blank screen.

"Charley, old buddy, you say Tracy Bakersfield put this together for you?" Bremmer had known her from the days Dresden had worked for Channel Three.

"Yes."

"And she believes you?"

"She believes what's on the tape."

There was another pause. Bremmer used to smoke and looked like he wanted to again. "Okay. I can do this much for you, Charley. I can get a short item in my column for tomorrow. There's still an hour and a half before they lock up the first edition. I wanted to write something about the shooting. I guess you've given me a local angle." He grinned the way he always did when he said something witty, but his uneasy expression quickly returned.

"*Muchas gracias, amigo,*" Dresden said.

Bremmer waved his hand. "Don't thank me yet. I've gotten you out of a lot trouble over the years. Now I'm probably going to get you into some."

6

Bushy Ambrose emerged from his lodge, followed by several men in both uniforms and suits. His stride was brisk, reflexively if reluctantly matched by the others, rendering their walk a military procession. They headed down the slope in the first hour of sunlight of a very cold morning, their destination the helipad where Marine One, the president's helicopter, and an escort chopper waited, their crews already aboard.

Ambrose's breath came in quick, short puffs of vapor, not from strain but from purpose. He was not only in command but was actively commanding. They had agreed upon a plan, had drawn up a set of actions requisite to implementation of the plan, and were now commencing to carry them out. The troops were moving. The battle was joined.

There was a squeaking whine as the pilot of the escort ship started his engine. Ambrose raised his hand in protest and the noise abruptly ceased. The pilot sat waiting, chagrined.

"You're sure he'll do it?" Ambrose said to Jerry Greene, the president's media adviser. "You're sure he won't foul this up?"

"Hell yes. I told you. I've had the man to my house. I know him.

After we had him at the inaugural he even switched political parties. This'll be an ego trip for him. He'll be with us all the way."

Columnist David Callister, licking his lips in an irritating habit, intruded upon the conversation, as he intruded upon everything. Ambrose tolerated him only because he was one of the president's closest friends and because he was a powerful news media figure. And the media were of paramount importance at this juncture.

"We shall simply overwhelm him," Callister said, with his Westchester County drawl. "Greene shall appeal to his friendship, and I to his patriotism and sense of history, such as he may possess."

"Does it really have to be done in New York?" said Ambrose. He was standing with legs at parade rest, arms folded tightly across his chest.

"If it's to be done exactly right," Greene said. "It's going to take several days to get set up here."

"Very well," Ambrose said, "but when you're done, bring him back with you."

"He might not want to come."

"Give him no choice. I don't want anyone who knows what we're doing wandering around the goddamn city of New York."

"You shall have to make an exception for me, laddy buck," said Callister. "I have to tape my television show tomorrow and my wife is counting on me for a dinner party tonight."

"I'd prefer you came back here with the others," Ambrose said coldly. He disliked being told whom he had to make exceptions for, he disliked being called "laddy buck," and he disliked very much having silly dinner parties made a factor in his calculations.

"Bushy, a person as constantly visible as I simply can't disappear mysteriously. And my television program is going to be a great help to us in this. Next week I'm having the good Dr. Kissinger on. International terrorism and kindred compelling topics."

"All right. Get back as soon as you can. And don't let yourself get cornered by reporters."

Callister sniffed, eyelids lowered and brows raised. He strolled off toward Marine One looking much the English gentleman off on a shoot. After a nod from Ambrose, Greene and the four-star general who was accompanying them followed. Ambrose then turned to Peter Schlessler.

"Go with them. Prevent trouble. Keep Callister in line."

"Yes, sir."

When they were aboard, Ambrose raised his arm and gave the pilots a flight deck "start engines" signal. The twin whines that followed grew to galloping roars and then merged into a single overpowering din. He loved that sound dearly, much as Hampton hated it.

The flight path of the two New York–bound presidential helicopters crossed that of Kreski's machine as it approached the Pennsylvania border not far from the Camp David mountaintop, the aircraft separated by six hundred or seven hundred feet in altitude and perhaps a mile in distance. In the bright morning sunlight the white and olive presidential colors were clearly visible, though Kreski was at first unsure.

But he had seen these helicopters in flight a thousand times, identifying them from even greater distances. What had given him pause was the possibility of the wounded president being aboard one of them, perhaps being taken to a hospital. Yet they did not seem to be moving with enough urgency for that. Judging by his conduct thus far in the crisis, Ambrose would not be moving the president about in this manner without several squadrons of helicopters flying escort.

The marine aircraft were obviously on some other mission, and it was very unlikely—indeed, impossible—that the president was aboard. Kreski thought of calling them on his radio, or better, discreetly tagging along behind to learn their destination and possible purpose. But he hadn't time for that. His duty lay with the investigation on the ground, with the picturesque little town of Gettysburg that soon rose to greet them from the winter yellow hills. As they landed, it occurred to him he might have been mistaken about the two other machines. Many helicopters, official and civilian, bore similar markings. He was more tired than he could remember ever having been. Instead of going to bed upon reaching his home the previous night he had sat up listening to Mahler, thinking, sipping but not finishing a glass of wine.

Hammond had come with him to Gettysburg and for a moment they were alone, the gusting wind swift over the hard, cold ground, chasing among the grave markers. Even without them, it would have seemed a place of death.

"It's so different now," Hammond said. "You'd almost think nothing had happened."

"Dick, I've not even been able to dream that nothing happened."

Some men were advancing toward them from the roadway opposite, U.S. Route 140, the Baltimore Pike. Most were state and local policemen, but among them Kreski recognized Special Agent Gibby, whom Copley had put in charge of the FBI field investigation. Kreski could have done without him this morning. He wanted to walk about the area on his own, looking at what he wished, free to talk to himself if need be. Free to think.

"Good morning, Director," Gibby said. "Did you get some sleep?"

"Some." In the bathroom mirror that morning, he had looked much the survivor of a prisoner-of-war camp.

"What can we help you with today?"

"Not too much just yet. I want to take a good long walk around the scene. I'll probably have some questions afterward."

"We've photographed the area from every angle. We have photographs of every vantage point that had a view of the president's speaking stand."

"I was sure you would, and I'd be grateful if we could have copies of them, later. But right now I need to do some solitary wandering."

He glanced about, then went to where the president's limousine had been, the deep ruts from its spinning wheels preserved in the hardened ground. The president's, Berger's, and Ambrose's footprints were preserved as well, though it was difficult to tell which was which.

Gibby and Hammond had followed behind him.

"You've taken impressions of these?" Kreski asked Gibby.

"Yes, sir. And others. From all around here. If you read our report, sir, you'll note we also have aerial photos of the entire area and tape-recorded interviews with just about the entire Gettysburg population. We've been very busy, director."

"I don't doubt it. I'm just thinking aloud, reminding myself of what I might want to look at later."

Kreski went slowly, solemnly, to stand where the president had stood. He gazed silently at the tower platform for a very long time, then let his eyes travel along the horizon, pausing briefly at various buildings, monuments, statues, trees, and stone walls visible from this point. They were too visible. Any shots from a second gun would have come from cover.

Or would they have? The grassy knoll in Dallas was a highly visible position. But everyone was looking at the stricken President Kennedy, their attention distracted by the shots from Lee Harvey Oswald's gun.

"Dick," Kreski said to Hammond. "May I have that clipboard?"

Atop the sheaf of papers attached to it was a finely drawn map of the scene, including the positions of all the principals. Kreski paid particular attention to the locations of all the Secret Service agents assigned to the detail at the time the shooting had begun. Still pondering the map, he set off on an examination of each of their positions, looking to see everything they could have seen from where they had stood.

When he got to the tower he swallowed and coughed, looking at the large depression made by the falling body of Agent Pribble. Everyone had forgotten about that poor devil. Huerta, rising from his hiding place beneath the tower floor, had shot the agent once. It was not a fatal wound, but the impact had knocked Pribble over the railing, into a twelve-story fall. Striking a very muddy patch of ground, Pribble had lived, but only by the barest of margins. He had suffered a fractured skull and broken the bones of every limb; had ruptured his spleen and damaged other organs. He was in a coma at the local hospital.

The agent was a heavyset man and the depression in the now frozen earth looked like a shallow grave. Kreski moved on.

Since news of the assassination attempt had first crackled onto his office radio monitor, Kreski's every thought and action had been made and taken in urgency, or at least with a guilty appreciation of the need for urgency. He put all that from his mind now, taking his time, staring at broken twigs on the ground and studying the fall of shadows from the morning sunlight. Walking at a stroller's pace from each place marked on the map to the next, he replayed from his memory the televised events that had taken place, in sequence—trying to imagine how they must have looked from each position, how much of the violence, how many of the victims could have been seen by each agent. The only point of reference visible to all was the tower.

At length, he moved along the outer perimeter of what had been the Secret Service security cordon, his path taking him along the shoulder of the Baltimore Pike. There had been four agents stationed in the vicinity: Evans, Ajemian, Ballard, and Storch. Retracing his steps, he decided that Ballard had the clearest view of the president at his limousine, but that Ajemian had the best sight of the buildings, monuments, and forest cover that might have harbored a second assailant.

Returning to Ballard's spot, he turned back to face the death scene and waved his arm at the assorted policemen and officials still gathered there to watch him. Hammond and Gibby broke from the crowd and began walking, then trotting, toward him. A half dozen uniformed policemen hurried behind. Kreski grimaced. He hadn't meant for everyone to come.

"I'd like to have someone standing exactly where the president stood when the firing began," Kreski said to a nearly breathless Gibby when the special agent arrived. Kreski looked to Hammond, handing him back the clipboard. "I need a rifle."

"I'm sure one of the state troopers has a shotgun in his car."

"No. A rifle. A deer rifle with a scope. I'll wager the first house you come to has one."

It proved to be the fourth house. The owner was at first terrified that he was being arrested. He then became surly when asked for the loan of his gun, but finally cooperated. The weapon was only a .22 caliber, but it had a scope and would suffice.

Leaving the others behind, Kreski cradled the rifle in his arm and started back up Baltimore Pike toward the center of town. At the Jennie Wade House, in Civil War days the home of a young woman who had taken a fatal bullet in the great battle, he stopped. This was the northern limit of the field of fire. It was also adjacent to the tower. The second shot would not have come from here. It would have had to have come from someplace between the tower and the southern limit of the field of fire, a structure a mile down the road from him housing a tourist enterprise called Fantasyland.

For the next hour or more, much to the mystification and, sometimes, consternation of the townspeople, Kreski clambered over rooftops, hunkered down behind walls, lay flat in depressions in the ground, each time bringing the borrowed rifle to bear and sighting through the scope at the distant policeman standing in for the president. Even with a scope, the assailant must have been a near perfect shot.

Working his way steadily south, Kreski remained dissatisfied. All the firing points he tried were either too exposed or offered no clear shot. The roof of the battlefield military museum at Baltimore Pike and the National Battlefield Park's Slocum Avenue provided the clearest shot of all, but it had been open for business and full of tourists.

Though not when the president was speaking. When the president comes everyone rushes to see. The building might well have been completely deserted. Kreski walked slowly around it, looking up at the rooftop. An ideal site, except that the shooter might easily have been seen by Agent Storch, if not Ballard, and would certainly have been seen by both trying to escape. The ground around the building was all cleared, parking lot and grass. It was a hundred yards to the nearest trees and brush, and Ballard would have had an open view of the entire distance. There was a large equestrian statue nearby, but the intervening space would also have been visible to both Ballard and Storch.

Kreski went to the sculpture, looking first at the chiseled name and then up into the stony eyes of General Henry W. Slocum, whose troops had given way to the Confederates on this ground in what initially had appeared to be the crowning southern triumph of the Civil War. From here, it was just a short dash into the trees. Kreski moved to the rear of the statue's base. The platform of the pedestal was just a few inches above his head. Sliding the rifle up onto it, he found handholds on the pedestal rim and a leg of the general's bronze horse. With a quick and painful pull of arm and shove of feet, he was flat on his belly next to the rifle, feeling very stiff and middle-aged.

Lying exactly in the center of this cold platform, he found he could not be seen from any of the positions that had been occupied by his agents. The statue was situated on too high a level. Raising his head and the rifle as the sniper might have, he had a glimpse of where Ajemian and Storch had stood. Ballard's post was directly in front of him. If the sniper had used the Slocum monument, he would have fired over Ballard's head.

But one or two quick shots, squeezed off just as the other gunfire erupted, might have been possible. They would have had to have been well-rehearsed snap shots, the work of a highly trained marksman.

Schultz had muttered something about horses—about a horse.

Kreski centered the standing policeman in the scope's crosshairs and mentally killed him several times. He tried it again with quick pop up, pop down shots. He had difficulty, but it could be done. What was the sniper to do after that?

He turned about and peered over the rear of the platform. They weren't perfectly defined, but there were two depressions in the ground just below, toe deep, as would be expected landing backward from a jump. Kreski took up the rifle and slid down the side of the base, careful to avoid stepping on any of the footprints.

There was a portion of a third footprint, just behind the other two and somewhat perpendicular to them, the mark of someone pivoting.

More marks led off toward the trees, disappearing in higher, drier ground just short of them. He searched carefully, but could find no shell casings, just some marks and scuffs in the ground alongside the statue that might have been made by feet. Yet would a sniper have paused to snatch up expended shells when it would have made him so visible to Ballard and Storch?

Kreski took out another map, a larger one showing the entire town and battlefield. Roads led out of Gettysburg in the manner of spokes in a wheel, a graphic depiction of its tactical importance as a key crossroads in General Lee's invasion of the North. Between the Baltimore Pike and Pennsylvania Route 116, the Hanover Road, to the north, was a long, heavily forested pie slice of territory that included Culp's Hill and other landmarks of the battle. A lone man could easily have made his way through it undetected. He might even have driven out of it in a car he'd hidden in the trees.

Kreski had left his two-way radio with Hammond so as not to be disturbed. Rifle and clipboard in hand, he began a slow walk back to the others.

Charley Dresden again awoke early, though not because of worry or alcoholic overindulgence. His wakefulness was born of sheer anticipation. Rubbing his eyes, he went to the rear door opening onto the kitchen porch, the only part of the house facing the road. As usual, the morning copy of the Santa Linda *Press-Journal* was not on the porch but on the driveway beneath. Though he was completely naked, he went immediately to fetch it. The light was still faint and, in any event, his few neighbors had seen many more startling sights about his house over the years. In Tiburcio, one accepted things.

Back in the kitchen, he wished Zack were up. He and Charlene had spent most of the evening in a long session of lovemaking by his small fireplace, and his skin was still atingle with memories of her body. He wanted the touch of her now, cuddling from behind, her breasts pressing against his back. But she had never been much for morning nudity. She liked sex only in the night. Mornings for her were created for sleep.

Restraining an impulse to turn immediately to Bremmer's column, he took the newspaper to his bar, laid it out carefully on the mahogany top, then opened the pages to the second section and began to read. He read every word of Bremmer's column. Not one of them was about him, or his idea, or even about the assassination. He glanced over the long column one more time, then smashed his fist down on the bartop and swore.

"What's wrong?" said Zack unhappily, from the bedroom.

"Nothing. Everything."

"Well, be quiet about nothing. And everything."

He sat down on the cold wooden stool. Perhaps they had sent him the previous day's paper. He turned to the front page. It was the correct date; the final edition. Bremmer had backed out. So much for fifteen years of friendship. Dresden went to the phone. What was ghastly dawn for the likes of Charlene Zack was a normal hour for the father of school-age children.

Bremmer's wife was a long time fetching him.

"I'm shaving, old buddy, what is it?"

"The item's not in your column," Charley said.

"It isn't? I put it in. Two long graphs."

"I have the final edition. There's not a word."

"I made it in time for the edition before that. It was the lead item. There was a headline that went with it. 'Tape Shows Hampton May Be Dead.'"

"Well, it's not there."

"Sorry, old buddy. I'll find out what happened and get back to you. Right now I'm standing here wearing shaving cream and nothing else."

"Excuse me, Paul. I just got a little upset."

"You always do. But no sweat. I'll be back to you."

Dresden hung up slowly. It shouldn't really matter that this had failed. If he was right, and he knew he was absolutely right, it would all come out. The world would learn sooner or later. One simply can't hide the president of the United States, alive or dead.

But that was not the point. Charley wanted the world to know that he was right before the fact.

Tracy Bakersfield had called him a little boy. Paul Bremmer was probably thinking of him in even less kindly terms. Zack was close to laughing at him, and not indulgently. But he was not acting out of childish compulsion, not anymore. This was one occasion when he had made a carefully considered judgment, and, once certain of something, Charley Dresden would not be turned back. Certainly not by himself.

He sat quietly for a while, then abruptly got up and went into the bathroom to shower. He was engaged in a game with the rest of the world, and he had to keep in mind that the rules were all his opponent's.

His secretary, Isabel, was startled to see him. There was no excess of work to justify her own presence in the office that early. He knew she took on typing jobs on the side and presumed the material on her desk amounted to one of them. He paid it no mind. Her paydays were much too irregular for him to complain.

"You didn't come back yesterday," she said.

"I went to the seashore."

"For the amusement park account?"

"No, to Villa Beach. Private business."

"Jim Ireland called. He said if you don't return that tape today he'll have a warrant sworn out for your arrest for theft."

Dresden laughed, and went into his office. While he waited for Paul Bremmer's call, he would actually do some work. With suit coat still on, an old eastern habit of his, he sat down at his desk and began to rough out some visuals of a roller coaster. He would have it roar into a tunnel, and then would fade to black and segue to the interior of the park's funhouse. He wondered if the amusement park had a funhouse. He had forgotten to ask.

Bremmer didn't call until midmorning.

"Sorry to take so long, Charley, old buddy. I was tied up having my fanny munched by the editor."

"What for?"

"It seems I exceeded the bounds of good taste in a recent column."

"You mean the one with me?"

"I'm afraid so. The night editor stopped the presses and had the item yanked. You made all of seventeen hundred copies. They were part of the run that goes up to the Bay Area. If you want to browse the newsstands up in San Jose or Palo Alto, you might find one."

"That wasn't the idea."

"I know, old buddy."

"I'm appreciative, Paul. I really am."

"I'd say 'anytime,' but I won't. Anyway, Charley, for whatever it's worth, I think you're on to something here."

"You're a friend, Paul."

After hanging up, he stared unhappily at the phone, having lost all interest in roller coasters and clients. Finally, he dragged his desk chair out onto the balcony outside his office, tilted back against the stucco wall, and contemplated the tops of the palm trees.

His friends believed him, or said they did. Two people in all the world. How many friends did he have? How many who could be of any use?

He snapped forward in the chair. He had at least one more friend. In San Francisco.

When he got off the telephone this time it was as a happier man. He had another move to make in this game.

"Isabelita. I'll be gone for the rest of the day."

"Don't leave the chair out there."

"I won't. Stand up, m'dear."

She made a face, then grinned, and did so. Gently, he patted her bottom. It had nothing to do with sex. It was for luck, an old ritual of theirs, when he needed a lot of it.

"*Con mucho gusto*, Charley. *Buena suerte*. Too bad this won't bring us any money."

Though an ostensibly full-blown meeting was in session, the Cabinet Room looked absurdly empty. President Hampton's faction was still absent. Those members present, including Vice President Atherton, had taken their regular seats in their red leather chairs with brass nameplates on the back, and this scattered them around the huge table. Atherton was reminded of the mad tea party in *Alice in Wonderland*, an impression reinforced by the secretary of commerce as she gave a report on the progress of talks on the new trade agreement with Italy. Nothing could have been more irrelevant to Atherton's mind. What had Nixon said at the height of the Watergate scandal? "I don't give a shit about the lira." Precisely.

When she was done Atherton thanked her, and then nodded to the attorney general, who gave a brief summary of the latest report on crime statistics. This was another irrelevancy. There was only one crime any of them cared about.

After that, they fell into silence. Atherton drummed on the table, wondering whether to adjourn the session, which had lasted slightly less than forty minutes. He was about to, when restrained by the discreet, patrician cough of Secretary of State Crosby.

"I've come into possession of a communication from the government of Nicaragua," he said, taking a single sheet of paper from the folder in front of him. "It was intended for the secretary of defense, but in the present confusion, it was mistakenly routed to me. I chafe at using the word 'mistakenly,' as the content seems more diplomatic than military."

"I think this sounds more properly a subject for the National Security Council meeting," Atherton said.

"I'd be inclined to agree, were it not for the fact that this matter has never once come up at any of our National Security Council meetings," Crosby said. "I thought there was an understanding that we would have no direct communication with the Nicaraguan government until it withdraws its people from Guatemala, Honduras, and Costa Rica."

"It's more than an understanding," Atherton said. "It's policy. There was a directive."

"Indeed," said Crosby, putting on the half glasses he used for reading. "Yet this Nicaraguan telex is a response. To an earlier message and to the present circumstance. It asks if the Cuernavaca telegram is still valid."

"What is the Cuernavaca telegram?" asked the secretary of commerce.

"It is a direct communication with the government of Nicaragua from the president of the United States," said Atherton. "Mr. Hampton has a friend in Cuernavaca who has friends in Managua. They talk."

"I knew nothing about this," Crosby said. "No one with a top-secret clearance in our embassy in Mexico City does either."

"This smells of secret deal," the attorney general said. "Just like Kissinger and Haig selling us out in China while General Abrams and Admiral Moorer were trying to beat back the North Vietnamese. We've lost more than one hundred and fifty American lives in Central America. He shouldn't be playing games with that kind of investment."

"There are rumors of a trade. They pull out and leave us Guatemala, Honduras, and Costa Rica free and clear. They get El Salvador free and clear and the Soviets take a walk. But those are just rumors. As I said. This is a subject for the National Security Council, presuming the chairman of the council wishes to bring it up."

"That's the president," said the commerce secretary.

"Precisely."

"What am I to do with this message?" Crosby asked.

"Shred all the copies I presume you've made," Atherton said, "and send the original on to the secretary of defense, with an explanation of how it accidentally came to hand. What happens next will be up to Henry Hampton, depending on his condition."

Atherton adjourned the meeting, noting that the next would be in the smaller Roosevelt Room, where their paltry numbers wouldn't look so ridiculous. As he went out the door, his aide Shawcross drew him aside.

"Steve Copley called. Philadelphia police, along with his agents, have found the place where Huerta was staying. And Walt Kreski seems to be onto something in Gettysburg."

"Where's Steve now?"

"En route to Philadelphia."

"I want to speak with him as soon as possible. And with Walt Kreski. And get Neil Howard. I think there's a strong possibility we're going to be holding a news conference soon."

At that moment Kreski was walking through the Gettysburg woods with his clipboard, a bent stem briar clenched in his teeth, his two-way radio affixed to his belt and turned on. Several dozen FBI and Secret Service agents and as many policemen had fanned out to either side of him. It was a manhunt, only two days too late.

There was another battlefield tower here, an older, smaller structure situated on Culp's Hill. It possessed a view of the cemetery and the Slocum statue and there had been an agent assigned to it, Calvin Perkins. He should have easily been able to see anyone fleeing from the statue, but in his report he stated that he noticed nothing except the gunfire at the cemetery. He said that, once the shooting had started, he had descended the smaller tower and approached the scene of action through the woods, but had seen no one or nothing until reaching Slocum Drive.

Kreski motioned to Special Agent Gibby, who, like Hammond, was staying close by.

"You say you searched the entire area surrounding the cemetery?"

"Sir. We searched the entire town."

"But around the Slocum statue?"

"Yes, all around there."

"But you didn't go into the woods?"

"Sir, we went as far as the longest conceivable rifle shot."

"And you made nothing of those footprints around the base of the statue."

"No, sir. There were a couple thousand people here. All over the place."

"But you will get me impressions of those footprints."

"Yes, sir. At once, sir."

Kreski nodded, and moved away, muttering to himself. There were times when he wished he were back working with the street cops of his youth. They had had none of these young agents' sophisticated training and superior education. As a consequence, they had been compelled to rely on mere thought.

He chided himself for the unfairness of that. Al Berger and Dick Hammond had never been street cops. And Berger had told him only a week before that he felt something was wrong, that something was going to happen. Berger had always been right.

Kreski was walking these woods in his best shoes, having presumed he'd have to appear before the president, or at least the vice president. Now they were soiled. The ground was hard, rocklike in places, yet somehow his shoes had become muddied and dusty. He walked on.

They were following the line of a creek that led north to a ridge identified on his map as Benner's Hill. The Hanover Road cut through the ridge and across the creek. He could see the highway as a thin gray slash just ahead. If his skirmish line of searchers reached it without finding any evidence of a sniper's escape, his theory was effectively destroyed.

His radio crackled. Hammond got to his first. He talked briefly, then looked over at Kreski.

"Pribble didn't make it," he said.

They stood for a moment, all of them, statues in the grass, only the wind and crackling static from the two-ways filling the silence. Pribble had been a man obsessed with firearms. Someone had told Kreski that he owned an original or copy of every sidearm used in World War II. If it had not been written somewhere, it should be: Beware first irony.

Ten dead now, with those who had expired during the night. How many yet to come?

Kreski relighted his pipe, then waved his arm. They moved on. They were all the way to the road when the word finally came.

"Director, this is Major Henderson, with the Pennsylvania State Police."

Kreski snatched up his radio. "Yes, Major?"

"I've got it, sir. Two tire tracks, leading from a small hollow out to the road. The car turned east."

"Where are you?"

"Just past the bridge over Rock Creek. It's on your map. Over by the Lincoln school."

"We'll be right there. Don't let anyone walk over those tire tracks."

Kreski knocked the ashes from his pipe in a windblown scatter over the road and then began trotting along the shoulder toward the Rock Creek bridge.

The tire marks were good, made by expensive radials from the look of them. The driver had not spun his wheels in panic but had driven out of his hiding place with care and deliberation. Kreski, bent over, walked slowly along them, finding three places where there was a perfect imprint of tread. He stood up straight.

"I know," said Gibby. "You want full impressions."

"It's been a long time since I've had to work as a detective."

"Director, you know what it's been like here. We've tried to deal with first things first."

"'The first shall be last.'"

"Sir?"

"Nothing."

"Shall I call for cars to take us back?"

"No. We'll walk."

"Why?"

"We might see something else."

They did not. But when they broke out of the trees back by the Slocum statue, they were confronted with another discovery. As an FBI agent who rushed up to Gibby explained, a check of the museum rooftop had been made, and a piece of torn cloth had been found caught on a shingle. He handed it to Gibby, who gave it to Kreski. It was a triangular remnant, yellow and white in color, emblazoned with what appeared to be the word "no" at one side. There was, however, a Spanish accent above the *n*.

"It's their flag," said Gibby. "It's La Puño."

Kreski studied the roof, then slowly turned, his gaze following the tops of the trees. The small tower by Culp's Hill was just barely visible.

"Dick," he said to Hammond. "I want to talk to Agent Perkins."

"He's on the vice president's detail. I think he's with Mrs. Atherton. She went down to Williamsburg for a few days to get away from it all."

"I envy Mrs. Atherton. When they get back I want to talk to Perkins."

Charley Dresden drove his old MG at top speed over the mountains and up the Bayshore Freeway to San Francisco without two things happening: the car did not break down and he was not stopped by police. One or the other occurred with such frequency on his journeys to the city that he had come almost to expect them.

He pulled into a parking garage on the side of Nob Hill, admonishing the car parker not to flood the engine or rely on the hand brake, then started on the two-block walk to the studios of San Francisco's Channel Six. Though there had been bright sunshine along the peninsula, an afternoon fog was settling on the city, obscuring some of its high-rise towers.

Charley was gladdened by it. When he had first come to California, at a time when there were still municipal fears of earthquakes and strict building height restrictions, San Francisco had been an Italianate city of hills and great vistas. The huge towers had rendered it just another Pittsburgh, with the lovely house-hugged hilltops that had been visible from Madeleine Anderson's apartment now just a wall of high-rises. He wished for fog every time he set upon the Bayshore.

He disliked San Francisco now for another reason. He and Maddy used to take early morning walks in a woodland park just down the street from the old mansion that had been divided into hers and other apartments. He had returned to that park out of nostalgic curiosity years after, on a hot day. The bushes beside the path were aquiver with naked, coupling men. Two of them had come after him. He had run, from his and Madeleine Anderson's sacred bower.

He only came to San Francisco now when business made it absolutely necessary, or when some new woman insisted upon it for an evening's entertainment. His business with Bill Jenks, editorial director of Channel Six, was absolutely necessary. It was his last good chance.

Jenks was Dresden's oldest friend in California. He had been a news reporter at Santa Linda's Channel Three when Dresden had first come there from New York. They had been companions of youth, drinking, gambling, chasing women, adventuring in the wilds, almost always together, sometimes in one of the station's mobile news units. Jenks had taken up with Tracy Bakersfield after Dresden's pursuit of her had so involuntarilly ended. Jenks had, in fact, been engaged to her for nearly a year. It was in that period that he and Dresden briefly ceased being amigos.

"The three of us cannot abide together," he had told Dresden in a somber conversation in a neighborhood bar. Yet Tracy could not bring herself to fully let go of her dear adopted brother Charley, just as she could not bring herself to fully cling to the brooding Jenks. If

Dresden was too much the little boy, Jenks was too much the opposite. She had waited until Jenks had taken a job as a widely traveling network correspondent, then broke the engagement by telephone when he was off on assignment covering a mass murder in Arizona. Like Charley, Jenks had never really understood.

Jenks' real name was Harrison William Jenkins, but one of the news directors he had worked for had ordered him to shorten it to something crisp and punchy. He had become a news director himself, after his few years as a network regional reporter, first at Channel Three in Santa Linda and then here at Channel Six. He had instituted nightly editorials at the end of the eleven o'clock newscast, writing and delivering them himself. He still gave the editorials, but was no longer news director. In television, one goes up or one goes down, but one never stays in the same place. Jenks' predecessor was now a vice president of CBS News in New York. Bill Jenks just wanted to stay where he was. So had Charley.

His office as a mere editorial writer was small, affording room for only one visitor's chair. Dresden sat in it uncomfortably. The door opened directly onto a main corridor, and secretaries and other station staff kept passing by.

Jenks sighed. It was how he began all his conversations. He was balding now, and had grown a very British-looking moustache. Such a somber, distinguished mien was an asset in Jenks' present job, but it made his friends wonder if he was unhappy with them.

"The story of the millennium, you said."

"Right here," said Dresden, patting his briefcase. A young woman with a clipboard came in and took some papers from Jenks' desk.

"You haven't yet said what it's about, except that it involves the president."

"The president's dead."

The woman with the clipboard returned and put the papers back.

Jenks sighed again when she had left. "Let's go find a place with beer," he said.

They went to one of the few bars in the neighborhood without ferns. It was a five-block walk, two of them uphill, but well worth it. There was a pool table in the back. Dresden remembered the saloon from their youth, though then it had had another name, and was not so clean.

He racked for eight ball while Jenks fetched two large steins of dark German lager. As Charley related his story, they played pool. Jenks jumped way ahead at first, even sinking a difficult bank shot, but his play deteriorated as he became engrossed in what Charley had to say. Missing badly a straight-in shot to a corner pocket, he stood a moment, sipping his beer. Jenks always looked concerned about something, even when asleep. Now his expression was that of a man contemplating nuclear war.

"You say Tracy wants me to believe this?" he said.

"No. Tracy has no idea I'm here. I just said Tracy believes it. Completely. She made the tape that proves I'm right."

Jenks took a quick sip and then his turn, missing once again. He chalked his cue. Dresden had hesitated bringing up the episode with Paul Bremmer and the Santa Linda *Press-Journal*, for fear it might scare Jenks off. But Jenks was his friend. He was Bremmer's friend too.

"Paul Bremmer believes it," Dresden said. "He put what I had to say in his column this morning. Unfortunately, an editor took it out. A question of taste. The beloved president."

"They killed it outright?"

"It made seventeen hundred copies."

"They didn't make it up here."

"I did. So did my tape."

Jenks put his cue back in the rack. "Let's go look at it, in living color."

The right rear tire on Dresden's MG blew just outside of Sunnyvale, sending him across three lanes of Bayshore Freeway and sideways up the shoulder. It must have been the twentieth time an automobile had come close to killing him in California. He was becoming used to the feeling. Though he had almost clipped a station wagon and been broadsided by a postal service truck, he was hardly rattled. But he soon became angry. The spinner hubcap was rusted tight and the spare in the boot was flat. After phoning for a tow truck, he made a quick call to his office.

"*Por que tarda tonto?*" Isabel asked.

"The frailties of the English automobile," he said. "I have a blown tire and a flat spare. I won't be back by the time you go home."

"Mr. Bolger from the amusement park called, twice. Mr. Novak from Channel Three called. Jim Ireland didn't call, but a sergeant from the Santa Linda police department called and asked you to give back the tape so he wouldn't have to go through the foolishness of making out a warrant."

"I had a copy made in San Francisco. I'll give them that."

"How did it go?"

"*Aun no lo se.* They looked at what I had, and said they'd think seriously about it, but they had to talk to the general manager. If he agrees, they may do something tonight. An editorial."

"So now you'll go back to making commercials, okay? You've got to do this week's ads for Freddy's Pizzas, you know."

"Okay."

"Oh. Two men came to see you this afternoon, Charley."

"Clients, or bill collectors?"

"*Quien sabe?* They wore suits. They sat quietly for about half an hour, then left."

"Did they say they'd be back, when they'd be back?"

"No. Just that they wanted to talk to you. They were polite, but very serious. They didn't even look at my legs."

Everyone looked at Isabel's legs.

"Probably bill collectors," he said, "from the Purple Gang in Detroit."

"Purple Gang?"

"Never mind. A joke. Don't work too late, Isabelita. See you tomorrow."

It was well past nightfall when he drove into the Tiburcio canyon, a brand new Michelin tire he couldn't really afford carrying the right rear of the MG over the bumpy surface of the road. He paused briefly at Cooper's saloon for his mail, but no drink. He hurried home in hopes of finding Charlene, encountering instead only the makings of a meal in the refrigerator and a hasty note. She had gone down to Monterey to meet with a resort developer who wanted her to handle public relations for him.

"He wants a Zack in his sack," Dresden muttered. He nibbled at the dinner, cold chicken and potato salad in November, then poured himself a whiskey and went up to the darkness of his hillside lanai.

The swing creaked as he sat on it. The lights of the cabins and houses below stretched along the creek like warm and friendly decorations, Japanese lanterns at some festive outdoor party. He supposed he felt happy, or at least excited. Bill Jenks had seemed sincere enough. It was a natural subject for an editorial. All Dresden needed was for his message to appear on television and then that would be that. It would be on the record. It could be on the late news that very night.

He drank to pass the time, finishing another whiskey by the time the eleven o'clock news came on. The reception was abysmal, but he could determine that it was the Channel Six anchorman speaking, and comprehend what he was saying.

The man went almost immediately to network feeds. There had been a White House news conference that day, Vice President Atherton flanked by the head of the FBI, the director of the Secret Service, and a number of aides. Atherton made a statement, and then the FBI director took questions.

They had found the assailant's hiding place—a cheap rented room in Philadelphia. They'd recovered from it material belonging to a Honduran guerrilla group called La Puño, "The Fist." It was similar to material recovered from a La Puño cell in Chicago. FBI Director Steven Copley said that a portion of what appeared to be a La Puño flag was also found on a rooftop at Gettysburg, within rifle range of where the president had been shot. Tire tracks believed to have been made by the getaway car were discovered about a mile away. Secret Service Director Walter Kreski said he accepted the possibility that at least two or more others in addition to Huerta were involved in the assassination attempt. Copley said a nationwide search was underway for the others who had taken part in the shooting, but he believed the conspiracy had been crushed and no longer posed a danger to the U.S. government. Atherton added that he hoped the news media appreciated how open the administration was being with the conduct of this investigation.

The questioning abruptly turned to the "slaughter" of Bonnie Greer and the others by the Secret Service. Demands were made as to why there wasn't a full investigation of that, and why Kreski was still in his job. Atherton started to say there had been a full investigation, but was drowned out by shouts and angry questions. A network correspondent then appeared on the screen standing in front of a large wall map in the State Department press briefing room. He said he had learned from sources that La Puño was heavily financed by the Iranian and Libyan governments.

After a commercial the station returned to local coverage. A state law enforcement official was interviewed vowing to hunt down every member of La Puño from the Oregon state line to the Mexican border. The San Francisco Board of Supervisors voted unanimously for a resolution condemning terrorism in any form. In an interview outside his San Francisco office, Senator Calendiari warned against trampling on the rights of innocent Hispanics in too zealous a search for La Puño conspirators.

Then came two more commercials, a lurid story on a sex killing in Oakland, and the weather. It would be unseasonably warm.

Dresden poured himself another drink. He thought of calling Tracy Bakersfield so that she might watch, but wasn't sure how well she could receive the station in Villa Beach. She would find out about it soon enough.

After an interminable sportscast dealing mostly with a 49ers' football game that had yet to be played, they came to Bill Jenks's editorial segment. Dresden's hopes rose with Jenks's first words and died with those that immediately followed. It was an editorial that dealt with the assassination attempt but was addressed to the need for gun control. There was no reference to Charley or his all-important question. Channel Six and every other station in the Bay Area must have come out for gun control a dozen times already that year. No one had yet seen the president and no one cared.

Dresden slammed off the television set and went to the drawer in the bedroom where he kept his handguns. He took out his .357 Magnum revolver. His impulse was to empty it into his television set, but he wasn't quite that drunk. After a huge swallow of whiskey, he turned his television back on and switched to the channel carrying "ABC News Nightline." Ted Koppel was interviewing State Department officials and the foreign minister of Nicaragua about La Puño. No one seemed to know much about it.

Drinking steadily, Dresden propped the barrel of the pistol on his knee and kept it aimed at the television screen, even as the "Nightline" show went off the air and a late movie began. Pouring yet another drink, Dresden let the film's voice drone on, listening instead to those inside his mind. The president was dead. The president was dead. The president was dead and the vice president was president and no one knew, not even the vice president.

He looked at the handgun closely, even turning the barrel toward his own face. Incipient death, implicit death, frozen in a piece of metal. Aiming the weapon away, he resisted a tremendous urge to fire it. He had last shot a pistol inside this house more than a year before, at a drunken party, when he and Danny Hill had decided to see which of them was the better shot. The target chosen had been the corner where walls and ceiling met just to the right of the big picture window overlooking the cemetery. A miss by either one of them would have shattered the expensive glass. Hill's shot, deafening in the enclosed room, struck wallboard about two inches off the exact center of the corner. Dresden's had been a bull's-eye. The next morning, he discovered that the exiting bullets had blown several shingles off the roof.

Zack had been furious. She'd hidden all his guns while he was at work, and it had taken him several days to find them. He promised her he would never do it again—while she was in residence.

Raising the pistol, he held the sight just beneath the joining point of walls and ceiling and squeezed the trigger, his ears ringing with the shattering noise and his mind's eye seeing the pink globules floating away from the president's chest. The president was dead.

Stumbling slightly, Charley went to the corner and found he had scored another direct hit, this time producing a long crack in the wall, though not the glass. He poured himself another drink. When Zack returned home she found him sleeping on the floor, a spilled glass beside him and a gun in his hand.

7

Because of the terrorist attacks, the police had barred the public from the congressional subway line that connected the Senate office buildings with the Capitol basement, and Senator Andrew Rollins was able to get a seat easily. He doubtless would have been given a seat even if the small, open cars were crammed full with senators returning to their offices from a vote. As the president's closest friend in the Congress, he enjoyed an unofficial power almost equal to the majority leader's. This was even truer with Hampton up at Camp David, wounded and incommunicado. Rollins was now the Senate's only real point of contact with the presidency.

He had flown by helicopter to the Capitol directly from a presunrise breakfast meeting with Bushy Ambrose and presidential political adviser C. D. Bragg. Rollins had at first been more than a little dubious about what they were about to do, but had come to be almost amused at the idea. Nothing that had happened in Hampton's two years in the White House, including the assassination attempt, had caused as much consternation on the Hill as this move was likely to. Rollins chuckled out loud, startling the man next to him, a senator from Maine.

"I would have expected you to be a little more somber, Andy, what with what happened to the president."

"Don't worry, Bill. The president's doing just fine."

"A few of us wouldn't mind hearing from him."

"Give the man time. He's in a bit of pain."

"Doc Potter's statement didn't say that."

"Doc Potter's statement was accurate enough. The president's going to make it. Or is that what has you guys worried?"

The senator from Maine was a frequent opponent of administration policy.

"For God's sake, Andy. What a thing to say."

"I'm just joking, Bill. Today is a day for jokes."

He slapped the startled senator on the shoulder as the little train slid quietly to a stop at the basement entrance to the Dirksen Senate Office Building. Stepping out, Rollins strode briskly along the concrete platform to the escalator, which led to elevators that took him up to the building's crowded main corridor.

It was the usual governmental carnival, assassination attempt or no. Markup sessions were underway on the big appropriations and revenue bills that had been deferred until after the election, and seemingly every lobbyist in Washington was now prowling the sacred halls of government. These ranged from eight-hundred-thousand-dollar-a-year tax lawyers in Brooks Brothers suits to farmers in overalls and "Cat" caps protesting further threats to dairy subsidies. Hurrying among them were staff aides both youthful and balding. And blond. The election had brought in a new load of college girls who doubtless wrote home about their brilliant new careers in Washington without mentioning that their unwritten job descriptions often called for sex with their esteemed public servant masters.

In all his years in the Federal City, Rollins had never understood the paradox. In New York, Chicago, or even Nashville, such women were rewarded with expensive apartments and whatever luxuries they might fancy, and frequently marriage to their patrons. In Hollywood, they were given parts in movies and television shows and a chance at careers. In Washington, they got sixteen thousand dollars a year and the right to slave at humble office chores for twelve hours a day. Yet they kept coming and staying, living in constant dread of being fired.

Rollins had once kept a secretary as a mistress, a former Miss Davison County out of Peabody University, a tall, tanned, dark-haired girl with long legs, a flat belly, and a face that was all eyes and smile. When then Senator Henry Hampton got himself elected president, however, Rollins had quickly put a stop to it, firing the young woman from his office but arranging a job for her on the Agriculture Committee. She raised no great fuss. It was how things were done.

The senator moved along with the crowd, smiling here, nodding there, exchanging a pleasantry or touching a shoulder, but never once stopping. These days, five minutes with Andrew Rollins was worth a large bonus to a lobbyist. Rollins liked lobbyists to earn their money with as much difficulty as possible. The Founding Fathers had, with much deliberation, structured the American government as an unwieldy and inefficient system, thus to protect democracy. Lobbyists represented an effort by impatient citizenry and special interests to hire their own government. Rollins, a constitutional conservative, resented that. So did Henry Hampton.

Security had been dramatically increased in the Senate office buildings, with Capitol police and other armed security guards stationed all along the corridors, impeding the flow. Rollins frowned at them, turning finally into the outer office of Senator Moses Goode, the very powerful chairman of the Senate Finance Committee and, though a black, a solid supporter of the administration.

"He has someone in his office right now, Senator Rollins," said the receptionist, as she hastily reached for her phone, "but I'm sure the gentleman will be leaving very soon."

She spoke a few quick words into the receiver. In a minute, a somewhat startled lobbyist for one of the accountants' associations emerged from Goode's office. As Goode appeared in the doorway, Rollins strolled inside, taking a seat on a leather couch. Goode, in shirtsleeves, eased into a chair opposite.

"The president's okay?" he said.

"He's fine. Just fine. Mose." Rollins paused for effect, but not because he felt hesitant. "I'd appreciate it if you could get the word out that the president is backing Senator Dubarry for president pro tem."

Goode's expression went from disbelief to shock to grimness. He was a leading candidate for that post, and had thought he had Hampton's backing. The caucus vote was just three days away.

"Why?"

"Because it's true. The president's backing Dubarry."

"Let me try again. Why is he doing such a stupid goddamn thing? Why do I suddenly feel something sharp inside my back? The president pro tem is third in line of presidential succession. No 'gentleman of color' has ever risen so high. I thought we had an understanding."

"The president is not forgetful of that. I wouldn't be surprised if he were to exert the full force of his office on behalf of any such ambition you might have in this regard—two years hence."

"But now he wants Meathead Dubarry?"

"Yup."

"How can he get the votes? Meathead'll be lucky to hold onto Armed Services."

"He will not hold onto Armed Services. That's one way we're going to get him votes for president pro tem."

"Who will get Armed Services?"

"Carl Pfeiffer."

"He's running for whip."

"Not anymore."

Goode stood up and went to his window, one of the few in the vast complex of congressional office buildings that actually had a view of the Capitol. He put his hands on his hips and spoke without looking at Rollins.

"What has Jake Owens to say about all this?"

"The majority leader, a man of acute perception and sound judgment, is going along with us. He's been given incentive. North Dakota will soon have more dams than Howard Baker ever dreamed of for Tennessee. And they're just appetizers. We're even going to put Owens's brother-in-law up for ambassador to Guinea-Bisseau."

Goode gazed out his window. "The vice president is behind me."

"You're our guy, not his guy."

"I'm nobody's 'guy.' I'm nobody's 'boy.'"

"True enough. You've just proved that by not asking the obvious question. Anyway, there's nothing the vice president can do with Owens and us together on this."

"What's the 'obvious question'?"

"'What's in it for me?' Which is to say, you."

Goode shook his head and returned to his seat. He propped his feet up on his coffee table and linked his hands behind his neck.

"Okay, Andy," he said. "What's in it for me?"

"You get to be whip. No 'gentleman of color' has ever risen so high."

"Me? Whip? You have the votes for this?"

"We will."

"You only have three days."

"Hampton got the Honduran military assistance bill through in two days."

"That was after the guerrillas killed our ambassador."

Rollins said nothing. Goode tilted back his head until he was staring at the ceiling.

"Nagging question here, Andrew. Has Meathead agreed to any of this?"

"He will. He hasn't heard about it yet. I'm going to tell him this afternoon."

"He could be drunk by then."

"That's the idea. I'm having lunch with Reuben Jackson. As you always said, Mose, administrative assistants run the country."

Goode sat up straight in his chair, and sighed. Then he slapped the tops of his thighs and stood up.

"Majority whip."

"Yes, sir, Mr. Whip."

"But you won't tell me why this is happening."

"When you find out, Mose, you'll approve."

Kreski had set aside most of the morning for his interrogation of agents Evans, Ajemian, Ballard, and Storch. He had worried how to approach them. Having read their reports, he was in effect asking them if they had erred or lied in them.

All four said virtually the same thing. They had not seen any second shooter or fleeing figure because they had immediately turned to Huerta's tower at the first burst of gunfire. Kreski believed young Evans without hesitation—because the agent had been the nearest to Huerta of the four and because it was Kreski's instinct to believe him. He listened to the most halting of the young man's answers without feeling the slightest itch in his gut.

Ajemian he thought evasive and prevaricating, but discounted this reaction. Ajemian came from a family of Lebanese Armenians. Kreski had lost an old and cherished friend in the 1983 bombing of the U.S. embassy in Beirut, and consequently bore a prejudice toward the Lebanese he fought constantly to keep out of his judgment.

Storch he believed because he had known the man for a decade and found his responses to questions about Gettysburg just as thorough, open, and forthright as hundreds of others he had made over the years. Storch made one erroneous assumption, however: that the Secret Service helicopter stationed overhead would have sighted anyone using the museum roof or the Slocum statue. Kreski reminded him that the aircraft had been ordered to stand off to the north because the noise from its rotors had interfered with Hampton's speech. Only Perkins atop the Culp's Hill tower might have seen the museum roof—if he were looking at it instead of the larger tower where everyone was shooting at Huerta.

With Ballard, there had been an itch in his gut. The man's answers were too perfect, containing no doubts or stumbles, uttered cleanly without downward glances. He was an inordinately handsome fellow, athletic, the product of private schools and an Ivy League college. He had served in the Army Rangers after graduating from Harvard Law, killing some people in the 1983 invasion of Grenada, and had joined the Secret Service for no reason Kreski could understand. He supposed the fellow had, along the way, developed a taste for violence.

Kreski called in Hammond afterward and both of them listened to the director's tapes of the interviews. Hammond found all four credible but said he would probably rate Evans and Ajemian lowest on the scale of credibility.

"Why's that, Dick?"

"Because Storch and Ballard are so professional."

Kreski relighted his pipe. He had not only given Hammond Al Berger's job but, within the space of a few days, had virtually accorded him Berger's place in his life, adopting him, as it were. Anyone to fill the void, he supposed. Such a painful void.

But Hammond was a good man. Probably the best in the Service. Now.

"I'm convinced, beyond any doubt, that there was a second gun and that it was fired from the base of the Slocum statue," Kreski said. "I don't understand why it wasn't noticed by at least one of the four agents there, especially Ballard."

"What about the roof of the museum? The La Puño flag? Storch should have noticed that."

"That confuses me. But it doesn't diminish my belief in the Slocum statue as the firing point. These bastards may have been all over the place, although it's not very logical."

"The FBI found no powder traces on that statue." Hammond drank thirstily from his cup of coffee. It was, to Kreski's knowledge, the man's only vice.

"The rain and wind took care of that," Kreski said.

"No expended shells. And no footprints leading to where shells would have fallen."

Kreski shrugged. The two sat silent for a long moment.

"My impulse is to give them all polygraph tests," Kreski said, finally. "I can't remember the last time I did anything like that."

"That's precisely why you can't test them, at least now, director. Everyone's looking for a scapegoat. If it got out that you yourself thought something was funny in the White House detail, you'd hand them the Service on a meat platter. Anyway, sir, I think all these guys are straight, including Evans and Ajemian."

"There've been times in all this when I haven't even trusted myself, Dick. It shouldn't have happened. There's no way this should have happened, if everyone did their job, did it right."

"There's no way the Reagan attempt should have happened, or the Ford attempt in 1975. Everyone did his job, Director. Huerta was dead within seconds. Al Berger did his job. He probably saved the president's life."

"But the second shooter escaped."

"For now, Director. The FBI's interviewing everyone who lives on Baltimore Pike, at least down to the Maryland line."

"And no doubt taking aerial photographs of every one of their roofs." Kreski glanced over the map spread out on his coffee table for a last time, then began carefully folding it. "All right, Dick, let's have lunch. When stuck, have lunch. The Washington way. We'll go to Dominque's."

Atherton and his group came into the morning cabinet meeting embarrassed that they had even less to discuss than they'd had the previous day. Ten minutes later, all this changed. The president's faction, led by Defense Secretary George Moran, trooped in, unannounced. They entered as though it were just a routine session, smiling and nodding in greeting, but taking their seats in order, as though they had lined up outside the door. Atherton felt like asking if they had come in a bus.

"We've been hearing about the fate of the farm bill," he said to Moran. "I'm so pleased you could join us." Moran ignored the darkness of his look.

"I'll cut it short and get to the point," said the agriculture secretary, closing the folder in front of him. "The farm bill is dead. The dairy lobby rides again. As things stand, all the old subsidies remain intact."

"That's unfortunate," Moran said. "The president had high hopes."

Atherton cleared his throat. "You've talked to him?"

"Yes," said Moran, glancing around the table. "A number of us have. That's why we're here."

He opened his briefcase and took out a sheaf of papers. The cabinet secretary came forward and, at Moran's nod, began distributing them around the table.

"It's a directive from the president," Moran said. "On how government is to be conducted during his, er, convalescence. I'll just go over the main points."

He waited until everyone had received his or her copy.

"The president didn't want to confer on this first?" Atherton asked, his voice as brittle as frozen metal. "Not even with me?"

"The president isn't able to do much conferring. The bullet that hit him nicked his left bronchial passage. The wound hurts like hell. For a while they've had a tube down his throat to help with breathing."

"But he's recovering?"

"He's just fine."

"If he was hurt that badly, why did Bushy Ambrose drive him twenty miles to Camp David?"

"Panic. Your driver might panic, too, if you got shot that way."

"But he needed a hospital."

"The hospital came to him. The best field hospital in the Eighty-second Airborne Division."

Atherton read the directive twice, the second time slowly.

"Each member of the cabinet is to continue to run his or her agency on a day-to-day basis," he said.

"That is correct."

"And I and my staff are to supervise the day-to-day operations of the White House."

"Right."

"And the military operations in Central America?"

"I will continue to run the Department of Defense on a day-to-day basis. The president will be apprised of any and all military developments—in Honduras and anywhere else. You will be briefed as well."

"And all contact is to be through Bushy Ambrose?"

"Much as it was in the White House before this horrible shooting."

"What about the arms control talks in Geneva?"

"They are to continue."

"What if there's a breakthrough?"

"I assume," said Moran, looking at Secretary of State Crosby, "that the president would be immediately informed."

"Through Bushy Ambrose," Atherton said. He leaned far back in his chair and folded his arms somewhat belligerently across his chest. No one else spoke. Atherton and Moran stared at each other like gunfighters.

Then Atherton smiled, though the expression did not reach his dark eyes. "You're sure you don't want to make use of the Twenty-fifth Amendment?"

Its language had come to be very certain in his mind, especially Section Three: "Whenever the President transmits to the President pro tempore of the Senate and the Speaker of the House of Representatives his written declaration that he is unable to discharge the powers and duties of his office, and until he transmits to them a written declaration to the contrary, such powers and duties shall be discharged by the Vice President as Acting President."

Moran's face turned almost crimson. "My answer to that question, Mr. Vice President, is, hell no!"

Atherton unfolded his arms, frowning. "I'm sorry. I meant no offense. I was thinking of the best interests of the country."

"The president is very pleased with the way you've handled things, thus far," Moran said, calming. "Let's just keep it that way."

"How soon do we get to see him?"

"As soon as possible."

"That means when?"

"Just as soon as it's possible."

Atherton sighed. "How about Bushy Ambrose?"

"Probably sooner."

The vice president leaned forward, glancing at the papers on the table before him. "There's a matter that's come up concerning Nicaragua that we're going to discuss at the next National Security Council meeting. Will you be attending National Security Council meetings?"

"That's something that wasn't put into the directive. For the time being, there will be no National Security Council meetings."

"What?"

"We will direct national security from up there. For the duration of the emergency. Until further notice."

Senator Rollins met Reuben Jackson at a discreet side door a distance down the corridor from the main entrance to Senator Dubarry's office suite. Without speaking beyond pleasantries, they went out a rear exit of the Dirksen Building, crossed the street and traversed a parking lot that abutted the rear of a nondescript building that housed the Monocle, a restaurant so favored by the powers on Capitol Hill that some called it the third house of Congress. It was here that they should have erected the security barricades. It was not too much of an exaggeration to say that more business was transacted in the Monocle's bar in a single day than was accomplished in a month of Senate committee hearings.

Rollins and Jackson were considered among the most powerful individuals in Congress and were instantly recognized by an immediately deferential maître d'. Rollins's secretary had made very definite reservations. As was Rollins's habit, they were exactly on time. But they were requested to wait a few minutes in the bar. The establishment was that popular and crowded. Such were the processes of government.

"Do you want to tell me now?" said Jackson, as a diffident bartender set down their Bloody Marys.

"No. I want to wait until you're pinned against the wall and I can shove a table into your gut in case you get antsy."

"Big stuff."

"Big stuff. The biggest."

The maître d' all but dragged two lingering congressional wives from their coffee and table, then waved frantically.

"Gird thy loins," said Rollins, taking up his glass. When they were seated, with Jackson's back to the wall, Rollins carefully glanced about the nearby tables. They were mostly familiar faces—familiar lobbyists—but they paid him no unusual attention. This was the most public place on Capitol Hill outside of the Rotunda, and it was altogether natural for Rollins to be meeting Jackson there. It would be assumed that their conversation was routine business. Rollins hunched forward and spoke softly.

"It's been two hours since I put out the word, Reuben. What have you heard?"

"Jake Owens stays majority leader."

Rollins nodded.

"Mose Goode becomes the first black majority whip in history."

Rollins nodded again, this time adding a slight smile.

"Carl Pfeiffer gets Armed Services."

"That's right."

"And we get fucked."

Rollins smiled again. "I'm told that happens to Meathead twice a day."

"Not like this. From what I hear, you guys are up to Spanish Inquisition fucking."

"Nothing of the sort, Reuben. But you've got the general idea. Maitland steps down as congressional honcho of the American military."

"Why?"

"Wrong question."

"All right. What. What do we get in return?"

"Maitland becomes Senate president pro tempore. He keeps the subcommittee on military construction. You get to be staff director of Armed Services, which is better than chairman."

"Pfeiffer agreed to that?"

"For now. In the Congress after this, he may try to bump you, but that's two years away."

"What else do we get?"

"Just about anything. Except the ambassadorship to Guinea-Bisseau. That's been promised."

"A ride for my wife in Air Force One?"

"A trip around the world in Air Force One."

"I'll write that down in blood." He paused, reminded of the president's blood. "Back to question one. Why?"

"I'll say this much. The honorable gentleman from Louisiana is about the most loyal supporter the president has, after me, Bushy Ambrose, and Mrs. Hampton. At least when Meathead's sober."

"I keep him that way. If not sober, loyal."

"As president pro tem, he will sit astride the presidential succession."

"Jesus, Andy, is the president critical? Dead? We're getting a few whispers."

"I can assure you on the most direct firsthand knowledge that he's not, and that he's not likely to be, as long as he stays up at Camp David until this is cleared up. Believe me, Reuben. He's as alive as you and I. But he got shot up, and Ambrose is scared shitless, and he's got to stay there."

"And?"

"And, the vice president, who's scared shitless himself, seems interested in invoking the Twenty-fifth Amendment. As president pro tem, Meathead would have to rule on any such action, along with the speaker of the House."

"The speaker is our sworn enemy. He wouldn't side with the vice president."

"Who knows what he'd do if he decided to screw us up. The present confused situation is certainly a golden opportunity for him. With Meathead in there, he'd have no chance to try anything."

"I wish you'd speak more respectfully of the Saviour of the Republic. As president pro tem, Meathead, uh, my boss, would be third in line for the presidency."

"I said the president's fine, Reuben. We just don't want any fun and games."

The waiter came to take their order. Rollins chose a seafood platter and Jackson decided on the restaurant's largest steak. When the salads arrived Jackson began eating his hurriedly, a man forever pressed for time.

"Have you heard all the rumors?" he asked, between mouthfuls.

"Most of them, I guess," said Rollins. "The one about the coup seems to have faded away."

"There's one that's really for real. The Judiciary Committee is going to appoint a special prosecutor to investigate the Secret Service."

Rollins stared at his plate. "I'm not sure that's such a bad idea."

"Bonnie Greer's death shall not go unavenged. Some good people are going overboard. You can't shoot network correspondents."

The entrées came. Jackson began carving into the steak. A blond woman lobbyist and a young staff aide on the Environment Committee seated themselves at the table next to them. Jackson waited until the two had resumed their conversation; the boyish staff aide was very excited and talked in loud squeaks.

"We've left out a part of the equation," Jackson said. "Monsieur Meathead *lui-meme*."

"It'll take both of us to persuade him."

"It'll take more than that."

"We'll fly him down the most luxurious whore in New York. A countess from the Hamptons. Someone featured in *W* magazine."

"Maybe one of those ladies who's been on the cover of *Embassy Row* magazine. But you'll have to persuade him of the logic of this as well. When he's sober, you know, he's still one of the shrewdest guys on the Hill."

"*Entendu.*"

Jackson munched a large bite of steak. "And that's not all he'll want."

"What else?" said Rollins, slightly irritated.

"The president."

"What do you mean?"

"It's going to take a call from the president. Private. Direct to Meathead."

"A personal call."

"He'll insist on it. He will, Andy. It has to be. Otherwise he'll think it's just you guys screwing around."

"Okay."

"You're sure? A call from the president?"

"How about this afternoon?"

"He may be asleep."

"Well, wake him up, damn it. It'll be the president of the United States."

> *My sorrow—I could not awaken*
> *My heart to joy at the same tone—*
> *And all I loved—I loved alone—*
> *Then—in my childhood, in the dawn*
> *Of a most stormy life—was drawn*
> *From every depth of good and ill*
> *The mystery which binds me still—*
> *From the torrent, or the fountain—*
> *From the red cliff of the mountain—*
> *From the sun that round me rolled*
> *In its autumn tint of gold—*
> *From the lightning in the sky*
> *As it pass'd me flying by—*
> *From the thunder and the storm—*
> *And the cloud that took the form*
> *When the rest of Heaven was blue*
> *Of a demon in my view.*

Charley Dresden was again in his old velvet chair, again watching the arrival of dawn, again drinking wine. But in reciting aloud, he had disturbed the peace. He heard Charlene move from the bed. In a moment she appeared in the doorway, barefoot, but otherwise wrapped in a robe.

"What were you saying?" she said.

"I was reciting a poem. Edgar Allan Poe."

"Edgar Allan Poe. 'The Raven.'"

"'Tis some visitor,' I muttered, 'tapping at my chamber door—
Only this and nothing more.'" He shook his head. "No. The poem I
was reciting is titled 'Alone.'"

She went to the chair opposite him, seating herself demurely. She
was extraordinarily beautiful, even when unkempt. Perhaps especially
when unkempt. It brought out her inherent wildness.

"You're not alone," she said. "I'm back."

"For now."

"For a long time. I got the resort account in Monterey."

"You're hiring on as the fellow's flack."

"I'm hiring on to nothing. He's an account, a client. And I'm
going to have more. As of today, I'm a public relations agency."

"Do you want to use my office?"

She shook her head firmly. "I'm going to have my own office. I'm
going to get one today."

He smiled, indulgently, the parent of a superambitious child.

"I mean it, Charley. I'm going into business. On my own."

"*Estupendo.*"

"Don't speak Spanish."

"Sorry."

"You're sitting here naked again, drinking wine, in the morning."

"The last scant edge of night. It's the most pleasant part of the
day."

"The rest of the day might be more pleasant if you didn't start off
with drinking."

"I hear nagging. It must be Mrs. Mercredes next door."

"It's me, Charley. You got drunk last night."

"There's not a person in Tiburcio who doesn't get drunk once in a
while, including you."

"Nobody else shoots holes in their walls."

Dresden glanced up at the ceiling corner.

"I've done that before."

"I know. And I've left you before. Charley, I don't want to live
with a man who gets drunk and plays around with guns."

"Okay."

"I mean it, Charley."

"Okay."

They sat. Charlene rubbed her eyes and then looked down at her
hands. She glanced at him. He was seated very elegantly in his
nakedness, legs crossed, wine glass held as though in preparation for

a toast. She started to speak, but didn't. The morning light had brightened some by the time she finally did.

"How did you make out in San Francisco? Isabel said you went up to the city."

"I don't know," he said. "They had nothing on the air last night."

"Why don't you give it a rest, Charley?" He had never seen her expression so earnest, or unhappy.

"I told you why."

"It doesn't matter that people think you're a screwball?"

"I know I'm not."

"Charley."

"You once told me I was the most unusual man you'd ever met, that I was a very special person.

"You are."

"You topped it off by saying you loved me."

"Maybe I do." She looked down at her hands again, then directly up into his eyes. "I mean to be a respectable woman, Charley. A very respectable, adult, sensible woman. No more Tahoe. No more on the bum."

"You've said that before."

"I mean it. Don't screw things up for me."

He sipped his wine, gazing at her over the rim of his glass. "Do you want to move out?"

"No, Charley. I don't want that at all. That's why I'm so goddamn unhappy."

Jenks did not call until long after Charlene, still angry with him, had left for Santa Linda. Dresden had fallen asleep in his chair.

"Your phone rang nine times," Jenks said. "I was going to give up on you."

"Maybe you should. I've had a half gallon of wine for breakfast."

Jenks paused, then sighed. "We ain't gonna no way do an editorial about what you got to say."

"That's your privilege."

"The general manager's decree. A matter of the majesty of the presidential office. The good news is that I can get you on the air with what you have to say anyway."

"On the newscast?"

"No. I guess this comes under bad news. In any event, what I can get you on is 'The Jimmy Moon Show.'"

"*Malchiste*," Dresden said, using the Spanish term for bad joke.

"The Jimmy Moon Show" was so notoriously sensational it made the "Phil Donahue Show" seem like a BBC documentary. Moon had actually once had Siamese twins on to discuss their sex lives.

"No joke," said Jenks. "They want you, amigo. I think they'd like to have you on tonight."

"Malchiste el grande."

"It's all I can do."

Dresden stared at his bare feet. If even his mistress was going to think him a screwball, he might as well be a famous one.

"Tell them I'll do it."

"They're having their morning meeting right now. It'll be an hour or more before they're done. Where can the nice producer lady reach you?"

"I'll be at my office. Fast as I can."

He arrived in his very best vested suit, a dark gray pinstripe he had bought at Brooks Brothers in Philadelphia on a business trip several years before. He also wore an actual, pressed, nonwash-and-wear blue shirt and a dark, striped guards tie. Isabel was very impressed.

"New client?" she asked.

"No such luck. I think I'm going to be on television tonight."

"Well, your old client, Mr. Bolger of the amusement park, has already called twice. He said he would like an expression of interest from you as to whether you would like to continue with his account. Freddy the pizza man would like his radio spots. Novak called from Channel Three. The *Press-Journal* real estate ad section would like its money. Frank's Used Cars would like to buy some TV movie time. And the police sergeant called and said he really does have a warrant."

"How nice. I'm going to San Francisco. It looks like I'm going to be on 'The Jimmy Moon Show.'"

"Terrific. I watch it all the time. Are you going to wear a dress?"

"Ho ho. Anything in the mail?"

"Two bills and yet another invitation to join the Chamber of Commerce."

"Sooner the Elks. Did those two mysterious gentlemen show up again?"

"So to speak. I saw one of them sitting in a car when I pulled up this morning. Maybe they're process servers."

"A process server would have served me by now." He went to the door and opened it slightly. "What kind of car?"

"I don't know. Chevy, I guess. Dark blue."

"No such car there now."

The phone rang. It was Freddy of Freddy's Pizza. Dresden shook his head and Isabel muttered something pleasant, hanging up. The next call was from Mr. Bolger. Dresden shook his head twice as hard. The third call was from Channel Six in San Francisco. Dresden leaped for the phone.

The "producer lady" sounded young, breathless, excited, and deferential. He supposed she was that way with all the show's guests, including sexually active Siamese twins. The requirements were simple. His would be a twenty-minute segment. He and Moon would talk about his tape, view the tape, and then take questions from the studio audience and those at home. Though the program aired at midnight, the taping would be at three-thirty that afternoon. Could he please arrive at three? He could.

"Do you need to pat my fanny?" Isabel asked after he got off the phone.

"I'm still going on yesterday's luck," he said. "I don't want to empty the well." He picked up his briefcase and started out the door, then hesitated. "On second thought, maybe I better. You know how the MG hates going to San Francisco."

She stood up, smiling. "After this, Charley, you get back to work, okay?"

The MG behaved itself, and Dresden was able to reach the studio well before three. He thought of stopping for a drink to bolster his nerves, but dismissed the idea. He needed to appear as sober and responsible as possible.

Jenks was in a meeting and not available. The station receptionist rang up the young woman Dresden had talked to and she appeared a few minutes later. A tall, starved, nervous stick of a girl, attractive, but wearing very thick glasses, she led him to a windowless room in which sat two others, presumably also guests on the show. One was a man wearing combat fatigues, though no military insignia. The other was a fashionably dressed and very striking woman, or possibly a man dressed as a woman, or possibly a woman who thought of herself as a man dressed as a woman. Charley said nothing to either of them, pretending to rummage through his briefcase.

Jimmy Moon looked the epitome of a well-dressed hayseed—a man twenty or thirty pounds overweight in obvious places, with a beefy, jowly face, florid complexion, and bristly hair, yet dressed in a stylish, dark brown suit that might have cost a thousand dollars. Like most Californians, he spoke with a midwestern accent, and in fact came from St. Louis. He had a loose, affable manner, but a mind and mouth like a snapping turtle's bite. His was the highest rated program in its time period in San Francisco.

He began Charlie's segment very circumspectly, reminding viewers and his studio audience of the details of the assassination attempt, then in gracious manner introducing Dresden.

"You are, sir, an advertising executive in Santa Linda?" he said, after Charley had seated himself.

"Yes," said Dresden, a trifle nervously. "I'm president of the Dresden Organization. It's an advertising concern that specializes in television production."

"And you've had previous experience as a broadcast journalist?"

"Yes. I was news director at Channel Ten in Santa Cruz, and before that was program director at Channel Three in Santa Linda. I was also . . ."

"I just want to establish that you're an expert on videotape and what shows up on the television screen."

"Well, yes, I suppose you can say that. . . ."

"And you've studied tapes of the assassination attempt at Gettysburg very carefully. Having done so, it's your belief that it was not a mere attempt but an actual assassination, that President Hampton is not at Camp David but is actually dead. That his aides are perpetrating a monstrous fraud and cover-up on the American people, that our most fundamental governmental institutions are being threatened by an evil cabal . . ."

"It's my opinion, having looked at the tapes, that the president suffered not just one wound, as the surgeon general stated, but two, and that the second one was in all likelihood fatal."

"All right, Mr. Dresden, we'll roll the tape."

The screen gave way to images that had not been a significant part of Dresden's tape—Bonnie Greer meeting her violent end yet once again in living color, in living rooms throughout the Bay Area. Finally, they came to the footage that Tracy Bakersfield had prepared, the slow motion torture of the president receiving his wounds and the pink blobs sailing slowly from his chest into his limousine. The tape stopped in freeze frame, then faded to black.

"And Mr. Dresden," said Moon, "you claim that those little pink balls are drops of the president's blood."

"They're large and pink because, in recording this from the original footage, we—my assistant and I—deliberately turned up the tint and color controls."

"Why did you do that, Mr. Dresden?"

"It exaggerated the size of the droplets and made them more visible. Otherwise, they'd be almost impossible to see on a home receiver. You need a very high resolution television monitor . . ."

"Yes. It's fascinating stuff, Mr. Dresden. Compelling. Riveting. Before we go any further, there's something I have to ask you. Is it true your father flew war planes for the Nazis?"

Dresden controlled himself, but only just. "It was my grandfather and it was for the Kaiser, in World War I. He became an American citizen. He was later in the motion picture business."

"But a German flier nonetheless?"

"Yes, but what . . ."

"The phones are all lit up and we'd better take a call. Sir or madam, identify yourself and let's have your question."

"Jimmy, this is Marinda Sue in Alviso. What I want to ask Mr. Dresden is this. As everyone knows, President Hampton and the Communists are in league . . ."

The remainder of Dresden's segment, perhaps eleven minutes all told, seemed three hours. When he was finally freed from the set during a commercial break, the man in the camouflage garb taking his place, he felt released from an inquisition. He left the television station as quickly as possible, not stopping to talk with Bill Jenks, rudely pushing past some people in the lobby to reach the revolving door to the street before them. Still hurrying, he moved down the hill till the studio was out of sight, halting finally for a traffic light. He was breathing heavily. In a way, he felt violated.

The light changed, but he remained at the curb. His breaths came more slowly. He'd been made a fool of, but perhaps that didn't matter so much. Actually, it didn't matter at all. What counted was that they had accepted his tape, and in a few short hours would be broadcasting it to hundreds of thousands of homes.

The tape. He had left his cassette with them. But Tracy had made him another copy.

After the traffic light again went through its cycle, he crossed the street, striding quickly. Now he could go home to Santa Linda. Tomorrow he would celebrate his triumph at Antoine's, at lunch. Charley Dresden had put his case on holy television. It would be up to Jim Ireland to disprove it. All television is real until proven otherwise.

He did not want to go home. A celebratory drink was in order. He turned into the first decent-looking cocktail lounge and ordered himself a large martini. A few sips into it, he had a wonderful idea. He had been trying to work up the courage for it for days. Now was the time. He went to the public telephone.

"I'm sorry, old buddy," said Paul Bremmer, once Dresden had located him and explained his need. "I'd do it if I could, but our policy on the confidential phone file here is carved in marble. And that especially goes for the private unlisted home phone numbers of U.S. senators. They fired a copy boy last week for giving out a number."

"You're sure, Paul?"

"I'm your friend, old buddy, as I think I've proved in recent days. But the editor's a real hard case on this. Why don't you try to reach Calendiari through his office?"

"It's not the senator himself I'm trying to reach."

"What?"

Dresden paused, glancing about the saloon. The damned place was filled with ferns.

"Paul," he said. "What about addresses? Do you have a written policy about giving out home addresses?"

"Well, now that you bring it up, I don't think I've ever seen such a thing. The old man's hang-up is phone numbers."

"I would surely appreciate knowing where the good congressman is now residing."

"Hang on and I'll see what I can find. Uh, friends for life and all that, old buddy, but I might point out that the favor quota for the week is getting kinda full."

"Duly noted. In the repayment book."

"Hang loose."

Within the hour, Dresden was out of the city and grinding the MG up into the hills. Perhaps it was only the martini, but he was feeling in love.

8

The house was situated far back among trees on the east side of the mountain road. It had a sweeping view of the Bay and, from the upper windows of its west side, a glimpse of the yellow vales and valleys of San Francisco horse country. Dresden drove past the driveway twice before realizing it was the place. The brand-new black and gray Seville parked in front of the three-car garage made it certain. The license plate bracket bore the name of Anderson Cadillac in Santa Linda. An annual gift from mommy and daddy, no doubt.

There was a Mercedes-Benz roadster, top down, parked next to the Seville, but it bore no U.S. Senate license plate. Calendiari maintained a local senatorial office in the small bayside city at the foot of the mountain. His winery's corporate offices were in San Francisco, and his family's holdings—comprising thousands of acres of vineyards in the Napa and Sonoma valleys—also included a large horse ranch in this country. Dresden hesitated, holding the MG at idle on the crown of the descending drive. He was still uncertain as to which of them he really wanted to see—the powerful senator who could help him press his case about the president's death, or Madeleine, now so far removed from his life, yet once its dearest treasure. He had last talked to her a little more than two years before. It had not been a happy occasion. There had been tears in her eyes, and anger in her voice—much like their first awful parting years before that, in that so youthful time of theirs in San Francisco. He well remembered the look of shock, anger, disgust, and injured pride when she had stumbled upon his clumsy, disreputable self-indulgence with her roommate in that cluttered kitchen of her hilltop apartment. To him, it had seemed a thoughtless but harmless indiscretion at first, but Maddy had taken it with fierce seriousness, marrying Calendiari not long after. Charley had devoted their subsequent few reunions, chance meetings most of them, to seeking her forgiveness. She had devoted them to withholding it, always behaving very much as Calendiari's wife.

He eased the MG down the drive and parked it discreetly to the side of the Cadillac. A flagstone path led to the front entrance of the house, two massive oaken doors that seemed to require a sweating slave and gong more than a mere doorbell. It rang loud interior chimes, audible despite the thickness of the highly polished wood. He stepped back, into the bright sunlight.

Charley expected a servant, but it was Madeleine herself, unchanged, tall and slender, blond hair falling across large blue eyes, the fairest of skin. She was dressed elegantly, in matching pale blue slacks, blouse, and hair ribbon, a gold belt at her narrow waist and a gold scarf at her throat. She stared at him a moment, hesitant, her lips parted but not in speech. Then she stepped back into the shadow of the hall, nearer the shelter of the heavy door.

"It's me. Charley Dresden."

"Yes. I see," she said. Her voice was softer than he remembered, and lower. But not happier.

"I need to speak with your husband."

"With George?"

"Yes. It's quite important. To me, anyway."

She stepped back still farther. He feared she might slam shut the door.

"He's not here, Charley. He's in Washington. You could have telephoned first."

"Your number's unlisted."

"Yes. It cuts down on the late-night calls from rejected swains in saloons."

"I only did that once, and it was years ago."

"George isn't here."

"May I talk with you then? I need some help."

"I have a guest, Charley."

"I won't take long."

They stared into each other's eyes. She finally surrendered.

"All right. For a few minutes."

He bowed slightly, borrowing some of the formality of his Prussian ancestors, and entered. She gave him a quick glance, then led him along the tile-floored hall, around a corner, and down into an enormous living room. One entire wall was given to floor-to-ceiling windows and sliding glass doors. A large sunlit terrace filled with flowers was visible beyond. The bay was crisply blue in the late-afternoon sunshine, and the hills and mountains on the other side clearly visible. A woman was seated on one of several couches placed about the room. She turned and smiled crookedly but pleasantly. She was as blond as Maddy, but unlike her—larger, tanner, healthier looking in an outdoor, western way, with wrinkles at the corners of her eyes Charley could see even at that distance.

"Stephie, this is Charley Dresden, an old friend. He just dropped in out of absolutely nowhere. I haven't seen him in years and years."

"Two," said Charley.

The woman kept smiling, extending her hand as Charley came near. "Stephanie Pernell," she said. Her speech was slightly slurred. There were the remnants of a gin and tonic on the glass tabletop before her. The ice had melted.

"You may even have met before," Maddy continued, her hostess's pleasantries failing to distract from a slightly troubled look in her eyes. "Stephie was at Santa Linda State when I was there."

"I still live in Santa Linda," Charley said. "Or work there. My house is in the mountains west of there. In Tiburcio."

"I live here. Down the road. My husband's Rob Pernell. The banker? He's in Japan. Always in goddamn Japan."

Dresden's eyes again went to her glass.

"Stephie," said Maddy, "we have to call George. That's why Charley stopped by. He thought George might be here."

"Take your time. I'll just finish my drink." She did so with one quick gulp, then held the empty glass very obviously in front of her.

· "Stephie. Rob's coming home tonight. What you could use most of all is a nap."

The woman didn't budge. "Plenty of time for that, Maddy. Plenty of time for naps when he comes home."

"He's been away a month, Steph. Why don't you try for a happy homecoming?" Maddy stepped forward and took the woman's glass.

"Charley, would you step out and see the view from the terrace while I go out with Stephie to her car."

Dresden nodded to the Pernell woman and did as he was commanded. As he let the glass door slide closed behind him, he glanced back and saw Maddy leading the woman away.

The terrace and garden were a splendor, perfectly designed and meticulously tended, obviously a matter of some pride to her. He wondered how much time she spent in this house—alone. Senators were always traveling. He paused before some of the flower beds and shrubs, recognizing few of them. Charlene would know what they were. Charlene would appreciate living in such a place. Dresden would not. It reminded him too forcefully of the grand house his father's failure had compelled him to leave in Westchester.

The air was cooler here on the shady side of the house; the breeze, when it blew, almost chilly. Those on the tiny sailboats below would be dressed warmly. Leaning against the stone wall at the terrace's edge, he stared down at their distant lives, guessing idly at their cares and secrets. If they looked up at the far remove of this ridge, they might imagine a reunion of two former lovers, but certainly not a conversation about a dead president.

There was color in Maddy's face when she returned, lingering disgust and frustration in her expression.

"If nothing else, you gave me an excuse to put an end to that," she said. "I think Stephanie's been drinking all day. She had four while she was over here. I probably should have driven her home."

"She didn't look that bad off."

"You'd know, wouldn't you, Charley? Well, she's that bad off emotionally. Her husband is away as much as George is, and she just doesn't know how to cope with it."

"How do you cope with it?"

"Very nicely, thank you. Now why are you here, Charley? Really."

"I'd really like to talk to your husband. I really would like his help. There's something he should know, would want to know."

"Well, you can't talk with him; not that he'd want to talk to you; not that I'd know where to find him. They're supposed to be conferring somewhere on the budget vote—on how they're going to manage it with the president wounded. George wouldn't be very happy to know you're here, Charley. I presume you know that."

"I know that."

"It's going to be bad enough when he finds out. Stephie will talk about it. She's really quite uncontrollable."

Maddy shivered. He felt an impulse to put his arm around her, and almost gave in to it. As though sensing his intent, she stepped to the side.

"I'm sure you want a drink, Charley. I'll give you one. Then you'll have to go. You're complicating my day."

Once back inside, it took her only a brief moment to bring him a glass of very expensive scotch whiskey, along with one for herself. To his surprise, when he seated himself in the place just abandoned by Mrs. Pernell, Maddy sat next to him. She was sending such contradictory signals.

"All right, Charley Dresden, friend of my youth. How can we help you?"

"The president's dead."

"What do you mean?"

"I mean he's dead. He was shot to death at Gettysburg, and I can prove it. I want your husband to know about it."

"Prove it how?"

"I've studied the videotapes. With an expert. We're convinced there were two wounds, not one, and that the second one was fatal."

He went on to explain in careful detail the technicalities of videotape editing and production and how they permitted minute examinations of visual and audial events. He proceeded to relate the details of the assassination attempt with similar methodology, interspersing electronics with descriptions of the gore, adding his own amateur criminology where necessary.

"That's appalling."

"Yes."

"You have all this on tape?"

"Yes. It will be on television tonight, on Channel Six. 'The Jimmy Moon Show.' I'm one of his guests. I taped the show this afternoon."

"George calls it 'The Jimmy Loon Show.' He was almost trapped into appearing on it once. How did it happen to you?"

"I more or less asked for it. There wasn't any other way to get what I have to say on the air."

"Truly appalling."

"It's all true."

"If it is, why aren't they telling us? Why would they keep something like that secret?"

"I'll leave it to people like George to figure that out. All I know is what I know. The president is dead."

She pressed the rim of her glass against her lips. He could see the years in her face now, but they had been kind to her. There was a bit of melancholy, perhaps, but nothing harsh. He hadn't asked if she had children. He could see no trace of any child's habitation in the room.

"What do you want me to do?"

"Watch the show. If you have a home recorder, record it. Tell George. Show him."

"Nothing about this will please him."

"I didn't come here to please him."

"Well, you're not going to stay here to watch 'The Jimmy Moon Show,' Charles Dresden. Don't get any ideas about that. I'm not sure I'm even going to turn that awful program on." Her gaze shifted to the windows. The advancing darkness had merged the bay with the shadows of the opposite hills. She took a deep breath, and then a sip of her drink. "Stay for dinner, Charley. I've had no company but Stephanie for days. It will be good to talk to you without interruption for once."

Since her marriage to Calendiari, they had met only in public places—cocktail parties, receptions, at Santa Linda's Channel Three when her husband had announced his candidacy for the Senate, in shopping malls, and once even at the beach at Capitola, their only really amicable meeting. But never alone. In their encounter at the beach, they had progressed no further than a few pleasantries when Zack had come upon them, impressed to learn that Charley knew a U.S. senator's wife. Madeleine had not looked impressed with Zack.

"You're sure this is all right?" he said.

"No, it's not all right. But since I'm to pay a penalty anyway, you might as well stay a little longer." She rose. "I'd better turn on some lights."

She turned on just one, added soft guitar music from a Wyndam Hill tape on the stereo, and then left him. He heard the small sound of her heels crossing the hard floor of a distant room. After that, more faintly, came kitchen noises.

He turned his attention to the music, a quiet, contemplative, solitary pleasantness, each note a tone struck in crystal. He drank and leaned back his head, inhaling the lingering scent of her perfume. Zack and Tracy Bakersfield were beautiful creatures of nature. Madeleine was a refinement, a distillate of the excellences of life. He remembered coming to her San Francisco apartment when no one was there, finding a note left for him taped on a bottle of jug burgundy. It had ended with "Poverty means you must drink wine instead of sipping it." Maddy always sipped of everything.

It had been Calendiari wine.

He went to join her in the kitchen, helping himself to some more scotch.

"We're having fettucine," she said. "I've come to detest Italian food, but pasta is all we ever seem to have."

"I recall you never cared for Mexican food, either."

"You know us Scandinavians. Just give us a piece of dried fish."

"Are you happy, Maddy?"

"You've no idea, Charley."

"I mean with everything, with your life."

"Perfectly, Charley. Everything about it has exceeded my wildest expectations. I've even been to a banquet in the Kremlin, did you know that? I made a very eloquent toast in my Santa Linda State Russian. And you, Charley? How is life with the remarkable Mr. Dresden?"

"Much the same as it's always been, I suppose. Not much different than when we, when we used to date."

"Then you're not very happy."

"Well, often that's true, Maddy. But I'm also often very content. And sometimes I'm quite joyous. I'm beginning to feel that way right now. It's so damn good to see you again."

She looked away, returning her attention to the preparation of the meal. She served it with an expensive wine, which they both sipped slowly, the conversation far outlasting the dinner. He talked mostly about Tiburcio, leaving out much mention of Zack. Maddy spoke of Washington, matching him anecdote for anecdote, the two places so antithetical. He followed her tale of the Canadian ambassador's bizarre arranged marriage with a recounting of a night in the Tiburcio Saloon and Grocery when a group of them at the bar became blood brothers with a drunken Indian and frightened the saloon's subsequent patrons with their unexplained bloody palms.

She laughed, the first time that evening. After dinner he asked for a brandy and she brought him what must have been one of Calendiari's costliest bottles. When he poured himself a second she did not complain, but she did object when, as their arms brushed, he reached and kissed her hand. She pulled it away almost violently. They had returned to the huge living room and were sitting on a couch. To his surprise, she did not leave his side. He stared into the amber iridescence of the cognac, fantasizing about what he desired to come to pass, then took a large gulp.

"I should go," he said. It was a flat statement.

A long silence followed. She kept her face from him, staring at the now dark wall of windows with only a few distant lights visible through it. She began turning her wedding ring on her finger as she finally spoke.

"If you go now, you won't get home in time to see your all-important television show."

"No," he said.

She sighed, too emphatically for simple resignation.

"All right, Charley. You can watch 'The Jimmy Moon Show' with me. But then you absolutely must go. You're upsetting me. I think I'm going to feel very bad about this tomorrow."

"Do you want me to go?"

"No. It's too late. Pour me a brandy too."

Watching "The Jimmy Moon Show" was a mistake, in every way a mistake. They had to forsake the warmth and comfort of the couch for Calendiari's study for a convenient television set. The room was cold, the furniture uncomfortable, the mood dispelled. Moon, his audience, and the general conduct of the program were more embarrassing, abusive, and humiliating than he remembered. The duration of the assassination tape seemed much shorter than before, though he could identify nothing left out. The audience reaction afterward was much more hostile than he recalled. There were even shouts and catcalls that he must have simply put out of his mind at the time. A commercial for a used-car dealer featuring a near-naked woman followed, and then another advertising a laxative. When the program resumed the man in the camouflage fatigues was sitting in Charley's place on the set. He held a hatbox on his lap that he said contained evidence that the enemy was using headhunters in the war in Central America.

"That is quite enough of that," said Maddy, rising and snapping off the set. Now the room seemed very cold indeed. "I still don't understand your tape. Those little pink flecks could be anything."

"Yes, they could. And I suppose at this point it might be just as well to leave it at that, except for my bet at Antoine's."

"Antoine's? The restaurant in Santa Linda?"

"I have a bet there with Jim Ireland, who owns Channel Three, a bet on whether the president's dead. I'll consider this show and tape my proof."

"A bet on the president's death? For what?"

"The stakes are whether I'm ever allowed to go into Antoine's again." He studied his brandy again, keeping his eyes from hers. It was his fourth. Why had he allowed himself to have so much to drink this evening? What other shameful thing was he about to reveal?

After a silence Maddy finally spoke. "All right, Charley. I'm not going to throw you out into the cold, or down the mountain. Henry's press secretary wouldn't be very pleased with news stories about guests getting arrested for drunk driving. You can stay the night. In the guest room. By yourself. Don't come pawing at my door. I'm going back to Washington tomorrow and I need an early start. I don't want you to bother me any more than you have."

She stood up, her expression very cold. She seemed infuriated by something, though not necessarily him.

She took him past the curving staircase that led to the bedrooms above and instead went down the hall to a guest room on the main floor.

"It has its own bath, through there," she said. "There are clean towels in the closet, disposable razors, toothpaste, toothbrushes, everything you need. I suggest you leave before the morning gets much underway. We have neighbors, and George has family nearby. Stephie Pernell is going to have enough to say as it is."

"Why did you let me stay on so late?"

She had kept her hand on the doorknob. "A number of reasons, Charley. Let's just say I was curious. I wanted to see if you'd changed any, or if I'd remembered you wrong."

"And?"

"You haven't really changed one bit, Charley." She looked down at the nearly empty brandy glass in his hand. "Not one drop. If you're desperate tonight, there's a bar in the family room next door. Don't take any more of the good scotch. George will ask. And, please, be out of here as early as possible."

"That's all? That's it for us?"

"Washington's my real home now. I'll be there tomorrow, where I really belong. It's been grand seeing you again, Charley. Just like old times." She smiled, as she might have when she had been a model during college. "Good night. And good-bye."

And she was gone.

He gulped down the last of the brandy, then waited a discreet minute or two before going into the next room and taking a bottle of the most expensive whiskey he could find, a rare, unblended scotch with an unpronounceable Gaelic name on the label. He thanked Calendiari silently. Then, after a sip of the smoky, foul stuff, he thought better of gratitude. A second sip was only slightly better. He could hear water running somewhere upstairs.

Returning to the guest room, he turned out the lights, undressed, and pulled a chair up to the window, which faced east. Trees and shrubbery obscured any view of the bay itself, but there was a diamond dust of lights on the opposite shore and enough of rising moonlight to limn the distant ridgeline.

The drinking had made him slightly giddy, appropriate for the absurdity of his situation. His "Jimmy Moon Show" appearance had been black comedy, rendering him ridiculous. He would be spending the night alone in the house of the most alluring of his long-lost loves—to no purpose, separated by an entire floor. He'd have Charlene's and doubtless Calendiari's anger to contend with nonetheless. His only consolation was this connoisseur's whiskey he could not abide and a sweep of night beauty outside his window he was too sleepy to appreciate.

The sheets were silk or satin—in any event, blissful. He sank his head back against the pillow. But before his eyes had fully closed he heard the click of the door opening and looked to see the silhouette of a woman's form just as it closed again. He heard the sound of her robe slipping from her body.

He started to speak, but she moved her hand to cover his lips. He pulled her head to him and kissed her gently, as she had liked to be kissed when still a girl in college. His hand went to her breast. Then he fell back.

"Maddy, I'm sorry. I've had so much to drink."

"Don't you worry, Charles Dresden," she said, sliding over him and sitting back as she rubbed his chest with her hands. "Madeleine Margrit Anderson will attend to your every lovely little care and need. Miss Anderson has managed to learn some very interesting things in her years. It's one of the niceties of married life, the many interesting things you can learn." She moved her hands farther down his body. "You just leave everything to your enchanting blue-eyed Ophelia."

The night beauty filled his mind as he closed his eyes, tightly, his senses overwhelmed by the ultimate intoxication. He tumbled and flew and drifted through a soft darkness. He almost slept.

"There then," she said, finally, lying closely against him. "It's done. The happy ending."

"I love you."

He held her tightly, his nostrils full of the scent of sex and her perfume and her cleanliness, a great happiness derived from the warmth of her small breasts against his chest, the coolness of her cheek against his, the gentleness of her hair against his brow. What a perfect creation she still was. Exhibit A in his case against mortality. He stretched out his body full against her and let his head fall slightly back against the pillow.

"You're a wanton," he said, stroking her cheek.

She murmured, "Only on very rare occasions."

"This was all too rare an occasion."

"It's the only one there's going to be. Let's go to sleep now, Charley."

"We can't. I want to talk to you."

She murmured again. "In a little bit."

"A little bit is all there is. If we fall asleep now it will be morning before we know it. You're going to Washington. Please."

"It means I won't be able to fall asleep in your arms. I used to fall asleep in your arms in that apartment in San Francisco."

"Most usually with all your clothes on."

"Not now."

"Not now. I took a bottle of scotch. I'm going to have another drink. Do you want one?"

"You truly think me wanton. God, Charley, the way you drink. The liver's our most forgiving organ, but when it finally turns on you, I'm told there's nothing more horrible."

"I made a promise to myself that if a doctor ever tells me my life is threatened by it I'll stop drinking."

"And?"

"One of these years I must see a doctor."

He poured them both whiskeys. She took hers without further objection.

"I asked you why you let me stay so long," he said. "Now I have another question."

"Why I'm here?"

"Yes."

"I more or less told you before, Charley. For a long time now I've wondered if I'd cheated myself out of something when I left you to marry George. You two are the only men I ever had, and you were so long ago."

"And George is getting rather bald."

"You're being rude and loutish, Charley. George was and is a very attractive man, more agreeable than you in many ways. It was always understood that I was going to marry him. I could think of no logical reason not to. Then along you came out of nowhere and upset everything, kicked everything sky-high. It was the craziest time of my life. Gloriously romantic. But it was very unpleasant too. That time with you was very disorderly, and painful. When we had our falling out it only made sense to go back to George."

"You two were married within a week."

"Yes. All very hasty. To Henry's consternation, completely unarranged. We just drove up to Stateline. Eloped. From time to time, though not very much in recent years, I've wondered if I was too hasty, made a mistake. If, as I said, I cheated myself. If there was something between us, something in you, I should have tried to hold on to. I went through this whole miserable evening now trying to decide whether I really wanted to find out."

"And did you?"

He could sense her smile. "George is the better lover, whiskey or no, *cherie*. He really works at it. But there is a tenderness in you, Charley. Something a little poetic. I really did cheat myself, I think. Maybe a lot. I'm glad I found out. I don't know why you were bent on being such a rakehell when you were young. Going through so many women. Being such a swine sometimes."

"I've tried to find a way to apologize to you for that awful night with your roommate. I've forgotten her name."

"You bounder. It was Corrinne."

"Whatever happened to her?"

"After a couple of years of sitting on men's laps, and other places, she got on a plane for Las Vegas one day with no money and a fifth of gin in her purse. I guess she survived, but I hate to think how."

"And the other roommate, the one who was going to marry that folk singer?"

"She didn't. He kept her a little while after he became famous, and then he stopped."

"There was another girl. The nicest. Very worldly. I used to sit on the edge of the tub and drink martinis while she bathed."

"She lives in the San Jose suburbs. Barbecue, cable television, four children, the lot."

"And you are Mrs. Senator George Calendiari."

Maddy stood up, stared out the window a moment, then looked down at him. "Very much so." She eased herself onto his lap, and drank, without coughing. "I've never cheated on my husband until now, if you'll believe that. Me a Washington wife and all. I never have. He's cheated on me. I don't mean sex really, though out on the campaign trail I'm sure that's happened once or twice. He cheats in the usual congressional way, by living this separate political life that takes up so goddamn much time, days and days sometimes, weeks. He even goes on those funeral trips abroad with the vice president. Very seldom do I get to come along."

She nestled against Dresden's shoulder.

"There's life in the old dame yet, Charley, but I think I'm down a quart. I worked it out, worked it up in my mind that I owed myself a fling, one fling, *c'est tout. Rien de plus.* Now, while I'm still in flower, and not when I'm older and haggard and someone's doing me a favor—or looking for one through me from my husband." She paused, rubbing her head against his cheek. "That it could be with you, Charley, the only other man there's ever really been in my life, that made it just about perfect."

"And safe. The past, not the future."

"I think I probably had my mind made up the moment I let you in the door."

"You had a guest."

"That poor woman. Her husband is more obsessed with his job than George is. Stephanie gets what's left over, and it isn't very much. She sells real estate, plays tennis, drinks a fifth a day, reads a novel a day, and sleeps with almost anyone who comes along."

"How do you cope?"

"I'm not sure. Perhaps I really haven't until now."

"Are you in love with me?"

"Wouldn't that be nice? No, Charley. I just wanted a happy ending. That's all we get, isn't it? Endings. All we can ask is that they're happy ones. We had no happy ending, you and I. I walked into that kitchen all those years ago and walked out and wanted to throw things and throw up and scream."

"And a week later, I read about your elopement in the Santa Linda *Press-Journal.* They tried to treat it as a normal society wedding. The bride wore peau de sois and tennis shoes. I laughed."

"No, you didn't. You cried. Confess."

"Yes. I cried."

"Happy ending, Charley. Happy memory. Happy night." She kissed him, sweetly and gently.

"And for this we must thank the president for getting killed."

She gripped his arm. "I think that whole idea of yours is ghastly and ghoulish and appalling and I don't want to hear another word about it."

"I'm sorry."

She studied him, the blue in her eyes very evident in the brightening moonlight. She still wore her hair ribbon and the color was the same. "I don't want to think of you as someone on 'The Jimmy Moon Show.'"

"I'm not. I'm someone on the Charley Dresden Show. I just wish I knew how it was going to come out."

She leaned forward to kiss him again, but he held her back.

"Wait," he said, and reached and untied the hair ribbon, pulling it gently away from her head and folding it in his hand. "Something of you."

"All right. You may have it. A souvenir of the past, brought up to date. But nothing to do with the future, Charley."

"'And all I loved I love alone.'"

"What?"

"Something from Poe."

"You understand what I'm saying?"

"I understand. Sadly."

Another kiss, then she held him closely, her loosened hair against his face. "Good night, Charley. That's all there is. There isn't any more." She slipped away, pausing at the door. "Good-bye, Charley. I'm going to have a very pretty sleep now. Please be gone when I awake." She vanished in silence.

When she had left he dressed hurriedly, slipping the hair ribbon in his suit coat pocket. He took the whiskey. He felt quite heady, a smitten schoolboy.

The front door clicked, locking behind him, causing a momentary pang, but he hurried on. Despite the cold, he left the MG's top down. He wanted to stay heady, but also awake. The car's engine started sluggishly, but once all cylinders were functioning, he gunned it vigorously, reversing the roadster up the drive and onto the road with great clamor, then roaring off into the mountainous night, leaving sound and echoes to dwindle in her hearing until there was nothing but silence and emptiness and sleep.

Dresden drove rapidly, using the danger as another spur to his alertness. It was an unfamiliar road, and he was constantly steering hard to make the curves. There were a number of cutoffs that led down to the broad freeway that followed the shore of the bay below, but he ignored them to remain on the heights, sustaining his ecstatic lover's mood with the sweeping view and whiskey. He turned on the radio, not minding the loud music it produced, even turning the volume nearly to maximum.

He'd managed more than forty miles before the radio racket was interrupted by a scheduled newscast, the announcer's voice booming loudly over the engine noise. The lead story was about the president. For an instant Dresden harbored the egocentric notion that it might have something to do with his "Jimmy Moon" broadcast, but it was something more consequential than that. For the first time since the shooting the president of the United States had granted a radio interview. That's what the newscaster said. It had been conducted over the telephone with a pool reporter from one of the networks. The president's voice had a painful croak to it, but it was his. The man that Charley Dresden had just sworn was dead to several hundred thousand television viewers was suddenly there in the dashboard, chatting warmly with the American people—in pain, he said, but alive and getting better.

Charley stared, horrified, at the radio dial, for too long. The MG hurtled onto the shoulder and the right front fender caught the guardrail and crumpled, the light from the headlamp disappearing. There was a great screeching and scraping from the side of the car, and the sound of the rear bumper falling off. Then the guardrail ended. By the time the MG bumped to a stop in the slender, sloping ditch that came after, the radio was no longer working.

9

Vice President Atherton did not simply pace his White House office, he prowled it like a zoo creature, making a circuit, moving around his desk, striding back and forth in front of the fireplace, sitting and rising, consumingly impatient. He ordered in Shawcross, Neil Howard, and Mrs. Hildebrand, singly and together, issued them commands, countermanded the commands, ordered them out, ordered them back again. Through it all, he placed phone calls, to nearly every member of the cabinet, to Admiral Elmore at the CIA, to the telephone number he'd been given for the president's makeshift command center at Thurmont, Maryland, and even to the Pentagon war room, where he tried to get patched through to Camp David, with no success.

At length, as Mrs. Hildebrand was making shorthand notes of a rambling stream of objections he was going to raise when and if he ever made contact with the presidential party, a buzzer sounded and the red light on his scrambler phone began flashing. It was Bushy Ambrose, who had had himself patched through the Pentagon war room to reach the vice president on the scrambler.

"Let me introduce myself," said Atherton. "I am the vice president of the United States. I'm one of the fellows who carries around a

'Gold Codes' card that lets me start nuclear war if the notion takes me. I'm the fellow who, according to your representatives, is in charge here at the White House. I have asked politely and otherwise to speak with the president for I don't know how many days now, but have been told it's utterly impossible because of the state of his health and for reasons of national security. So what do I hear at seven thirty-five A.M. this morning on CBS radio? The president of the United States chatting merrily away with some reporter! The government of the United States can wait. Interviews come first!"

Ambrose was uncharacteristically calm. "It was one reporter selected as pool, Mr. Vice President. It was over the telephone. The tape was made available to everyone. It was early in the morning because that's when the president has been at his best and this morning he said he was up to it. He felt it was imperative that he do this as soon as possible to reassure the American people he was all right. Like Ronald Reagan signing that legislation in the recovery room."

Atherton realized he was so agitated he was breathing like an asthmatic. He sat down behind his desk and waved Mrs. Hildebrand out of the room. He took two deep breaths, then resumed speaking, much more in control of himself.

"There are rumors that the president made calls around the Hill yesterday."

"He made one call. To Senator Rollins, who is one of his closest friends."

"A nice chummy chat. Did he find time to talk about the farm bill? The farm lobby's taking the Capitol by storm, and we haven't been able to raise a finger. How about the spending bills? Four of them came through conference yesterday with twenty-two billion dollars added."

"Senator Rollins is in command of the situation."

"Senator Rollins is preoccupied with the party leadership fight."

"He is looking out for the president's interests."

Atherton stood up. "So am I. I presume the president's interests include the talks in Geneva. The Soviets have asked if we don't want to suspend them. Our ambassador has asked Crosby for permission to come back for consultations."

"Telex him to stay put. We don't want the American people thinking the arms control talks are going to break down because of this."

"But they are breaking down because of this! And it's not exactly been quiet in Central America, either. Have you had any access up there to the cable traffic out of Honduras lately? They killed more than a dozen people in Tegucigalpa last night. Assassinations. Leftists. One of those Hughes Five Hundred black job helicopters we have down there dropped another crater bomb on the Managua airport. Someone firebombed two villages in El Salvador."

"Mr. Vice President. It was the understanding that we were to handle national security matters from up here. The secretary of defense . . ."

"Do you want me to shut down the State Department? We're getting official protests! Cuernavaca's not the only place Managua sends telegrams, you know!"

"How do you know about that?"

"I'm vice president of the United States, that's how! Look, Bushy. I don't care if it's the president, or you, or me, or Winnie the Pooh. But someone has to be running this government! And not from some treehouse in Maryland!"

There was a long pause.

"All right, Mr. Vice President. I'll be down today to give you a briefing, a full briefing, on Central America."

"When?"

"This afternoon. After lunch. No, for lunch. We'll have lunch in my White House office. At twelve-thirty sharp."

"What about the president? When do I get to talk to him?"

"I'll make sure he calls you. At one-thirty. Sharp."

After hanging up, Atherton leaned far back in his leather chair, exhausted. In a perverse fantasy, he was back on the Capitol steps at the inaugural, being asked by Justice June Standish of the United States Supreme Court to take the oath of office as vice president. In his fantasy, he refused.

He groaned, and leaned forward far enough to flick a switch on his telephone intercom, summoning Shawcross, Howard, and Mrs. Hildebrand again. Except for his wife and daughter, whom he'd shipped off to Williamsburg for the duration, they were about the only human beings in Washington in whom he had any trust left.

They filed in as might errant pupils entering a principal's office. Mrs. Hildebrand sat the closest to him, as she considered her due.

"Bushy Ambrose is coming down to have lunch with me at twelve-thirty," Atherton said, his hand over his eyes. "He's going to brief me on Tegucigalpa and such like. At one-thirty, the president is going to call."

"About Central America?" Howard asked. "We're going to get questions at the press briefing."

"About everything. Nothing." Atherton dropped his hand, blinking. "Who knows? For God's sake, Neil. What matters is that I'm finally going to get to talk to Hampton. What matters is that he's alive."

"Did Ambrose explain what the hell they're doing making Meathead Dubarry president pro tem?"

"I let that subject pass. Whatever they're doing, I don't want to be seen opposing it. Which reminds me. Mrs. H., get me Senator Goode on the phone."

She went quickly to a telephone on a side table near the fireplace.

"Well," said Howard, hunching forward. "I had the radio interview taped and I've listened to it three times. It sure sounds like the president. A little hoarse, maybe, but that Virginia gentleman drawl comes right through."

"Thirty years in Colorado and he still says 'oot' for 'out,'" said Shawcross.

"I've no doubt it's the president," Atherton said. "And you have no idea what a relief that is to me at this juncture. There was never a time in my life when I wanted so very much not to be president of the United States."

Howard smiled, and glanced at Shawcross.

"If you mean that, which I doubt, don't ever say it in front of a reporter," he said.

Atherton darkened. "Don't patronize me like that, Neil. I'll say what I damn please." He was interrupted by Mrs. Hildebrand, who motioned to a telephone on his desk. "Hello, Mose?" he said, after picking it up. "This is Larry Atherton."

"Yes, Mr. Vice President. How are you, sir?"

"Fine. I understand that there's been a change of minds and that now you're a candidate for whip. Is that correct?"

"Yes, sir. I thought you were aware of it."

"Well, there's been a lot of confusion around here. I just want to make sure this is what you want, Mose."

"It is, Mr. Vice President."

"In that case, I want you to know I'm behind you and behind the president on this one hundred percent. And I want you to make that clear all over the Hill."

"Yes, sir. Thank you. It sure was good to hear the president on the radio this morning."

"You've no idea, Mose. Good luck in the caucus. Not that you'll need it."

Atherton hung up and covered his eyes again. "Any new develop-ments in the investigation? The way things are going, I wouldn't be surprised if they found one of those little La Puño flags on top of the Empire State Building. Or in the Sistine Chapel."

"Nothing new," said Shawcross. "It would help if Steve Copley or someone could produce a confession."

"Precisely," said Atherton. "But it's too late to get one from Man-uel Huerta."

Walt Kreski was in his office, a room he'd not visited much in the last few days. On his stereo, soloist Peter Serkin was in the midst of an electrifying recorded performance of Ravel's Concerto in G, the only work the composer had produced that he couldn't play himself, because of its complexity and speed. On Kreski's desk was a computer printout his secretary had just brought him.

He read it through twice, then sat staring at it, thinking hard. The record had just ended when there came a knock at the door and Dick Hammond entered, on time and as requested. He carried a briefcase. Kreski had his own waiting at the side of his desk. They were shortly to ride out to National for a flight to New York in a Treasury Depart-ment Lear jet.

"What's that?" Hammond said.

"A list of agents in the Washington office with a proficiency in Spanish," Kreski said.

"I could get you three out of the White House detail right now. Hernandez. Garcia. Maria O'Brien."

"The list includes Evans, Ballard, Storch, Perkins, and three oth-ers who were at Gettysburg, including Al Berger. And you." Kreski folded the printout into a careful square and put it in his desk drawer, locking it. "I'm going to use some DEA people in New York to do the interrogating. In fact, this whole thing is supposed to look like a DEA show, which is all right with them, because they've been wanting to talk to these Hondurans, anyway."

"You're not bringing in Steve Copley?"

"Steven is having the time of his life rummaging through La Puño artifacts in Philadelphia. And anyway, I can do without Bureau help. They'd only start taking aerial photographs of Manhattan."

He rose, and reached for his raincoat and briefcase. "We're late. I've got to be back to testify for the Judiciary Committee this after-noon. I don't dare be late for anything anymore."

"The president was very high on you and Al Berger and the Service in his interview this morning."

"Yes, he certainly was."

"It helps."

"I hope."

The jet's engines had already been started by the time they reached National. They received special clearance from the tower and were wheels up within two minutes of the aircraft door's closing. Kreski watched the familiar landmarks and buildings slip by his porthole of a window, then looked away. It would be a short trip to Manhattan, but he had a feeling the journey still before him was going to be very, very long.

The two companies of reinforcements from Fort Bragg arrived at Camp David in a long, dusty convoy of large "deuce and a half" trucks hauling disassembled Quonset huts in trailers along with a great deal of electronic equipment. One of the companies was a long-lines signal unit that would shortly be setting up a microwave tower and satellite dish, connecting with the worldwide STARCOM network. It suggested a sort of permanence and military-only communications.

The convoy had been on the road all night and was several hours late, owing to breakdowns of two of the new "Hummer" command vehicles with which the Pentagon, in one of its more idiotic decisions, was replacing the tried and trusty Jeep. The men were tired, hungry, and irritable—and put to work at once. They were all "volunteers," in that the commanding general of the 82nd Airborne Division assumed that anyone who joined the airborne had perforce volunteered for whatever the military might ask of them, but two of the men had made a particular point of coming when they didn't have to. The division commander delighted in leaving units behind during important operations as a form of punishment and disgraceful example. He had done this for three of the "exercises" in Central America and the second Grenadan invasion. This time he had selected the 59th Signal Long Lines Company to set up a STARCOM hookup and had pointedly left the hardcase 58th Signal back at Fort Bragg to pull dirty details. The outfit contained too high a percentage for his liking of alcoholic sergeants near retirement, short-timers who had failed to reenlist, ROTC officers, and transferees with funny 201 files. Yet, two men of the latter category, PFC Corboy and Sp/4 Macchi, had gone to the first sergeant to ask for transfers to the 59th just so they could take part in the protection of the president. They'd already just transferred to the 82nd from a unit at Fort Meade.

SFC Albert Benney, who ran 2nd Platoon for the 59th, neither liked nor trusted such enthusiasm. He rewarded it appropriately, with the nastiest jobs he could dream up until the enthusiasts began griping and grousing and shirking like normal grunts. Upon arriving at Camp David, his choice for Corboy and Macchi was between helping to erect the 204-foot microwave tower and digging a platoon latrine. Not wanting to trust new men to tower construction, he assigned them the latrine detail. When they were a third of the way through he had them relocate the site a hundred feet or so for better drainage. Then, when they were close to finishing the job, he told them they were on permanent garbage detail for the duration of the Camp David operation. Not once did they complain.

At Kreski's request, the questioning of the three Hispanics took place in a holding room of an annex to the main city jail, a grubby, shabby chamber smelling, like most jails, of urine, sweat, vomit, and disinfectant. It was Kreski's notion that the suspects would feel more at home and relaxed here than in the startlingly pristine and architectually bizarre surroundings of the new Federal Detention Center where they'd been kept since the night of the Gettysburg shooting. However aesthetically pleasing, the Federal Center was imbued with all the mighty presence, authority, and mystery of the national government. Seated at a stained, greasy table surrounded by federal drug agents and, at Kreski's request, a couple of NYPD narcs, they were among their own kind—if Kreski's suspicions about them were right. Kreski and Hammond remained quiet in a far corner of the room, simply observing, perhaps mistaken for people from the local prosecutor's office.

Kreski quite literally understood much more Greek and Latin than Spanish, but was able to follow the conversation as it proceeded both in that language and English. Despite efforts to get all three to respond to questions, two of the Hispanics deferred to the third, a somewhat older and much larger man who was the only one of them who had admitted to being Honduran. His answers followed a pattern. Anything to do with the assassination attempt drew either monosyllabic replies or sullen silences, with anger, frustration, and not a little paranoia evident in the man's gleaming dark eyes. Questions concerning narcotics produced voluble exchanges that ultimately seemed to follow the rules or at least understandings of an oft-played game. Finally, in Spanish, the Honduran asked to speak with the chief DEA agent in private. Kreski nodded.

Afterward, the agent gave Kreski and Hammond a full report and his best assessment of the interrogation in an office borrowed from one of the NYPD narcotics detectives. It was almost as foul-smelling and looking as the holding room. Kreski assumed it was also frequently used for conversations with suspects. He lighted his pipe. It had warded off many evil vapors in its time.

"On the Gettysburg shooting, on the ambush setup for the vice president's motorcade, we get the same shit as in their initial statements," said the agent, a thin, weary man with a scar and thick mustache named Jackman.

"They know nothing, nothing about Huerta, nothing about the vice president's visit to New York, nothing about the rifles on the rooftop. They say they were holed up in the building waiting for a big delivery of cocaine due in from Colombia." He shifted in his chair, planting his elbows on the filthy desktop. "We were waiting for it too. Still are."

The agent looked from Kreski to Hammond and back again. There were all kinds of cops in the federal service, and Kreski and Hammond didn't seem to be his kind.

"These people are from the Charo family," the agent continued. "I know them. By 'family' I don't mean they are all related. The leaders are Colombian, father and son, but there are all kinds, Mexican, Guatemalan, Honduran. Madeiro, the one who did most of the talking, offered a deal. Pull them off the assassination rap and he'll give us the name of the ship. I told him to give us the ship, and then I'd see what we could do. If we connect, well, hell, like I told your people in the beginning, I don't think these are politicals. I think the only presidents they're interested in are the ones on fifty- and hundred-dollar bills."

Kreski puffed his pipe, a signal to the others to wait. "I agree with you," he said, finally, quietly. "If I had prosecutorial jurisdiction, I'd recommend reducing this to a narcotics case. At least for now. But we're just Treasury, not Justice." He smoked some more, waiting as much as they were for his next words to come. "Still, I work for the president. I report every day to his chief of staff and the vice president. I'll see what I can do. In the meantime, be as encouraging as you can with that Madeiro about the drug shipment. If there's a score, I would be very interested in knowing."

They left New York in more than sufficient time to make the congressional hearing as scheduled, but then something unscheduled happened. As the Lear jet was climbing to altitude above the smoky smear that was northern New Jersey, a call came in from the National Park Service at Gettysburg. This was the treasury secretary's personal plane, and it had its own radio telephone.

It was the superintendent of the National Battlefield Park. "Director Kreski? We've just had a musketball man—you know, one of those scavenger hunters with metal detectors? Well, he just brought in something interesting, something that I think has to do with the shooting of the president."

"What's that, Superintendent? A weapon?"

"Yeah, there's a pistol in here. But a lot of other stuff too. He found a small toolbox. Brand-new from the looks of it. He dug it up in the woods north of the Trostle farm, you know, over by Cemetery Ridge?"

"I don't have a map of the battlefield with me, superintendent."

"Well, it's in woods and all but not far down the road from where the president was shot. It was locked, but we broke it open. There's a revolver in it, some letters, in Spanish. Some other papers. And ten thousand dollars in U.S. currency. Hundred-dollar bills."

Kreski lowered the receiver to his lap and sighed. Richard Lawrence, the first to attempt a presidential assassination, tried to kill Andrew Jackson because he thought he was the king of England. John Wilkes Booth murdered Lincoln as an act of war. Lee Harvey Oswald was a misfit trying to make a mark on history, or anything. Sirhan Sirhan was a Palestinian fanatic who was convinced Bobby Kennedy was going to become president and that Bobby Kennedy had sold out to Israel. Now there was Manuel Huerta, "Honduran patriot."

"Do you know what a president of the United States is worth now?" Kreski said to Hammond, wearily. "He's worth ten thousand dollars." The director lifted the phone.

"Sorry, Superintendent. I was passing on the news. Was there anything else in there? A small flag that said La Puño?'"

"No, sir. Just the things I said."

"Well, lock that box up somewhere and don't let anyone touch it. I'll be there as soon as I can."

"Uh, sir. It's against federal law to bring those metal detectors onto park grounds. Should I have the rangers arrest this guy?"

"No! You'd only scare the hell out of him. Just keep him there for questioning."

"I called the State Police. Is there anyone else I should notify?"

"Certainly. You should notify the FBI. You should have done that immediately."

After hanging up the phone Kreski rubbed his eyes, then looked to the younger man across from him who'd been waiting so patiently.

"One of those souvenir hunters with a metal detector dug up a toolbox that appears to be Huerta's," Kreski said. "It has a handgun in it, some letters in Spanish, and money."

"Ten thousand dollars."

"Ten people dead. That's a thousand dollars apiece."

"Huerta's dead too."

"Yeah. Go up and tell the pilot he'll have to divert to the closest field he can find to Gettysburg. If there isn't one at York I know there is at Harrisburg. And tell him to radio ahead for some ground transport."

"But what about the Judiciary Committee hearing? Technically, you're under subpoena."

"You go ahead and be my stand-in. If the honorable chairman makes a fuss, tell him that at this juncture I consider his subpoena an obstruction of justice."

The vice president lunched on avocado stuffed with shrimp and iced tea—except for the lack of a glass of chilled white wine, a very California meal. Bushy Ambrose had a small steak and cottage cheese, followed by coffee. They ate at a small table near the windows of Ambrose's office. The chief of staff had had an easel set up next to them bearing a large map of Central America. From time to time, he would set down his fork and wave a pointer about to better identify a location or emphasize a point.

It was a very military briefing—exact, detailed, boring, and totally useless to Atherton. He didn't want to hear about how many right-wing guerrillas the d'Aubisson movement had amassed around Aca-jutla or that loyalist forces had pushed all leftist insurgents back across the Patuca River. His only interest concerning the region was the nature of the Cuernavaca talks with the Sandinistas and how far they had progressed. Ambrose would say, tersely, only that they had pro-gressed not at all. The president had merely opened'an avenue of communication that might prove helpful in the future, he said. Am-brose would not discuss the president's condition in any more detail than he already had by telephone. In response to Atherton's inquiry as to Mrs. Hampton's well-being, he stated only that she was holding up better than expected, and expressed her thanks to Atherton for his kindly attentions the night of the shooting. From there, the conversation degenerated into idle pleasantries and from there into silence. Atherton and Ambrose had had more informative conversations when they had lunched simply for social reasons.

Both kept an eye and mind to their watches. Ambrose's was apparently the most accurate. He looked from its dial to the telephone just at the instant it rang.

"The president asked me to join you on an extension," Ambrose said, "in case he has a problem with his voice."

"Of course," said Atherton, as politely—if dishonestly—as possible. He picked up the receiver much as he might a ticking bomb. His hand was trembling again, as it had not since the first horrible night.

"Mr. President?"

"Larry, Irving told me how worried you were. I'm sorry I wasn't able to call before this."

The voice was the president's. There was a definite hoarseness, a slight lack of resonance, and an unexpected nasal quality to certain words. Otherwise it was the same as always, the exact tone, the exact inflection.

"I appreciate your making the effort, Henry, what with all you've gone through."

"Should have done it before this. I look forward to rejoining you in the White House, as soon as this terrible business is over and the doctors let me. When they don't have me sleeping I've been rereading the collected papers of Lincoln. Inspiring, Larry, inspiring. I've always admired the man, as you know, but never so much as now. It must be getting shot." Oddly, he began to laugh at the strained, bad joke, and then began to cough.

Embarrassed, Atherton looked to Ambrose, who ignored him.

"Mr. President," said Atherton. "Irving and I have been talking about Central America, and your communications with Managua."

Ambrose glared. "I told him everything is well in hand, Mr. President," he said. "Especially the military situation."

"Yes, Irving," said Hampton. "Well in hand."

Atherton had to play his card now, or not at all.

"Mr. President," he said, "some of the legal staff, and congressional staff, have raised the question of the Twenty-fifth Amendment. In light of the seriousness of your wound and length of convalescence, they . . ."

"What's that? What Twenty-fifth Amendment? Uh, what was that, Larry?"

"Mr. President," said Ambrose, speaking very loudly, as though to drown out anything Atherton might yet have to say. "We've tired you enough. The vice president thanks you. I thank you. I'll see you very soon." He hung up the phone, and glared at Atherton.

"How dare you bother the president of the United States when he's in that condition with a question like that?" Ambrose asked. "Are you so ambitious you'd try to have yourself declared acting president at a time like this?"

"Especially at a time like this. Colonel, someone has to be president, and that man is not functioning as one."

"All I can say, Mr. Vice President," said Ambrose, throwing some papers into his briefcase, "is that it's going to be a long time before you talk to 'that man' again." He snapped shut the briefcase and snatched it up. "I'm going back to Camp David. I'll contact you when it's appropriate."

He walked out of the room in a perfect impersonation of the head of a military tribunal departing a court-martial. A moment later a Security Council aide and army major entered and took up the map and easel. They waited for the vice president to precede them before leaving the office and locking the door behind them.

Charley Dresden nearly stumbled through the door to his office, hobbled by fatigue and the painful stiffness of several injuries. He startled Isabel, more with his appearance than the odd hour of his arrival. He feared she would think him drunk, which he still was, a little.

"My God, Charley! Have you been in a fight?"

He slumped into a chair, wincing. "With a guardrail and a ditch. I had to leave the MG in a garage up in Cupertino. It needs a new radiator and front axle, among other things. Many costly things."

"Your face is all cut up, and your hand's bleeding."

He looked down to where a streak of crimson had soaked through the bandage wrapped around his left hand.

"I patched myself up with the first-aid kit they had in the tow truck. I'm worried most about my knee. It's getting a little swollen, but it still seems to work. Most of me seems to work."

"Didn't you have yourself X-rayed?"

"A hospital didn't seem in order. They have policemen in those emergency rooms, you know, and I wasn't sure I was up to passing a blood alcohol test."

"Where were you?"

"Visiting an old friend. A wonderful old friend. I thought I'd come back early and get a head start on a very busy day. And now it's almost noon."

"Your beautiful suit. It's ruined."

There were huge tears at one knee and elbow. The suit coat was smeared with blood, oil, and grime.

"Yes. I'd better tidy up a little. We can't go to lunch with me looking like a derelict."

"What do you mean 'lunch'?"

"At Antoine's. As far as I'm concerned, I won my bet. I proved my point, on television, no less. Or didn't you watch me on 'The Jimmy Moon Show'?"

"Yes, Charley. But the president was on the radio this morning. Jim Ireland called up to crow. He said he'd be magnanimous in victory and have the police withdraw that warrant. He said he was even going to pay off your tab at Antoine's, in honor of your never being able to have one there again. He was quite the smart ass."

"We'll have lunch. That alleged radio interview doesn't change anything. It can't possibly be real."

"Charley, are you loco? I've been taking calls all morning from every screwball in California. There've been UFO people, Kennedy conspiracy people, Manson family people, right-wing nuts, left-wing nuts, and every other kind of nut. One woman complained that the FBI had hidden a microphone in her vagina and wanted you to find it. Other people have called saying they're from the FBI, or the Secret Service, or the CIA. A lot of people just called up to swear at you. You're not very popular, Charley. I wouldn't go into Antoine's if I were you. And I'm sure as hell not going there with you."

"Did I get any serious calls?"

"You bet. Mr. Bolger called from the amusement park."

"I'll get right back to him."

"Don't bother. He said he called to tell you he doesn't want you to handle his account. Freddy came by for his pizza commercials. I gave them to him."

"How could you? I didn't write any."

"I did. I took some copy from a couple of years ago and just changed a few of the words. Freddy said it was fine. What can you say about pizza?"

"Thank you."

The phone rang. Isabel answered quickly, listened with some exasperation, replied in a long stream of near-violent Spanish, and hung up.

"See?" she said. "You're even getting Chicano screwballs."

"Anyone else? A call from a Mrs. Calendiari?"

"No. Your friend Charlene Zack called. Said she'd call back. But I don't think you'd better hang around for any more calls. Why don't you stay home for a few days? You've got no work to do. And besides, you should see a doctor. If you hang around here, someone's going to throw a rock through the window or something. My brother Tomas said I should get out of here. I think he's right, Charley."

"Very well. Can you give me a ride to Tiburcio? I've got to try to start my other car."

"Sure, Charley," Isabel said. She lived on the west side of Santa Linda, and it wasn't all that far over the hill into the Heather River valley and the Tiburcio Canyon.

"We'll take the electric typewriter," he said. "You can use it at home, for whatever you need to. We'll get a fresh start next week. No sense leaving it here to get wrecked."

He stood up, finding himself in severe pain. "I'm afraid you're going to have to help me with the typewriter, Isabelita."

"I'm going to have to help you with you, Charley. I'll come back for the typewriter."

She drove a seven-year-old Chevrolet that her brother, a mechanic, had carefully selected for her. It needed paint, but, to Charley's knowledge, had never once broken down. She drove very swiftly and expertly, glancing nervously at him from time to time, smiling when he caught her at it, but looking worried when she returned her attention to the road, even more so when her eyes went to the rearview mirror. The calls that morning must have been quite frightening.

The shade of the tall eucalyptus trees reached for them as they wound into the canyon. The striking beauty of the little town and its majestic surroundings had a distracting, relaxing effect on Isabel, but Dresden was stricken with quite another impression. Tiburcio now seemed strange to him, a different place, one he had experienced only vaguely. He felt for no explicable reason a foreigner, an outlander, almost a time traveler—though he had left the town only twenty-four hours before.

Isabel started bearing to the right, following the main road into the town center, but Charley motioned her left onto a cutoff, onto the back road. Rumbling over an old, steel-reinforced wooden bridge, they climbed a sudden hill and then followed twists and turns until at length they came to the steep hillside that harbored Charley's house and yard. The sunshine on the gravel of his drive and turn around was warm and bright.

"*Muchas gracias*, Isabelita," he said. "I'll call you first thing next week."

"Charley." She put her hand on his, holding him in the seat. "Just listen to me a minute. I like you a lot, okay? A lot. I think you're a very smart man. My brother Tomas thinks you're a loser and a screwball, but I know better. You made a lot of money two years ago and gave me a lot of it and I'm very grateful. My little sister's going to college thanks to you."

She leaned closer. Her dark eyes had never seemed so large, or earnest.

"But Charley. Something's gotten into you and you gotta get rid of it. You're drinking worse than I've ever seen you. You're paying no attention to your work. You've got your mind set on this screwball idea of yours about the president and you won't let go. You drive all over the place like a crazy man and now you almost got yourself killed. You gotta let go, Charley. You've gotta snap out of this before it's too late. If you don't, you're never going to get any work in Santa Linda again, or anywhere. They're going to make you into a joke. And I'm going to have to quit and go to work for some computer company. I don't want to do that, Charley, but I will."

He pulled free his hand, but only to squeeze hers. "Don't worry, Isabelita. You won't have to."

"Take care of yourself, Charley. See a doctor."

He lingered on his porch as she drove away, then withdrew into the sanctuary of his house. It, too, seemed strange and different—long his habitation, but now a very temporary one, merely the place where he had languished for the years that had interrupted his relationship with Madeleine Anderson. This was most importantly Charlene Zack's house, the abode she had shared with him for so long, yet would do so now with a sort of stranger. He was someone else. He was the man he had been, the fearless young fellow from the

East who would take California by storm and return to his homeland a conqueror. He no longer belonged in this place, but he knew not where to go. Or how.

There were further retreats for him, still, sanctuaries within sanctuaries—his whiskey, his mountainside, the deliriously remembered ecstasies and tendernesses of the night before, memories that belonged to him and no one else, that would forever be his most priceless possession now. He would resort to them. But first he must indulge a sudden, raging compulsion.

When he had left Maddy's house it was with the firm resolve to honor her request, to let their happy ending be an ending, to let her recross the barrier that had separated their lives. During the night drive along the mountain ridge, until it had been truncated by his mindless accident, he had allowed himself no thought of ever speaking to Madeleine Anderson again. But now, beset by fatigue, pain, and love, he could think of nothing else.

He went to the phone by his favorite chair and window and dialed the number rapidly, but there was no answer after six rings. Calming himself, he dialed again with the utmost care and slowness, this time letting the ring repeat itself seven times, and then ten. To no avail.

She was gone, en route to Washington. He had no idea of her ultimate destination or how he might discover it, and her. It was a problem he must postpone. She was likely still on an airplane, with hours of flying over this enormous country still to go. So he went to his whiskey, his mountain slope, and his reveries. Drinking against the increasing pain in his leg, he remembered savoringly the look and feel of hers. He remembered the softness of her voice, and her touch. Reminding himself of her hair ribbon, he took it from his coat pocket as he might a religious relic. He put it softly to his bloodied cheek. Again he drank. In the sunlight he dozed, and then slept. The sun had moved to the other side of the canyon and long shadows were climbing toward him by the time he awoke.

This would not do. He was a man who lived by actions. Whatever his future with Maddy Anderson, there were more immediate matters to attend to.

Beginning with guns.

While fetching his best scotch from the bedroom bureau drawer where he kept it, he noticed that Zack had again taken his pistols, as she had done the last time he had fired one in the house. On that occasion she had hidden them in a burlap sack stuck behind a board in the garage. Knowing her nature, he guessed that this time she would do something as different as possible. After a few minutes pondering he ruled out the house. It was too small to afford many hiding places. That left this end of the property, either the flower garden or the lanai.

There were no fresh diggings in the garden. The space behind the loose bricks in the lanai base yielded nothing. The wooden mulch bin contained only mulch. There was an old refrigerator set at the back of the lanai that had never worked in all the years he had owned the house. He found the handguns in a cardboard box stuck behind some plant food boxes in the useless freezer compartment. Her six thousand dollars was in there as well.

It would be just as well to leave everything where it was. Then Charlene would not be provoked and he would be content knowing exactly where his weapons were. He would take just one, a small .32 caliber automatic, which he could keep easily at hand beneath his mattress or behind some books in his bookcase. This was California—Tiburcio. There'd been murders here, and junkie homosexual motorcycle gangs.

He started down the slope to the house and discovered he was not alone. His neighbor, Mrs. Mercredes, a dark-haired woman passing from middle age to elderly, was at her fence. His bloody face, torn suit, whiskey bottle, and pistol stuck in his belt did not seem to faze her. She spoke as calmly and simply as passing the time of day, though her subject was not a happy one.

"Charley, was that you shooting off a gun night before last?"

"I guess it was, Mildred. I'm sorry."

"Herbert's arthritis is hurting him bad lately, and he has a hard time sleeping. You woke him up in the middle of the night, and he never was able to get back to sleep."

"I'm really sorry, Mildred. I didn't know. It won't happen again."

"I don't mind during the day, Charley. But not while Herbert's sleeping. It's hurtin' him really bad."

"Don't worry."

He reminded himself to buy Herb a bottle of Frenet Branca, the only really effective treatment he'd ever known for arthritis.

His next mission was the Armstrong-Siddeley. He and Danny Hill had reassembled the ancient car's engine, but it had not been started in days. He slid behind the wheel and, with a prayer to the gods of fools and antique cars, turned the slightly bent key and depressed the starter button on the dirty floorboard. It produced only a groan. He waited patiently, then tried again. Three diminishing groans were followed by silence.

There was nothing for it but to wait for Danny Hill to come home from work. There was no place to do that but the Tiburcio Saloon and Grocery.

Steve Copley had reached Gettysburg just ahead of Kreski, in time to have the contents of Huerta's toolbox set out neatly like museum exhibits, which someday they might be. He had managed, with his agency's famous if not always effective efficiency, to have the Spanish of the letters translated into computer-typed English. There were three: one to a friend or colleague identified only as Emiliano, one to the nation of Honduras at large, and one to his dead wife, Dolores. They were all political—stridently anti-Communist—ending with proclamations of devotion to General Diaz, the Honduran president, and the government cause.

The pistol was expensive, a top-of-the-line Remington .38 caliber six-shot revolver, fully loaded, with a six-inch barrel and a box of cartridges. The currency was in neat, bound stacks of hundred-dollar bills, quite crisp and new. Making the only immediate contribution he could, Kreski put arriving aides to work tracing the bills' serial numbers through Treasury headquarters in Washington.

"Walt," said Steve. "Let's take a walk."

It was a pleasant afternoon for it. They went out onto the battlefield, halting finally by an old brass cannon, rendered green with age, one of a battery facing the Confederate lines. Letting his eyes follow the line of the barrel toward the distant horizon of dark trees, Kreski could almost sense rebel soldiers there. He turned to look at Copley's handsome, well-groomed face.

"Bushy Ambrose is right," Copley said, running his hand back and forth over the top of the cannon.

"About what?"

"The investigation. We've got a big pile of paper and it's nearly all bullshit."

"What do you mean?"

"You were up in New York today. Those Hispanics we busted— they're strictly a narc case, aren't they?"

"That's my belief."

"Precisely. The firearms we recovered in New York were a plant, Walt. A ridiculously obvious plant."

Kreski said nothing. He began to walk slowly away from the cannons, in the direction they were aimed.

"I think the Chicago action wasn't much different," Copley said. "Our suspects are just illegals. Kitchen workers. Like thousands of others. That La Puño material was a plant too. It all came so easily. And I went for it."

"So did I. So did the entire country."

"Well, I think we were wrong, unless I'm proved otherwise, and I don't see that happening. We assumed this La Puño, if there really is a La Puño, was part of the leftist guerrilla movement, the Communist underground, a Sandinista proxy. But Huerta was, or so it appears, a right-winger. Did I tell you about the report I got from Admiral Elmore?"

"I didn't know you had talked to him. I didn't realize he had stirred himself to become interested in this case."

"He produced a file on Huerta. Late this morning. The man was Honduran, all right. He was a lieutenant in the national guard. He owned a one-hundred-sixty-acre farm. Got burned out—his family wiped out—by the Communists. If there was a plot—and I think that ten thousand dollars says there was a plot—it was a right-wing one."

As they strolled over the hard ground and spongy grass their pace picked up. It was as though they had someplace to go.

"Did I show you the inventory on Huerta's place in Philadelphia?" Copley said.

"You haven't mentioned it."

"It's in my car. In my briefcase."

"I'll look at it."

"The place was clean. No ammo, no brasso. Just some La Puño stuff that may or may not have been planted later. And something else."

"An autographed portrait of General Leonard Wood," said Kreski.

"Who?"

"General Leonard Wood. A compatriot of Teddy Roosevelt's. He used to confiscate the Cuban treasury whenever we were displeased with their fiscal policies. He also made visits to Nicaragua."

"He was a Republican?"

"I don't know. I suppose so. His was a Republican era."

"My much-vaunted Princeton education didn't include General Leonard Wood. Where did you go to school, Walt?"

"Isn't it in a file? The University of Toledo and Columbia Law."

"You were a New York street cop."

"Of a sort. For a while. What did you find in Huerta's apartment?"

"Room. Bathroom down the hall. Really squalid digs."

"What did you find?"

"Back copies of *Mercenary Magazine*. More than a year's worth. He was only in that room for a few weeks."

"I suppose that's not illogical. Not implausible. Was there anything else?"

"A lot of newspapers. *Philadelphia Inquirer. Washington Post. The New York Times.* Top-drawer publications full of Central American news. Señor Huerta was not your ordinary wetback. He even went for a high grade of sex magazine—*Penthouse.*"

"You said he was there several weeks."

"We also found a copy of *The Isle of Pines: A Conservative Manifesto.*"

"A book?"

"Of a sort. Mostly a polemic."

"I don't recall seeing it on the *New York Times* best-seller list."

"It's by Peter Ashley Brookes. He published it himself. It's about his great-uncle. The man ran a plantation on Cuba's Isle of Pines in the nineteen-twenties and -thirties and Brookes saw it as a utopian model for the rest of Latin America. The place was run almost along Communist lines, as far as the workers were concerned, except instead of slaving for the state and the common good of the proletariat, they did it for the plantation. An owe-my-soul-to-the-company-store sort of operation, although I gather it was pretty fairly run. Free medical care and all that. Otherwise, the plantation was strictly free-market capitalism, a law unto itself that tolerated no interference from the Cuban government."

"Are you sure you never heard of General Leonard Wood?"

"This great-uncle was quite an inspiration to Peter Ashley Brookes. Are you familiar with Brookes?"

"We had to assign a detail to him during the inaugural. President Hampton gave him some sort of official post on the committee. He owns a lot of mines out west. And I guess he's a big friend of the president's."

"Supporter, not friend. There's a difference. Brookes is one of the richest men in Colorado. Richer than Joe Coors or any of those fellows James Watt used to work for. Walt, he not only wrote this *Isle of Pines* book, he's the principal bankroller of *Mercenary Magazine.*"

"I thought that was published by that ex-Army Ranger, Phil Marcy. We've had to check out some of his people. Quite a few loose screws."

"Peter Ashley Brookes is the principal bankroller of *Mercenary*, and three or four other magazines. He's the principal bankroller of the Yorktown Foundation and about six other right-wing groups here and in the West. He's put up the money for Marcy's 'humanitarian aid' expeditions to Honduras. Most of this isn't even his own money. After his mother died he seized control of her foundation from his cousin. When she was alive the organization supported wildlife conservation. Now he's got it promoting strip mines. It's amazing how much influence a few million or even a few hundred thousand can have if you put it in the right places—magazines, foundations, lobbying outfits, direct mail campaigns."

They were almost across the field, nearing the line of dark woods.

"And Huerta had both Brookes's book and magazine in his hideaway. Of that you're making much."

"Listen," Copley said. "Brookes is a Princeton man. I'm not taking this lightly. But his various outfits have been strongly opposing the president on Central America. They say Hampton's lost the stomach for continuing the war. They don't like it."

"Enter Manuel Huerta? Foreign policy by the bullet?"

"I'm not talking to you officially, Walt. I'm just thinking out loud. But I'm getting tired of the way things are going. Every time we take a step we stumble over something new and get sent off in a different direction. I'm beginning to feel like a mouse in a maze and I don't like it. I want to be back in control of this investigation. We're being led around, Walt. And we don't even know by whom."

"Although you're making a very strong suggestion."

They were at the woods. Kreski turned and began walking back, his hands in his pockets. Copley half scampered to catch up.

"I'm just thinking aloud, Walt. But what seems to be happening is a very elaborate undertaking. It requires some resources. A lot of resources."

"Well, Steven. I'd be very careful where you did that thinking aloud."

"I am. Anyway, let's see what the evidence technicians come up with. And your banknote experts."

"At the moment, I'm inclined to put Mr. Brookes's book and magazine in the same category as those La Puño flags."

"I'd like to talk with him."

"You haven't grounds. Not legally."

"I'm going to mention him to the vice president, and Bushy Ambrose."

"And the president, of course. He probably knows more about Mr. Brookes than all of us."

"And the president."

Atherton met with the Nicaraguan ambassador in the Roosevelt Room. It was directly off the West Wing's main lobby, should he wish to suggest the ambassador's swift departure, and had another door which exited in the general direction of his own sanctuary, should he wish to make his own. There were no windows, assuring discretion. Yet it was a very formal room, imparting prestige and the power of the American government. It had long been a favorite of presidents for awing and cowing visiting newspaper editors and other potentially hostile groups. If nothing else, they always left impressed and subdued.

The vice president and the Sandinista took facing seats at one end of the room's long conference table. The ambassador had arrived at the Northwest Gate completely unannounced, an affrontery, and given the terror that all Latinos now struck in White House guards and sentries, reckless as well. Official diplomatic car or no.

Atherton had tried frantically to reach Merriman Crosby. The secretary of state had gone off on some supposedly urgent business and was not readily available except by car phone, from which there was no response. Instead, the vice-president hastily summoned the deputy secretary and the assistant secretary for Latin American affairs. The chairman of the Joint Chiefs of Staff was available, but Atherton sensed his presence would not be helpful, though he ordered him to stand by. He also summoned the staff director of the Senate Foreign Relations Committee, an old acquaintance who knew everything there was to know about the Sandinistas. Until this succor arrived he had to hold off the Nicaraguan as best he could with the help of Richard Shawcross and Mrs. Hildebrand, without great success.

"Given the present tensions, the state of uncertainty," said the ambassador, a small, expensively dressed man with a razor haircut, "these incidents, these provocations, are worse than ill timed. They are very dangerous. As your secretary of state would say, we are extremely concerned."

"And as I have been trying to make clear to you, Mr. Ambassador, I know little about them. All I have, essentially, are cables from our embassy and your government's protests, which have been forwarded all day. In any event, it seems to be a matter of only one as yet unidentified helicopter."

"No helicopter operating against my government need be considered unidentified, Mr. Vice President," said the ambassador, whose name was a memorable Miguel de la Tanchez Sanchez. "And it was not just that one crater bomb. There has been a general escalation of violence all through the region—when we are trying to do our best to keep hostilities to a minimum! And all this talk in your news media of this terrorist group 'La Puño.' We know nothing of such an organization!"

"Señor Tanchez Sanchez. I do not run the American news media. I do not run the Honduran government. I certainly do not run this one. Our president is incapacitated. All I can suggest—what I would most strongly urge on your part—is patience. The same kind of patience we are urging upon ourselves in this building every day."

Mrs. Hildebrand, who had left the room, returned, looking somewhat agitated.

"Mr. Vice President," she said. "Deputy Secretary Derwin and Ambassador Bell are here."

"Well, send them in."

She glanced meaningfully at the still open door to the lobby.

"There's another matter . . ."

Atherton excused himself, closing the door behind him. Derwin and Bell were waiting in an alcove. The former was a very large man and the latter quite the opposite. Both wished to whisper, and it was difficult for Atherton to follow them without bobbing his head.

"Sanchez is in there?" Derwin said.

"Yes," said Atherton. "Raising hòly hell about that black job helicopter."

"Castro is on Havana television with a harangue about our trying to expand the war," said Bell. "He says if that's what we want, we'll get it."

"Where the hell is Crosby?" whispered Atherton. The Secret Service agent at the entrance desk was watching them.

"At the Soviet Embassy," said Derwin.

"Why is the secretary of state at the Soviet Embassy? The Soviet ambassador comes to us. That's why we gave him back his parking place in the State Department basement."

"Because that's where Crosby is taking a telephone call from Moscow, from the Soviet foreign minister."

"Why didn't he call here?"

"I guess they're not sure of what's going on here," said Derwin. "They're sure of what's going on at their embassy."

"Why didn't Crosby tell me?"

"I was to tell you. The secretary didn't want to speak to you himself until he knew what was on their minds."

"And Castro's threatening war?"

The diminutive Bell shrugged. "At the least, it's a profound escalation of rhetoric."

Geoffery Beck, director of the Senate Foreign Relations Committee, arrived. Though he was a frequent visitor to the White House, the Secret Service took a long time with his credentials.

"What's up, Larry?" he said, when permitted to join the others. The two State Department men nodded to him with much deference. "My secretary said 'Nicaragua.'"

"I have Tanchez Sanchez in the Roosevelt Room."

"This afternoon I threw him out of my office."

"That probably accounts for his disposition," said Atherton. "It is not agreeable."

"Castro's threatening war," Bell said.

Neil Howard appeared. He'd been running down the corridor.

"Crosby's on the phone. Your office. Hot stuff. The Russians."

Atherton started to walk away with him.

"How do we respond to Castro?" Bell asked.

"Issue the same kind of statement we did last time he said something outrageous."

"Deeply concerned," said Bell. "What do we say to Tanchez Sanchez?"

"What was that General McAuliffe said to the Germans at Bastogne?"

"'Nuts,'" said Bell.

"Actually, it was something less printable than that," said Derwin, something of a historian. "They used 'nuts' for the newspapers."

"Don't say anything less printable," Atherton said. "But say something like nuts. I'm getting tired of the goddamn Nicaraguans."

Atherton waved his blessing, then moved quickly down the corridor, Howard scurrying after.

"They did it, by the way," Howard said. "Meathead Dubarry won president pro tem in the caucus fifty-three to two. There's no way that can be overturned when the new Congress meets for the formal vote in January."

They rounded a corner, startling a secretary, who scuttled out of the way.

"What about Mose Goode?" Atherton asked.

"Not quite so decisive—thirty-nine, twelve, three."

"That could come unglued. Then everything would come unglued."

He swept into his office, where Mrs. Hildebrand, who had somehow preceded him using another corridor, was by his desk, holding the phone for him.

"Secretary Crosby, Mr. Vice President."

"I know. Thank you."

"There's something else," Howard said. "One of the networks on the evening news said there was a report that the assassination attempt may have been a right-wing plot—an American right-wing plot."

"What?" said Atherton.

"An American right plot. On the networks. One of them. I didn't catch which one. Let me run back."

"Run back," said Atherton, taking the telephone and dropping wearily into his chair. "Merriman, what's going on?"

"I should say to you at the outset, Mr. Vice President," said the secretary of state, "that this is not a secure telephone line."

"As you are speaking from the Russian Embassy," Atherton said, evidencing even more weariness, "I would assume that to be the case."

"The Soviet premier has agreed not to suspend our talks in Geneva. He is, in fact, prepared to make an offer. The withdrawal within six months of all Soviet intermediate range missiles now deployed in Eastern Europe."

"What?"

"I should discuss the entirety of his proposal of it with you in person," Crosby said. "I'll be there shortly. I said we'd make a response by noon tomorrow Moscow time."

"As that will be five A.M. our time, you'd best get here shortly indeed," Atherton said. "Please."

He lowered the telephone receiver to its cradle gently, staring at it strangely, then looked up. Mrs. Hildebrand was again at his side.

"What?" he snapped, then added, "Excuse me. What is it now, Mrs. Hildebrand?"

"I canceled your luncheon speech at the homebuilders convention tomorrow. Was that all right?"

"Precisely the thing to do, as always. Cancel everything else tomorrow. Clear decks."

Another phone rang on his desk. It was his wife. She was tired of Williamsburg.

"I'll be there as soon as I can, baby. But it's going to be a few days. Just hang on, please. No. Don't hang on. My war room phone is flashing. Hang up. I love you. Good night, baby."

In the war room, speaking coldly and matter-of-factly, as always, was the chairman of the Joint Chiefs of Staff.

"I'm sorry to find you working so late," said Atherton.

"Lately, sir, I seem to be working around the clock," said the general. "But of course, that's why the Congress keeps voting for our generous retirement benefits."

"Is this about Nicaragua?" Atherton asked. "I've got something more important. A new Russian arms offer."

"I have something different, sir. In Korea. Some firing on the DMZ. Casualties."

"American?"

"Two enlisted men wounded. One critical. Three ROK enlisted men killed. Twelve ROK wounded, including a major."

"What's the situation now?"

"Quiet. Stable. They claim we started it."

"General. Colonel Ambrose has made it very clear that Camp David is to handle all national security matters."

"Affirmative. The Eighth Army is on Def Con Four by order of the president —through Mr. Ambrose." Atherton had never heard a Pentagon military man call Ambrose "colonel." "It was Mr. Ambrose, sir, who advised you be informed."

"How nice. Thank you, General. Please keep me advised."

He hung up, and buried his face in his arms. Someone new came into his office. It was Shawcross.

"What?" said Atherton.

Shawcross hesitated. "I think it can wait until tomorrow," he said.

"Good," said Atherton. "You have just spared yourself from a firing squad. We have a Nicaraguan diplomat being extremely unpleasant to us in the Roosevelt Room. Castro is threatening war. The
Soviets are offering to pull their missiles out of Europe. The North
Koreans started shooting on the DMZ. What in the hell is going
on?"

"They're taking advantage," Shawcross said. "They're trying to
screw things up."

"Then they're carrying coals to Newcastle," said Atherton. "I'm
about to lose my mind."

"They're also doing what we're doing," Shawcross said. "They're
trying to draw out the president, hoping to get some handle on what's
going on."

"I hate every Communist who ever lived," Atherton said. "I hate
every one of Bushy Ambrose's ancestors who ever lived."

Neil Howard rushed into the room. "Larry! Mr. Vice President.
The president is on television! On the news!"

Charley Dresden's evening meal was precisely the same as his
lunch—three boneless chicken dinners eaten from a napkin on the
bar of the Tiburcio Saloon and Grocery. He washed them down with
bourbon and water, as throughout the afternoon he had washed his
thoughts. As soon as the first in the late-afternoon, early-evening cycle of news broadcasts began, he instructed, not requested, Cooper to
turn on the television set. He then instructed Cooper to keep it on
until instructed otherwise. He was compelled to expend nearly all the
capital of his local prestige, influence, friendship, foul temper, and
dangerous reputation to enforce that command as locals and visitors
were not giving a damn about television, news, or the president of
the United States and sought instead to entertain themselves with the
jukebox, or merely to speak loudly within Charley's hearing. At one
point Cooper asked for his gun, in a practiced, friendly-angry manner—to be returned only when Charley was ready to leave the bar.

His hands began to go numb, a consequence of drinking he'd not
experienced in years. He had Cooper stop the bourbon and bring
him coffee until feeling was restored. He went to the men's room,
had another cup of coffee upon returning, and then asked for the
procession of bourbons to resume.

The presence of the president's speaking face on local and network
television news did not surprise him in the least, especially when the
first anchorman informed his audience that the footage was a tape

provided by the White House and not a live broadcast or even a network recording. Dresden had expected something on videotape almost as soon as he had heard the president's voice on his car radio. This was a television age, not a radio one. And more things were possible on television than the people who had rattled steel sheets for rain sounds and fired pistol blanks next to microphones in the 1930s and 1940s for radio had ever imagined.

It took two broadcasts of the videotape for him to notice a small shaving cut on the president's left cheek—which had not been visible in the assassination-attempt footage. Something to be expected of a badly injured man perhaps, but not one who was regularly shaved by his own barber. Dimly, Dresden recalled noticing such a shaving cut on Hampton's face months—indeed, more than a year—before. He'd seen it just once, and as his memory stirred it came to him that it was also on an occasion when the president was incapacitated by injury.

The third run revealed to him the fact that the president's hair had grown detectably longer and fuller in only about a week's time. There was also a somewhat bloodshot right eye and a twitch to the left. These were also, perhaps, to be expected. What was not were the cutaway shots of the videotape camera or cameras—one to the presidential seal, one to a map of the western hemisphere, and another to a glimpse of the American flag flying over the grounds of Camp David—a sure sign of editing. What need of editing a four-minute prepared remark by a practiced politician and speaker? Even with the hoarseness, the voice came forth evenly and strongly.

It also struck Dresden that the lip movements might be out of sync, but that he conceded to himself was an inexact and very subjective judgment. His overall assessment was very firm and clear, however. The tape was phony. It was not the president's voice he was actually hearing. Though the content of Hampton's remarks was as disingenuous, vague, meaningless, and convincingly crafted as always, nothing diminished Dresden's conviction. It made him feel very bitter. When Danny Hill finally entered the bar, having worked overtime, Charley was speaking grimly.

"'There exists an obvious fact that seems utterly moral: namely, that a man is always a prey to his truths,'" said Dresden, as Danny Hill dropped heavily onto the stool next to him.

"Come on, mate, no poetry," said Hill. "Not another night of Edgar Allan Poe. Not even Robert W. Service." He ordered two hard-boiled eggs for himself, and a cold bottle of Hamm's beer.

"That's not poetry," said Dresden, sipping his whiskey. "Not Poe. It's Albert Camus. 'The Myth of Sisyphus.'"

"The dumb son of a bitch who kept rolling the rock up the mountain?"

"He wasn't dumb. He was doomed to it. The experience defines doom. Oddly, Camus found that he must logically be happy."

Hill bit into one of his eggs, and looked along the bar.

"I've been repeating that line over and over," Dresden continued. "For several days now I've been rolling that rock up the mountain and it keeps rolling back down on me. But it's the truth. I'm right. I know it. But I am victim to being right. I am prey to my truth. My truth is rolling that rock back down on me. And I keep coming back at it like an idiot, an imbecile."

"You're not an idiot. You're so smart you sometimes scare the hell out of me. You're also just a little crazy. And tanked to the gills."

"I am crazy because I pursue the truth. If I accept the lie, I am sane and normal."

"Look, Charley. I'm not in the mood, okay? I got heavy problems. I'm five months behind in my alimony and my wife's family is getting nasty about it. I think her brothers are fixing to come down here again. It's not the money. They've got three grocery stores in the valley. It's a point of honor. They're Portuguese."

"The Portuguese are an eminently civilized people. I've had their wine."

"Last time they beat the shit out of me. Charley, if they show up, can I crash at your place?"

"As I've always told you, Daniel, you are welcome to stay at my place anytime, for any reason. Even if my place is just a ditch by the side of the road."

"You read too much Steinbeck."

"He's why I moved here. It's Albert Camus who's making me think about other places."

Hill belched, though he covered the indiscretion with his hand.

"I've got a problem, too, Danny. I ripped the MG apart on a guardrail last night. I've got to get the old Hawk started."

"That battery's too old for a jump. It'll take a push. Will Coop loan us his pickup?"

"He will if you drive. Sure."

"Are you sober enough?"

"Sure. You bet."

"Oh oh," said Hill, as some people entered the saloon.

"What is it?" said Charley, looking into a new bourbon. "Your ex-in-laws?"

"No. It's your lady. Zack. With a gentleman friend."

The man was tall, very well dressed, and handsome. Charlene glanced along the bar, greeted Dresden with a faint, worried smile, and then took the intruder over to a table. Only then did she come to Charley's side. Their relationship had rules, and to Charley's mind, she had just broken one. The main one.

"Where've you been?" he asked.

"That's a fine question coming from someone who's disappeared for nearly forty-eight hours. You didn't call. You didn't return my calls."

"Had an accident on the way back from the city. Had to spend the night with a friend."

He had spent a fair portion of the day struggling with the problem of reconciling the fact of Charlene and their mutual residence with a now-consuming passion for Madeleine Anderson. The mental effort, little assisted by whiskey, had produced only frustration and guilt. Now he had the solution. Ritghteousness, and—in his current state of recklessness—cruelty.

"Who's the stud?" he asked, lifting his glass.

At first she was silent, scaring him. He avoided her eye. When she leaned close he almost flinched.

"Look you son of a bitch," she said, her voice lowered, but not enough. "That gentleman is a client."

"Ah yes. 'Client.' The perfect word."

She leaned closer still. "If he weren't here I'd smash your face, Charley Dresden. He's a developer. From Texas. He's opening a shopping mall in Santa Cruz in the spring. He's already interested in hiring me for the publicity on the grand opening and I brought him down here because he said he'd heard about Tiburcio and wanted to see the place and because I convinced him that you were the best person in Santa Linda to talk to about advertising."

"Did you really?"

"Look, you stuck-up, arrogant, Eastern college boy looney-tune jerk. I wouldn't let him talk to you now about directions the hell out of here. You're drunk. You're unshaven. Your clothes are filthy. You look terrible. You smell terrible. You are terrible! I hate you! You wreck everything!"

Conversation along the bar and in much of the room had stopped. Domestic disputes were great sport in Tiburcio, and one coupled with the prospect of violence between two large males—one with a reputation for gunplay—made this a major event.

But Charlene put an end to it. Pausing to restrain tears and regain her composure, she returned to her somewhat startled guest and spoke a few quiet words. They quickly left.

"I think maybe I'd better not spend the night at your place," Hill said, "in-laws or no."

"Why not?" Dresden said. "I'm going to have the house to myself."

"No, you're not."

"You don't think she's going to bed down in Santa Linda with that big Texas bankroll?"

"You know if I ever said something like that, Charley, you'd kill me. I don't know what's wrong with you, but you ought to have figured out by now that that woman is in love with you—more in love with you than anyone would deserve, but especially you. I'm not the best person to speak on the subject of holy matrimony, but it seems to me you're screwing up the opportunity of a lifetime."

Dresden said nothing.

"Anyway," Hill said. "I'm sure you're going to find her home, in the bedroom, alone, with the door locked."

"In that case, you can have the living room couch. I'll sleep on the floor, or on the bar. I'm so tired I could sleep in the toilet."

"You look like you have. There are times, mate, when it's hard to remember you're supposed to be the town gentleman. Come on, let's get that car of yours started."

10

Walt Kreski had walked the halls of Congress countless times before, but always with something of a sense of guardianship and proprietorship, notwithstanding his lack of day-to-day jurisdiction. On occasions when the president or a foreign head of government addressed a joint session, he was the Capitol's absolute master. No one moved through its labyrinth without the approval and authority of his agency. The president moved only as he was instructed.

Now Kreski felt a prisoner of the Congress, himself constrained to follow direction, an accused person heading with little relish to a place of judgment, a person summoned.

Hammond walked quietly at his side. Three other agents, bearing files and briefcases, followed. Kreski had last testified on the Hill on behalf of a bill strengthening a counterfeiting statute, and had been treated with much deference. Now he was tantamount to culprit. The White House congressional liaison office had told him he could count on the fairness and objectivity of perhaps half the committee investigating the Gettysburg shootings, but no friendship. From the rest of them, he could expect only hostility and grandstand plays to the public.

But, as he kept reminding himself, he had no complaint. The

president had, in fact, been shot and those people killed. He ran the agency whose sacred mission it was to prevent that. He had allowed Schultz and too many others to put in too much time during the election campaign. He had read the advance field reports and not asked whether there was a crawl space in the observation tower. He had approved the security plan for the Gettysburg event, almost routinely. Hampton went regularly to Civil War battlefields.

If he had assigned a man to the Slocum statue, if he had made a more careful study of the tower's structure, if he had for once insisted that the president accept more bodyguards in and around his car, this might not have happened.

But he could not have prevented Schultz's tragic action. The man had been returned to a normal schedule after the election and should have had a normal night's sleep. Tests had found no trace of alcohol or drugs aside from some medication for a minor allergy. It was simply and starkly a gruesome accident. The man's sense of urgency combined disastrously with a slip of the foot on wet metal. How could he have foreseen that? How could his conduct of the operations of his office have prevented that?

Increasing noise ahead warned of what awaited him around the next corner of the hall. As he turned it, he was assaulted by glaring batteries of television cameras and lights arrayed along one wall like the bizarre weaponry in the recently popular science fiction war movies. Along the other side was a long line of ghoulish public and congressional staff, waiting their turns for a seat in the hearing room. From some of their expressions, he might as well have been Lee Harvey Oswald.

The chamber itself was jammed and even more oppressive—and ominous. The press were crowded around a long side table looking much like what they were: a jury. The committee members sat in two raised, curving banks as might stern judges, their staff aides and counsels positioned behind them like so many bailiffs and officers of the court. There were more television cameras. Several were aimed at an easel bearing a stack of enlarged, mounted photographs just to the side of the witness table. The front one was of the fallen bodies of the dead and wounded at Gettysburg, Bonnie Greer's the most prominent. He was in for about as comfortable a time as the French Protestants on St. Bartholomew's Day.

The first question came from a pleasant-looking, bald, bespectacled congressional veteran who smiled, glanced down at his notes, and then said: "Mr. Kreski, can you give us one single reason why you should be retained as director of the United States Secret Service?"

Kreski reddened and stared down at the microphone on the green tabletop before him. It was, save the ceiling, about the only focal point in the room that spared him from having to look at another human face. He could not remember when he had experienced such a naked moment. He could not understand why some more just and reasonable member of the committee did not at once intercede on his behalf. If this lout felt justified in such flagrant political posturing and personal abuse, was the silence of the others a reflection of the depth of the public's outrage over what had happened? Much of Washington was oblivious to the national mood, but seldom the Congress, not when that mood was angry or fearful.

"Sir, I serve at the pleasure of the president of the United States and the secretary of the treasury. Neither gentleman has asked me to resign or called my conduct of my office into question."

"That dead young woman would call your conduct into question!" shouted the now-livid inquisitor, half rising from his seat and thrusting his arm out at the easel.

Finally, someone came to Kreski's rescue.

"Mr. Chairman," said another member. "If we could dispense with these pointless theatrics, I'd like to ask the director to explain his defiance of our subpoena and refusal to appear at yesterday's hearing."

"Sir," said Kreski. "I sent Mr. Hammond in my place. He's as knowledgeable on the matters that concern you as I am. As I believe he made clear, I was out of town yesterday, in New York and Pennsylvania, working on the investigation."

"So Mr. Hammond explained, but is it not correct that this is essentially an FBI case?"

"The Bureau has principal jurisdiction over investigation of the federal crimes committed in the attack on the president. There are state and local charges involved also. The Secret Service has a number of responsibilities. We've also been asked personally by the White House chief of staff and Director Copley to assist, and we have our own internal investigation to pursue."

"Did you find anything so important as to risk a contempt of Congress citation?"

"Sir, I would hope that the Congress might be reasonable and responsible enough to withhold its contempt for the time being. We have just experienced a major assault upon the government of the

United States. What we accomplish in the next few hours, days, and weeks is crucial. We've made progress, a lot of progress, including yesterday."

"Have you established the Nicaraguan connection?" demanded a member from the left of the back row of committee seats, but the extreme right of the political spectrum.

"Sir, we have no evidence of the involvement of any foreign government."

"You mean as yet."

"Sir, I mean no evidence. We have, however, learned a great deal more about the apparent assassin, Manuel Huerta, and about how . . ."

"What about the second gun?!"

". . . and about how the crime was committed. I must remind you gentlemen that this is, in fact, a criminal investigation. There is no more important criminal investigation underway in this country. If you don't wish to prejudice this case, I would respectfully suggest that if you have any further questions concerning evidence that you close this hearing from the press and public and proceed in executive session."

That happening, of course, was very far from many if not most of the minds of the committee members.

His initial inquisitor was now on his feet, however, reddened bald head awash in perspiration. Kreski realized how much he himself was sweating.

"We don't need to be in executive session to demand an explanation for what happened to these poor innocent bystanders!" thundered the man. "Look upon that woman's brutalized body and face, Mr. Kreski. Is there an answer to that that can be hidden by executive privilege!"

"Sir, I said executive session, not executive privilege. That is something only the president can invoke, and he has not."

"Yes, well. Anyway, look at her!"

The questions got no worse, but few were much better. They trailed off, however, as the television camera lights began to go out and the press pens slowed and stopped. At length, the chairman asked Kreski the most responsible and reasonable, fair and objective question he'd been posed that morning. It was also the one he'd dreaded most.

"Director," he said. "As matters now stand, having examined the evidence and learned as much as you have at this point, would you recommend to this committee, to this government, any changes in procedures that might prevent this kind of attack from happening again? Do you think there are any serious flaws that need to be corrected?"

Kreski remembered a long-ago television interview with one of his predecessors. He inexplicably could not recall which one or whether the congressional inquiry had had to do with the Reagan shooting in 1981 or the attempt on President Ford's life in 1975 but the man had been asked exactly the same question. His response had been that, given the strictures imposed upon security by the egalitarian nature of the republic and the political openness of the democratic process, there was nothing he could or would change. It was an easy and not irresponsible answer.

But Kreski could not give it.

"There have been nearly a dozen and a half successful and unsuccessful attempts upon the lives of American presidents, Mr. Chairman," he said, "starting with the attack by a lunatic house painter named Richard Lawrence on Andrew Jackson here at the Capitol in 1835. In nearly every case the responsible security authorities have said there was nothing they would change. But after every attempt, there have always been changes and increases in security measures."

The television lights, following suit, came back on. Looking to the press table, he saw the ballpoint pens busy again.

"There are many new measures I might recommend, and probably should," he continued, "to try to prevent what happened to President Hampton. But you run up against some problems. One has to do with the inclinations and dispositions of the presidents themselves. They don't like being separated from the people. They don't like to appear cowards. They have an intrinsic urge to mingle and press the flesh. Another has to do with the basic values of the country. The American people feel they own this city, the Capitol, and certainly the White House. You remember the uproar in 1985 when it was suggested that Pennsylvania Avenue be closed in front of the White House for security reasons. Everyone screamed. You can't erect a Kremlin in the Federal City."

All the television lights were on and the pens were moving furiously.

"Let me put it this way, sir," Kreski added. "The president's current situation at Camp David is almost ideal from a security point of view. He's more or less invulnerable to everything but a nuclear attack. But, once he recovers, when we're sure the immediate threat has been neutralized, he has to come back down here. As his chief protector, I'm not comfortable with that, but the American people wouldn't have it any other way."

Several reporters rose from the press table and began pushing their way through the knot of people gathered at the doorway. They were bound for the nearest telephones.

To Atherton's mind, one of Jimmy Carter's stupidest acts as president was getting rid of the official presidential yacht *Sequoia* as a gesture of humility and egalitarianism. It had impressed the voters about as much as the Georgian's insistence on getting off and on Air Force One carrying an empty garment bag over his shoulder—this from a man who made such frequent use of the White House's elegant tennis court.

Hampton, to Atherton's joy, had defiantly insisted that the government buy the boat back again, federal deficit or no. The vessel was simply too valuable for impressing VIPs, heavy lobbying, rewarding worthy supporters and subordinates, and secret negotiating. It was unsurpassed as a presidential retreat, a restful and pleasurable sanctuary affording the ultimate appreciation of the Potomac's beauty and the capital's magnificence, not to speak of discreet indulgence in the trappings of power and high office. It was a floating Camp David one could repair to in minutes whenever one wished.

The vice president now so wished. He had been left in charge of the White House, if not much else, and the yacht was an extension of the White House. As though on a whim, he had commandeered the craft for most of the afternoon and now sat on the afterdeck enjoying a warm drink as it glided down the Anacostia River from the Navy Yard, heading for Haines Point and the wider Potomac. The Secret Service hadn't liked the idea much. Gun-toting agents were crowded into two escorting power craft, and one of the navy's larger patrol boats was following along behind like a nanny, as though assassins were going to attack by submarine. Atherton could still be described as more than a little apprehensive at times, but he had lost the terror he had felt immediately after Gettysburg.

As Atherton had requested, the *Sequoia* turned upriver upon reaching the Potomac, slowing and easing over to the embankment at a small wooden dock protruding from the greensward of West Potomac Park. FBI Director Copley, clad in a nautical enough blue blazer and familiar Burburry's raincoat, clambered aboard and was directed aft. The yacht's powerful engines shuddered the deck as it churned away from the dock and the captain changed course downriver.

As the vice president had also requested, they were left quite alone, with security men, stewards, and crew keeping a respectful distance. They were well practiced at it.

"First things first," said Atherton. "Have you been able to penetrate Camp David?"

"Yes," said Copley. "Today." He smiled. Atherton nodded appreciatively, and with some amazement.

"The president is there?"

"He, or someone who looks very much like him, was observed sitting on a terrace, bundled in blankets."

"Observed from close up?"

"No, but someone who looks very much like Daisy Hampton was with him, along with a short person who could only have been Bushy Ambrose."

"Anything else?"

"Not yet. There's been a lot of helicopter traffic. There's a lot of military up there, but also a surprising number of civilians. I don't know where they're all sleeping. Or coming from."

"Anyone peculiar?"

"Not that we know of. Unless you count David Callister as peculiar."

"Just some of his recent columns."

"Walt Kreski is being hanged, drawn, and quartered on the Hill today," Copley said. "He made a big mistake in not showing up yesterday."

"Shawcross is up there for me. I expect I'll get a report when I get back to the White House."

"It was a real inquisition, but he said something that might be helpful."

"About the Twenty-fifth Amendment?"

"Not quite. But he said the president can't stay up at Camp David forever. He said it's great for security but bad for the American people."

"What a wonderful fellow. Neil Howard's logged more than a hundred newspapers now that have said the same thing in editorials. The *Post* this morning was complaining about excessive secrecy and a paralysis of government."

"I saw it. 'ABC News Nightline' last night brought up Woodrow Wilson and his stroke."

"Bushy Ambrose as Edith Galt Wilson."

Atherton turned to look along the railing at a barge and tug approaching from downstream. The *Sequoia's* helmsman steered away, though staying within the channel markers. One of the Secret Service boats moved up as a screen.

"Anything else?" the vice president asked.

"Kreski and I have talked about a possible connection with Peter Ashley Brookes. Finding his book on the Isle of Pines and back copies of *Mercenary Magazine* among Huerta's effects was an interesting enough development, but Kreski didn't seem awfully excited by it."

"For God's sake, Steve. It's hardly enough to swear out a warrant on."

"You saw the treasury report on Huerta's bankroll."

"Yes."

"All the banks it came from are west of the Mississippi. One is in Denver and Brookes is a director."

"You couldn't get a warrant on that, either."

The barge, shoving a large wave before it, came slowly by, its tug chugging noisily. It wasn't close enough for anyone aboard to recognize Atherton, although the Secret Service must have had a dozen weapons aimed at it.

"Anyway," said Copley, after the noisy tug and barge had passed. "Kreski's thinking about it. I feel obligated to at least make a field investigation."

"Discreetly. Decorously. After all, Brookes's been one of the president's strongest supporters."

"Of course. But this will have to include wiretaps."

"Just clear it with the attorney general and follow proper procedure. Have you released any information about Huerta's effects to the press?"

"No. Nothing."

"Why don't you give out the inventory? Without comment. Clear it with the attorney general, of course. And keep Walt Kreski informed."

"It would be interesting to see what Brookes might do."

"It would be more interesting to see what Bushy Ambrose might do."

The sudden, loud crack of a gunshot drove both men to the deck, Atherton painfully bruising his elbow. Copley jerked out his pistol. They lay there, breathing heavily and looking frantically about, until finally the ranking Secret Service agent on board ran up to them. He looked both startled and sheepish.

"I'm sorry, sir. Really sorry. One of our men slipped on the deck and his weapon discharged."

"My God," said Atherton. "They're going to do it again!"

Charley Dresden awoke on his living room couch, in severe pain. Much of it was from his auto accident injuries, but most was from his Olympian hangover. He could not have absorbed another ounce of alcohol and lived. He was not altogether sure he had.

Slowly, his mind cleared. It intensified his discomfort, but brought thought.

Danny Hill, spared any visits by vengeful brothers-in-law, had spent the night in his own house. His prediction had proven correct. Zack was at home, asleep in the bedroom, and the door was closed, though not locked. There was no sign or sound of the Texan. Dresden had not disturbed her, allowing himself to fall quickly unconscious on the couch without pausing to turn off the one lamp she had left lit. When he finally heard her stir he did not speak or even move until she was out of the house and driving away. Presuming she was going to return—and she had spent too little time getting out of there to have done any packing—he would thrash it out with her that evening or night. He would find a way to apologize meaningfully, to adequately compensate her for the insult and hurt of his outrageous behavior, to restore civility and amicability between them, though it was clear their relationship had irrevocably changed.

What was not clear was whether it had ended. In his pain and fuzziness, Madeleine Anderson Calendiari now seemed rather far away; Tiburcio and his memories of the night before too near. He went back to sleep. He slept until he could no longer. He discovered it to be nearly noon.

When he felt well enough he sat up. The time, he realized, had come to confront reality. He had to stop this nonsense about the president, just give it up and let it all be over. As he had said to himself, it really shouldn't matter who was president. How many had come and gone without making the slightest difference to life in Tiburcio? To his life? Unless the country were on the brink of major war—and, despite all the hysteria on television, that did not seem to be the case—they could be left to thrash this murky business out all by themselves in Washington, three thousand miles and a civilization away from California. He need only proceed to the bath and bedroom to clean, repair, and dress himself; go into Santa Linda and his office, crank calls or no; and life would return to normal. If Madeleine Anderson was to be found anywhere in his future, he could not reach that place by means of this obsessive and pointless pursuit of the truth behind a video tape.

He showered, tended to his cuts and scrapes, wrapped tape around his sprained knee, and dressed himself in what had been his second best suit, now promoted, if only for the proprietary feel of it.

But then he made a mistake. He decided his hangover needed treatment as well and made himself a Bloody Mary with what little remained of his gin. As he sat by the cemetery window drinking it, his mind wandered, then fell into a familiar track. He reached for the telephone.

Tracy Bakersfield was not at her beach house. He tried the university and found her there but teaching her class and unavailable. He left a message and sat down to wait. He was not all that certain she would return the call, given her attitude on the obvious subject. If she did, that fact alone would serve as a statement. If she didn't, he would leave it at that. It had all come down to one call.

He still had half the drink when the phone finally rang. Tracy's voice was very quiet, very serious—not hostile, but without any of her usual cheerfulness.

"I was expecting your call," she said.

"You saw the president's tape, then."

"Yes. Who hasn't?"

"I think it's been extensively edited."

"It looks like that."

"I think it has new sound on it. I think the president's lips were out of sync."

"That's certainly possible."

"I think that wasn't the president's voice. Tracy, I think I'm still right."

She made no reply. He waited, realizing that the whole game turned on her response to his next question.

"Tracy, are there any facilities on campus for making voice analysis, voice prints?"

"Yes. There's a lab used by both the police school and our speech therapy department." She said nothing further. He paused again, selecting his words.

"I hate to impose upon you any further," he said. "But it shouldn't take much time. If you can help me again, I'll make you this promise. Even if we come up with something, I won't bother you about this again. Not ever. And if the results are negative, I'll drop the whole thing. I promise. I was on the brink of doing that today anyway."

There was only silence.

"We already have the president on tape speaking at Gettysburg," he said. "It ought to be easy for me to scare up one of his television appearances last night."

She sighed. "You needn't bother. I've already done that. I had voice prints made and an analysis done." Another sigh. "Charley, you are right. The prints don't match. There are many similarities, but they aren't the same person."

"Bless you."

"I have it all in an envelope for you. But come by for it soon. I want to go home."

"I love you."

"Charley, please. Stick to your promise. I don't want anything more to do with this."

The swiftness of his arrival depended entirely on the cooperation of the Hawker-Siddeley, and Danny Hill had warned him it probably wouldn't start again without another push. Yet, after the briefest of groans and a slightly longer, coughing sputter, the old engine caught with all cylinders. The gods were with him. Perhaps he was their instrument after all.

Tracy did not linger with him long at the college and refused to let him walk her to her car. He gathered she wanted the envelope out of her sight as soon as possible. But she gave his hand a hard squeeze when he shook hers in thanks and farewell.

He stopped by his office, Isabel's fears notwithstanding. If it had been broken into, there was no evidence of it. Everything looked just as before. The landlord had not had the furniture hauled away or the lock changed. There was even some mail on the floor, but, pushing it apart with his foot, he saw nothing that looked like a check. More normality.

Sitting at his desk, he spread the contents of Tracy's envelope out before him, studying the two voice prints and the markings she had made on them. There was also a typewritten page of notes she had made from the technician's analysis. The phone began to ring but he ignored it, reading the notes over several times and reexamining the prints. From the looks of it, to his layman's ken, what she had given him might even be admissible as evidence in a trial, however little prospect there seemed to be of anything like that.

The telephone ceased. He sat back a moment and pondered. The data was lacking in only one respect. He had only one copy of each sheet. Isabel had the typewriter and his video recorder might not be working, but their small Xerox machine was. He went to it and, fiddling with the contrast control, made copies until he was satisfied with the quality, producing three duplicates of each page. The originals he returned to Tracy's envelope, placing sets of the copies into envelopes from his office supply. One set he'd keep as a backup, perhaps having someone in Tiburcio hide it for him in some safe place. The others he'd mail to people, though he had no clear idea yet as to whom.

Dresden had just put everything into his briefcase when the telephone resumed its nagging summons. He made a face at it and started toward the door, then halted. The odds were overwhelming that the caller was just another crank but it could be Zack or Isabel, or Tracy calling with something to clarify or add. It might be some police authority who had caught Charley's appearance on "The Jimmy Moon Show" and become interested in his theory, or Mr. Bolger of the amusement park deciding to retain him after all. If it were through some extraordinary fortune Maddy Anderson who was trying to reach him, he could never forgive himself. He would shoot himself.

He caught the phone on the sixth ring.

"Hello. The Dresden Organization."

"Is this Mr. Charles Dresden?" It was a man, who seemed to be calling from a great distance.

"Yes. That's why this is called the Dresden Organization."

The man then identified himself as a reporter in the New York office of one of the most sleazy and scurrilous sensation-mongering supermarket "news" magazines in the country. Dresden got ruder.

"Please, Mr. Dresden. Hear me out. Our San Francisco stringer told us about what you had to say on 'The Jimmy Moon Show' out there and we're very much interested."

"Even though the president has appeared live and almost well on television since then?"

"Especially because of that. We'd very much like to talk to you about it. We can have our San Francisco man meet with you whenever it's convenient. Even tonight, if need be."

"No, thank you."

"We're prepared to pay you well. Say, a thousand dollars?"

"A thousand dollars? That tape of the shooting isn't all I have, you know. I now have evidence that the president's appearance on television last night was a phony. It was a heavily edited and dubbed tape that they rigged for the occasion. It was the president's face, sure. But the voice belonged to someone else. I have proof of that. Actual voice prints."

"Well, Mr. Dresden, if you can show us that, I'd have to say our interest would change to downright enthusiasm! And that figure I cited would change to ten thousand. Or more! Who knows?"

And there he'd be on the cover, along with Liz Taylor entering another fat farm and a picture of some headless animal. Charles Dresden, just another looney-tune from the land of the bunny rabbits.

"Triple no thank you. Good-bye."

He hung up the phone hurriedly, as though the man's hand might somehow reach out for him through the receiver. He left the building just as hurriedly, upset by the risk he'd almost run. He should have ended the conversation after the first "no thank you." He should not have told the man anything. They could have recorded what little he did say and might well run some vague sort of story anyway, anything to justify some not-so-vaguely sensational headline.

A few minutes before he'd felt so confident and smug about what Tracy had given him he'd thought of going to Antoine's in search of Jim Ireland and the ultimate showdown. Not now. As he drove by the restaurant and Channel Three's studios in the Hawker-Siddeley, both places seemed to have an eerie cast to them, and made him shudder. He needed friendship and security, and that lay west over the ridge in Tiburcio. Though he had picked up the phone in wild hopes of hearing Madeleine's voice, he desperately needed Zack.

She was not home. She did not appear by anything that might be construed as dinner time, nor an hour after that. Dresden had contritely and assiduously avoided even the thought of drink as he waited, but his agitation became too much for him and he broke his resolve, mixing some Coca-Cola with an inch of old Greek brandy. It was the last liquor he had left in the house.

He took his glass up to the lanai and settled into the swing. Its view of the road was ample, but the cars that came along were few, and none stopped or even slowed. It was getting cold. This would not do. There was nothing for it but the Tiburcio Saloon and Grocery. If Zack were interested in any kind of reconciliation, she would know to find him there. Leaving a light on in the living room and over the kitchen door, Dresden drove the short, familiar distance that his car could by now doubtless manage all by itself.

There were few at the bar and no one brought up Charley's indiscretions of the night before. He forced himself to drink sedately, filling the time by playing the jukebox and joining in the general conversation. He did not ask to have the television set turned on at news time, nor did anyone else. Twice he had to fight off the impulse to telephone his house, in the last instance quite resolutely. It was no way to deal with his difficulties with Zack, which involved much that could not or would not be spoken. If she was home, she could have no doubt as to where he was. If she was there waiting as impatiently as he, not wanting to risk another encounter in the bar, closing time wasn't that far off. She most likely would not be there, and he didn't want to submit himself to the loneliness of an empty house before he had to.

That much, at least, he was spared. At about twenty minutes to midnight, Danny Hill came in, breathless and anxious.

"It's happened, Charley," he said, standing at the bar without pulling up a stool and shaking his head as Cooper began to reach for a bottle of beer. "My ex-wife just called. Her brothers have worked themselves up into a fucking fit with the vino and are headed down here."

"You sound scared this time."

"If you think I'm scared, you should have heard her."

"No problem," said Charley, reaching for his keys. He pulled off the one to his kitchen door. "If Zack's not there, use this. If she is, she'll be glad to put you up on the couch. You're as much her friend as you are mine."

"*Muchas, muchas gracias.*"

"We'll tell them we haven't seen you all night," said Cooper.

"No. That won't do," Dresden said. "We'll tell them you went off with some housewife from Santa Linda. A woman in her fifties with a big car. They'll believe that."

"You're not coming?" Hill asked.

"Not yet," said Dresden. "If Zack is there, tell her I'm here, and that I'll be along. Unless she wants to join me here."

"Okay, amigo. I think I'll leave by the back."

It was full into the middle of the night in Washington, yet Kreski was in his living room, in his pajamas, Mahler playing mournfully on his stereo and an untouched glass of wine on the table before him—something to stare into, not to drink.

His wife appeared in the doorway, tying her robe.

"Again?"

"Yup. Can't sleep. Again."

"After what they did to you in Congress today, I don't blame you." She sat down beside him and took his hand in hers.

"It was worse seeing it replayed on television. They left out every significant and responsible thing I said. I came across looking like an incompetent war criminal."

"I couldn't watch it. I turned it off. You didn't wake me when you came in."

"One of us should sleep. I'm told they have even worse planned for tomorrow. One of our men somehow managed to fire off an accidental round this afternoon on the *Sequoia*. The vice president was using it. Why the hell he thought this is a time for yacht cruises is beyond me."

"That certainly wasn't your fault. You were testifying."

"Some bleeding heart idiot in the House is even suggesting that we be disarmed except under special circumstances, like British police. The hell with them. They won't have me to kick around tomorrow. I'm going to go out of town. I probably won't be back until the following morning."

"Why, Walt?"

"In the sacred name of the investigation. I'm going to try to talk to a man in Colorado. The famous Peter Ashley Brookes."

"On the late news, they said that one of his books turned up among that man Huerta's things."

"Yes. Copley decided it would appease the press to release a list of the inventory. He should have gone into public relations instead of the law. He's certainly better at it than I am."

"Shouldn't his people be talking to Brookes?"

"I'm sure they are. Or will be. I just want to talk to him myself."

"Why?"

"I have the strong sense that Copley wants me to, and I don't know why. Maybe I'll come up with an answer. Also, it falls within my authority to do so and I'll admit I'm for any excuse I can get to avoid going up to the Hill tomorrow. Besides, damn it, I can't think of anything else to do with this rotten damn investigation. Every door we've opened has led to another door, but in the end they've led nowhere. All my astounding tire track discovery has produced is an

APB for six different kinds of big cars that use that size radial. All the agents' stories check out. But we have to keep at this. I've got to keep doing something."

"You do what you feel you must, Walt. That's always been good enough for me."

"And I've always counted on you for that. But this time it may get me into trouble. I probably won't survive this, you know. Politically. My career may soon be at an end. It may already be. The first question today was whether I should keep my job."

"We'll survive it in all the other ways. You just make sure you do what you must."

He smiled, wearily, and kissed her cheek. "My problem is that I can't seem to figure out just what that is. I've never before felt so stupid and helpless. And scared. I try to keep it from everybody, but I'm scared to death. I don't think this thing is over."

"The investigation? Of course not."

"I mean the assassination attempt. I think Bushy Ambrose is right. Politically wrong, politically crazy, but right. I think the president's still in great danger, and if I were Mr. Atherton, I'd go find myself a fort too. I keep telling him that. I tell Shawcross that. They sent Mrs. Atherton to Williamsburg, but otherwise I'm ignored. I guess we no longer give the orders."

"Walt. Come to bed. Around here I give the orders."

He surrendered, though it would do no good. She had no idea the things he still saw when he closed his eyes.

By closing time neither Danny Hill's brothers-in-law nor Zack had made an appearance. Dresden resigned himself to the obvious. She, at least, was not going to appear. He was condemned to return to a darkened house, an empty bed, a snoring Hill on the couch, and not even the makings of a decent drink. That was the only thing he could remedy. He bought a bottle of bar whiskey from Cooper on the tab, and slowly walked with it out to his car, the saloon's last customer. The night sky was extraordinarily clear and starry. Gazing up at it, he thought he might restore his spirits with a walk.

Better than that would be a drive, to a place he'd not been in weeks. As he started his car, he wondered if the old Hawk would be up to it, but the engine commenced with such encouraging vigor he decided to take the risk.

He repaid the automobile with kindly driving once he had turned up onto the mountain road. The surface became quite rutted and stony in the steep switchbacks that began after he passed the entrance to Tiburcio's now abandoned silver mine, compelling him to slow nearly to a stop on the turns to protect the car's old suspension. But wheezing like an aging runner, the Hawker-Siddeley finally bounced onto the grassy summit.

Stepping out into the odd quiet of the windless night, he glanced about. Often this place was used by lovers, but none were in sight or hearing. What was in view was his world as seen by the gods. To the east, shimmering in its valley, was Santa Linda in the only manifestation of beauty it ever displayed. Below, to the west, Tiburcio was a friendly cluster of warm and tiny lights. The glimmer on the far distant horizon to the north was San Jose. To the southwest, were it daylight and the weather still this clear, a glimpse of the sea would be visible through the saddle of a mountain pass.

Dresden felt what he always did atop this mountain, a sense of awe that such a place existed and a sense of exultant possession. There was also a reaffirmation of his faith in the sufficiency of this magical kingdom, his.

What had provoked this madness in him, this compulsive fascination with a distasteful mystery in a dreary, forbidding Washington that could scarcely be imagined from this California prospect? Television had done it. Television had intruded all this unpleasantness upon him. It was his life's work. It had also been his father's death. He had stubbornly, proudly, refused to abandon it, refused to accept his father's defeat, and now television was extracting a terrible price. Tiburcio, his advertising agency, Zack, Isabel, Tracy, they were all he had, and he was losing them fast.

Perhaps. Perhaps not quite yet. He eased himself onto the car's left front fender, opened his bottle, and drank. The alcohol, he supposed, was part of the evil television was working upon him. Like most everyone in Tiburcio, he had indulged in drinking as a recreation, but usually with some care and wisdom. Two years before, when he had been so successful and made such a remarkable amount of money, he had drunk only white or rosé wine, and often not even that. Now, in the mad course of a few days, he'd been driven to flooding his system with the poisonous stuff like a lush on a bender. He may well have become such a lush.

That could be determined on the morrow. This night he would accept the whiskey's exhiliration and solace at least one more time. For it was, after all, a momentous occasion. He was at last coming to terms with the requirement of making a resolute and final decision. He could wait no longer.

The Greek historian Herodotus had written of the village elders of ancient Persia that it was their custom to deliberate on important matters while drunk and then reconsider them in sobriety. If they through inadvertence came to a conclusion while sober, they would often reflect again upon it after having become blotto. Dresden was putting his morning's decision to the same set of tests. Without haste, moving his gaze from point to point in the panorama around him, he consumed something approaching half the bottle. It was enough. He was done. He was still sure. He'd do it. He'd quit this thing, and forget President Hampton ever existed.

He went to the boot of the car where he had locked his all-important briefcase with the tapes and voice analysis inside. Retrieving it, he climbed a slight rise at the edge of the clearing that gave way to the mountain's steepest slope. With a gleeful, echoing shout of liberation, he swung the briefcase and flung it spinning into the void. Then, after one last ceremonial swallow of whiskey, he hurled the bottle after it.

His joy diminished to mere sleepiness by the time he reached the bottom of the mountain and the canyon floor, but there was much contentment.

It was not long-lasting.

All the lights were out at his house, including the one over the kitchen door. Silently cursing Danny Hill, and his own tipsy state, he struggled for a long time trying to get his spare key in his door, before discovering it was unlocked. He entered quietly, for, in happy surprise, he had found Zack's Triumph parked in its customary place in the drive. Waiting a moment for his vision to adjust to the darkness, he made another meaningful decision. Whatever Zack's mood in the morning, he would, without waking her, slip into their bed. Hill's occupying the couch would provide excuse. He was in no mood now for the hard floor.

But Hill was not on the couch. He was for some reason sleeping on the rug near the living room doorway. Perhaps he had managed somehow to become drunk, though Dresden could hear no sound of snoring. Stepping carefully over his friend, he proceeded to the bedroom, where he was made curious again. Zack, though naked, was not in the bed but kneeling as though in prayer against the foot of it. But one did not pray with one's arms hanging behind one. In sudden consuming terror, he reached frantically to turn on the light, wishing instantly he had not, wishing now for a thousand million things that could never, ever be.

She had been shot, a hole as neat and round and large as the one he had put in the wall by the corner of his window, in the middle of her back, another less well-defined crimson circle at the back of her head. The bedclothes were red with blood. With trembling hand, he reached to touch her shoulder, as though this were all some macabre joke she would end by leaping up and shouting, "Surprise!"

She did not. In response to the urgent grasp of his fingers on her cold flesh, her body fell back, legs bending stiffly at the knees, her horrible bloody mask of a face staring upward at him as her head came to rest by his feet.

Staggering backward, numb now, he turned on another lamp and went to his friend Hill, peering down in horror. Danny was fully clothed, though his shirt was badly torn. His shirt was all by which Dresden could recognize him, for his face had been beaten into a jellified red, purple, and greenish lump with only one dead eye visible. Dresden began to retch, the angry gods taking back the whiskey as they had the lives of these two dear, innocent people. He swore and cried, uselessly. There was no one to hear.

After the sickness came paralysis. Dresden stumbled to his couch, closing his eyes, not moving—after a moment not able to move. He decided this could not possibly be happening to him. He was still on the mountain and drunk, having some sort of delirium. Or he was in Maddy Anderson's bed, tormented in sleep with guilt for having broken faith with Zack.

He opened his eyes and the bodies were still there in the stark lamplight, unmoving, as though they had always been there and would always be, permanent fixtures of his house, of his life. That they would be, forever and ever and ever, no matter what desperate means he might use to drown the memory.

His life. It had been rendered a useless, pointless, rapidly perishing commodity, worth a few days or hours. Or minutes. He had thought he could simply back away from whatever the terrible secret was he had been pursuing, that the decision to ignore it would make it cease to exist, or at least exist only in some immeasurably distant place far beyond all his horizons. But the keepers of that dreadful secret had reached through all time and space and limit and found his small life and tried to smash at it as one might some skittering insect's, as they had smashed Charlene's and Danny Hill's. They had heard his small, ridiculous, inconsequential voice raised in feckless protest at what they were doing and decided to silence it with the most expeditious ruthlessness. They had nearly succeeded. They had missed him only through mischance. A second blow from them could come at any moment. A gunsight might be centered on the back of his head that instant, the tiny pull of a finger all that was required to destroy him.

He bolted for the light switch and then stood in the sudden darkness, his breathing heavy in fear as he waited for his vision to adjust, as he waited for his mind to work. Sweat was covering his chest and neck. His hands tingled.

He had to flee at once. His shock, anger, and helplessness had first combined in frustration, and a compelling urge to do nothing more than call the police, to summon the forces of law. But that would be utter madness. They would look no further than one suspect: Charles August Dresden, who was still known throughout the canyon as the man who had shot Curley Lewes, who had fought with Zack the night before just after Cooper had taken his gun away, who had now been drinking for hours in the saloon and upon returning home had found his woman naked with his friend. There would be no search for mysterious strangers. If the true killer or killers didn't gun him down, he'd just be meat for the police. He'd pass this night either dead or in some filthy, sour-smelling cell.

Unless he left immediately; but he was utterly without refuge. There was literally not one place he could think of to go. He had friends—he could imagine no better friends—but it was to them that the police would turn first.

His ultimate destination did not yet matter. His first need was to run, as the frightened beasts of the mountains had run the night of that long ago forest fire. His car was just outside, the gas tank nearly full.

That was more madness. In so odd an antique British car he might as well be driving a fire engine with the siren screaming. He had bought the Hawker-Siddeley as an advertisement for himself, a symbol of his differentness and contempt for the conventional life. There was always a price for that and now he was paying it. He could take Zack's Triumph, but it was hardly nondescript either, and for no reason would he now go back into the room where her body lay to rummage through her things for the keys.

He must go into the mountains on foot. He knew them well. He knew hiding places and tracks along the ridgeline that could take him far to the south before he'd need to descend to the highway. Yet, leaving both cars in the driveway would advertise that decision as well. They'd be out after him with dogs and helicopters in hours.

Dresden forced himself to make his thoughts come faster. Whatever he did, he could not go just as he was. There was a canvas over-the-shoulder bag he had used back when he had been a regular flyer on commercial airlines. He dragged it from his front closet shelf and then went to the door to the garden, dropping to his hands and knees and quietly easing it open.

Nothing stirred in the heavy shadows, though he could hear a dog barking at some distance. Crouching, he moved up the slope to the lanai, pausing as he reached it to listen again for any hint of menace. Then he hurried to the old disconnected refrigerator, rising carefully and opening the freezer compartment. The box was still where she had put it and he had left it. Searching its contents with his fingers, he pulled out his .38 Smith and Wesson revolver, a long-ago gift from a onetime police friend, and the .357 Magnum, along with a heavy box of cartridges. Dresden hesitated, then, in considerable self-disgust, reached into the box once more, removing the thick stack of currency that had been Zack's so short-lived good fortune. He was now a thief, and it was all the worse that he was stealing from the dead, his own beloved dead.

If she had told anyone else about the money, its absence would be another weight on the scales against him. But his need for it was great and desperate. He stuffed it into the bag.

He had decided what he would do. Stepping off the side of the lanai, he slipped down the hillside and through the cemetery, returning along the road to the front of his house, and then to the side of his car. For a few seconds, he would have to expose himself, announce himself, but he had no choice.

The Hawker-Siddeley, still faithful, started at once. He gunned the engine, backing out of the driveway in a churning spray of gravel, then roared off down the road with a protesting squeal of tires, maintaining his mad speed around all the curves and bouncing over the old wooden bridge with such violence he feared it would buckle. When he reached the main road he pushed the old car to its maximum, nervously keeping it there all the way to the crossroads and the now-deserted Mexican beer bar. He turned onto the highway to Santa Linda, but instead of continuing on, he killed his headlights and swerved into the bar's dirt parking lot, steering the vehicle around behind the little building and halting where he was nearly hidden from view, though he could see a fair stretch of both the highway and the Tiburcio road.

To his amazement, no other car came speeding after him. Nothing drove by at all. He waited five minutes, and then five minutes more, and then a full quarter hour, but the roads remained empty. This puzzled him, but changed none of his plans. Taking a deep breath, leaving his headlights off, he slipped the Hawker into gear and turned back toward Tiburcio. Reaching the town's darkened center, his headlamps still dark, he slowed and eased to a stop beside Cooper's closed saloon. He had to expose himself to one more risk. It was foolish, terrifyingly so, but vitally necessary. If they knew of him they could know of Tracy Bakersfield. He would not let them do to her what they had done to Charlene, not if he could get to her in time.

There was a pay telephone in front of the building, the only one in the town. Dresden left its door open to avoid turning on its light. All sounds now seemed frighteningly magnified—the frogs peeping and croaking along the creek, the coin dropping through the phone box's mechanism, the dial clicking, the ringing on the line. When someone finally answered and he spoke, his own voice seemed to boom throughout the canyon, although he spoke in what was not much more than a whisper.

It was Tracy's husband who had answered, without much happiness.

"Bill, it's Charley Dresden. I've got to talk to Tracy. It's really, really urgent."

Kluggerman had always been amazingly cordial to Dresden when he called, no matter how odd the circumstance. He must have loved Tracy to an extraordinary degree to be so tolerant.

He was not so tolerant now.

"Charley," he said wearily, "are you even dimly aware of what time it is?"

"Yes, of course. Damn it, I wouldn't be calling you at this hour if it wasn't really, really urgent. I think Tracy may be in trouble."

"What kind of trouble?"

"I don't have a lot of time, Bill. Just get her on the phone and let me tell her about it. Hurry. Please."

Kluggerman sighed, displeased, but once again tolerant. There were times when Dresden was infuriated by the man's essential goodness, but not now. "All right, Charley. This one last time. Wait."

As he did so, Dresden began to feel a touch of returning confidence, but it did not last long. A new sound intruded upon the quiet, a distant murmur that increased, soon recognizable as an approaching car. In a moment, he could see the first flicker of headlights far down the road.

"Charley," said Tracy. "You said you wouldn't do this."

He crouched down against the side of the booth, bringing pain to his injured knee.

"Just listen to me, Tracy. And do what I say. They killed Charlene and Danny Hill. They came for me, but I stayed away until very late. So they killed them. Their bodies . . ."

The car was slowing. Its headlights seemed monstrous, all-seeing eyes, illuminating all before them. He had stupidly left both of his pistols in the bag in the Hawker-Siddeley.

"Charlene? Do you mean your—friend?"

"Yes, my woman, my girlfriend. She's dead. They shot her."

"They?"

"Someone. Someone who may know what you and I have been doing."

The car had stopped at the edge of the road, not much more than a hundred yards distant. It was pointless trying to hide himself. Crouching against the glass of the booth, he must be as visible as some zoo animal in its cage.

"Charley? . . ."

He would have only a few seconds if he made a run for the Hawker, but it could be done. There was still a chance for escape—if he was willing to abandon Tracy. He might never be able to make contact with her again. She might not be alive the next day.

"Charley? Are you there?"

"Yes. Now listen. I think they might come after you. If they could track me down, they might also know about you, about what you did for me, about what you know. I may have been followed for days. I want you to leave as soon as possible."

Now the car's lights went out. Dresden told himself it might only be a Tiburcio resident, returning home after a late night. But Zack and Danny were dead. He should run. Now.

"Have you been drinking, Charley?"

"Damn it, Tracy. Listen to me. They murdered Charlene and Danny Hill. It was awful. Their bodies are still in my house. Now I want you and Bill to get out of there. Go anywhere you don't usually go, but go. It could mean your life. Please, believe me. It'll be on the news tomorrow, but tomorrow could be too bloody late."

She paused. "I believe you. It's in your voice. It always is when you're truly serious, Charley. But I'm not sure I can convince Bill. Have you called the police?"

He could see no movement along the road, but if his fears were correct, he had by now lingered too long. At least he would die a little nobly. His death was worth Tracy's life.

"I can't call the police. They're going to think I did it. I need to get away. You, too, Trace. Please. I have to go. Now. I don't know when I'll talk to you again."

"Charley . . ."

"Good-bye, Trace. I love you in all the ways there are."

He hung up, the sound of her voice calling out his name echoing in his mind. Her last word. He would cherish it—for however long he had left.

Now he ran. It was all he could do. He was in his car and driving away in a blurred instant. He kept his headlights off until he was around the long curve at the end of town that took the main road over the creek and toward the mountain. He could see no lights behind him. He might yet be able to carry out his plan.

His rearview mirror was still empty when he reached the mountain road and slewed the Hawker onto its rough dirt surface for the second time that night. On this climb, however, he went no farther than the entrance to the mine. He got his car inside the wire fence, then closed the gate behind it. At the opening in the mountainside a wooden barrier had been put up, warning away intruders with a strident but pointless KEEP OUT! Charley drove through it, wincing as splintered wood and nails scraped at the Hawker-Siddeley's sides. He proceeded on through the tunnel until it steepened and he came to a second wooden barrier, this one proclaiming DANGER!

"Right," he said.

Beyond this obstruction, the shaft plunged into the depths of the mountain. There had been heavy rains that fall and in such weather the bottom of the shaft flooded. It was one of the reasons they had decided to close the mine. It might be weeks or months before they found his car, if ever.

Letting the engine idle, he took his canvas bag and a flashlight from it, then stood a moment, his hand on the roof. It was an awful thing he must do, but he was losing much this night. Depressing the clutch with his foot, he reached, straining, and shoved the gear lever into first. Then he stood up and, hurling himself back, yanked his foot off the pedal. The Hawker ground furiously ahead, thudding against the barrier, but it was less substantial than the first and quickly gave way. The car rumbled on, swerving and crunching noisily against the tunnel walls, but the descending shaft was so narrow it served as a guide. As the car moved away, so did the light. Dresden stood in darkness, listening to the terrible noises until they culminated in an enormous splash. He turned on his flashlight, shouldered his bag, and began what was going to be the longest walk of his life, or so he hoped.

Clicking off the flashlight as he emerged into the starry night, he noticed that his friend the moon had returned, though now a much different moon from that which had lent its glow to his final interlude with Madeleine Anderson. It seemed cold and lifeless now, drained of all its sentimental qualities, a stark sentinel staring blankly as Charley passed through the gate and started his trudge to the top of the mountain. He had to return to the summit to regain the only thing now of any use to him. Whatever all-powerful, all-seeing force had reached out and stolen life from Zack and Hill had taken everything that Charley loved and valued, everything that constituted his own life. He could never go back. Tiburcio, his house, his friends, his loves, California—everything his long years there had given him had all been snatched away, forever beyond his reach. He'd have to wander the earth for the rest of his days, however long or few, a faceless, unknown man, Tiburcio existing only in his memory. But if he'd luck enough to somehow find it, he'd at least have that briefcase, and the power its contents gave him.

As the road steepened, the pain in his leg increased until it produced a severe limp, and then almost a stagger. Perhaps he might not make it after all. Perhaps this mountain would prove to be as far as he would ever come.

Kreski tried to use the long flight to Denver for sleep, but achieved only unpleasant thoughts and a heightened sense of discomfort. Following his own policy for Secret Service personnel traveling civilian, he was flying economy class, a self-inflicted, humbling punishment. The difference between Air Force One and this was as profound as that between first class and steerage on one of the old trans-Atlantic luxury liners. After so many years attached to the presidency, it sometimes came as a shock to him how mere citizens lived. He'd have to get used to it—soon, if the Congress had what looked to be its intended way.

He was traveling alone, just another anonymous face and suit in a cabin crowded with distracted businessmen. His only connection with Washington was a pocket beeper he carried that could be activated with a call through the Denver office. His only other trappings were his identification badge and pistol. His hope was to come upon Peter Ashley Brookes as circumspectly as possible, and not spook him with what might resemble an investigatory assault. If Kreski was able to arrange a conversation, he wanted it to be as relaxed and revealing as possible. Aside from being rich, ruthless, and slightly crazy, Brookes was an extremely smart man.

There were a number of things Kreski should have been attending to in Washington. Mrs. Atherton, bored with Williamsburg and worried about her husband, had returned with her daughter to the capital, which was not in need of two more such highly visible targets. Agent Perkins had, of course, returned with her, and Kreski had not yet interviewed him about Gettysburg. A stolen car recovered by Philadelphia police not far from Huerta's hideaway proved to have tires matching the imprint taken from the battlefield on the other side of the woods from Perkins's tower. A fingerprint report was probably already awaiting Kreski. He had undoubtedly taken another step higher on the ladder to the hangman's scaffold by dodging the Congress again. Ultimately, they were going to get him, and the longer he put them off the more vicious they would be about it.

But this Brookes matter was beginning to make him itch.

Like so many men of his circumstances, Peter Ashley Brookes required a shimmering office tower to perceive his own success and power. Brookes's building, a slab-sided shaft with a black, mirrored finish, was one of the highest in Denver. His personal office, as the lobby guard informed Kreski, was on the very top floor, but Kreski wouldn't be able to go there. It was forbidden.

Kreski's government badge got him past the lobby guard, and to within two floors of Brookes's aerie. There he was passed from a receptionist to a succession of secretaries and assistants and finally up one floor to a youngish man whose manner suggested he was a high-ranking member of Brookes's praetorian guard.

He had a large corner office with an outsize photograph of Brookes mounted on one wall. There were no other decorations.

Once again, Kreski displayed his badge.

"Do you have a warrant?" said the man, politely but coldly.

"No. I'm not here to arrest anyone. If Mr. Brookes could spare me a few minutes, I'd appreciate talking with him."

"Mr. Brookes sees no one without an appointment."

"Very well. I'd like to make an appointment."

"We'll get back to you."

"An appointment for today. I have to get back to Washington."

"I'm sure that would be impossible."

"Sir. This concerns an attempted assassination of the president of the United States. I'm the director of the U.S. Secret Service. I'm not here to solicit contributions to the National Gallery of Art."

"Fine. Get a warrant."

Kreski wondered if he might have been wiser to have come with an army of agents. He had once enjoyed power enough to have this man hauled out of his office without explanation. Perhaps he still did. But he'd make one more try with an oblique approach.

"Sir," he said. "This is a highly sensitive investigation, but it's also one that's under the utmost scrutiny. Whatever I do, whomever I see, whatever results—it's all going to end up in the public record. I'm sure Mr. Brookes is quite cognizant of that, but it strikes me he's probably not even aware that I'm here. What if it turns out he would have wanted to talk to me? Would you like to give that some thought? Before the *New York Times* reports that he hid from an investigative officer?"

The man's expression softened, though not by much. "I'll see," he said. "But he's extremely busy."

Kreski was led back out to a reception area to wait, guided to a chair near the outer door. Brookes's assistant returned with unexpected swiftness.

"He wants to talk to you," he said, somewhat agitatedly. "Immediately!"

As Kreski had expected, Brookes's office was outsize beyond all reason, incorporating two corners of the building and reaching at least a hundred feet from the enormous double entrance doors to the far windows. The pillars encasing the structural girders were obscured by statuary, life-size sculptures of soldiery taken from various periods of world history. A free-standing mural served to separate a conference area from the rest of the room. The long painting was a vivid rendering of a varicolored jungle reminiscent of Rousseau, except for the fact that the figures moving among the jungle growth were not animals but combat troops. Otherwise, the huge chamber held little furniture or decoration. Brookes's slab-topped desk was on a raised dais at one of the far corners. His was the only chair and he sat facing away from the windows. The Denver haze and smog had obliterated what otherwise would have been a sweeping view across the city to the mountains.

Brookes was tanned and lean, looking much younger than his age, which was forty-eight. Kreski supposed he skied and otherwise spent a set period of every day in violent exercise. He had a dark mustache and longish gray hair that, like President Hampton's, was probably trimmed every day. His light blue eyes were unusually clear, almost transluscent, like faintly tinted glass marbles. It was as though one could look through them into the man's mind, though with Brookes, one might not want to.

There was nothing on Brookes's desk but a large inset telephone console. To his side, however, was an elaborate computer terminal, its large, brightly hued screen fully aglow. It was like coming upon the chairman of General Motors with a wrench in his hand. Brookes snapped off the computer, then swiveled back to glare at Kreski, who was smiling.

"What's so funny?" Brookes asked.

"I'm sorry," Kreski said. "I would have thought you'd have a few thousand people on the payroll who could do that for you."

"This computer is programmed for only one man to operate. Me. It accesses everything I own."

And doubtless much, much more, Kreski thought. He was still standing. There was no chair within reach, as Brookes doubtless intended.

"I'm very busy," Brookes said. "I don't want to hear what you want. Let me tell you what I want. I want to know why I'm being investigated. I want it stopped. Immediately!"

"I know nothing about any official investigation. I just want to talk with you."

"No official investigation? There were federal agents at all three of my foundations in Washington this morning. There were agents talking to my neighbors. I don't even know my goddamn neighbors! The closest one is half a mile away."

"What federal agents?"

"From the Federal fucking Bureau of Investigation!"

"As I made clear to your people, I'm director of the Secret Service. I don't initiate FBI investigations."

Brookes waved his hand disgustedly and swiveled away. "You're all the goddamn same."

Kreski sighed. "With all due respect, sir, may I have a chair? I'm told that even the KGB occasionally lets its prisoners in the Lubyanka have chairs."

The reference to the Communists worked. Brookes abruptly stood up and started toward the opposite corner, where two curving couches were set by the windows. "Sit," he commanded.

Kreski did so thankfully, stretching out his long legs. Now they were arranged as equals, though Brookes still managed to dominate. The light from the windows illuminated his crystalline eyes eerily. Kreski had to look away.

"Who planted all that stuff about me in the press?" Brookes said, before Kreski could speak. "I was talked about on the news last night, on 'Today,' 'CBS Morning News,' 'Good Morning America,' and that goddamn Ted Turner outfit this morning. Just because that Honduran had a copy of my book. What if he had a copy of one of Bill Buckley's books? Would you have people talking to Buckley's neighbors too?"

"The only one from my agency who's talking to anyone is me, Mr. Brookes. I'm afraid that what set off the news media was the fact that Huerta had all those back copies of *Mercenary Magazine*."

"And who dropped that on them?"

"The Bureau released the inventory of Huerta's possessions to the media. They'd been screaming for information."

"The *Washington Post* had a story this morning listing all my other activities in addition to *Mercenary Magazine*—as though Huerta were on all my boards of directors. Has anyone bothered to find out if this guy could even read English? I'm being set up, Krepski! I don't like it. Keep it up and I'm going to fight back! Fights with me are not a lot of fucking fun."

"I'm sure they're not, sir. And my name is Kreski. As I've been trying to make clear, Mr. Brookes, I don't consider you any kind of suspect. I came because of your expertise on Central America. You have many interests there."

"I have interests in Korea, Saudi Arabia, South Africa, and Canada. You want my expertise on the skiing in Quebec?"

"It's not germane. You bankroll a lot of rightist guerrilla groups. Do you know of any terrorist or paramilitary organization down there that might go by the name of 'La Puño'? On your side, or the other side?"

Brookes's eerie eyes gazed steadily into Kreski's without falter. "None. 'La Puño.' The Fist. It's not political or military sounding enough. Or poetic, like the 'Shining Path,' that Marxist outfit in Peru. 'La Puño' is the kind of name one of the cadre leaders might take for himself. It's like 'El Toro,' 'El Monte,' 'El Cicatriz.' Macho stuff. There might be a couple dozen 'Puños' in Honduras alone, though I never heard of any."

"Give me a motive. What kind of Central American would be crazy or desperate enough to try to kill the president of the United States? Why? What possible benefit could accrue?"

"On the Marxist side, they've got people fanatical enough to see wasting Henry Hampton as the ultimate triumph. And the place is crawling with Cubans and KGB who want to keep things destabilized. But I can't see the Sandinistas wanting to pull it off. It wouldn't suit their purposes at all."

"And on your side?"

Brookes frowned.

"Okay. There's talk Hampton was trying to cut a deal with Managua. There are a lot of Salvadoran landowners in exile who don't like that one fucking bit. But none of my people would get out of line. All of our groups are assisted by Washington. Our job is to pick up the slack when the Congress gets pricky. I say all this to you because I'm sure you know it already and just want to see how up-front I'll be with you."

Kreski certainly did not know any of this, but he didn't admit to it. He pondered his next question, but took much too long.

"All right, Kreski," Brookes said, standing. "That's enough. You're keeping me from my computer. I'm just warning you. I want you bastards to knock it off. I'm a friend of the president, you know. Been one of his most generous supporters. If just one more trenchcoat turns up at any of my operations I'm going to get Hampton on the phone and have him put some teeth marks in your backsides."

"If you can get the president on the phone you're a much better man than I am. I've been trying since the shooting."

"He's on television every night and he hasn't talked to the head of the Secret Service?"

"He's spoken to Senator Rollins and the vice president, very briefly. To my knowledge, no one else."

"Well who the hell is running the government?"

Kreski shrugged. "Ask your computer. I'm sure it knows much more than I do."

On the swift elevator ride down to the street-level lobby, Kreski found his spirits improving. This long-distance digression hadn't been a complete waste of time. The itch he'd been feeling about Brookes had vanished.

And now he had a new one.

The motel out on New York Avenue northeast of the Capitol was missing some lights from its marquee and had what looked like an abandoned car parked opposite its office door. But then, the guests didn't come there for the ambience. Senator Rollins and Reuben Jackson pulled their car up as close as possible to the police unit that waited for them at the curb, its Mars light revolving slowly, as though to proclaim there was no real emergency here.

"He's got a couple of cuts and bruises," the officer told them. "I don't know whether they did that to him or if he got them falling out of bed. He's got a bad-looking gouge on his wrist from when they pulled off his watch. Should we take him to a hospital and have them look at it?"

"We'll take care of that," said Jackson. "What else did they take?"

"They dropped his wallet—I guess when they saw who he was. But there's no money in it. Oh, yeah, they also took his pants. We couldn't find them anywhere."

"Thank you, officer," Jackson said. "Where do we find him?"

"Room twenty-eight. Second floor."

"Will this go on the public record?" Rollins asked.

"Just a routine report," the policeman said. "Unless he wants to file a complaint."

"I'm sure he doesn't," Jackson said.

Motel employees stood silently and sullenly in the littered lobby, waiting for the unwelcome visitors to leave. White people had intruded upon their evening, disrupting the orderly flow of their business, commerce that could not be transacted in the presence of police. Rollins and Jackson hurried on.

"Stole his pants," said Rollins disgustedly, as they climbed the stained, carpeted stairs. "What the hell did he come out here for? I told you we'd fix him up with any woman he wanted. Not that he's hard up. Your outer office is getting to look like one of those Baltimore girls-girls-girls bars."

"I guess he felt the need for a little strange."

"Strange he got. A lot of strange."

The shade had been knocked from the cheap bedside lamp, flooding the small, dirty room with a harsh glare. Senator Dubarry, dressed only in his underwear and one sock, sat on the edge of the bed, holding his face in his hands and rocking back and forth, muttering. There were two not quite empty glasses on the table, but no bottle. Dubarry's friends must have taken that too.

A black policeman stood in the corner of the room, looking unhappy.

"We'll take it from here, officer," Jackson said. "Thanks for all your trouble. It's appreciated."

The man lingered, though it didn't seem he was looking for a tangible expression of that appreciation. "He's got a bad gash on his wrist."

"Just put in your report that the gentleman declined treatment," Rollins said. "We'll take him to his own doctor. I hope he didn't give you any difficulty."

"No, sir. He's too drunk. If he had, he'd be in jail now, and you'd have to wait till the morning to get him."

"I understand," Rollins said.

Jackson began gathering what remained of Dubarry's clothes. He shortly found himself pulling a moist sock onto the senator's sweaty foot. His country was asking much of Reuben Jackson.

With Jackson's raincoat over Dubarry's head, and the night's darkness and a returning rain shower shielding them from any passing motorist who might recognize them, they quickly shoved him into the rear seat of Jackson's car. By the time Jackson completed his U-turn and was heading back toward Capitol Hill, Dubarry was snoring loudly.

"Where shall we take him?" Jackson said. "I don't think it's a good idea to bring him home to his wife. She's been threatening to go back to Louisiana as it is, and that would surely make the gossip columns."

"Let's go to his doctor's. We can tell him he got drunk and took a nasty fall."

"His doctor will certainly believe the drunk part. He's been warning Meathead, er, the senator, about his liver for years."

"Somehow we have to keep the Senate and the public convinced that this man actually could serve as president of the United States. I wish we could keep him at Camp David until we get January behind us."

"Can't do that."

"Nope. Things look funny enough up there as it is."

"Besides. Meathead is still a key player on the defense budget. He's got a big subcommittee vote on the Stealth bomber tomorrow."

"How can you worry about national security at a time like this?"

                    *   *   *

Bushy Ambrose took a full report from Senator Rollins over his secure phone, then hung up the receiver carefully, turning off the scrambler. He sat back in his chair, very satisfied, relaxing his posture for the first time that day.

"Andy Rollins has just executed damage control on Meathead Dubarry. The bastard got himself rolled by some colored hooker in Northeast."

"That guy has the most understanding wife in America," said C. D. Bragg, who, with Schlessler, had become a constant presence in Ambrose's cabin.

"Maybe she's hoping he'll get a heart attack."

There was a knock at the door, not the sentry's.

"Come in!"

Jerry Greene entered, looking uncomfortable. He sat down heavily, shaking his head. "Our friend wants to leave," Greene said. "He wants to go back to New York."

"We all want to leave," said Bragg.

"Tell him he can't," Ambrose said.

"I have, endlessly. He says this place depresses him. He says it reminds him of the Catskills, only there's no chopped liver and no one in his right mind goes to the Catskills in November."

"Tell him it's okay. Appeal to his patriotism."

"I think we've exhausted that quality in his case," Bragg said. "There wasn't much to begin with."

"This is the presidency, for God's sake," said Ambrose. "He's taking part in history. Doesn't that mean anything to him? Anyway, he hasn't been up here all that long."

"I think he's afraid it's going to be a lot longer."

"He's got that straight," Bragg said.

Ambrose frowned. There were too many people involved in this who weren't used to taking orders. "What would appeal to him?"

"I don't know," said Greene, scratching his head nervously. "Maybe he's horny."

"We could get a hooker up here from Baltimore," said Bragg. "Or we could fly in one of Dubarry's office bimbos."

"No, I don't want to do that until it's really necessary. There are too many civilians up here as it is. And once we bring them in they can't leave."

"What else turns him on?" Bragg asked.

"Money," said Greene. "He likes money a lot."

"We're paying him a hundred thousand dollars as it is," Bragg said.

"He says he can make that in a month at the Catskills. And he gets chopped liver."

"Tell him we'll double the sum," Ambrose said. "And we'll have some chopped liver brought in. Anything to save the republic."

12

Kreski returned earlier than he had expected, his plane settling onto the runway at National Airport in full daylight. To his surprise, Steve Copley was waiting for him at the gate.

"To put it mildly, I'm curious about what you got," Copley said, as they started down the concourse.

"To put it mildly, you certainly are curious. Your boys came down with pretty heavy feet on Brookes. I think you spooked him."

"There was a bit of overkill, but we were trying to spook him, to see what he might do. The lads are getting impatient with the way this is dragging on, and Brookes looks like a live one."

"I believe the man is clean in this."

"Why?"

"Let's just say he has honest eyes."

The airport was crowded and there were people all around them, including some walking immediately behind.

"Let's wait until we're a little more secure," Copley said.

"I'm supposed to have a car and driver waiting."

"You did have. I sent him back. I thought we could chat. Are you going back to your office?"

"Yes. Although I suspect there are a few congressmen on my door-step with a noose in their hands."

"I have some good news for you on that score. Atherton's people on the Hill took a nose count. You've got a one-vote margin on the committee, providing you don't provoke them by absenting yourself again."

"Do you have any other news?"

"Just what's in the papers, and on the networks. Nothing you can believe."

"I always believe the Federal Bureau of Investigation. Your people have found nothing more?"

"Let's wait until we're more secure."

Copley had a car waiting in the cab lane. When he and Kreski appeared the driver got out without a word and walked away. Copley slipped behind the wheel. The engine was already running.

"How did you know I was going to see Brookes today?" said Kreski as Copley sped them onto the George Washington Parkway.

"I didn't. I learned after the fact. We had agents all over Denver."

"He noticed."

"But he didn't show any signs of panic? You didn't pick up anything odd from him?"

"Nothing beyond his known oddities, and the strong impression that he's not involved in this. I didn't think he'd agree to talk with me, but he was surprisingly cooperative—considering."

"You don't think there's any connection between his many inter-esting activities and La Puño, if there is a La Puño?"

"He's quite certain there's no such thing, unless it's the name of some guerrilla leader. Right wing or left wing. In any event, not an organization. Admiral Elmore said more or less the same thing."

"Brookes probably has better information."

Copley slowed the car as they approached the entrance ramp to the 14th Street bridge. "You said the office, right?"

"The office. Agent Perkins should be waiting for me, presuming Mrs. Atherton has released him to my custody."

"Your custody?"

"A joke. He's been volunteering for overtime duty with her so much you'd almost wonder if they're having an affair. I've been try-ing to get him in for a chat about Gettysburg for days."

"Do affairs like that ever happen? I've always wondered."

Kreski smiled. "Then I'm sure you've found out. In any event, I worry less about wives than I do about the daughters. Secret Service agents often are the only men in their lives."

Copley switched to the far left lane, proceeding on toward the center of Washington once they were across the Potomac.

"My office is on 18th Street," Kreski said after Copley had gone a block too far. "As you may recall."

"Sorry. I wasn't thinking. I mean I was thinking. We're going to go ahead with our field investigation of Brookes. And I'm going to make penetrations of his mercenary groups."

"I'm surprised you didn't do that years ago."

"I did. But now it's time for another look."

"Do you really think you're going to turn up anything? Aside from the usual right-wing crazies and survivalists? We made a couple of runs at his people in Florida last time the president went down there and couldn't even find any neo-Nazis. They were mostly ex-military helping out with black job work for the Special Functions Force. The most dangerous people we identified down there were some of Admiral Elmore's Cubans."

Copley swung the car left onto Constitution Avenue. "And?"

"By dangerous, I mean bureaucratically. The admiral didn't appreciate our intrusion."

"Well, I want to know who's swimming in Brookes's many ponds these days," Copley said. "You think there's nothing because he has honest eyes—though, frankly, they give me the creeps. This may be another one of your famous hunches that turns out to be absolutely correct. Walter Kreski's intuitive genius. But I have to keep after Brookes. I can't think of anything else to do. And I don't want to be hauled before a congressional green table, either, to tell them I'm at a dead end."

Kreski was silent for a long time. "Steven, I think we've both been pursuing a dead end from the beginning," he said finally. "We've been looking for the president's assailants, just like homicide cops. We should have been looking for whoever it is that's been planting all this false evidence—La Puño flags, Brookes's book and magazines, the funny money, all of that."

"What do you mean?"

"We should be trying to find out how they've been doing it. How that ridiculous scrap of a La Puño flag got onto that museum roof."

"Maybe Manuel Huerta put it there himself. He may have been

planting things on orders, to throw us off his compatriots. If you really believe everything we've collected is a plant."

"As Brookes pointed out, we haven't even determined if Huerta spoke English. That's why I'm interviewing Perkins, Steve. And those other agents. I'm afraid the possibility exists that someone in my agency is involved in this—if not the assassination attempt, at least the laying of these false trails. I'm not talking to Perkins idly—because I've nothing else to do."

"You have something specific?"

"Let's just call it one of my famous hunches."

"God help us if you're right."

"God help us, period."

Kreski found Hammond waiting outside his office, but not Agent Perkins.

"The Congress is really raising hell, director," Hammond said. "We've had calls from five committee chairmen plus a visit by the sergeant at arms. He had another subpoena."

"Never mind that. Where's Perkins?"

"On detail. Special orders."

Kreski picked up his office radio's microphone. "I'm going to have him pulled. I wish I could have Atherton pulled. I'm beginning to think he's lost his mind. Cruises on the Potomac. Banquet speeches. And he picks the hotel where President Reagan was shot."

"I suppose he's thinking of appearances. A show of normality. The government is in the safe hands of a cool, calm, competent 'acting president.' This is billed as a major policy address. He's going to talk about Central America. An opportunity to show his stuff."

"And another opportunity for some shooter's symbolic act." Kreski swore, then clicked on the microphone. But he hesitated. After a moment he relaxed his thumb. "Perkins would be with Mrs. Atherton, at the VIP reception?"

"Yes, Director. SOP."

"I don't want to startle anybody." He replaced the microphone on its hook. "We'll go up there ourselves. Get us a car."

"And driver?"

"Negative. Just us."

The hotel should have been just a few minutes away, up 18th Street and Connecticut Avenue, but there were delays. The evening traffic was heavy, and a three-car rear-ender accident at the intersection with Connecticut compounded the congestion. Backing out of the vehicular confusion, Kreski tried making a detour down a narrow side street, but encountered a double-parked truck.

"My biggest failure when I leave this job," he said, "will be that I never had traffic enforcement in the District of Columbia placed under the control of our agency."

"Here comes the driver. Shall I have a few words with him?"

Kreski honked his horn. "That's few words enough," he said. "Anything more will just delay us further."

The driver made an obscene gesture, then climbed laconically into his cab, started the truck, and slowly chugged away, Kreski all but pressing his own car to the truck's bumper. Hammond again looked at his watch.

"The reception should now be over. They'll be filing in to the head table shortly. Should I check that?"

"Affirmative. Discreetly."

Hammond spoke quietly into his microphone. After a brief conversation he replaced it.

"There you are. The vice president should be speaking by the time we arrive."

"If this bastard in the truck doesn't get a move on, the vice president will be home in bed by the time we arrive. If something else doesn't happen to him. I don't know how we're going to do it, but we got to impress upon him the importance of increasing his security. The country's in damn serious trouble. The president's wounded. If something happens to Atherton, the next in line would be the seventy-seven-year-old speaker, and after him Maitland Dubarry, God help us. As of January."

"Speaking of security problems, Meathead got himself rolled by a prostitute in Northeast. He even got cut up a little."

An opportunity came to get around the truck, and Kreski seized it, slamming down the accelerator and roaring by. The driver made another obscene gesture as they passed.

"Don't we have a detail on Dubarry?"

"A one-man tail. Dubarry kept him at arm's length so the guy wouldn't interfere with his social life. I guess he was able to evade our agent using one of those side doors he has."

"I want a full unit on him. At all times."

"Director, we're spread kind of thin."

"Spread us thinner, even if you have to start emptying non-Washington field offices. He may be Meathead Dubarry, but he will shortly be fourth in line for the presidency of the United States. I don't want any more casualties."

Kreski's car radio, set to the agency's main frequency, crackled into life. The voice of Special Agent Leonardi, in charge of vice presidential security, urgently but quietly requested backup teams at the hotel. He gave the code phrase they used for "death threat."

"Son of a bitch!" said Hammond.

Kreski clicked on the siren and set it at a high-frequency warble, weaving flat out through the traffic in Connecticut Avenue like a fighter plane cutting through an enemy bomber formation. He should have driven like this all the way. Reaching the hotel, he ignored the side entrance where the vice president's motorcade waited—and where former President Reagan had taken a bullet in 1981. Instead, bouncing his car over the curb, he sped down the curving drive to the main doors leading to the lobby. It would be the quickest route to the ballroom. With other agents hurrying behind, they bounded up the rising escalator, pushing people out of their way in thorough Secret Service fashion. At the doors to the ballroom, they stopped, and walked in as though all was normal.

The guests, glittering in evening gowns and black tie, still sat at the crowded tables, but were talking excitedly. There were only a few empty seats at the long head table that curved along the dais opposite, but they included those where the vice president and his wife would be sitting. Leonardi, one of Kreski's most trusted veterans, hastened up to him.

"Where's Atherton?" Kreski said.

"In the kitchen."

Bobby Kennedy was shot in a hotel kitchen. Kreski started to make his way down across the huge ballroom floor, Leonardi at his side, Hammond just behind. Kreski paused. "Dick. Secure all the doors. No one in or out. No one."

"Yes, sir." Hammond turned quickly away.

Kreski, moving on, lowered his head to Leonardi's. "Explain this. Quick."

"'Seashore,'" Leonardi began, using the detail's code name for Mrs. Atherton, "opened her dinner program and a note fell out, in Spanish. She doesn't speak Spanish so she handed it to Secretary of State Crosby next to her, who does."

"And?" said Kreski, pushing aside a waiter.

"It translated as, 'Now you will die, for our victory.'"

Kreski swore. "Was it signed?"

"Yes. With the words, 'La Puño.'"

The director swore again, and quickened his pace. "The 'you' in 'now you will die,' was it the singular, 'usted,' or the plural, 'ustedes'?"

"It was 'ustedes.'"

"Okay. We're going to have to shut this place down. I want everyone in the room interviewed, and all, I repeat, all hotel personnel held in quarantine. Damn, half the waiters here must be Hispanic. Have the secretary of state make the announcement."

"Director, you better talk to the vice president first. He wants to make his speech. I've tried to get him out of here, but he won't budge."

Atherton was standing by a stainless-steel serving table, a cordon of Secret Service around him, weapons drawn.

"Walt," said the vice president, sharply. "Get these thugs of yours away from me! I've got to make my speech."

"Mr. Vice President, with all due respect, what you've got to do is get the hell out of here at once. If you won't leave voluntarily, we'll carry you out."

"You do that and I'll have your job, Walt. You're in enough trouble as it is."

"If I have to lose my job in order to perform it, sir, fine. But I'm going to perform it."

Atherton pushed his way between two of the agents to stand face to face with Kreski. When he spoke his voice was lower, but angrier.

"Will you stop thinking of yourself and your procedures for one minute and think about your damned country?" the vice president said. "We have a military crisis in Central America, Mr. Kreski. We have a political crisis in this country. Ambassadors from most of the world's nations are out in that audience, Mr. Kreski, including all the Latin American ones. The Soviet ambassador is here. Now do you want to show them, show the world, show the people of America that the vice president of the United States, at the moment the only visible representative of constitutional authority, can be kept from speaking out on the most critical foreign policy issue now facing this nation by any crank who scribbles a note?"

"We don't know it's a crank, sir."

"Who in hell else can it be? You've said yourself this La Puño business is a fraud. How many assassins send death threats first?"

Kreski looked down. "Some of the mental cases do. There's always a risk."

"There's risk in everything we do. You have to balance it with the needs of the country. Remember what you said to that congressional committee? The president is safe up at Camp David, but the American people want him down here." Atherton moved even closer. "If I leave here now, Walter, I know exactly what you're going to do. You're going to turn that ballroom out there into a Secret Service version of a 1920s speakeasy raid. Do you realize the international outrage that's going to cause, the panic it'll cause here? What it might unleash or provoke in Central America?"

Kreski stared into Atherton's dark, glittering eyes. "I'm going to do what I have to do."

"I'm not going to let you. I promise you I'll leave the instant my speech is done. No curtain calls. No opening jokes. You can station agents at every table if you like. I don't care if you have a man with an Uzi sitting on my dinner plate. In fact, considering what's on the menu, I wish you would. But I am going to make that speech. This is America, Walt. Teddy Roosevelt finished his speech."

"While wounded."

"I'm wearing my Kevlar vest," Atherton said, patting his tuxedo front. "You see, a Washington stuffed shirt."

He gripped Kreski's shoulder in manly fashion, then propelled himself forward toward the doors to the ballroom. Kreski gave a slight nod and the cordon of agents reformed and hurried to make a protective accompanying wedge around Atherton. Kreski quickly motioned to Leonardi.

"I don't want any agents sitting on Atherton's plate, but I want at least half a dozen within reach of it—hands on weapons. And the instant he's done, get him out. Tell Dick Hammond."

"Yes, sir."

Kreski hesitated, then spoke again quickly. "Where's Mrs. Atherton?"

"Shawcross had her taken upstairs. She was nearly hysterical."

"How much security do you have up there?"

"None now, sir. As soon as they administered a sedative, I had her sent home. With the vice president's approval. She was really in bad shape, director. She's been upset for days."

"Sent her home how?"

"I broke out one of the limousines and a couple of chase cars."

"You busted a vice presidential motorcade? You violated procedure like that?"

"Sir, she was a basket case! And I'm taking that death threat seriously."

"How long ago did they leave?"

"I gave the order just a few minutes before you arrived. They should be out of here now. We held an elevator."

"Who'd you give the detail to?"

"Agent Perkins."

Kreski bolted, not for the door to the ballroom but a side exit leading to a service hall. He knew the interior of this hotel better than he did that of the Treasury Department. A back stairs took him to another service corridor and an unmarked door opening onto the lobby. Loping through the milling guests, he was in his car within a minute, squealing away from the curb and out the drive, careening across Connecticut Avenue. He tried raising Perkins on his radio, but there was no response. He wasn't sure which route Perkins would take to the vice presidential mansion—if he went there at all—but Kreski would use S Street.

He swerved onto it and sped up the hill. He was just gliding down the other side by the Irish ambassador's residence when he heard the sharp, shattering crack of an explosion off to his right. At the bottom of the hill, skidding right onto Massachusetts Avenue through a red light, he could see the harsh bright flicker of flames ahead, somewhere by the long bridge across Rock Creek Park.

The blast had been of such violence it had obliterated several sections of the concrete bridge railing and buckled the roadway. Four vehicles had been demolished—the vice presidential limousine, the rear chase car, a small sports car that had been caught passing by in the opposite lanes, and the square, blackened, flattened, nearly atomized remains of what likely had been a small van. It had been parked at the side of the bridge halfway on the sidewalk, doubtless as though stalled or in distress, a four-wheeled blockbuster bomb.

A few blocks down, Kreski could see the lights of the huge British Embassy still aglow. Just beyond was Observatory Hill and the Vice President's House. "Seashore" had almost made it home.

There were other victims. Two other civilian vehicles in the opposite lanes had been hit and were slewed to the side, their occupants screaming and crying. A short distance ahead the lead Secret Service car, badly damaged but not burning, also sat sideways. Kreski could see two figures moving in it.

He went first to his chief responsibility. The vice presidential limousine, like all those in the White House service, was heavily armored, but this bomb could have destroyed an entire building. Mrs. Atherton's body was a mangle, her head and a dangling arm extending from the crumpled rear door. In the front seat two blackened bodies, hunched over but sitting as though staring ahead, were still aflame.

Kreski glanced through the vacant gap where the bridge railing had been, into blackness. Whoever had detonated the device was by now long gone north or south on Rock Creek Parkway. Dodging around still burning debris and litter, Kreski hurried up to the lead car of the detail. The man in the right-hand seat appeared to be badly injured and was moaning, but the driver, Agent Dunne, seemed merely stunned.

"Car bomb," he said, between breaths. "Caught us broadside. No chance."

"Are you all right?"

"Yeah. Think so. Kelleter took some metal. He's bleeding."

Kreski could hear nearing sirens, approaching from both directions. Georgetown Hospital was not far. He touched Agent Kelleter's shoulder and looked into his face. The man looked back, nodding, then groaned.

The director stood up. "Where's Perkins?" he asked.

"He was driving the limousine," Dunne said. "I guess he bought the farm."

Kreski looked back to the blackened, flame-flickered form framed by the twisted windshield of the limousine. Now there were two Manuel Huertas.

13

Dresden needed to rest his travel-weary body and too slowly healing injuries, and also to take a careful look around him. If he was correct that Charlene's killers were not pursuing him, a great many police agencies surely were. He was extremely lucky to have gotten as far as he had.

He was in St. Louis, at a downtown hotel where he hoped to find a working television set, and a reasonable expectation of not getting rolled or murdered during the night, but one cheap and nondescript enough to avoid credit card routines and eyebrows raised at the roustabout clothing he had acquired on the road. His only request was for a room with a view of the street, and it was granted without comment. The hostelry was not one to attract conventions, and the mailboxes behind the elderly desk clerk were filled with keys. Dresden's room proved to be small and dank, but the television did function and the window overlooked the hotel's entrance, dismal vista as that was.

He dropped his bag in the closet, leaving the Magnum in it. His other pistol he carried in his belt at his back. His money was in his boots and the videotapes and voice prints in the deep pockets of the army surplus field jacket he had bought in Amarillo. He had also bought some army-issue gloves. The cold was probably normal for the Midwest, but he found it numbing.

An hour's limping amble about downtown St. Louis's scruffier streets produced no sign of anyone who seemed interested in him except for a couple of shivering prostitutes and a slowly moving police car that hesitated only briefly before continuing on. He paid it no apparent attention, though it made his back turn wet with sweat. Finally, he made his way to a more respectable district, took a decent meal in a coffee shop, and bought some newspapers. He also, without much guilt, bought a fifth of Early Times.

The newspapers were full of stories about the bombing in Washington that had killed the vice president's wife. The *Chicago Tribune* had pages and pages of them, including a short but very gracefully written biography of Mrs. Atherton. She was near Dresden's age, had grown up in Carmel, and was a graduate student at Stanford at about the time Charley had been dating a girl there. He wondered if he had ever met Mrs. Atherton when she was young. The accompanying photograph was of a beautiful woman, but it did not jar his memory.

He turned back to the front page again, and the three-column photograph of the wreckage of the vice president's limousine. The bodies had been removed by the time the picture had been taken, but it was wrenchingly apparent what must have happened to the victims.

He now had a bond with the vice president of the United States of America, a bond of the most intimate and terrible sort. Two women, dead, by the same hand.

There was nothing about himself in any of the Midwest papers. Journalistic interest in the Tiburcio murders appeared to have ended at the California line. The *Los Angeles Times* had run a long story under the headline: "Ad Exec Sought in Double Murder." Mrs. Mercredes was quoted calling him a violent man with a love of guns. Dresden had several times suppressed an urge to telephone one of his California friends. He began to wish he had not sent Tracy away, though he could not be certain she had actually gone. A quick call— just long enough to hear her voice if she answered—would tell. He looked to the old black dial telephone on the night table.

It was too dangerous. Everything was too dangerous. He dialed. It rang seven times. There was no answer.

He limped to the television set. It was time for the television news.

They were showing footage now many hours old of the smouldering auto wreckage on the bridge. Mrs. Atherton's remains, encased mummylike in an orange-colored body bag, were seen trundled away on a wheeled stretcher through the glare of television lights to an ambulance. With sirens wailing and warbling constantly in the background, police, detectives, Secret Service agents, FBI, even soldiers armed with automatic weapons, swarmed everywhere as the cameras and lights swept back and forth. Helicopters rattled overhead. The director of the Secret Service, looking both furious and tearful, refused questions. Other officials tried to push reporters away. A badly wounded Secret Service agent was limbered past the battery of television lights and a hand reached out angrily and smashed the camera's view into darkness when it focused too closely on the injured man's stricken face. There were shouts, more sirens, more helicopters.

They cut to a sudden, jarring shot of a hotel doorway, which Dresden quickly recognized as the one former President Reagan had exited from before being shot some years before. From it came Vice President Atherton, his handsome face ugly with grief. The glimpse of him was brief. He vanished behind the dark forms of Secret Service agents and into his car. The news anchor, if somberly, boasted that this footage was exclusive. They ran it again.

After a commercial for a line of Japanese cars, a White House correspondent did a standup report with the Executive Mansion unusually distant in the background. As she explained, the Secret Service had permanently closed Pennsylvania Avenue from 17th Street to 15th Street, and had set up a barbed-wire perimeter around LaFayette Square. All public tours of the White House, the correspondent dramatically announced, had been permanently canceled.

A sudden loud crash sent Dresden leaping clumsily from his chair to press himself against the wall. The sudden sound had come from the street. He pulled his revolver from its place in his belt and peered around the drapes, exposing just the edge of his face. An old ironbound stake truck, laden with junk, was thumping along the pavement. It had struck a deep depression in the concrete opposite the hotel entrance.

He had forgotten about cities, real, gritty midwestern cities. Letting his breathing subside, he returned to his chair, his attention at once snatched back by the television screen. There was videotape footage of the president speaking, expressing his sorrow at Mrs. Atherton's death and his deep affection for her and her husband, his faithful right hand.

It had been three weeks since the Gettysburg shooting. It was nearly Christmas.

*   *   *

Kreski had once more sought the late-night solace of his living room, but there was no classical music on the stereo. His eyes were fixed on his television set. He had tuned to the continuous news broadcast of the Cable News Network, and what he was watching was his own professional death. In deference to the others in the house at this late hour, he had kept the volume at a barely audible level, but it would not have mattered had he turned the sound off entirely. Every image that appeared on the screen imparted the same message: The Secret Service was guilty of catastrophic failure, and that failure was Walter Kreski's.

His wife, as he feared, and yet hoped, entered the room, tying her robe.

"I'm sorry," he said. "I didn't mean to wake you. I turned the volume . . ."

"You didn't wake me," she said, putting her hand gently on his shoulder. "I've been awake since I went to bed. I've just been waiting for you to join me. When you didn't after all this time, I decided I'd better join you."

Kreski stared at the flickering colors of the screen.

"We accomplished one thing tonight," he said. "We established that the van with the bomb was parked on the bridge exactly five minutes before Mrs. Atherton's car left the Hilton. We have witnesses who passed the spot just before the van was parked and just after. We have the time down exactly. Whoever did it was given precise information from someone at the hotel."

"Not very precise, Walter. They didn't know the vice president wasn't in the car."

"No, but they knew Perkins was. Perkins was the target. That lovely woman died because of one of my agents, because someone turned him, and was now trying to effect some damage control. Perkins was the key to the Gettysburg shooting. I don't have proof. Not yet. No proof of anything. But it fits like a box. I'm quite sure Perkins was the 'second gun' at Gettysburg. He was on a competition rifle team in the army. According to his two-o-one file, he could fire one shot for windage and then empty an entire magazine into a bull's-eye at a thousand meters. A thousand meters! I'm amazed the president's alive."

His eyes were on the television screen but his mind was elsewhere. His wife, watching his expression carefully, waited.

"They beat us, Babs," he said. "They got through us. I don't know if they were Latins or Russians or homegrown traitors, but they penetrated us. We did our best, we followed all the right procedures, but they beat us and almost killed the president and vice president of the United States." He coughed. It served to distract from the catch in his voice, and his near tears. "But Babs, I'm close to something now. I think I can trace it back to them. I . . ."

She took his hand, knowing what was coming next.

"No point," he said. "All irrelevant. All moot. They beat us, and they beat me. . . ." He sighed. "Babs, I'm going to get the sack."

"Walter, I knew that was going to happen just as soon as I heard about poor Mrs. Atherton."

He gripped her hand tightly. "I'm to see the attorney general at ten tomorrow morning." He looked at his watch. "This morning. His secretary didn't state the reason for the meeting, but it's obvious. And I checked with some people. I'm to resign at once, pension or no. There'll be wholesale transfers of practically everyone in the White House detail and the Washington field office. The new director will be Marv Jellicoe of the San Francisco office. The vice president's known him for some years. Atherton ordered all this. I don't blame him. If it was my wife, if it was you, I'd fire me too. I'd probably kill me."

"Walter," she said, "it's not the end of the world. You can go to work with my brother anytime you want. And if you don't want to live in Florida, you can do something else. Frank Holcomb called up this afternoon. He said that, whatever happens, you're to consider the offer he made to you six months ago still open, and you're to name your own salary."

Holcomb was president of one of the largest branch banking chains in Virginia. The job he had offered Kreski was vice president for personnel management and security.

"That's very kind of him."

"He didn't mean it as charity. You happen to be very good at your work. For heaven's sake, didn't *Time* magazine call you the best Secret Service director in memory?"

"They called me the 'most intellectual.' And that's a crock. They were just impressed by my taste in music. I was probably listening to Berlioz when I approved the advance plans for Gettysburg."

"Walt. What I'm trying to get across to you is that Frank Holcomb is your friend. You have lots and lots of friends, all over the country. There are a lot of people who are on your side in this."

"What's on my side in this is Mrs. Atherton's dead body."

"Walter. If I didn't know you better I'd say you were feeling sorry for yourself. And that's something I've never seen before."

"Okay. Forgive me."

"Forgive yourself, and whatever happens tomorrow, let's get on with our lives. There's a lot of happiness out there, a lot of future. You don't have to take that job with Frank Holcomb. We don't have to stay here, though I certainly wouldn't mind. But there are all kinds of things we can do."

"I'll call Frank. In a few weeks, maybe a few months, I'll probably gratefully accept his offer. But at the moment, there's only one job I'm interested in. The job I have now. I want to finish it. I want all this over with. I want the killings to stop. Babs, I'm going to have to clean out my office tomorrow. What if two days after I walk out of there the president gets it for good, or it's Atherton himself who gets blown up?"

"That would be horrible, but there'd be nothing you could do about it."

"That's the problem. There's a hell of a lot I could do about it, that I can do about it right now. With Steve Copley's help, I'm convinced we can shut these people down. But all I have left is a few hours."

His wife took his hand in both of hers, turning slightly on the couch to look directly at him. "I was once asked by a reporter from the *Washington Post* if you had any faults, Walter Kreski. I, of course, said you didn't, except perhaps when you forget to pick up your socks. But that's what your fault is. You're faultless. You simply won't accept fault. You won't accept it that anything could go otherwise than the way you planned it. You Secret Service people have this wonderful deity complex. Only you have the power to prevent death. The president's life is your sacred trust. If something goes wrong, and somebody gets hurt, then it's the Apocalypse. I think you're the most wonderful man on this planet. But I don't think you're God. God doesn't leave His socks on the bedroom carpet."

He smiled.

"You did your best, Walt. You're being treated unfairly. A lot of people are. We're going through a horrible time. You did your best. You did right. You have a terrific record. Accept it. Let Marv Jellicoe have his try. And let's move on to the rest of our lives."

She rose, and then kissed his forehead.

"I think I got through to you."

He smiled, less sadly this time. "You always do."

When she was gone he returned his thoughts directly to where they had been before she had joined him—to a pondering of his agency's personnel list, to a mental examination of his department's defenses in search of the weak spot where they'd been penetrated, where rot, corruption, or treachery had burned their way through. Marv Jellicoe or not, fired or not, he was going to resolve this.

Bushy Ambrose was waiting at the edge of the floodlit helipad, wearing nothing warmer than a suit despite the December night's bitter mountain cold, his legs spread slightly apart and his arms folded. The helicopter appeared as a tiny light in the north sky, an oddly moving star. Ambrose tilted his head back to watch the machine's approach. It was as though he were commanding it to come to him, to pull it to Earth.

C.D. Bragg was at his side. On this trip, he had sent Jerry Greene and David Callister. The latter was beginning to make him very nervous. He was spending entirely too much time in New York.

"They're burying Mrs. Atherton Wednesday," Bragg said.

"I know. Shawcross called this afternoon."

"Are you going to go?"

"Negative. I don't think the vice president would appreciate my presence," Ambrose said, "and I wouldn't leave here in any case. The members of the cabinet will go—except for the secretary of defense, and Jim Malcom. We still have Central America to worry about."

"Should I go?"

"Where?"

The helicopter's light was a great glare in their eyes, a seeming visual manifestation of the machine's now near deafening roar.

"To California!" shouted Bragg. "To the funeral!"

"Hell no! I need you here!"

Ambrose wondered what had possibly entered Bragg's mind. Like everyone else, he had been up on this mountain too long. There was such a long time yet to go.

The helicopter settled gently to the ground, the pilot killing the engine the instant the skids touched the surface of the helipad. As it subsided in a chuffing whine, Jerry Greene scrambled out, carrying a very large briefcase. No one came out after him.

"Where's Callister?" Ambrose said, as Greene approached.

"He decided to stay in New York."

"You were there to prevent such decisions," Ambrose said.

"He has a lunch with his publisher tomorrow," Greene said. "He thinks his wife is getting suspicious about what's going on up here. He said she'd really think it funny if he stood up his publisher. They meet for lunch every month come what may."

"Bullshit," Ambrose said. "He's just tired of pulling this duty. Not enough pâté de fois gras up here."

"Maybe so, but he was a big help," Greene said, lifting up the briefcase. "Thanks to him we got everything we needed. No muss, no fuss."

"How high up did you have to go?" Ambrose asked.

"Not high at all, thanks to Callister," Greene said. "The only one we dealt with was a studio librarian. He turned on so much charm I don't think she paid any attention to what we were after. We were out of there in an hour. I was afraid we'd have to go out to that warehouse they have in New Jersey."

"If you were out of there in an hour," said Ambrose, "why are you getting back this late?"

"More chopped liver," said Greene. "And a case of rock 'n' rye."

"Rock 'n' rye?" said Ambrose.

"He claims it's good for his throat," said Greene. "We've got to do something about that voice."

They started up the walk toward Ambrose's cabin.

"Are you going out to California for Mrs. Atherton's funeral?" Greene asked.

"Does no one around here think?" Ambrose said. "Of course not. There's no point in irritating the vice president, and that's all I'd do. We're up here to serve and protect the president. That's why we never leave."

"Almost never," Greene said.

"When Atherton comes back he's going to have to hole up too," said Bragg.

"Yes," said Ambrose. "I think it's finally dawned on him how dangerous the situation is."

"Observatory Hill isn't very easy to protect," Bragg said.

"Unfortunately, that's not where he plans to hole up," said Ambrose. "He said it's too painful being in the house where he and his wife were so happy."

"When he was home," Greene said.

"Where's he going?" Bragg said. "Out to that National Park Service retreat in the Shenandoah?"

"No such luck," said Ambrose. "Until further notice, the vice president of the United States is going to live in the White House."

14

Dresden arrived in Washington wearing his suit. The Federal City was a formal place, and he didn't want to look in any way out of the ordinary, though in the seedy bus terminal and seedier surrounding neighborhood he looked so presentable he drew glances, as though he were a government official, or a mark for a mugging. Pausing only to choose a hotel from the Yellow Pages and make a room reservation from a public phone, he hurried west into a more respectable district, where he could deal with his most immediate need: new clothes, most particularly a warm, lined trenchcoat; decent gloves; and the sort of dark, pin-striped suit that he had seen so many congressmen and White House officials wear on the Sunday morning television talk shows. For an extra fifty dollars the haberdasher he found on Connecticut Avenue agreed to have the alterations on the suit completed by the following morning.

The hotel he chose for himself was the best in Washington, the palatial Willard, just around the corner from the White House. It was not the sort of place one would expect to harbor a desperate fugitive from the hills of California.

Checking in, he made what could prove either a very smart or extremely foolish decision. Defying the instincts that had guided him all the way across the country, he registered under his own name, using his only remaining credit card, a revolving charge card from one of California's larger banks. He had been wise enough to keep up the monthly interest payments. The desk clerk treated it—and him— routinely. If Dresden had put down a large cash deposit, he would have marked himself in the man's memory. His calculations now all had to be based on presumptions. He presumed that the police would not be checking every hotel registry in the country; that they would not have expected him to travel three thousand miles to this place just five blocks from the FBI building. In St. Louis he had been too much the paranoid desperado, costumed like a drifter on the run. He meant to spend some time here in Washington, and to do so he must be the substantial citizen. All substantial citizens used credit cards.

His elegant room was a startling surprise. It overlooked not only Pennsylvania Avenue but, just beyond the rooftop of the Treasury building, the White House itself, the view centering on a curved, half-moon window that was part of the president's third-floor family quarters in the East Wing.

It was darkened, and rightly so. The president was dead.

Dresden waited for several minutes after the bellman had departed, then left himself. He needed freedom, needed to walk. His injuries still pained him, but he found the exercise good therapy, each outing extending the time and distance he was able to walk.

There were armed guards in the side doorway of the Treasury building. Concrete barricades topped with barbed wire extended all the way across Pennsylvania Avenue, with uniformed police and men in civilian overcoats stationed behind them. A block beyond, parked in front of the White House, was a turreted armored personnel carrier equipped with what looked to be machine guns and a small cannon. Dresden took all this in with a few quick glances, but otherwise paid them little apparent attention.

He felt like shouting, bellowing his defiance at his faceless, ruthless enemy till the sound echoed off the marble facades of all these symbols of government, the supposed government of the people. But this was the impulse of the aging youth he had been in California. He had changed. As he had loved Charlene, as he had loved his wildness and freedom, now he loved vengeance.

With limping swagger, he swung about and started a long walk toward the Capitol.

The skies were lowering and gray, but they had been so all day, and there had been no rain. It seemed God's contribution to the funeral—ambience without interference. It was cold, but that was fitting. Watching Special Agent Calvin Perkins's earthly remains put to rest in the sacred ground of Arlington Cemetery was a chilling moment for Walter Kreski. He would not deny, he did not resent the man's honorable gravesite. Perkins had won the Silver Star in Vietnam and probably deserved better for his courageous deed, saving the lives of four of his comrades, risking his own four separate times to do so. What Kreski resented was the man's death and his everlasting silence.

Even if Perkins still lived, there would be little Kreski could do to make him reveal his secrets. Kreski was now a common, ordinary, powerless citizen. He had a vestigial importance for the remainder of this somber ceremony. But at its conclusion he would descend this hill of yellow winter grass and white crosses and disappear into the Metro subway, just another man in a raincoat.

His thoughts had drifted. The report of the rifles of the honor guard startled him. As his head snapped up, his eyes caught the gaze of the vice president opposite him across the small dark square into which the coffin had been lowered. The vice president's eyes held so much grief and commiseration. Kreski had felt a duty to tell Atherton of his suspicions, his hard evidence and strong belief, concerning Perkins. But he had held back. The man had been told too many terrible things in too short a time. It would gain no good to tell him more. Steve Copley, who stood at the vice president's side, had agreed.

Perkins' widow, a small blond woman wearing large tinted glasses, had been given the folded flag. The ceremony was over. Some began to drift away. Most waited at a respectful distance for their turn to speak a few words to her. Kreski waited also, but all he could bring himself to do was touch her shoulder. She reached and touched his hand, but looked away. There could be a dozen reasons why she avoided his eyes, including the worst. It was pointless to speculate. This poor woman would now be gone from his life. He tightened his grip briefly, hoping she would take it as an expression of sympathy rather than pity, then stepped away. Copley caught up with him partway down the slope.

"You're a dutiful man, Walt. Coming here."

"It's an obligation that goes with the job, even though I no longer have the job."

They walked a moment in silence.

"I argued with the attorney general and Shawcross about that,"

Copley said finally. "But the Congress was screaming for blood. The vice president had no choice."

"I understand that."

"He didn't want to do it. He really didn't."

"That's good to know. There was something of that in his face just now."

"Ambrose concurred in the decision. In the president's name. Did you get to speak to Perkins, before the bombing?"

"Not a word."

"Damn."

"Indeed."

"We're going to go full press, Walt. We're going to turn this town upside down."

"Start with my agency."

"We have."

"And the White House. Shake it good."

"We're doing that too, Walt. And Camp David."

"That won't be easy."

"I've got men in there."

They had reached the parking lot at the bottom of the hill. A tourist bus moved slowly by.

"What are you going to do?" Copley asked.

"I'm going to go to work for a bank. But not for a while. For the time being, I'm just going to rest and think."

"You have that coming."

"I suppose I do."

"If there's anything we can do. Ever. Any of us. Just ask."

"Consider that reciprocal."

They shook hands, Copley reaching to grip Kreski's forearm.

"I wish we could make it be a month ago, and tell the president not to go to Gettysburg."

"So do I."

They looked at each other, but said nothing more. Kreski turned and walked off toward the subway entrance. Somehow, this conversation had brought a finality to everything. His job was truly gone. That Copley still had his, that he still had full powers to pursue the investigation, emphasized this as nothing else could—nothing else save seeing Marv Jellicoe sitting at his desk.

Near the subway entrance, a tourist came up to Kreski and asked for directions to the Kennedy graves. As Kreski turned and pointed the way up the hill, the man spoke again, with lowered voice.

"Mr. Brookes wants to see you, urgently," he said. "Get off at the Rosslyn stop. There will be a blue Buick sedan parked around the corner. He'll be in the back."

Kreski simply stared.

"It's important," the man said. "He wants to help." He looked up the hill in the direction Kreski had pointed, then smiled. "Thanks a lot."

Kreski moved on quickly, not looking back. He had had no intention of getting off at Rosslyn, but when the conductor called out the stop, he found himself almost leaping from his seat and hurrying up the escalator from the platform. Peter Ashley Brookes was better than nothing, and nothing was all the government of the United States had left him.

The car pulled away from the curb the instant Kreski had slid into the rear seat and shut the door. The driver moved into the traffic flow heading toward Key Bridge and Georgetown just across the Potomac, but on the other side, he abruptly spun the wheel left. He followed M Street to the Canal Road intersection, completed a skidding U-turn, sped back to the Key Bridge, and in a minute or so was on the Virginia side heading down the ramp to the George Washington Parkway.

"The road's clean, Mr. Brookes," he said, with a final glance at the rearview mirror.

"Thank you for coming, Kreski," Brookes said. "I wasn't at all certain you would."

The man's eerie eyes seemed just as crystalline in the shadowy interior of the car as they had been in the light.

"To tell you the truth, neither was I."

"I need your help."

"Your man said you wanted to help us."

"Help you. No one else. I'll get to that later."

"What is it you need from me?"

"They're trying to pin this on me," Brookes said.

"I think you're exaggerating."

"They're planting evidence. A yellow flag with 'La Puño' on it turned up at one of our encampments in Florida. I've made sweeps. They've bugged my telephone system. They've tried to access my computer system."

"Who do you mean by 'they'?"

"You tell me."

"I haven't the faintest idea. The appropriate agencies are pursuing an investigation. Ever since the vice president's wife was killed, they've been pursuing it hard. If they're making it difficult for you, I'm sorry, but these are very bad times."

"Kreski, I said they're dropping little yellow flags. I want it stopped. I want you to help me stop it."

The driver moved the speed up to sixty-five, even though the limit was fifty. He must have known the road. The upper reaches of the Parkway had only four access ramps. Police were scarce, and some motorists indulged themselves with seventy or better, many of them from the Central Intelligence Agency upriver at Langley, which had its own private access ramp.

"I'm a private citizen, Mr. Brookes. An out-of-work private citizen. I can't stop or start anything."

"Yes, you can. You can find out who's behind the shooting of the president, and get everyone off my ass. I've been doing everything I can to help this administration from the very beginning, and I'm not going to have it dump on me for an easy out from this assassination mess. I'm a fucking patriot, Kreski. There aren't many of us."

"Mr. Brookes. Until a few days ago I was director of the United States Secret Service. I was working in full cooperation with the Federal Bureau of Investigation and a dozen other police agencies. We were getting absolutely nowhere. And now you're asking me to go out on my own and solve everything, when I no longer even have a permit to carry a gun."

"You weren't getting absolutely nowhere, Kreski. You were getting somewhere. They were just a couple of steps ahead of you. And when I said 'they' were trying to pin this on me before, I sure as hell was including the Federal Bureau of Investigation."

"I can't think of anyone more clean in this. It's my agency that was dirty. I'm sure one of my agents was involved at Gettysburg. He was killed along with Mrs. Atherton. Since then, Director Copley has been coming down hard on everything. If that includes you because of Huerta's having your book and magazine, I'm sorry. Believe it or not, he's coming down just as hard on the White House staff."

"That's bullshit, but it's beside the point. I agree with you that you're not going to accomplish anything here. I'm not a stupid man, Kreski. I want you to go down to Central America. There's a lot to learn there—about Huerta, about what went down. I've got people in five countries down there. We can be a lot of help."

"If there's so much to learn, why don't you just find out for yourselves?"

"I want you to find out for yourself. I want you to believe, Kreski. And then I want you to come back and tell the country. The Congress may have hung you out to dry, but you've got twenty years of credibility in the United States of America and there's a lot of that left. Whatever you find out, whatever you believe, you can make others believe."

Kreski simply shook his head. They were passing the McLean-Chain Bridge Road exit. The CIA's was coming up. For a moment, Kreski wondered if Brookes would have them turn off there, if that was his home away from home while in Washington. Admiral Elmore was one of the most blunt and direct men in government when he chose to speak out, but he could also be oblique—damned oblique.

"Mr. Brookes. This is probably the strangest conversation I've had in my entire career."

"Kreski, I'll level with you. I'm a strange man."

Kreski said nothing. Brookes startled him with a sudden reach to the floor of the car, but he pulled forth only a briefcase. Snapping it open, he took out an envelope, and set it on the seat between them.

"I said I wanted to help. If you go into Central America, here's help—ten thousand dollars."

"For God's sake, Brookes. You're bribing a federal officer."

Now Brookes smiled. "As you just said, you're not a federal anything anymore. This is a retainer. Expenses will be heavy down there. You may need every cent of this."

Kreski stared at the envelope, but did not touch it. "Ten thousand dollars. It works out to exactly the same amount that turned up in Huerta's strongbox."

Brookes swore and reached back into the briefcase. He dropped a sheaf of bills, held together with a rubber band, onto the seat beside the envelope. Then he reached into his pocket and dropped some change there too.

"All right. There's $11,000.52—a nice odd number. Nothing for the damn FBI to seize upon as another 'coincidental' clue."

"I can't touch it," Kreski said.

"Yes, you can. Look, I'm used to working with the federal government, at least in this administration. I don't know how to work against it. I don't know how to deal with its working against me. I need you, Kreski."

They sped by the CIA exit doing at least seventy-five. The next exit would be the last, the Capital Beltway.

Brookes shoved the money closer. "And I'm all you've got, Kreski. You're not done with this, are you? You're not going to go out of office with your ass kicked in for something you didn't do. You want what I want."

"Let me think about it."

"Take as long as you want, as long as it isn't longer than a couple of days. And take the money. If you don't want to throw in with me, send it back. But I want your decision to involve some overt action. Send this back or get on an airplane. I'm not going to let you just slide away into the shadows. I want you to think about this. I'm not going to let you out of this car without the money."

"Unless you plan to shoot me, how are you going to accomplish that?"

"All right. I'll just mail you the money. Maybe they're watching your mailbox too. Maybe they, whoever in the hell they are, would be just as happy to pin this on both of us. Like you said, it was your agency that was dirty."

Kreski stared into Brookes's ghostly, expressionless eyes, then looked down at the money.

"Very well," he said, placing everything including the fifty-two cents in change in his pocket. "I'll get back to you. One way or the other."

Brookes's arguments were persuasive, but Kreski felt he had just stepped into a rubber boat on a wild, rushing river.

By the early December nightfall, Dresden's mood had utterly changed, the triumphant feeling of defiance become one of frustration and loneliness. He may have succeeded in placing himself in the midst of his enemy, but as he passed the armed policemen, as he glanced at the faces looking at his, that fact had become a source chiefly of fear. In the darkness the federal office buildings seemed even larger, monstrous and ominous. He had walked and sat and pondered, but his mind had proved incapable of any sensible plan or idea, every possible course of action seemingly leading only to his likely capture, arrest, and doom.

Returning to his hotel, he found the thought of his empty room also depressing, but he had to rest his leg. There was a restaurant up the street. He went first to its bar, carefully and painfully propping his leg over the empty stool beside him. Two Manhattans offered some cheer. He made himself eat a substantial meal, which warmed him, but its solitary consumption saddened him, especially when he paid the bill, using money that belonged to Charlene, that she should now be spending.

Still unwilling to return to his hotel room, he headed up 15th Street past the heavily armed barricades again, this time proceeding north and west until he came to DuPont Circle and one of the few districts in Washington that resembled a real city. Despite the cold, street musicians were playing in the park. Couples walked by, hand in hand. A panhandler approached him, a grizzled old man. On a whim, Charley gave him a twenty-dollar bill, thinking Charlene might be pleased. Startled, the man was speechless. Feeling pleased himself, Dresden moved on, lest the fellow decide to attach himself. He passed a policeman, who paid him no attention whatsoever.

On the other side of the Circle, following Massachusetts Avenue into the district known as Embassy Row, he found his depression returning. Here resided more power and authority, sinister because of its foreign nature, haunting because of the gloomy old mansions that housed it. His leg began to bother him again, but the pain served to drive him on.

At last he came to what he'd been seeking, the long bridge with blackened pavement and sidewalk—police sawhorses with small flashing yellow lights set in front of the empty space in the concrete railing.

Here his enemy had struck as they had struck at him, only with more viciousness and violence. He stood gazing into the darkness of the deep ravine the bridge traversed, a curving road winding below. They were out there, somewhere, everywhere. If they could reach out to kill the vice president of the United States, how safe could he be? How safe could anyone in the country be? They may have been the ones who shot the president, or maybe they were the president's men. For all his theories and beliefs, he could not say for certain who they were. That was a source of their power.

The flashing yellow lights were reflecting off his trenchcoat. Standing in this now notorious place, he would be dramatically visible to every passing motorist, a man in a raincoat, intermittently illuminated with a golden glow.

His limp worsening, he kept walking. In time he came to an odd complex of huge old Georgian and modern office structures, encompassed by a high wrought-iron fence, windows ablaze with light. It was the British Embassy. Farther on, around a curve in the road, a gate marked with floodlit ships' anchors and many armed men proclaimed the Vice President's House. Dresden wanted to pause a moment, to speak a few silent words of sympathy and shared grief to the house at the top of the hill, but he dared not. The armed men were already watching him.

On the way back, he stopped at a liquor store on Pennsylvania Avenue a few blocks from his hotel and he bought a fifth of Jack Daniels Black. Once returned to his room, he rang room service for ice. As he waited, he stood at his window, sipping some of the whiskey neat and warm.

There was something troubling. That half-moon window on the third floor of the White House was now brightly lit.

There was a knock at the door. Expecting only a bellman, he forgot the pistol in his belt at his back. Opening the door, he was quickly reminded. There was a man with a stern face and a neat dark suit. He held up a black leather case, letting it drop open to reveal a most official-looking badge.

"Secret Service," the man said.

15

Dresden stood speechless, fighting to hold back any sign of the terror that possessed him, struggling to look merely startled. Questions without answers raced through his mind. What if the man stepped into the room? How could he hide the pistol at his back? Would he have to use it? Could he?

The agent made a visual examination of the room with quick glances, but remained at the doorway.

"Sorry, sir," he said, with no real courtesy in his hard, flat voice. "But these upper floors were to have been cleared this afternoon. You'll have to leave."

"I've been out all day," said Dresden, amazed at the calmness of his reply. "No one told me."

He supposed that, after all, he might look a fairly normal business traveler—standing there in stocking feet, with tie askew, shirtsleeves rolled up and a glass of whiskey in his hand. His new briefcase was on top of the dresser, beside some newspapers. All the scene required was a copy of *Penthouse* or *Playboy*.

"They should have told you at the desk. Anyway, you'll have to move out at once."

Dresden decided a touch of indignation was in order, if he could muster it. He took a deep breath.

"Just where am I supposed to go? Do you know what time it is?"

"The hotel may have other rooms available on the lower floors. You may have to go somewhere else. That's not our concern. We just want all the rooms on these floors cleared. Now."

"What's this all about?"

The agent gave him a contemptuous look. "Security." He pocketed his badge, lingering a moment. Dresden feared the man would stand there in the open door until he was packed and ready to go.

"Let me go to the john, will you?" Dresden said. "I'll be out of here in a couple of minutes."

The agent hesitated, then grimaced, and moved away down the hall. Dresden closed the door quickly. He was packed, with both pistols rolled in his dirty laundry, and fully dressed in five minutes. He flushed the toilet, in case the agent was at the door listening. Then he left, frowning at every security agent he encountered. There were many.

The desk clerk, apologetic, offered him a room on the fourth floor, overlooking Fourteenth Street. Dresden, expressing weariness and resignation, nodded acceptance. He would check out the next day and find a place farther from the prowls of the Secret Service. To do so now might look too suspicious. So much of everything he did now seemed suspicious.

Dresden slept little that night, keeping his smaller pistol beneath the pillow beside him. The next morning he moved to the Embassy Row Hotel just up Massachusetts Avenue from DuPont Circle, having remembered it from the previous night's long walk. It was at the juncture of a variety of neighborhoods—rich and poor, bohemian and professional, drug culture and straight. Brer Rabbit had his choice of briar patches. There was even a Metro subway station just at the corner, should a more distant hiding place suddenly become necessary.

Checking his bag and briefcase, he took the Metro to a public library where he'd been told he could find out-of-town telephone books. His choice was the Manhattan Yellow Pages, and the listings for theatrical agents. He noted the names and numbers of some of the larger agencies—enough for a thoroughgoing start. Then he went to pick up his new suit at the Connecticut Avenue shop. When he returned to the hotel a room was ready for him, a very elegant one.

First there were a great many telephone calls to make to New York. There were three entertainers who did first-rate impersonations of President Henry Hampton. The best, or at least funniest, was Reggie Sands. As Vaughan Meader had been John F. Kennedy, and Rich Little had been Richard Nixon and Ronald Reagan, Sands was Henry Hampton, his caricature a perfect rendering of the president as stuffy antebellum Virginia gentleman with a flair for rhetorical excess. The next best was Bobby Dandridge, who gave a more rollicksome impression of Hampton made all the funnier by the fact that Dandridge was black. The most technically perfect mimicry of Hampton Dresden had ever heard was by a comic named Howie King, but he suffered from the fact that he apparently wrote his own material and it wasn't very good.

Dresden started with Sands, calling a major talent agency that, as he expected, didn't handle Sands but was able to refer him quickly to the agency that did. With his call there, Dresden penetrated no further than a woman assistant. Posing as the programming chief of a major Bay Area independent television station owned by a large communications conglomerate, Dresden said his group was planning to put together an hour variety special for syndication and wanted Sands as one of the headliners.

The assistant treated him as though he were a gas station operator who had inquired if Sands might be interested in a weekend job.

"Mr. Sands is already under contract with NBC," she said. "And he's in Las Vegas through New Year's. Who did you say you are?"

He reexplained, asking if she might recommend any impressionist as good as Sands at doing characters like the president. She was insulted, saying there was no one in Sands's league, but suggested the names of Bobby Dandridge and Howie King as good second-raters and someone named Frankie Ford as a last resort. Dresden thanked her, trying to sound as blasé as possible.

Charley was certain it could not be Reggie Sands. He was too much a star, too recognizable, and had performed at fund-raisers for Hampton's opponent in the presidential election. Still, in the insanity that had descended upon the nation in the last month, anything was possible. Dresden made some calls to Las Vegas. Sands was, indeed, appearing there, twice nightly.

Dandridge's agent was friendly enough, reporting that the comedian was working in Atlantic City, but he became not a little hostile at the suggestion that Dandridge might be interested in doing a President Hampton routine. "I can't think of anything that would be in worse taste right now, can you?" he said.

He was right, of course. At this juncture, nothing could sink a black comedian's career quicker, or deeper. Unless the performance were given entirely in private, in a Camp David recording studio.

But a call to Atlantic City confirmed Dandridge's booking there. The resort manager even complained that Dandridge had already won more than twenty thousand dollars at the blackjack and craps tables.

Next, Dresden tried the number he'd been given for Howie King's agent. There was no answer. The call to Frankie Ford's agent was answered almost instantly, and not by the agent but by Ford himself. He said he had a three-day gig at a Holiday Inn in Toledo, but was free after that and would be out on the coast as soon as Dresden could send him a ticket. Charley, who was using the name Larry Costa, said he would double-check the audition schedule and get right back to him.

It was clear the president's recording team was not using Frankie Ford. It was something of a wonder that the Holiday Inn in Toledo was.

Howie King's agent still did not answer on Dresden's next attempt. He read through the morning *Washington Post* for a few minutes, then tried again, and then again. This time he connected. Dresden went through the full Larry Costa routine, making a significant addition. He mentioned a specific amount of money. He guessed that, even as a second-rater, Howie King probably made a fair income from nightclub work and would want at least fifty thousand dollars to appear in a syndicated television special. Dresden offered thirty-five thousand and waited for the agent to commence haggling. To no avail.

"When did you say you'd want him?" the agent said.

"We tape next month."

"Couldn't promise you a thing."

"I'll make it forty-five thousand. It's only two days' work, after all."

"I don't care if you make it a million. Howie's not available."

"You mean he has other commitments?"

"Don't I wish. I mean he's not working. He's on vacation."

"When will he be back?"

"He didn't say. He just left a message on my answering machine a couple of weeks ago saying he'd been working too hard and needed to take a break. Just like that. Haven't heard from him since."

"Look, we'd really like him for this show. We'll make it fifty thousand dollars. That's the most I can budget."

"And I wouldn't accept a penny less, Mr. Costa, but I'm not kidding. Howie took a powder. Maybe he's been on the road too long. Or maybe it's his health. He was coming down with a cold or something."

"A cold? You mean he was getting hoarse?"

"What?"

"Hoarse. Coughing. There's a lot of that going around."

"Yeah, he was a little."

To himself, Charley said "Bingo!" To the agent, he said: "That was a couple of weeks ago, you said. I'm sure it's cleared up by now."

"You'd think, but I haven't heard a word. Yours isn't the only offer I've had to turn down. I've tried to reach him myself. Tried his apartment here; his place out in Hampton Bays. Tried his hangouts. He likes Miami. I tried around there, but nobody's seen him."

"Well, I'm sorry it's not going to work out," Dresden said. "Thanks anyway."

"Wait a minute, Mr. Costa," said the agent. "Give me your number and if he shows up in the next few days I'll get back to you."

"I'm on the road myself," Charley said. "I'll call you in a few days. Let's hope he appears. We'd really love to talk to him."

Dresden hung up. He knew perfectly well where Howie King was, and it certainly wasn't Miami. He was at Camp David, performing regularly—at least with his voice. All Dresden had to do now was prove it.

But that wasn't all. There were other questions he had to answer. It was a month now since the assassination attempt. How much longer did they intend to do this? And why?

The *Washington Post*, he knew, was not about to open its clip files to just anyone who walked in off the street. But there was another resource in Washington that contained newspaper files from all over the country—the Library of Congress.

Dresden identified himself as a free-lance writer preparing an article on the assassination attempt. The files on President Hampton's illnesses and hospitalizations had apparently been much examined in recent days.

He signed for the files with his own name. He was beginning to be a little cocky about that. But he made a great pose of taking copious notes from the clips, despite the swiftness with which he was able to obtain all the information he needed. President Hampton had previously been hospitalized three times—the latter two occasions involving bronchial pneumonia and some tests, stemming from unexplained chest pain, that showed nothing serious. In aggregate, his hospital time had come to eleven days. Somehow, Dresden was going to have to acquire eleven videotapes, and find the footage that was accompanying Howie King's spurious words.

He stepped out onto Independence Avenue, before him the Capitol and its grand, white dome rising from the leafless trees of its surrounding park. Just across the street was a newly erected security post manned by police carrying submachine guns. The sun was beginning to pale behind a veil of high cloud. Dresden still felt confident, still pleased with himself.

He started toward the senatorial office buildings, set in a row down the avenue, pausing before the first one. There would be a directory at the guard's desk that would tell him where he could find what he needed to know.

Guards. There were three of them. And a metal detector. To either side, the corridor was roped off. He had his pistol in his belt.

He paused, glanced at his watch, and then, as though remembering an important, forgotten appointment, strode outside again. On the sidewalk, his frustration colored his face. The damned gun. A pistol had taken his father's life and now one had almost undone him. He walked rapidly away from the Capitol down 1st Street, turning right at the downhill corner. He remembered a Metro subway station, and a vast agglomeration of various newspaper boxes at its entrance. Reaching it, he stood perusing the front pages until he was sure he was alone. Then he inserted a coin and opened the *Washington Times* box, which was nearly full of unsold papers. He waited a moment, glancing about to reaffirm his temporary solitude, then quickly snatched the pistol from his back and shoved it deep beneath the bottom paper in the stack. He let the box door close with a slam. For the next few minutes at least, the revolver might as well be in a bank safety deposit box.

As befitted the ranking opposition member of the Foreign Affairs Committee, Senator George Calendiari's office was in the Russell Office Building, the grandest of the three. Calendiari's office was, in fact, not far off the main corridor, facing away from the Capitol but toward the Mall and the western sunset. Dresden walked by the open outer door to the reception area twice, the second time lingering. The impulse he'd been barely resisting called for much more than this. His mad desire was to stroll right into Calendiari's office and casually seat himself across the desk from his past rival, just as they had sat across from each other at the best table in Antoine's in Santa Linda years before, when Calendiari, playing cigar-smoking young gentleman to cigar-smoking young gentleman, had taken Dresden to dinner in an attempt to talk him out of his fling with Madeleine Anderson. It had been an affable evening, with Calendiari explaining his carefully laid plans for his and Madeleine's future and his urbane understanding of Charley's ever-changing interest in a wide variety of women. Charley, equally as urbane and amiable, had agreed with everything Calendiari had said, and they had parted that evening something of friends. The next night Dresden had taken out Madeleine again.

The danger now was so tantalyzingly near. Charley stepped across the threshold and up to the receptionist. She looked as though she might have just walked off the campus of any state college in California.

"Hi," said Dresden, smiling. "I'm from Santa Linda. They told us back at your district office that we could get passes to the public galleries here."

She was friendly, but did not smile back. "Yes sir, that used to be the case. But the public galleries are closed now. You know, because of all the trouble."

"Are you sure? They told us we could get passes here. Is the senator in? We met him last year, at the county fair."

It occurred to Dresden he was much too well dressed to be playing such a rube, but the discrepancy seemed to escape her. She was very young.

"The senator's out of the country," she said. "In Brussels."

"Brussels?"

"For the NATO meeting. I'm sorry, sir. Maybe they'll open the galleries again after all this quiets down." She brightened. "In the meantime, you know, you can watch the proceedings on television. See if your hotel has C-Span."

He smiled again, backing away. "I'll do that. Thank you. Thank you very much."

He took a deep breath of freedom once out in the street, walking away as quickly as was seemly and possible with his injured knee, turning the first corner he came to. His idiocy knew no bounds. Doubtless every staffer in Calendiari's office read the local California papers. How many headlines might that receptionist have seen—"Ad Exec Kills Common-Law Wife," "Love Triangle Spurs Double

Murder," "Love Slaying in Tiburcio Hills"—how many front-page pictures? He must stay away from this place. There would come a time and need to talk to George Calendiari, but not soon, and not here.

A few people were on the street near the subway entrance, but none paying any attention to the newspaper boxes. As calmly as possible, Dresden reopened the one for the *Washington Times*, taking a copy from the top and reaching underneath the stack for the pistol. It was still there, but the hammer caught on something as he attempted to pull it forth; caught, and then suddenly released with a loud, terrifying report, the gunshot's echoes rattling along the building walls.

Dresden's impulse was to turn and run in a frantic descent of the escalator steps moving into the dark, slanted subway tunnel. But a survivor's instinct stayed him, constrained him to take his paper and let the box door snap shut, looking up as startled as everyone else. He saw three Capitol policemen hurrying down the street, guns drawn. Like others, Charley stared at them, anxiously, inquiringly, but they rushed past. One halted at the subway entrance, his movements all urgency and uselessness as he whirled about in search of the sight of a fleeing gunman, then hurried down into the tunnel depths. After waiting a moment, Dresden followed, standing content on the slowly moving escalator step as he watched the policeman's back disappear far below.

Back at the Embassy Row, he remembered that Maddy had said she and Calendiari had a house in McLean, Virginia. He called information, but the number was unlisted. He called the senator's office, but the receptionist refused to give out the number—and made him nervous. He quickly hung up.

As a youth growing up in Westchester, when his father had been sufficiently affluent for the family to dwell on the social periphery of the upper class, Dresden had been able to learn many things about his betters, especially debutantes. One was that they had their own system of communications, of phone listings and addresses.

Gulping the rest of his drink, he pulled on his coat and hurried out the door. There was still time before the library closed.

"Could you tell me where I might find a copy of the *Washington Social Register*?" Dresden asked the woman behind the desk.

She stared at him. He wondered how much his breath smelled of bourbon.

"Sir, they no longer publish *Social Registers* by city. They stopped doing that years ago. It's all in one big volume now. For the whole country."

His Westchester life was so long ago.

"That's what I'm looking for. Where can I find it?"

She glanced at her watch and then directed him to the appropriate shelf.

It was a thick and heavy volume, so resembling a telephone directory it belied its own exclusive purpose. He thumbed through the pages quickly, looking for the Calendiaris, and finding none whatsoever. He looked through all the names beginning with "CA," to no avail. He looked through all the Cs. He looked through the Andersons, and the Andersens. Nothing.

Dresden closed the book and then his eyes. Some things hadn't changed at all since he'd left Westchester. He supposed they never would. George Calendiari may have been of one of the wealthiest families in California, but he was Catholic, an Italian, the grandson of an immigrant, and worse, a politician. Maddy, more aristocrat than any woman he had ever known, was the daughter of a car dealer.

Charley brought the book to the desk, shaking his head.

"I don't understand," he said to the woman. "I'm trying to find an old friend. He's quite well known here in Washington, yet there's no listing for him."

"If he's prominent, here in Washington, then you shouldn't be looking him up in the *Social Register*. You should try the *Green Book*."

"The *Green Book*?"

"Yes, the *Washington Green Book*. It's much more important than the *Social Register*. In Washington, at least."

It was, in any event, much more useful. Among all the diplomats, cabinet officers, remittance men, and distant cousins of prominent New York, Boston, and Philadelphia society names, he found the Calendiaris very quickly, complete with McLean phone number and address. He wanted to thank the librarian profusely, but she had seen enough of his face as it was.

Back in his room he dialed the number. The woman who answered spoke with a heavy Spanish accent. Mrs. Calendiari was not home.

He turned on the TV news, watched the sports and weather, and called again. Mrs. Calendiari still was not home. She was going to a reception and then to a dinner party. She would not be home until late. Was there a message?

There was not. Apologizing in Spanish for the intrusion, Dresden hung up. He went to the dresser for a whiskey, but halted suddenly before he reached it. The president was on television again. He was no longer in a robe and pajamas, but a turtleneck sweater, tweed jacket, and raincoat. His shaving cut was gone and his skin no longer sallow, but slightly flushed, as though from the crisp weather. He was speaking outside, though in such a closeup shot it was impossible to tell from where. His voice, his inflection, was still perfect, but still hoarse. He was remarking on a sudden and welcome upturn in his condition, probably brought on by the interlude of warm sunshine. He waved and smiled and said all was well. Dresden looked hard at the screen, burning the clothes and face into his memory before the president's image abruptly vanished and a coffee commercial took his place. Now Dresden would need another tape. He would have to keep pace with these people.

After dinner, he tried Maddy's number again. There was an answer after just two rings, and this time there was no Spanish accent. The voice was full of sleepiness and some uncertainty, but it was the dearest sound he had heard in days. He hung up after she repeated the word "hello" three times. He did so regretfully, with shame and guilt, but with purpose. He would hear that voice again. But he would have to wait.

16

Dresden slept badly, awakening shortly after four A.M. He went to the window, pulling the drawn curtains aside. Nothing moved in the street. He went to his bag and took out the Magnum. He'd now have to walk about the streets of the nation's capital with that huge cannon stuck in his belt. As the episode at the newspaper box attested, a firearm was likely more liability than help. But he did not want to leave it in his room, at risk of it being found or stolen. It was now his only weapon. He had no hope of acquiring another without the possibility of bringing serious trouble upon himself, and he still felt a certainty that before this was done he would have need of a gun.

Dresden turned on the television set. A program advertised as an all-night news show was on, but the news set was composed of couches and ferns, and the person being interviewed was a motion picture actor who had written a book confessing his homosexuality. Charley slumped into a chair and drank and watched, the large pistol on the table beside him. He was glad when the actor was replaced by a motion picture actress who confessed to nothing more than her next film.

At length, the all-night talk was replaced by an early-morning network news show. There was a report of famine in Southeast Asia.

There was more rioting in Manila. The vice president of the United States was meeting with the prime minister of Canada about Central America. There were unconfirmed reports that Secretary of State Crosby was going to announce the breaking of diplomatic relations with Nicaragua and El Salvador over La Puño and the refusal of those two governments to admit to its existence and their connection with it. A new rise in the prime rate had driven stock prices down.

Dresden dozed. When he awoke the main morning news program had come on the screen, and with it, the same actor with the same book confessing his same homosexuality. Charley stared bleakly. The weatherman talked of bad storms on the Pacific Coast and unseasonal cold in the Midwest. Dresden thought of Tracy Bakersfield huddled in her beach house, great gray waves crashing along the pier. Where was Tracy? On impulse, he dialed her number again. He let it ring a dozen times or more. There was no answer. Was he to take comfort in that?

Dresden slept. When he awoke again the morning news show was in its last minutes. Over news film including footage of the starvation in Cambodia, there was a slow roll of credits. At the fifth name, Dresden almost leaped out of his chair. It was that of a one-time protégé of his, a man he had hired as a production assistant in Santa Linda who was now a network producer. The man had been so grateful to Charley for his first chance and start in television that, after joining the network and hearing of Charley's decline, he had twice called to offer him a job. Had Charley wished to leave California for New York, he might have taken it, but at that time, as in all times, leaving his life in Tiburcio was too great a price.

But now this man's gratitude could be of real use. He snapped off the set and opened the curtains. It was snowing, a faint, wet snow falling from a bleak gray sky. It was December. He was in Washington. He was looking at the morning of a joyless day.

Perhaps. He gave his producer friend time enough to have concluded what Dresden expected would be obligatory after-show postmortems, and then called the network number in New York. He had to go through three people, but he reached his friend.

"This is you, Charley?" said the man. "Charley Dresden? I haven't talked to you in five years."

"It's been too long," Dresden said. "I just caught your show and it reminded me, so I thought I'd call. I'm on the road."

"You're here? Here in New York?"

"No. I'm down in Washington." The instant he said that he regretted it. Until that moment, no one had the faintest idea where he was. Now his secret was shared by an important executive of the most-watched television network in the country.

"You left California?"

"For the time being. I—I need a favor. I'm putting together a news special and I need some videotape footage, some file footage."

"You're doing a special for Channel Three? Or are you with some-one else?"

"It's an independent production. I need some file footage of some old presidential White House talks. Stock stuff. Your network owns one of the television stations down here. I wondered if you might possibly—if you don't mind, and I'd sure appreciate it—if you might ask your people here if they'd loan me some of that stuff. I mean, to make a copy. I'll buy my own tape. I'm just in a jam, and I don't know where to turn. The government's no help. We've got a real deadline. And I really need it. I'd really, really appreciate it."

"I'm sorry, Charley. But I can't do that. There's a policy against that. Everything is strictly in-house. You're right. The station there is one of our owned and operated, but their tape files are theirs. We use our own."

"You're sure you couldn't get them to bend the rules? I really am in a jam."

"Charley. No."

"Well, I expect to be in New York in a day or two. Is there any chance you might be able to help me out with your files up there?"

There was a long pause.

"Charley. I better tell you this. I get the Santa Linda paper. My mother sends it to me. Charley, I saw your picture on the front page. I read the story. Charley, I . . ."

Dresden hung up immediately, furious with himself. He could trust no one. He must do all this himself.

The black man behind the counter looked at him with an expres-sion composed of equal parts of shrewdness, incredulity, and fear.

"Mister," he said, "the best car I've got available is a 1983 Chevette. Are you sure you've come to the right place, I mean, the place you thought you were coming to?"

"I'm just in town on business," said Dresden, smiling, but looking a little apprehensive, deliberately apprehensive. "I saw your ad in the phone book. Your rates seem quite reasonable. I'm not a man to waste money."

"You're gonna pay with a credit card?"

"No, with cash." He would carry on with this feigned parsimony as long as it served to explain his presence in such a place. "I don't believe in paying interest to credit card companies."

"And you'll bring the car back? This ain't some scam?"

"Name your deposit."

"A hundred bucks."

Charley took out his wallet, peeked into its recesses, and slowly pulled out a hundred dollar bill, as though it amounted to his grandmother's entire fortune. He shoved his wallet quickly back into his suit coat's breast pocket. If the car rental agent was worried about the anomaly that was Dresden, Charley was infinitely more worried about the neighborhood and what might await him in it.

The agent stuck the money into a pocket, not a cash register. Charley wondered if he'd get it back. But that, of course, didn't matter.

"No mileage charge," the agent said. "But you buy all the gas."

"Understood," Dresden said.

"The car runs," the agent said.

"I certainly hope so."

"And you'll bring it back?"

"Yes. But I don't think it'll be after dark."

"You got that right, my man." The agent handed him a key with a dirty plastic tag attached to it. "It's the red one out in back. It's a stick shift and it slips out of second sometimes, but otherwise she be dynamite."

He had planned to head north immediately. Instead, he bought a street directory and drove to McLean. It was just up the George Washington Parkway on the Virginia side of the Potomac. Nearing the town, he passed the CIA and turned onto Georgetown Pike, following that to a road called Sandra Court, a cul-de-sac. It looked dangerous. Though their rear yards were well wooded and spacious, the houses were close together where they fronted the street. In this old, bright red, and certainly cheap-looking car with District of Columbia plates, he was noticeable to half a dozen houses, including the Calendiaris'. He rounded the circle of the cul-de-sac hurriedly, hastening to where Sandra Court interesected with Georgetown Pike. He found a place on the shoulder of the road where he had a distant but clear view of the Calendiaris' big house. Slumping down behind the wheel, he waited, more than an hour.

Maddy's garage door opened automatically, a bright yellow Mercedes-Benz roadster with a black top backing out as soon as the door was fully retracted, and the door sliding down again the instant the car had cleared the garage. She wore a blue kerchief and trenchcoat and paid him no attention as she wheeled onto Georgetown Pike at the first interruption in traffic. He waited for two other cars to take up the interval, then followed. She took two more turnings, and led him into what he took to be the village of McLean. Mercedes, Volvos, and expensive Japanese cars seemed to be the rule.

She pulled into a dry cleaners. That certainly didn't suit his purpose. Neither did the Crown bookstore she visited afterward. Bookstores were very quiet places, and he half expected her to scream upon seeing him. Then she went to what appeared to be a gourmet supermarket. That would do.

The store was crowded with very wealthy-looking people shopping for the holidays. He waited for Maddy to take a number at the meat counter, then moved up beside her. He was about to touch her arm, but thought better of it. Instead he pretended to be just another customer, and spoke quietly.

"Is there a place we can talk? Maddy, I've got to talk to you. I'm quite desperate."

She stared at him, her expression frozen—not in contempt, not in fear, but far from anything remotely friendly. He might have just said something obscene to her, or admitted poisoning her pet dog.

"Charley, you promised you'd never see me again."

"Yes, I did. And I stuck to that. Even though it tore me up. I fell in love with you all over again, Maddy. I almost called you several times. I always hung up. But now I'm in trouble."

"You called me last night, didn't you?"

"Yes."

"Get away from me, Charley. Get out of here and leave me alone. Forever."

"Maddy. It's me. Charley. The other love in your life. Your dear friend. And I'm in the biggest trouble of my life."

"We get the California papers. They say you're a murderer."

"Maddy. Let me talk to you, please. For fifteen minutes. For five minutes."

She dropped her ticket into a plastic box atop the meat counter.

"All right," she said. "Outside. In the parking lot. Don't give me any problems. There's a county police station just down the road and the firehouse is right across the street."

"Maddy, I wouldn't harm a hair on your head."

Grim-faced, she preceded him past the checkout counters and out the door, which opened for them automatically. She kept walking, back toward where she had parked the Mercedes.

"Is there a bar nearby?"

"A bar? No."

"A restaurant?"

"Several, but none where I wouldn't be likely to run into friends. George is away. This is most inopportune."

"I know."

She stopped at the side of her car. "You said five minutes."

"Whatever you can spare me. Maddy, I didn't kill that woman. She was a dear, dear friend. I didn't kill that man. He was a friend, a good friend."

Her expression softened, though not into friendliness. Not into warmth. There were the faintest tears in her eyes.

"We didn't think that you had, Charley. Not George. Not me. But I don't want any part of this, your trouble, or any part of you. We have all kinds of problems as it is. We don't need more."

"The whole country has a problem. That's why my friends were killed."

She looked down at the pavement. The snow was still melting as it touched the blacktop, but it was now falling more thickly. She unlocked the door on the passenger side.

"Get in, Charley."

He did. As she sat behind the wheel, he said, "I thought you didn't want to go to a restaurant."

"We're not," she said, turning on the engine with a sudden roar. She backed up. "We're going to a place where we won't be bothered. I'm going to trust you, once again, Charles Dresden. Trust doubtless misplaced."

She drove rapidly out of the village, following a road called Old Dominion Drive.

"Explain it to me," she said. "Who killed your friends?"

"I can't say anything for a fact; nothing in court. But I'm convinced it's the people behind the assassination, someone involved in the fraud they're perpetrating at Camp David. Probably someone working for the president. The late president."

"The same sort of nonsense you were telling me back in California?"

"But it isn't nonsense. That's why I've come here. To get back at them. They killed Charlene and Danny Hill. They tried to kill the vice president and they got his wife."

"George is a good friend of the vice president."

"I know."

"Is that why you're bothering me? You want to make contact with the vice president?"

"Not yet. I have almost all the proof I need. But not enough, not yet."

They drove without speaking, till the highway began to switch back and forth in sharp curves in rolling, hilly countryside, horse fences on either side.

"All right, Charley, say it."

"What?"

"You want me to help you. To get you out of this."

"I can't get 'out' of this. But I need your help. Desperately."

"You've no one else."

"No one. All my friends are in California. Out there, I'm a dead man."

"All right. Don't speak. I want to think."

He didn't. At length they came to a traffic light, and a brown and white sign that announced GREAT FALLS PARK. She followed the access road past a closed National Park Service ticket booth and into a parking lot that held only one other car. The elevation was higher here and the temperature colder. The snow was adhering to the ground.

As he stepped out of the roadster, he heard a vague roaring sound. He glanced at her.

"It's the waterfall," she said. "You're not carrying any liquor, are you? There's a ranger on duty in the visitor center and they're very strict about liquor here. You could get yourself into trouble you don't need."

"I've nothing with me, Maddy."

She led them down a lane that seemed to parallel the river. They kept on until he could hear the falls at full, crashing volume. In a moment they could see them. They were the most spectacular sight he had seen since Niagara, years before, a mad rush of blue-green water tumbling tumultuously around and over great boulders, falling in huge steps to a wide, deceptively serene-looking pool amidst steep, granite walls. She took his arm as they descended a stony path to rocks at the water's edge.

"I brought you here because this is the place where I come to make decisions. I made one a few days ago. Now that you're here, now that you've brought all this dreadful mess with you, I've got to reconsider it."

He stared at her, unspeaking. The cold had brought a flush to her cheeks. She had never looked more beautiful.

"Charley. I've decided to divorce George."

He put his arm around her shoulders, but she stiffened. She did not pull away, but he saw ample reason to keep his embrace loose— friendly, comforting, but formal.

"It has nothing to do with you, Charley. No, that's not quite true. You're a symptom. That night in California, that was a symptom. But you're not the cause. I don't need you in my life, Charley. My problem is that I no longer want George in my life."

"You won't believe this, but in a way, I've always liked George. I was, I suppose, rotten to him, didn't respect him at all, but I liked him. He was always a gentleman to me."

"A very old-country-type Italian gentleman, Charley. You have no idea what that can be like."

"Well, perhaps not."

"It can be goddamn hell. They're one of the wealthiest families in California. But George is just like his wealthy Italian old-country-gentleman father, who in too many terrible ways is just like George's unwealthy Italian old-country-peasant grandfather. We have all this money, Charley; all these houses. But the only help I've had is cleaning women whom I finally persuaded George to have come in every day. All the kitchen work, anything that doesn't have to do with cleaning toilets, that falls to me. On purpose. The kitchen is where the woman belongs, in the old-country way, just like his mother. And on top of all this has been Washington and Congress and politics. Trips for the vice president. Trips *with* the vice president. Trips to NATO and every other place. Trips back to the district almost every weekend. Trips to fund-raising dinners. It's a truly horrible life here, Charley Dresden, with Senator George Calendiari. The only saving grace is that his old-country mother is convinced it's his constant traveling and politicking that has kept us from having children, and not some dreadfully un-Catholic Nordic chastity on my part. When he is home he drops his underwear and socks at the foot of the bed and expects me to pick them up in the morning. When he's done with his newspaper he drops it on the carpet. I'm supposed to pick it up. He smokes cigars, and in all our married life he's never emptied an ashtray. Not once. When the cleaning women aren't there I'm supposed to answer all the telephone calls. And sometimes he gets them all day—and night."

"I don't think you're guilty of dreadfully un-Catholic Nordic chastity."

"Of all the things you could have said at this point, of all the thousands of words you could have spoken, you just picked the very worst ones."

"I'm sorry. I'm truly sorry."

He thought she would pull completely away, but instead she relaxed, coming closer to him, her soft, fine golden hair brushing his face.

"Damn you, Charley."

"I didn't mean what you think I mean."

"I know what you mean. I wish you hadn't miraculously appeared today. I wish you would miraculously disappear. Forever. I had it all figured out. I was going to tell him right after the holidays. I have it all figured out. I've got to leave and he's got to learn to shift for himself. But he shows absolutely no disposition to do so. Not for even a few minutes a day. Like all these goddam politicians, like everybody in government. Like these great Washington journalists, who are the worst of all, he thinks he's God. He thinks he's running the country, bearing all the burdens of the world. I've had enough. More than enough."

Dresden was wearing gloves, and she was not. He took both her hands in his. He stared at her eyes until she finally looked up into his.

"I understand," he said.

"If I help you, by having George help you, it'll mess everything up. I'll be taking on a big obligation to him, and I don't want to owe him anything ever again."

"I understand that. I won't lie to you. I want your help anyway. I need for you to obligate yourself to him. I know you may cut me off forever because I'm saying this, because I'm asking so much. But I need you. I need George."

"Just to meet with Laurence Atherton."

"That's not all. I need to go to New York, for the rest of the proof. I need you to come with me. I've no one else I can ask."

She put her head against his shoulder.

"That's all I can say. I've nothing more to say," he said. Gently, he pulled her closer. "I don't know what's happening between us. I don't understand what's happening to me. I never harmed anybody. I just get a little crazy about things."

"Where are you staying, Charley? Where are you hiding out?"

"At the Embassy Row Hotel."

She looked up, her eyes brimming with tears, but a brave sort of smile on her lips.

"You're a most stylish fugitive."

"It works out."

Now she pulled so close to him he could feel her breasts.

"Help me, Charley. Help me every way you can. Help me the way you want me to help you."

"Maddy, I'd kill for you."

She stepped back. Her expression was all frozen again, as it had been in the store.

"Once again, you've said exactly the wrong thing. Now I'm losing my trust in you. Now you're scaring the hell out of me, Charley."

Maddy's hard look into his eyes was searching, doubting, fearing.

"Be in your room at eight P.M.," she said. "If I decide to help you, to be with you, I'll come then. If not, not. And that will be it with us, forever. You understand that? No popping up at meat counters."

"Yes."

"All right. I'll drive you back to your car. Then I'll do some thinking. A lot of thinking. Damn it all, Charley. Why are you and George the only men in all my life I've ever loved?"

"Because I'm damned lucky."

"For once you've said the right thing. But I haven't made up my mind. I'm not sure I'll come. I don't think I will."

"My life has been run by other people ever since the president was shot. I'll abide with whatever you decide. I promise. Now I'm going to say the wrong thing again, Madeleine Margrit Anderson Calendiari. I love you."

She closed her eyes, an invitation. He kissed her, gently, as gently as the falling snowflakes. Her lips were sweetly dry and warm.

"I still don't think I'll come," she said.

The knock at his hotel-room door came at nine-twenty P.M. He reached for his pistol, then thought better of it, and hurriedly slipped the big revolver into a dresser drawer. The new bottle of whiskey atop the dresser he didn't bother to hide. If it was Madeleine, the pistol would frighten her away. The whiskey she wouldn't like, but would expect.

If it wasn't her, he was probably done for anyway. He hesitated, then swung open the door. She carried a small overnight case.

"I wasn't going to come," she said, stepping into the room. He closed the door quickly. "I really wasn't. I made up my mind. Then I got the call from Europe. It wasn't even George; just some staff aide. He said George would be delayed two days because he had to go to Bonn for some meeting with the German defense minister. He said George would have called himself, but it was the middle of the night over there and he'd gone to bed."

She set down her case, glancing at the whiskey bottle as he helped her off with her coat.

"It just made me so goddamn mad," she said. "I've already been alone in that house for four days. And he wouldn't even make the call himself."

She looked again at the whiskey bottle and went to an armchair, taking off her shoes and then leaning her head back and closing her eyes.

"Make me a drink, Charley. I don't intend to become a drunk like my friend Stephanie Pernell. That's one of the reasons I have to leave George. But now I really need a drink. I don't intend to become a whore like Stephanie either. That's why I've come to you. I need a man, but I don't want to start picking up strangers. Somehow, with you, I still feel like an honest woman."

He handed her a glass filled with ice and scotch.

"I don't know I'm at all in love with you, Charley. I didn't really believe you when you said you'd fallen for me again."

"I meant it."

She smiled, wearily. "Your problem is that you've stayed in love with all the women you ever loved."

He smiled sadly.

"I'll have this drink and then we'll make love, Charley. I'll go to New York with you tomorrow. I don't know what's going to come of all this—what's going to become of us. I just wish you weren't in this awful mess." She drank, with need and haste. "Do your best when you make love to me. Your very, very best. You owe it to me."

17

Kreski's last flight to Honduras had been aboard Air Force One five months before, during President Hampton's much-publicized two-day visit to American troops in the camps and compounds in the combat areas along the Nicaraguan and El Salvadoran borders. Then they had been escorted by what seemed half the U.S. Air Force, including an AWACS radar mother ship and a squadron of F-15s.

The chief fear then had been of ground-to-air missiles, and even worry of an actual attack by aircraft. The El Salvadorans only had some Soviet Yak-28s and a few leftover American Blackhawk helicopters, but the Nicaraguans were flying MIG 21s, OH-6s, and Alouette IIIs. Happily, they had restrained themselves, confining their response to the president's visit to a nighttime strike at a Honduran army base hours after Hampton had left the country.

Now, whatever the Nicaraguans' mood, Kreski's only protection was the neutrality of the Mexican airliner in which he was a passenger.

The approach into Tegucigalpa was the same as it had been in Air Force One, and just as unnerving, flying straight in from the coast and low over the city and the murky little river that divided it in two, touching down on the lip of the high, hazy plateau to the west that itself was bordered by steep mountains.

He was one of several Americans to come down the aircraft's steps, and no one seemed to pay him any particular attention. There was military everywhere, mostly Honduran—the officers in crisp khaki uniforms, the enlisted men in rumpled, sweaty fatigues, nearly all wearing sunglasses.

At customs, he found himself being studied by an American wearing a military beret and camouflage fatigues, though no rank or insignia. The man also wore mirrored sunglasses and carried what looked to be a NATO-issue 9 mm Beretta automatic on his webbed belt.

Kreski glanced away, but noticed the man move to one of the Hondurans in business suits. In a moment the man in fatigues had disappeared and the Honduran was approaching Kreski. The heat and humidity had not bothered Kreski, but suddenly he began to sweat. He had no wish to begin—and end—this visit by being placed under arrest, or worse.

The Honduran, a good foot shorter than Kreski, smiled. "You have cleared customs, señor," he said. "You are free to go."

Once outside, he was beseiged by a swarm of taxi drivers. Brookes had told him he would be met at the airport, but had said nothing about the mob of jabbering cabbies. One pushed his way through the others, however, put his hand on Kreski's bag, and said all he needed to: "Señor Kreski. *Hemos reservado una habitacion*"—"We've reserved a room."

It proved to be not in a hotel, but in what in Tegucigalpa passed for an expensive residential high-rise, and it was not a single chamber but a one-bedroom apartment, with kitchen, bath, large living room, and balcony. The taxi driver had unlocked the door, handed him the key, set his bag just inside, and left. It was not until Kreski had closed the door behind him that he noticed the man in the chair near the balcony door. He was well dressed and very Latin, with very large dark eyes and a thick mustache. When he stood up he was as tall as Kreski. He was also very light complexioned.

"Señor Kreski. I am Señor Sandoval—Jorge Sandoval Mejia. Welcome to Honduras."

Kreski shook his hand. "You work for Peter Brookes?"

"Let us just say we have many mutual friends. Would you like some refreshment?" He nodded to a bar with many bottles. "Something cooling? There is an excellent local rum. To drink rum is to help the economy of this poor region."

"I'll have a rum and tonic, then."

Sandoval moved to the bar. "And I will join you, but with a rum and Coca-Cola. They have changed the formula for Coca-Cola, unfortunately, but the drink is still called a Cuba Libre, correct?"

Kreski nodded, but remained standing. Sandoval returned to his chair.

"Cuba Libre. A wonderful phrase, but unlike the drink, the reality goes sour. Do you speak Spanish well, Señor Kreski?"

"Well enough to get by, I suppose."

"But not well enough to tell that I am not Honduran. My accent is Cuban. I am an American. I grew up in Florida. My father owned a hotel in Havana. He went to Miami after Battista was overthrown and got a job as a waiter. Shortly after that he was headwaiter and soon he was managing the hotel. Finally, he owned his own hotel again, though not a large one. Sadly, he returned to Cuba, at night, with old comrades. Several times." Sandoval raised his glass. "Cuba libre. One time he never came back."

Sandoval drank, staring at Kreski over the rim of his glass.

"Now I own the hotel," he continued. "And some other things. When I can, I try to be helpful. I am here to be helpful to you. We will introduce you to anyone you want to meet. We will take you wherever you want to go. The taxidriver who brought you here will be waiting outside and will be at your disposal whenever you are in Tegucigalpa. When you want to go out into the countryside we will provide more rugged transportation and additional protection."

"When and why will I be wanting to go into the countryside? Into the war zone?"

Sandoval smiled. "The war zone is everywhere, señor. You are a policeman. You will go where you think you must, where your instincts and the evidence leads you. But we strongly suggest that you include three items on your itinerary. One is to join me and a Colonel Victores of the Guardia Nacionale for dinner tonight. He is a most charming gentleman, a very pleasant and interesting conversationalist. He may also be the only honest policeman in the country, his only corruption being that he is heavily in the pay of Americans."

"You mean the CIA?"

"I merely said Americans, not the American government. We also strongly urge you to visit Huerta's village, where he had his farm and where his people were murdered. And we would like you also to go to the town on the coast where he was last seen before he turned up several weeks later as a corpse in Gettysburg, Pennsylvania. This town will be the most difficult to visit, for there is a large American military presence in the area and frequent fighting. We will do all for you that we can."

He stood up, draining his glass and returning it to the bar.

"In the meantime, you should find everything here that you might need."

"I was expecting a hotel. Is there a place nearby where I can get American newspapers?"

"I will have the *Miami Herald* brought here every day. I will have this morning's brought to you this afternoon. Also, the Mexico City English-language paper, and the most reliable newspaper published here in Tegucigalpa—if your Spanish is good enough to follow it."

"Probably not."

"*Bueno.* It isn't reliable enough." Sandoval started toward the door, then halted. "Did you bring a weapon, señor? Probably not."

"Definitely not."

"We will provide you with one. Weapons are plentiful everywhere now in Honduras—in Central America. As numerous as the insects. You will need one."

"As you say. I'm familiar with them."

Sandoval paused just once more, this time with his hand on the doorknob. "I would suggest also, señor, that you keep off the balcony, though the view is very pleasant when there is no haze. And that you not go for aimless strolls on your own. As I say, weapons are everywhere in Honduras, and everywhere is in its way a war zone. Until tonight, then. I will pick you up at ten P.M. The restaurant is not far."

Maddy drove, insisting on it after examining Dresden's injured knee and other wounds when they awoke in the morning. She insisted also on his returning the aging Chevette, though the rental agency's neighborhood clearly frightened her, and on using her bright yellow Mercedes for the New York trip instead. His argument that it was conspicuous was not persuasive. She had become used to many things. She would stay with him, but she would not part with her car.

"You're speeding," he said. "It won't help at all to be stopped by the police."

"Everyone speeds on the New Jersey Turnpike. Who can blame them? This must be the worst stretch of countryside in America."

"They named one of the rest stops after Joyce Kilmer."

"Only in New Jersey would they name a urinal after one of America's great poets." She smiled at him and briefly took his hand. Her fear and trembling of the night before had disappeared. He sensed an excitement in her. He supposed it was not because she anticipated or appreciated the danger they were rushing toward. It was that they were breaking utterly free, however temporarily, from her world, the world of Washington, the world of George Calendiari. She had begun her estrangement, thrillingly, and with love. However tenuously, she'd grabbed hold of some tangible happiness. She was delightful. If it weren't for all the corpses strewn about in his all-too-vivid memory, it would have seemed they'd been brought together again through some wonderful act of divine intercession.

He'd been glancing back at the following traffic with some frequency, paying particular attention to those who stayed too near too long, but he'd seen no one to alarm him. A state police cruiser had taken note of Maddy's California license plate, but that was logical. It said U.S. SENATE.

"We'll be in New York within the hour," she said. "We can have a late lunch. You don't know how much I'm looking forward to that. Washington hasn't quite got the knack of great restaurants yet, especially in Georgetown, where we congressional ladies are always having to go for our socializing. But now, a genuine first-class New York meal."

"I'm afraid it'll have to be a cheeseburger," he said, "and here in New Jersey. We won't get to New York until tomorrow."

"But Charley, we're almost there! You said we would stay at the Plaza."

"It'll have to wait one more day. There's a stop I have to make in New Jersey. I was going to do it on the way back, but it's important, and I don't want to chance having to miss it. We could run into trouble in New York. We can run into trouble in a lot of places."

"What sort of 'important stop'?"

"You don't need to know. It involves the commission of a felony."

"Charley!"

"I didn't exactly advertise this as a Club Med vacation. Don't worry. I'm not going to involve you. While I'm attending to business you can wait at the motel. I'll be back by morning."

"What business? What do you mean by felony?"

"Breaking and entering. Burglary. I want to acquire some videotapes that don't belong to me. It's vital that I get a hold of them. They'll be more convincing than anything I can say—especially to the vice president."

"Convincing of what?"

"Of everything I've told you. You'll see when I get back. If I get back." He should not have said that. The uncertainty returned to her eyes. "I'll get back. Don't worry. If I can be here with you now, driving down the New Jersey Turnpike instead of being chained to a toilet in some California jail cell, anything is possible. Everything is possible. We'd better turn off and find a motel soon. The place where I want to go isn't far, if I remember it correctly, and as this will be of the late-night variety of business, I could use a little sleep beforehand. After last night, you could too, couldn't you, Madeleine Margrit Anderson?"

She returned to smiling. "After last night, dearest darling Charles August Dresden, I am deliriously in need of a little sleep. But let's try for a Holiday Inn, at least. I dread the thought of one of those little cinderblock wall places."

"A Holiday Inn will be fine. To make it absolutely perfect, take off your wedding ring."

She pulled off her left glove, revealing a naked hand.

"You didn't notice," she said. "I took it off last night. For good."

There was a local telephone directory listing for the network's New Jersey warehouse, but it took Dresden nearly an hour of mostly useless driving in the fading daylight before he found the place. The building reasonably resembled his memory of it—a large, one-story structure with a two-story annex, the network's logo on a huge sign at the front. There was wire fencing at the rear and sides, but the parking lot by the entrance was open to the street. He left Maddy's car at the curb, out of view of the entrance, and strolled toward the door, briefcase in hand, looking his very best impression of an important television executive.

Nodding to a security guard standing just inside the doorway, Dresden continued on to a young black woman at the front desk.

"I'm Mr.—uh—Ireland from Los Angeles," he said, as matter-of-factly as possible. "I was supposed to meet some people from the news division here to look at some tapes." He glanced at his watch. "I may have the time wrong."

"Just have a seat, sir. I'm sure they'll be along soon. They've got two lanes of the Holland Tunnel closed this week and New York traffic this time of day's bad enough with four."

She went back to her work, which didn't appear to amount to much, as Charley seated himself on a vinyl-covered chair, crossed his legs, and tried to look as significant and impatient as possible. A man in a short-sleeved shirt came down the corridor pushing a cart laden with cases of videotapes, but otherwise there seemed to be little activity in the building. Dresden glanced irritably at his watch. He guessed that the security guard post here in the small lobby was probably manned twenty-four hours a day and that there might be an additional security man on duty overnight. Probably a librarian or clerk, too, just to provide the network with full-time access. The network news operation and the network's New York owned-and-operated station both maintained huge tape libraries. This warehouse in New Jersey was archives. But if the aging Soviet president were to die in the middle of the night, this is where they would come for footage of him standing with Khrushchev atop Lenin's mausoleum in the 1960s, and they would want it fast.

After twenty minutes, now ignored by the security guard, Dresden returned to the woman at the desk.

"Is there a phone I might use? I just want to make sure they've left. The way my week's been going, I'm probably here on the wrong day."

"Sure." He might just as well have asked to browse among the tapes.

Dialing the recorded weather report, he asked the tinny voice that ultimately responded for the office of the former protégé he had called from Washington the previous morning. He then engaged in a spurious conversation that ended with him in a high state of exasperation. Finally, regaining his composure, he hung up.

"I have the right day," he said to the young woman. "*They* had the wrong one."

He looked again at his watch. As he did so, he stole a quick look about him. There was a file records room, probably containing the main tape index listings, just off the corridor to his right, an older woman looking slowly through one of the drawers. Adjoining it was an office that looked unoccupied. No other employee was in view.

"Thank you very much," he said. "I'll see you in the morning."

The guard opened the door for him. He had earlier presumed his effort that night would entail wire cutting, window smashing, and other dangerous difficulties. He decided now he would use a direct, frontal approach, and that it might even be fairly easy.

Maddy was awake when he returned. The motel was closer to cinderblock than a first-rate Holiday Inn, and she was not comfortable in it. He supposed she had not slept well. He felt no need for sleep at all. He could go the night, and might have to.

"You took a long time," she said.

"I had trouble finding the place." He sat down on the bed beside her, taking her hand. "I'm afraid I'm going to have to stick you here a fair bit longer. I think I can manage this nicely. But I want to wait until after midnight. I'll come back for you as soon as I can."

She sat up, brushing a tumble of blondness back from her forehead.

"No, you won't," she said. "You're not sticking me anywhere, Mr. Dresden. Especially here. I'm coming with you."

"No, Maddy."

"You asked my help. You're going to get it."

"No, thank you. There's some potential rough stuff in this."

"You told me about the rough stuff in the beginning."

He reached behind his back and took the heavy Magnum pistol from his belt. "I didn't tell you about this."

She stared at the weapon as though he had just shown her a severed hand. Finally, her expression firmed. She took a deep breath. "What do you want to tell me about that?"

"It has no past that you need worry about. I just need it now. I'm going to use it tonight."

"Charley? What the hell do you mean?"

"I didn't say fire it. I said use it. Now, do you still want to come?"

She bit down on her lip. "Yes. Damn you to hell, Charley Dresden. There's nothing safe about you whatsoever and never was. But, damn it, yes. I'm coming with you. It's my car. It's my me. It's my us. I'm coming with you."

Maddy only looked as though one had to carry her across puddles. As Charley was coming to remember, she was of stronger stuff than that. In many ways, of stronger stuff than him.

Colonel Victores, as Kreski had suspected, was the diminutive man in the business suit and sunglasses who had instantly cleared him through customs and passport control that afternoon. He was still wearing sunglasses, but was now dressed in a dark suit, expensive white shirt, and dark tie. A large gold ring was visible on his right hand. Kreski detected a slight bulge beneath the man's coat below his armpit. It was a professional observation, professionally understood. From the very beginning, he and Victores had absolutely no doubts about one another.

At first the conversation was entirely social. They talked of what the colonel called the unusually clement weather, of the red snapper that was the catch of the day from the coast, of international police officials they knew in common, of the terrorism that plagued the hemisphere and their general inability to do anything about it, of the beauty of the ash-blond English lady at the table next to them, of South American versus European soccer, of the beauty of the dark-haired Argentinian woman across the room, and then, at last, of what Kreski needed to know about Manuel Huerta. The colonel took a thick envelope from his suit pocket and carefully set it upon the tablecloth.

"Here it is," he said. "It is not all that is in our files. You do not wish to carry all of that with you. But I think you will find this a most useful distillation. It is facsimiles, as you say, 'Xeroxes.'"

"Should I look at it now?" said Kreski, pulling the envelope toward him.

"I was told, Señor Director, that discretion was a great virtue of the American Secret Service."

Kreski nodded to him without speaking, slipping the envelope into his pocket. "Can you tell me, Colonel, as we sit here, during this most pleasant evening, whether there is enough in here to justify my coming? Does this say anything of La Puño?"

The colonel leaned back in his chair and smiled. "What might be in there that is of value to you, that might or might not justify the expense of your journey, is for you to decide, Señor Kreski. As for 'La Puño,' I view that as one of the great amusements, the big joke, of this entire affair. Your people have continually talked about it. References to it have gone back and forth in your diplomatic dispatches. Your news magazines and newspapers are full of talk of this underground group 'La Puño.' Your secretary of state threatens an all-out war over it. But it is a great joke. La Puño there was. La Puño was one man. You shot him to ribbons on a tower in Gettysburg, Pennsylvania. 'The Fist' is old, dead, rotting meat. He is no more."

"What do you mean?"

"'The Fist,' 'La Puño,' was never something written down on paper. It was not intended to be. It was what Manuel Huerta called himself, what he wished to be known as in the slums and villages. It was both sobriquet and threat."

"He was a crook?" Kreski asked. "An extortionist? An enforcer?"

"An avenger, Señor Kreski. It is all in the distillation. His people were well off, of El Salvador. They were, as your journalists say, 'Garks.'"

"I beg your pardon?"

Sandoval smiled. "Their slang for oligarch, Señor Kreski."

"When the Communists toppled the government there, they scattered," Victores continued. "Those with the most money went to Brazil and Mexico, a few to Europe. Manuel and his brother came here, with their families. They acquired that small but thriving farm, and Manuel joined our Guardia Nacionale. His father had been a colonel in the El Salvadoran army. We made Huerta a lieutenant. He was a good one; too good. Very thorough. But it was all vengeance. It always came back to that."

Kreski remembered the bodies at Gettysburg.

"Huerta ran what you people would call a 'death squad.' He made strikes only across the El Salvadoran border at first. Then he took to looking for El Salvadoran leftist infiltrators on this side of the frontier, murdering them singly; leaving their bodies in the middle of streets at night. We made the mistake of transferring him to the East Coast. Then he just contented himself with Honduran leftists. And any Nicaraguans he could find, any he might suspect of association with the Sandinistas."

"And they struck back?"

The colonel swatted an insect upon his face. A tiny trace of blood was left when he took his hand away.

"Oh yes, Señor Kreski. It is done all the time. It is the basic nature of the war here. Huerta's farm and family were burned out. The families of others in his unit were hit too. They talked of crossing the border into Nicaragua for revenge. This would not be allowed. You understand? All of this war is by arrangement. Huerta and his men were not part of the arrangement. Not in their particular demeanor."

He signaled the waiter for more ice. Kreski could hear loud but engaging music from somewhere down the street.

"Our government strongly disapproved of these activities," Sandoval said, finally joining the conversation. "So did the Honduran government. Contras, sí. Guardia Nacionale, no. President Hampton had just reinvoked the unfortunate fate of the poor Catholic women in El Salvador. You may recall.

"We had just elected Emiliano Madeiro Ramon. You recall that your president came down here to campaign for him, to put the muscle of the United States behind the forces of moderation. You were here. I believe we may have met then."

"Probably so, colonel. We get very busy on such occasions. Forgive any lapse of memory."

"Of course. *No importante.* Huerta was an embarrassment. Now, we might bring such people to trial, or shoot them outright, or promote them to colonel, depending. Then, it was just a few months ago, policy was merely to dismiss them. Huerta was cashiered. He languished about his village until his people were buried, and then he struck out on his own. If he had been vengeful, he then became a fanatic. If a 'La Puño' grew from that, *quien sabe?* But at that time, he was all it was."

Kreski wiped his brow. This country seemed to grow hotter with the enveloping darkness.

"Señor Kreski," the colonel asked, all smiles, with an innocent curiosity in his eyes. "This name 'La Puño' has been in all your news journals. This country crawls with American journalists, with journalists from all over. There are many, many; very, very costly television camera units. You find the people everywhere—in the hotel toilets. In the jungles. On the front lines. They talk to official government spokesmen. They talk to leftist guerrillas from across the border. They talk to the nuns from Maryknoll. They talk to local newspaper editors. Mostly they sit in restaurants or cantinas and talk to each other. But they never ask about 'La Puño,' true or false. They never ask about Huerta's real background. The reports I receive— what I read in these two big American newspapers—all say Huerta was a poor farmer opposed to American policy in Central America."

Sandoval smiled, and sipped his rum drink. "But that is only fair, my colonel. Huerta was opposed to American policy in Central America. As he had come to learn about it, as we have all come to learn about it."

"But these journalists never ask to learn more. They keep writing the stories they bring with them. They talk to each other. They try to learn nothing. Is this always so?"

"Mostly," Kreski said.

"Why?" asked the colonel. "Are they ideologues?"

"To some degree. On the edges. But that's not it."

"Well, please, Señor Director. What is it? Why is this so?"

"Colonel. I learned a whole bunch of things working for the Secret

Service. But that's something I've never been able to figure out. I suppose, like most of us, they want a job with rules to follow. But there are no real rules for their job. They have to think for themselves. For some of them, that's hard."

The colonel grinned, then frowned. "Too bad we depend on them so much."

The dark of night. The cold outside and the warmth of the interior of the Mercedes. Pulling up at a stop light, he leaned to kiss her cheek. He kissed his fingertips and touched them to her breast.

She looked at him, those clear blue eyes pondering, assessing, knowing. She took his hand again, and squeezed. Then she sat back, against the window.

"What we do tonight will give me no choice but to stay with you to the bitter end."

"You can get out now. I'll stop the car and let you out. I'll get the car back to you. If you want, I'll get out. You've already done more than I've a right to ask."

"Damn you, damn you, Charley Dresden. You've screwed up my life once again."

The security guard, confronted by two extremely well-dressed people pounding on the door, snatched his consciousness back to full attention and hurried to open the door. Though he had grown up in a neighborhood of Jersey City where all norms and abnorms of human behavior could be witnessed on any weekend night with the temperature above zero, he was very surprised when Charley stuck the big gun in his ribs.

"I want you to take us into the tape room," Dresden said, pulling out the man's pistol from his holster. "Now."

The man's eyes widened with very genuine fear. It was probably the first such incident in his career as a security guard, certainly while working for the network.

"Yes, sir," he said. "No problem, sir."

There were two others in the huge chamber, one behind a desk and a second man filing tapes from a cart. They looked up, uncertainly, perhaps presuming Charley was an unexpected visitor from the network offices downtown.

"Tell them this is no joke and to do everything I say," said Dresden.

"Do everything he says," said the guard. "He's got the biggest gun in the world."

"Get against the wall, in the back, behind the shelves," Charley said.

They hurried to it, Charley pushing the guard after them. The other two held up their hands.

"That's not necessary," Charley said. He glanced around. As he would expect at any kind of television facility, there was a large roll of gray gaffer's tape on a shelf. The stuff of stagehands and floor directors, it was used for everything from sealing tape cartons and film cans to marking lines on studio floors to holding scenery together. It was about the strongest adhesive tape made.

Handing the two revolvers to Maddy, who held them a little clumsily, he quickly bound their captives' ankles and wrists. He made the three sit down against the wall.

"This is going to take a long time and they're going to get antsy," he said, "Just shoot the first one that moves."

She glanced at him, but kept steely control of her countenance. Settling into a chair, she took the pistol in both hands and held it in her lap, aiming it directly at the head of the man opposite her. He closed his eyes.

It took Dresden more than two hours to complete his work, but when he was done he was very satisfied with it. He made a package of the tapes he was taking and then returned to the filing room. Maddy was obviously nervous and seemed on the verge of becoming very upset, but this had only produced a very similar response in the four, who had stirred little from the positions in which Charley had left them.

"We're going to leave now," he said. "I'll call someone from the network in fifteen minutes to come out and free you."

In the car, Maddy talked frantically, almost hysterically, about how terrified she had been to have to sit for such a long time holding a loaded gun aimed at human beings. By the time they were speeding over a nearly empty George Washington Bridge, her fear and excitement had turned to a desire for love. It was not until they awoke the next morning in their room at the Plaza that Dresden remembered to call the network as promised.

18

The maître d' had given them a table in the northeast corner of the Edwardian Room, with a view of Central Park through one window and of Fifth Avenue across the fountain plaza through the other. There were many other couples there at breakfast, some very attractive, all looking extremely wealthy. Dresden and Maddy were attracting a few admiring looks. Charley returned his attention to Madeleine. "My father used to come here. This was his kind of life. I had fully expected it would also be mine."

"You look like you belong."

"Spuriously. Spending money I took from a dead woman, and soon I'll be running out of it."

A waiter appeared. They both ordered seafood dishes. It was late in the morning. He also ordered a bottle of champagne.

"I may run out sooner than I thought," he said.

"I have money," she said. "A lot."

"This isn't how I meant to return to the Plaza Hotel."

"Stop it, Charley. Enjoy yourself." She reached and touched his hand. "I feel all aglow."

"So do I. Are you still frightened?"

"A little. What sort of craziness is on the schedule for today?"

"We're going to look for a comic named Howie King."

"I've heard of him. He's an impersonator. Will we have an easy time finding him?"

"The object is not to find him. We have to establish that he's gone—and when he left. And how."

"Will that be easy?"

"I don't even know his address."

The waiter brought their champagne, with a decorous smile.

"So what are we going to do?" she asked, when the man had left.

"Actually, it may be easy. First we're going to call the subscription department of *Variety*."

The village of Ahuancha, just forty miles from the El Salvadoran border, was in a lush, green valley attained by crossing a forested ridge over a rough, dirt track. They were in two Jeeps: Kreski, Sandoval, Colonel Victores, and a Honduran national guardsman driver in one—the American mercenary in fatigues, beret, and mirrored sunglasses Kreski had seen at the airport in the other, accompanied by two murderous-looking Hondurans in combat dress, but also lacking insignia. They were heavily armed, and their Jeep led the way. The mysterious American had not said a single word to Kreski on the entire journey.

"Who is he?" Kreski asked Sandoval, as they bounced, slowing, around a steep, pitted curve in the road. The preceding jeep didn't slow a bit, until the American in the beret saw he had to wait for them. He had done so several times on the trip out from Tegucigalpa.

"A friend," said Sandoval. The colonel, riding in front with the driver, nodded.

"But I mean, who is he?"

"If he wants to tell you, he will. It is not for us to do so. Feel safe with him, however, Señor Kreski. He is very, very good. He fought twice in Vietnam, and has been coming here for many, many years."

The American in the beret was carrying an M-16, two pistols, and a half dozen hand grenades. Kreski had been provided with a 9 mm Beretta automatic. In Washington it would have made him feel very confident. Here, he felt rather helpless.

They roared into the village of Ahuancha, a long trail of dust hanging in the air behind them, at the height of the heat of the day. When they stopped it was to utter stillness. What few people had been squatting in doorways had withdrawn inside, doubtless wonder-

ing whether Kreski's party was government or guerrillas, and feeling equally uncertain about either possibility. After they had sat there
a moment, looking about but taking no threatening action, a few
faces appeared in the paneless windows, and two children stepped out
in the roadway, staring. They were barefoot, and skimpily clothed.

"You said Huerta had a prosperous farm here," Kreski said.

"For Honduras, this village is quite prosperous," said Sandoval.
"For some regions of Mexico, it would be quite prosperous."

"Huerta had a large house, with louvered glass windows," said the
colonel. "It was outside the village, up on the plateau."

"Who would you like to speak with?" said Sandoval.

"This visit was your idea," Kreski said. "I'll speak to anyone you
suggest."

"I would suggest the mayor," said the colonel. "He knew Huerta
well."

"And the head of the local agricultural bank," said Sandoval. "It's
a credit bank, up in that green building across the village square. You
should also talk to the police chief, and any of the villagers you
choose. I will be your translator."

"They won't even come out of their houses," Kreski said.

"They will be happy to talk to you," said the colonel. "We will
make them so."

In the Jeep ahead of them, the mysterious American sat staring
forward, the M-16 held upright on his knee. His Honduran companions were talking volubly among themselves, one of them glancing
back at Kreski's party.

"I'll talk to them all," Kreski said. "But first I'd like to go on up
and see where Huerta's people were murdered. I'm still curious about
his motivation."

"Oh, he was much motivated," said the colonel. *"Mucha locura."*

He shouted something in Spanish to the lead Jeep, and instantly
both vehicles jerked into motion, speeding up the grade and leaving a
dust cloud that drifted over the village square.

The bodies had, of course, all been removed and buried, but despite the passage of so many weeks, the ruination of the Huerta
granja seemed just as intensely recent as it must have when he had
first come upon it after the attack. Kreski could still smell the stench
of the charred wood. He looked at the skeletal remains of the rafters
and walls, and kicked at the debris. In the long building that had
been the main house, he noted some burned remnants of furniture

and kitchen utensils, but nothing else. No clothing, books, or papers. Many acres of the farm's fields had been burned as well.

"This fire was very intense," he said. "Gasoline?"

"Sí," the colonel said, nodding.

"But there are no traces of books or any other reading matter. Nothing. Not even gasoline would do that."

"Lieutenant Huerta was not known as a great reader."

Kreski looked around. "All the buildings are burned badly. They were all flamed at the same time, right? It was a hit by many men."

"Apparently so, señor."

"What did they do to the family?"

Sandoval looked away. The colonel shook his head.

"His wife was raped, many times. Then her throat was cut. The brother was beheaded, and his *conjones*, his privates, were stuffed in his mouth. One child was bayonetted. Others were simply shot. One had his head beaten in. There were other atrocities."

"Why?"

"Simply revenge. And to send a message."

"Why the rape?"

"A special insult."

"Huerta must have been especially hated."

"We are all hated, señor. On all sides. Huerta was especially famous. He should not have called himself La Puño. He should not have murdered so many people in the night. There are enough official ways to do it, legally, in the light of day."

"And who claimed credit for this?"

"A local Honduran group of leftist terrorists—La Izquierda Honduras. But there is no such group. We think the name is something made up by the El Salvadoran government. To keep them from blame for such things."

Kreski kicked again, sending a piece of charred wood spinning into some high weeds.

"All right," he said. "Let's go back to the village. I will talk to those you suggest. But I would like to start with some villagers."

The colonel smiled. "*Muy bien*, Señor Director."

Copley, summoned to the White House, was directed by a marine guard to the windowless situation room in the basement. The vice president was there, alone except for his aides Shawcross and Neil Howard. Those two took little note of his arrival, their attention riveted on Atherton, who was pacing in random direction about the room. The passage of time since the bombing seemed to have worsened his condition rather than eased it. There were dark hollows under his eyes and a gauntness to his cheeks. The vice president's shoulder muscles were hunched, and he kept smacking a fist against the palm of the other hand.

"Steven, Steven Copley," he said. "Here at last."

"I was going to come at seven P.M., my usual time," said Copley. "Is something wrong?"

Shawcross gave him an odd look.

"Precisely," said the vice president. "Something wrong. Where is Kreski?"

"As I told you yesterday, Larry," said Copley "he took a plane to Atlanta and changed for a flight to Texas. We lost him in the damned Dallas–Fort Worth airport."

"Find him. Is he at Camp David?"

"No, Larry," Copley said. "I told you. Our people report no one new at Camp David."

"What about Dubarry, our would-be president?"

Atherton paused at the map display. The huge topographical map of Central America that had been there for weeks had been removed. In its place, at Atherton's order, was one of the Washington metropolitan area. Jagged circles had been marked on it.

"We found the apartment house in Rosslyn where they'd been keeping him, but he'd moved by then. He was sighted boarding a train at Union Station, a westbound Amtrak to Chicago. We put an agent on at Martinsburg, but he was no longer on the train."

Atherton turned to look at Copley hard, his eyes weak but glittering.

"They took him off in Maryland, then. He's at Camp David!"

"Not that we've been able to detect, Larry," Copley said. "They're just trying to keep him out of trouble until January, until the vote for president pro tem of the Senate."

"They mean to make him president of the United States!" said the vice president. "After they blow the rest of us up! Where's the speaker?"

Copley glanced at his watch. "In his office in the Capitol. He's been there every day."

"Find him!"

"The speaker?"

"Precisely!"

Shawcross looked at Copley, shaking his head.

* * *

Finding Howie King's address did prove simple. Dresden called *Variety*'s subscription department, using King's name, and complained that he'd not received a copy of the trade paper since he'd moved. He asked what address they had him listed under. The woman on the other end gave him the addresses of three Howard Kings in Manhattan. Charley seized upon one—a street number in the West Seventies just off Central Park—and said that was his address. He then churlishly demanded that she see to it that his copies got through, hanging up angrily.

It was easy to determine that the two other addresses were not those he was seeking. One was for a Howard King theatrical agency in the West Forties. The other was in the East Village. Both were listed in the telephone directory. The one just off Central Park was not.

They stopped first at a discount electronics store on Fifth Avenue, buying an expensive and highly reliable Sony pocket tape recorder, which Charley had Madeleine place in her purse, with the microphone facing out. Then they took a taxi to King's building. It was old, mostly Jewish, a little worn at the edges, but, like all New York real estate property in that area, very expensive and something of a prestigious address. It had a doorman, who courteously admitted them; and a uniformed security guard at the lobby desk. They went up to him and, with a slightly irritated tone, Charley asked him to ring the King apartment.

"Mr. King isn't here," the man replied. "He's away. He's been away for some time."

"So I gather," Dresden said. "I've been calling him every day for weeks. He has an engagement with my television studio and has simply not appeared."

"Well, I don't know anything about that, sir."

"I'm sure you don't. Did he leave any word as to where he was going? When he might return?"

"No sir."

"Have you called the police?"

"The police?"

"Yes, the police. This is most irregular. A man who's being paid what I'm paying Mr. King doesn't simply not show up."

"Well, it is a little odd, his going away like this. When he left other times he always gave us notice. Had us hold his mail in the office. Things like that. This time, he just left. But I don't think you need the police."

"Did he say anything, to anyone? Where he was going?"

"No, but he . . . well, I don't know I should be discussing this with you, sir. Mr. King is a very important man."

Dresden sighed with much exasperation. "I don't know what it might take to overcome your undue discretion, but if this will help, here." He handed the guard a fifty-dollar bill. "I need to find Howie King. He's holding up my production. It's a very expensive one and he's making it even more so."

The guard studied Dresden's face a moment, then quickly slipped the bill into his pocket. He glanced at Maddy, whose well-dressed blond beauty seemed to help convince him that Dresden was who he said he was.

"Well, sir," he said. "He left under kinda peculiar circumstances. He looked happy enough. I mean, he looked like he was going willingly. But it was with a bunch of men. One was an army general. The other was that TV talk show guy, you know, the one with all the big words."

"William F. Buckley?"

"No, the other one. David Callister. I could tell it was him easy. He looked at me like I was a piece of dirt."

"Thank you," said Dresden, turning. "I'll call Callister's office."

Out on the street, looking for a cab, they halted, as Maddy switched off the machine.

"Does this help?" she said.

"It certainly helps us decide what to do next."

Kreski talked to at least a dozen people in Ahuancha, ranging from the mayor and police chief to a woman doing laundry in the little river and the small boy with her. His Spanish was poor, but he guessed that Colonel Victores was giving a fair and honest translation. All those he spoke to said more or less the same thing, though the mayor and police chief tried to belittle the ferocity and effectiveness of the guerrilla raid and the villagers tended to speak with some contempt of the mayor and police chief.

The consensus was that, though there was some affection for the women and children of the family, the Huerta brothers were considered something of local tyrants, engendering a dislike aggravated by their being outlanders from across the border in El Salvador, and people whom it was always expected would bring trouble on the village. They confirmed that Huerta liked to be talked about as "La Puño." After the killings and the mass funeral, Huerta had remained in the village, drinking in the local cantina day and night, still wearing his Guardia Nacionale lieutenant's uniform though he was no longer entitled to it. After a few days some Guardia officers who were friends of his came to see him, and a few days after that, a tall man named Jalisco, apparently Honduran, arrived in a relatively new American car. He and Huerta spent several hours drinking together, and by evening Huerta left with him, never to return.

All of the villagers, excepting the two officials, asked Kreski if there would be more trouble for Ahuancha now that Huerta had shot the president of the United States. Kreski assured them there would not, though without any inner certainty. From the way the Central American conflict was proceeding, it was not a pledge he could have made with certainty even if Huerta had never set foot in the United States.

"What can you tell me of this Jalisco?" Kreski asked Sandoval as they drove out of the village.

Sandoval said nothing, nodding to the colonel, who finally turned in his seat.

"Juan Pedro Jalisco," the colonel recited, as though from some memorized police record. "Born in either Mexico or Guatemala. Active with the FDN and the Contras in the Reagan days; with the right-wing El Salvadoran refugee groups and the American mercenaries in this stage of the conflict. He showed up with Huerta in Barra Mono a week or so after they left Ahuancha. It is a fishing port on the east coast near the Nicaraguan border. Jalisco had something to do with shipping—the merchant marine, or warehouses. We're not sure. He knew boats. Our suspicion is he got Huerta into the United States by boat."

"We will take you to Barra Mono tomorrow, if we can," said Sandoval, coughing from the dust thrown up by the Jeep ahead. "Maybe not for a few days. There has been some fighting there. I know that does not worry you perhaps, but the American military in the town will be touchy. We don't want them to inhibit you."

"Jalisco was also involved in some smuggling in this part of the country," Colonel Victores said. "We are not altogether certain which side he truly served, if any. We do not know if the American military approved of him or not."

"We're certain they don't approve of him now," Sandoval said.

The sky was turning a dirty gray, but the heat seemed only to intensify. Kreski assumed coolness would come only with the rain the skies were promising. He noted neither Jeep carried a canvas top.

The rain struck no more than ten miles down the road, a good distance yet to go before the main highway to Tegucigalpa, a few large dollops impacting on the dust like bullets amidst a heavy scent of jungle and ozone, followed by a crashing deluge. Kreski, like the colonel, wore khakis, but Sandoval was dressed in a civilian shirt and gray slacks. All of them were quickly and utterly soaked, but the feeling at first was less one of discomfort than of relief at the coolness. The Jeeps slowed as the road began to mud up in places. After a while the coolness turned more to cold, and Kreski began to wish for his hotel room and one of those rum drinks.

"*Lo siento*," said the colonel, shouting to make himself heard over the downpour. "The weather this time of year is always unpredictable."

Suddenly the lead Jeep lurched to a stop and, at a command from the American in the beret, began to back up rapidly, wheels spinning. Kreski supposed it had something to do with an obstruction in the road, but he saw the American suddenly dive from the vehicle into the roadside brush as orange bursts brightened the gloom ahead and the sound of gunfire crackled in the thundering deluge.

The American in the beret, rolling, fired his M-16 in response as his driver slumped over the wheel. The other Honduran in the vehicle skipped to the opposite side of the road, firing his weapon.

The American looked back at Kreski's Jeep, shouting: "Get out! Get down!"

Colonel Victores was already in the act of doing so. Kreski and Sandoval leaped over the side and flattened themselves in the mud. As Kreski looked up, he saw their driver scamper into the brush. In a moment, both Honduran soldiers and the American in the beret had disappeared into the heavy growth.

The firing ahead became more frequent and closer. Pulling out the Beretta, Kreski at length saw three, then four, shadowy figures dodging along either side of the road toward them, firing short bursts. The colonel, just ahead of Kreski, his feet almost in Kreski's face, got off two quick shots from his pistol, hitting no one. Kreski held his own fire, waiting with teeth hard against his lower lip as the dark figures came nearer. As Kreski should have expected, one of them abruptly halted, reached down, and then threw a grenade, which landed in the lead jeep, the following explosion knocking it askew, setting it aflame despite the heavy rain.

Kreski, gripping his automatic with both hands as trained, raised his weapon and squeezed off three careful rounds, the last one hitting his target in the chest and whipping him backward. The man had been about to throw another grenade, and it went off just behind him, lifting his body and wounding one of his comrades. At once there was a great cacophony of gunfire coming from the jungle on both sides of the roadway. The other attackers fell, but the gunfire continued, moving away. More shadowy figures appeared, backing out of the brush, but they fell too.

When at last there was silence the rain magically began to abate, as though it had been a special effect written into the script for which there was no longer any need. As it dissipated, leaving only a ground mist, the American in the beret and his two companions stepped out into the clear, weapons smoking and held at the ready.

"The dumb bastards should have used a Claymore," said the American in the beret. "Don't nobody know how to ambush anymore?"

He and his companions began examining the attackers' bodies, kicking each hard in the head with their boots. One they kicked and pulled to his feet. He appeared only slightly wounded but very much afraid.

The American looked back at the burning jeep, swore loudly, then turned to the wounded prisoner and shot him in the face. He crumpled without a sound.

The American joined Kreski and the others, who had risen from the road covered with mud.

"Why did you kill him?" Kreski asked.

"We got only one fucking Jeep now," the American said. "There's no room for the bastard."

Whatever complaint Kreski might have uttered was precluded by his remembering and looking at the man he had himself shot. He had an impulse to go and look at the body, but a stronger desire not to. Despite all his years in the police and the Secret Service, he wasn't much hardened to killing, especially when he was the killer.

"That was excellent shooting, Señor Director," said the colonel. "You may have saved our lives."

The American in the beret nodded and grunted what Kreski assumed was a similar compliment.

"Who were they?" Kreski asked.

The colonel shrugged. "In this country, they could be anyone. Bandits, drug smugglers, El Salvadoran infiltrators, leftist guerrillas, anyone."

"They were fucking Nicks," said the American in the beret, putting a fresh clip into his weapon. "Nistas, with fucking AK-7s. Come on. Let's get the hell out of here."

It was the most voluble he'd been on the entire trip. When they were all crowded into the cramped, remaining Jeep and churning down the road again, the human lumps left in their still, contorted positions on the track behind them, he lapsed back into silence. In fact, no one spoke until they reached the outskirts of Tegucigalpa, and Sandoval suggested a place for dinner.

Maddy was right. David Callister and his wife were listed in the *Social Register*, as she and George Calendiari were not. The copy made available to them at the public library on 42nd Street was that year's, and it showed three addresses—one on Park Avenue, one in Bermuda, and one in Pound Ridge up in Westchester. Dresden wrote them and the accompanying telephone numbers down, then returned the book to the librarian.

"I know him," Maddy said, as they came down the library steps into the crisp cold. "I mean, I've met and talked to him at several parties. We were seated next to each other at a dinner party once, but with him, it's hard to tell how much attention he pays to other people. He does all the talking. He might remember me."

"I'd remember you, even if you never said a word."

She took his arm as they turned up Fifth Avenue toward the park and the Plaza. The sky was clear and the sun was bright. The city looked almost beautiful.

"Dare we make these calls from our room?" he asked.

"Charley. If we're able to track down David Callister, it's not going to matter where we call from. If everything you believe is true, all that will matter is that we're able to get away from him again. Fast."

"I'll take care of that."

"Besides," she said, pulling him closer. "Going back to the room has other advantages."

They tried all three numbers—Park Avenue, Westchester, and Bermuda, in that order—but reached only rude servants who would tell them nothing.

"Perhaps I should have said it was the White House calling," said Dresden, exasperated.

"Let me try," she said.

But the response was largely the same. The servants politely took down the message, but gave no information as to where Callister was or when he'd be returning.

An hour later they were having scotch and water in the Plaza's Oak Bar, physically more content but otherwise frustrated.

"Charley. I have an idea. Haven't you noticed something different about New York?"

"It's more expensive."

"It's always more expensive. I'm talking about the shoppers, all the limousines at the curbs, the lights, the season."

"It's almost Christmas."

"Exactly. I think we should buy a present for Mr. Callister and deliver it personally to his Park Avenue place."

She emerged from Saks Fifth Avenue carrying a large gift-wrapped box in a shopping bag.

"What are we giving him?" Dresden said. "A dozen copies of *The Preppy Handbook?*"

"Nothing so heavy. Two dozen pairs of Jockey shorts. I hope in a size several times too small."

"Maddy. People from his background make a point of not wearing Jockey shorts. They wear boxer shorts. De rigeur."

"I'm well aware of that," she said, grinning mischievously. "Come along, Santa."

Callister's doorman admitted them without hesitation and with considerable deference, but, in the lobby, they encountered the same sort of security attendant they had in Howie King's building. This one was younger, much better dressed, and considerably more officious.

"I'm Madeleine Calendiari," Maddy said. "This is my husband, Senator Calendiari."

The Italian name did not overly impress the young man.

"We wanted to drop off our Christmas present for the Callisters before we left New York," Dresden said. He decorously slipped the man a twenty-dollar bill. "They're not in, apparently, but if you could take good care of it until they return . . . ? They will be back by Christmas, won't they?"

"As a matter of fact, no sir. I can send it upstairs to their apartment, but they'll be away until after the first of the year."

"Oh dear, not at their place in Bermuda?" Dresden said.

"We could never get this to them in Bermuda in time," said Maddy.

"Mrs. Callister is in Bermuda," said the attendant. "Mr. Callister is traveling."

Dresden retrieved the box, ignoring the money still in the attendant's hand. "Oh, well. Perhaps we'll run into him back in Washington."

"He didn't say where he was traveling, sir. But you might . . ." The young man appeared reluctant to say anything more to strangers, no matter how well dressed. His principal job was protecting residents of the building from strangers, though it also included providing every assistance to residents' friends.

"Might try sending it to the house in Pound Ridge?" Dresden asked.

"Yes, sir. I presume you have the address. Mr. Callister said he'd be stopping by there this weekend."

"We'll do precisely that," Dresden said. "Thank you very, very much."

Outside, unable to find an available cab, they decided to walk.

"Damn," Dresden said. "It's three days until the weekend."

"Charles," said Maddy, affecting an Eastern tone. "I think we can find something to do for three days in New York."

19

North of White Plains there was snow on the ground. When Dresden turned the yellow Mercedes off Interstate 684 at the Katonah exit some twelve miles farther up the road, the snow cover was thicker and more was falling. Under leaden skies, everything seemed black and white—old white colonial homes with dark roofs and windows set in fields of white amidst the stark silhouettes of winter trees, the highways a moist black where the snow was not sticking.

Charley drove in the easy, practiced manner of a man who knew where he was, though he had not been in Westchester for more than fifteen years. They followed the shore of a large and pretty reservoir that extended for several miles, passed through a small village that consisted of little more than post office and general store, then headed up a set of sweeping curves to the top of a high ridge. Turning onto the highway that ran along the summit, Dresden proceeded perhaps a mile and then abruptly pulled into the long, curving drive of a large estate. There was a separate four-car garage with an apartment above it, several outbuildings, including a summer house, and hedges indicating a formal garden. The main house was almost large enough to be called a mansion, an antique of genuine colonial architecture that established it as possibly two centuries old. Charley continued along the drive slowly, passing under the porte cochere at the house's entrance and then coming at length to the highway again, pausing at the open gate in the stone wall and looking back.

"It has thirty-five acres running all the way to the stream at the bottom of the valley," he said. "There's a pond with a waterfall, a stable with six stalls, a fifteen-foot-deep swimming pool, and the grape arbor is made of cedar wood, if it's still there."

"Is this David Callister's house?"

"No. Just a place from my past."

"You knew the people who lived here?"

"We were the people who lived here." He gunned the Mercedes' engine, wheels slipping in the snow until they had gripped the firmness of the highway again. "My father killed himself sitting in a car parked on the back drive."

She sat silently, glancing back one quick time, and then staring straight ahead. The snow had now stopped, and there was an unfolding break in the clouds visible above the hills on the horizon.

"Don't be overawed," Charley continued. "We rented the place. My father never saved enough money to buy anything. The real owners were one of those Russian émigré families. They didn't charge us all that much, really. The place was a little run-down and difficult to care for. They had a hard time finding renters. I loved it, though. When I was made to leave Westchester I felt like those émigrés must have when the Bolsheviks drove them out of Russia."

"With so many bad memories, why did you want to come back here? Was it just to impress the California car dealer's daughter?"

At the crossroads he turned onto a different highway, heading south.

"It was to impress myself. To remind myself of our old status. When we deal with Callister tonight I want to feel as confident as possible."

"Tonight?"

"It will be the best time to catch him unawares, and to be sure of not being interrupted. Or so I hope. First, I'm going to take you to dinner at Emily Shaw's Inn. It's one of the more pleasant experiences to be had around here. What comes after won't be pleasant at all."

En route to the restaurant, they first located the Callister home and drove by it twice. It was set well back from the road, but they could see a number of tire tracks in the snow-covered driveway. There were lights aglow in many of the windows. Someone besides a servant or two was at home.

It was fully dark when they left the inn. Maddy stiffened as they waited for the attendant to bring their car, and from more than the cold. He sensed she wished the dinner were the concluding event of the evening.

"Cheer up," he said. "This is the last part of the ordeal. Then we make our escape—from many things."

She merely shivered. At Callister's door, holding the spurious gift box from Saks, she took a deep breath and relaxed, preparing herself for her part in the nasty business that was about to follow.

"Just be careful how you hold your purse," Charley said. "We need every word of this on tape."

After another deep breath she rang the bell. After a fairly long wait, a woman who appeared to be a maid or housekeeper responded.

"I'm Mrs. Calendiari, the senator's wife. I just want to drop this Christmas package off for the Callisters."

The woman opened the door further. "Well, Mr. Callister's home tonight," she said. "Won't you come in?"

She hadn't noticed Charley, who'd been standing in the shadows to the side, and looked somewhat startled when he entered behind Maddy.

"This gentleman's a friend of mine," Maddy said. "My host for the weekend."

"I'll tell Mr. Callister you're here. He's in his study." The woman went to a large, paneled door a short ways down the hall, and knocked. There was a response they could not hear, and she entered.

"Mr. Callister," she said. "There's a Mrs. Calendiari here. She says she's a senator's wife and has a present for you."

He replied with some churlish muttering, and then said, more loudly than he perhaps intended, "How in hellfire would anyone know I'm here?"

When he appeared at the study door, dressed in cardigan sweater, button-down shirt, gray flannels, and tasseled loafers, his expression was at first very disagreeable, and then one of puzzlement. It was the first time Dresden had seen the commentator without his television personna. He had expected the aloof, almost supercilious, patronizing contempt that was Callister's trademark. Instead, there was only irritability.

The maid started down the hall.

"Mrs. Calendiari?" The voice at least was aloof—and mellifluous and refined.

"Do you remember me?" Maddy said. "We sat together one eve-ning at dinner, at the Canadian Embassy, as I recall."

"I remember vaguely. They had some ghastly French-Canadian folk singer for entertainment. You've brought me a present?"

"It's from George."

The maid had disappeared, shutting a distant door behind her.

"Oh yes. On the Foreign Affairs Committee. Atherton's friend. Is this some sort of unamusing joke? I just savaged your husband in a column a few weeks ago."

He stopped talking, his look of puzzlement become one of alarm. Dresden had taken out his Magnum pistol.

"Get into the study," Charley said, stepping forward.

"Is this a robbery? If so . . ."

Charley shoved him. "I said get into the study."

He did as bidden, a jab from the barrel of Dresden's pistol urging him on. When all three were in the room, Charley closed the door and locked it.

"If you are Mrs. Calendiari," Callister said, some of his arrogance returning, "and as memory serves, you look to be, you and your husband are in a great deal of trouble. If you are simply robbers, take what you want and leave quickly. You will still be in a great deal of trouble."

Dresden looked past Callister to his huge, mahogany desk. It was covered with newspaper clippings—not copies of Callister's columns but news stories. From the size and form of them, Charley guessed they were transcripts of presidential speeches and press conferences.

"Where is Howie King?" Charley asked.

Now Callister's expression turned to astonishment. His voice be-came very cautious. "Who are you?"

"Just consider us the political opposition," said Dresden.

Eyes darkening, Callister looked to Madeleine. "Your husband is a friend of the vice president's. Is Atherton involved in this?"

Charley went up to Callister and jammed the gun barrel into the man's stomach. "Where is Howie King?"

Callister gagged slightly, staggering backward. "I don't know what you're talking about."

"Yes, you do. The last time Howie King was seen by anyone was leaving his apartment building in New York in the company of your-self, a general, and a couple of other men I presume were White House assistants."

"How do you know that?"

"Where is King? At Camp David?"

"I've no idea. Our visit with him was brief. It had to do with national security. We were thinking of using the man as a double for the president until this period of danger is over, but it didn't work out. He doesn't really resemble President Hampton at all."

Dresden struck Callister hard across the mouth with the pistol, causing him to fall to the floor. He lay there, staring upward in fear and hatred, blood flowing from his rapidly swelling lip. Charley knelt over him and placed the gun's muzzle directly between Callister's eyes.

"You don't seem to understand how serious I am about this," Charley said. "I'm wanted for two murders in California, as you probably know."

"Don't know. Don't know anything about you."

"Like hell you don't." Charley pressed the muzzle hard against the bridge of the other's nose. "I didn't kill anyone, as you also must know. But I'm willing to do so now. It's all the same to the police. Those two people were dear friends of mine. They've got some biblical justice coming."

"Biblical . . . ?"

"Damn you! Answer me! Is Howie King at Camp David?"

"Yes." Callister's speech was slightly slurred from his injury.

"He's an impressionist, a professional imitator. You've been using him to simulate the president's voice. It's actually been King speaking in those telephone conversations, those radio broadcasts. You've dubbed his voice onto old videotapes of Hampton and passed it off as the real thing. Isn't that so?" He pulled back the hammer of the revolver.

"Yes."

"And the president is really dead, isn't he?"

"No."

"Damn it, Callister! A straight answer!"

"He was alive last time I saw him. That's the truth."

"When was that?"

"Weeks ago. After the shooting."

Dresden paused. William McKinley and James Garfield had been mortally wounded, but both had lingered for some time. Hampton may not have died instantly. But surely he was dead now. King's continuing performance attested to that. Dresden got to his feet. "I think you're lying about the president," he said. "But I have what I want."

Callister sat up, rubbing his mouth.

"I'll deny all of this," he said. "No one will believe you."

"Are you David Callister, the columnist?"

"Of course."

"Thank you for saying so. Now you won't be able to deny anything."

Callister looked at Maddy and then at her purse.

"You have this on tape."

"Of course."

"You won't get away with it. You've committed at least three felonies coming in here tonight. I'll have the police on you the instant you leave this house. I'll claim the tape as property you stole."

"I grew up here. I know ways out of this county the police would never dream of."

"Who are you?"

"If you truly don't know, Mr. Callister, I'm sure there are people at Camp David right now who can tell you."

Callister looked again at Maddy. "You've ruined your husband's career."

"There are a lot of careers that are going to be ruined before this is over," Charley said. "Including yours. Mrs. Atherton lost more than a career."

"We had nothing to do with that."

"That can be debated at some other time, maybe before a congressional investigating committee." Dresden returned the heavy pistol to his belt. "We're going to leave now, Callister. Fast. I suggest you sit here quietly for a while. Think very carefully about what you do after we go out that door."

Once in the car, as they sped down a back road toward the Connecticut line and the Merritt Parkway, Maddy began to cry. "Why did you have to hit him like that, Charley?"

"So he'd take me seriously. Really seriously. He did."

"But you were so vicious. That gun. God, what have you gotten me mixed up in?"

"Maddy, the whole country's mixed up in this. Do I have to say it again? Mrs. Atherton didn't get off with a pistol whipping. My friend Charlene is very dead."

Her crying ceased, but apparently not her tears. She kept wiping her eyes with the back of her glove.

"I'm scared, Charley. I've never been this scared."

"Play the tape back. I want to make sure we got everything. We've been lucky so far, but my luck has lately developed a habit of running out on me."

"Will the police be after us?"

"He won't call them."

"You're sure?"

"Callister's friends will come after us, all right. Don't worry about that. And when they do it won't be with the police. My hope is that by then we'll be safely in the Vice President's House."

"You've got us all in the same boat with you now, don't you? Me. George. And soon the vice president."

"It's not my boat."

He drove on. He offered her no words of comfort. She'd made her choice, just as he'd made his. It wasn't supposed to be easy. It was going to be anything but that, as she would have to make herself understand.

When the call finally came for the trip to Barra Mono, it was from Sandoval. He met Kreski in the lobby of the high-rise before sunrise the next morning and drove him up to the airport, proceeding on to the military side of the field and halting near a small helicopter parked slightly apart from a long row of others. It was painted olive drab, but bore no markings whatsoever. Sandoval did not get out of the car.

"There's your machine, Señor Kreski. I have business in Tegucigalpa today and won't be coming with you. He is a good pilot. You will be in good hands. You should be back tomorrow. I will see you then. *Buen viaje!*"

They shook hands with much macho firmness, brother veterans of combat now. Kreski took up his small canvas bag and hurried toward the little helicopter, whose pilot swung open the door for him. He was wearing a flight helmet, but Kreski recognized him immediately. He was the American who had been with them on the trip to Ahuancha, the killer in the beret, the "merc."

"Put this on," he said, handing Kreski another helmet. "Plug in the mike and we can talk on the intercom. Let loose of the mike button when you're through talking or you won't be able to hear a fucking thing I say."

"I've used radios before."

"Yeah. I guess you have."

As Kreski adjusted the helmet and fastened his seat belt, the other man started the engine with a whine that quickly grew into a muffled, shuddering roar. With a slight movement of his hand, he lifted the helicopter several feet off the ground, spoke a few words into the microphone to the military air controller, then tipped the small aircraft forward slightly and began a swift climb into the emerging sunlight in the east, following a course over the city. It was one of the few times of the day one could see the mountains around Tegucigalpa, their tops clearly etched against the sky. In an hour or so they would be lost in the haze and smog of automobile exhaust.

"What kind of helicopter is this?" Kreski asked. "I've never seen one before. They didn't have any around when I was down here with the president."

"It's an OH-Six. In Nam we called them the LOCH, light observation combat helicopter. They manufacture them now as the Hughes Five Hundred. You can get two of them into a C-One-three-one. Can fly them onto an enemy field, offload them and attach the rotors, and have them in combat in sixty seconds. They're great shit for clearing airfield perimeters. They carry a forward-firing chain gun and two rocket racks. We used them in 'Nada in eighty-three."

"What are they used for down here?"

"Everything from road interdiction to bomb drops to nightstalker black jobs. You know, 'training missions.'" He grinned.

"Does this one belong to the U.S. military or Peter Ashley Brookes?"

The man ceased grinning. "Ain't saying."

"I've figured out who you are."

"I would have thought you'd done that right off. The fucking libs have dragged my ass up to Congress enough times to testify about our activities."

"You're Mason Barren, editor of *Mercenary Magazine*."

"Managing editor. And I go by Mace Barren. You should know that. I'm sure you guys got a sheet on me."

"As a matter of fact, I was reading it just a few weeks ago. Born 1938, Rawlins, Wyoming . . ."

"It was 1939."

"Worked as a truck driver, strip-mine dynamiter, Forest Service fire fighter. Drafted in 1962, went through OCS, joined the Special

Forces, served in Panama, did two tours in Vietnam, never got above the rank of captain."

"Wrongo. Last tour I held the temporary rank of major. Lost it when I quit the army eight years short of retirement."

They were well east of the city, following a river that wound alongside the slopes of Honduras' central plateau. The sun had risen high enough to brighten all the ground below them. Barren tapped one of his instruments, then leaned back again, glancing about the skies around him in the manner of a World War I fighter pilot.

"Then you became a free-lancer in South Florida, working with anti-Castro Cubans. Then you disappeared for a while."

"I went to 'Gola. No big thing. Worked with Savimbi. You know, 'training.'"

"How did you get into 'journalism'?"

"I tried writing books, but I couldn't get anyone to publish them. Too right wing. Too gory. I finally had one published myself. Mr. Brookes didn't think it was too right wing, or too gory."

"You boasted once you'd probably killed more than a hundred men."

"I never said that. I said fifty. No Americans."

They lapsed into silence, which Barren seemed to prefer. In the gathering heat of the increasing sunlight, Kreski found himself dozing. At length, he slept.

He awakened to hear Barren's voice in his earphones, swearing. "Look at all this shit. Might as well be back at Fort Bragg."

They were still by the plateau, but the terrain was descending, and the green of the coastal plain was visible in the hazy distance ahead. Barren, however, was looking out the side window, straight down. Shading his eyes, Kreski did the same on his side.

Everything was camouflaged, but they were flying at an altitude low enough for much of it to be visible. Acres of army tents. Clusters of trucks, "Hummer" combat terrain vehicles, armored personnel carriers, light tanks, rocket launchers, missile launchers, radars, anti-aircraft gun emplacements. In a long nearby clearing, Kreski could even see the outlines of a few combat fighters. There were doubtless more hidden from view.

"There was hardly any of this around on the presidential visit," he said.

"Yeah, there was. They just kept you away from most of it because of all the fucking press you had with you."

"To what point? The American public has a pretty good idea of what's happening down here. TV and newspapers have been full of it for months. They know how many Americans have been lost, almost as many as in Lebanon."

"They don't know shit."

"They know there's a war."

"Don't I wish. Mister, there's been a 'continuous joint training exercise' with the Hondurans, Guatemalans, and Costa Ricans going on ever since the El Salvadoran government fell—nearly two fucking years. There's been one kind of training exercise or another going on since early in the Reagan administration. In the last fourteen months we've put enough conventional force into this sector to wipe the ass of the 'Nistas all the way to Managua."

"Sandinistas?"

"I call them 'Nistas. The Contras call them 'Compas'—short for Compañeros; that's like 'comrades.' They also call them an Indian name, *Perros quacos*. Mad dogs."

"There are mad dogs on your side—our side."

"There are mad dogs in all those skunk works around the Pentagon too. We've got gunships that can put a cannon round in every square yard of a football field quicker than a man can run across it. We used them in 'Nada. You should have seen the piles of chopped-up feet. We've got gas bombs that spread an explosive cloud over an area bigger than a city block that go off with enough implosive force to suck the lungs out of a 'Nista's nose. We've got antipersonnel grenades that fire hundreds of plastic flechettes that can dig into a man's guts without ever showing up in an X-ray. We've got two combat divisions, every kind of commando and black job unit imaginable, all kinds of tac air, and two naval task forces. We could win a war here in a week. All Hampton has to do is give the word and the 'Nistas disappear. But he's refused to do it, and ever since he got shot up everyone down here's been sitting on his ass. We haven't had a single decent combat action—black job, free-lance, nothing. The Pentagon even has a hold on cross border recon. But I tell you, one coded message from the Pentagon war room and the 'Nistas are piles of raw meat."

"What about the Cubans?"

"They're already here. They were in 'Gola. They were in 'Nada. No big shit."

"What about the Russians?"

"They were in Nam. They were in Laos. They were in fucking

Korea. No big shit. They're what we're fighting. That's why we're here."

Now it was Kreski who preferred silence. He saw uniformed men moving about the ground, many of them turning to watch them pass overhead, but without alarm. A question should have occurred to him many miles before.

"How is it we can overfly all these installations with such impunity?" he asked.

"Got clearance radioed ahead," said Barren. "And we're flying a prescribed course."

"How do you get this kind of clearance as a magazine editor?"

"I'm part of the team. I'm a lieutenant colonel in the Alabama National Guard."

"Are you from Alabama?"

Barren turned and grinned again. "Hell no."

They had been following the steep-sided valley of what Barren identified as the Patuca River. Without warning, he made a sharp turn to the right and began climbing to skirt the top of a high ridge that blocked their way to the south. He crossed at a shallow saddle, descending the long slope beyond into a lush, green valley. A twisting path among the trees ahead proved to be a wide river.

"This is the Coco," Barren said, as the helicopter chattered across it. "Welcome to Nicaragua."

"What?"

Barren said nothing more. He was busy. Dropping the chopper to treetop level, he flew a zigzag course parallel to the river, veered off to the right until he was over a dirt road, and followed it at red-line speed among flashes of gunfire from the ground until he was roaring along the main street of a town. The central square quickly appeared, a military vehicle of some sort parked next to it. Barren fired off a few rounds from the chain gun with indeterminate effect, then lifted over a rooftop and fled the area by the most direct route possible, crossing the river shortly after.

"Just got the urge," he said. "That town was Balana. Never liked the place." He turned the helicopter back north toward the ridge line. "Don't tell anyone. I might lose my commission in the Alabama Guard."

This time he stayed to the south of the ridge, which quickly grew into a range of mountains—the Montañas de Colon. The only diversion he made after that was to turn south briefly on another road, sweeping over a procession of a few dozen people and pack animals, moving slowly up from the border. They looked up at the helicopter, but did not flee.

"Campesinos," he said. "Probably okay. People have been leaving Nicaragua every day since the 'Nistas took over. Sometimes there's a 'Nista infiltrator with them, but there's no use wasting 'em just for that."

Lifting the machine once more, he set it on a compass heading for the northeast, and kept it there. The mountains at length slid away to the left, and the ensuing green flatness shortly afterward revealed a line of blueness on the horizon. It proved to be a wide bay, opening onto the sea.

"Laguna de Caratasca. This whole 'exercise' is 'purple,'" Barren said, using the Pentagon term for a joint operation involving all the armed services, "but this here's navy country. Swift boats, PVs, and landing craft in the bay. Destroyers and frigates off shore. And the USS *Iowa* task force on station in blue water. The ground perimeter's held by the marines."

"They know we're coming?"

"Fucking A. Otherwise we'd be nothing more than a few pieces of burning flesh and aluminum in about five minutes. They know who you are. They know you're no longer with the White House. You've got clearance because you're listed with us, TDY."

"Who are we going to see?"

"Any marine or navy intelligence officer who will talk to you. They got some good shit on Jalisco." He paused to throttle back on the helicopter's speed and speak a few words on the radio to someone on the ground. "Look, Kreski," he said, coming back on the intercom. "I can answer any question you have about Jalisco, at least about his operations down here. But Mr. Brookes wants you to get everything from the straight official shit. So I'll take you to it."

They swept over the trees toward a cleared landing zone containing perhaps a dozen other helicopters, all with marine markings.

"Just keep this in mind, Kreski," Barren said, settling the machine onto the ground in a great cloud of flying dust. "As long as you're in country, you are with us. That means especially me, Sandoval, or Victores. You ain't no longer a Fed."

"Understood," Kreski said.

A jeep driven by a marine lance corporal jounced them up a road to a gathering of camouflaged tents, halting before one of the smaller ones. Barren led them inside, past two enlisted men working at typewriters, and up to a desk where a marine major in combat fatigues with rolled up sleeves was sitting behind a table piled with paperwork. Except for mosquito netting, the sides of the tent had been rolled up to reveal the trees and tents around them. There was a vague breeze from the sea.

"'Colonel' Barren," the major said, in a greeting that amounted mostly to grunt. "Up our ass again, I see."

"All part of the program."

"This Kreski?"

"You got it."

The major looked up, then nodded at a canvas camp chair. "Have a seat, sir." As Kreski did as bidden the marine officer pulled a file folder out from a stack of them.

"You want to know about Juan Jalisco."

"Whatever you can tell me."

The major opened the folder, but kept its contents from Kreski's view. "Juan Pedro Jalisco, born 10 January 1943, Veracruz, Mexico. Also resided in Guatemala and Belize. Been in and out of this region since the overthrow of Somoza in 1979. Worked for underground organizations believed associated with Roberto d'Aubisson in El Salvador. Active in right-wing Contra groups here and across the border. Worked for U.S. government . . ." He paused. "That's classified."

"I understand."

"Main thing is, he's shown up at one time or another with every outfit down here that isn't Commie. For a while we were afraid he was spying for the Compas, but couldn't find a trace of any link to them. He's strictly right-wing."

"Was he involved with any organization called La Puño?"

"Nothing in here about that. But hell, there's a hundred of these outfits down here, a lot of them just bandits and smugglers. So who knows." He paused again. "Here's what you're looking for. Jalisco arrived in Barra Mono 29 September in company of Manuel Huerta, former lieutenant Honduran National Guard. Jalisco and Huerta departed Barra Mono in a small vessel with unknown crew, likely a fishing trawler, 3 October. Vessel never returned."

He looked up, smiling. "Next we saw of Huerta was in *Stars and Stripes*. You guys sure know how to shoot the shit out of a bastard."

"Not soon enough."

"Yeah." The major returned to the folder. "Here's what you're really looking for."

He handed Kreski an eight-by-ten black and white photograph. It was of a fat man lying on a beach; on second look, not really a fat man, but a swollen, dark-haired, bare-footed body, the bloated flesh having burst open some seams of its clothing. It was lying face up, half in the water.

"Juan Pedro Jalisco," the major said. "The body washed ashore about twenty miles up the coast on 5 October. Two bullet wounds in the head."

"Identification's positive?"

"That's only kind we ever make. Otherwise, they stay unidentified."

"You made a report on this?"

"Yes, sir. All the way up through fleet headquarters to NavInt."

"What happened to it?"

"Mr. Director, sir, that's a question we never ask."

20

Harpers Ferry, West Virginia, more a museum than a town, was built on and about a steep hill at the spectacular confluence of the Shenandoah and Potomac rivers. The two FBI agents on watch there had little interest in the scenery. They drove and parked about the town, seldom leaving their vehicle, observing the tourists, the townspeople, and the National Park Service workers, looking for anyone and anything out of place—looking for people like themselves. Their compatriots were doing the same in other towns along the Amtrak line between here and Washington. The orders had come from Director Copley himself, but that made them no less peculiar. If a U.S. senator wanted to shack up out here with the woodsies, it wasn't exactly a federal crime.

No one of any interest had gotten off the morning train, and the afternoon train had not even stopped. The tourists all went to the visitor's center, and to the fire house where John Brown had made his last stand, and prowled the musty antique shops on the long main street that climbed to the top of the hill. A dark green army sedan came by, but it proceeded across the river and out of town. The agents began to long for duty escorting tours of the J. Edgar Hoover Building.

Finally, making a patrol along the highway that led west from Harpers Ferry to Bolivar and Charles Town, a car moving fast in the opposite lane caught their attention. The sun was low in the sky, but the woman in the back was vividly obvious with her brilliant red hair.

"Do you think she fits the profile?" said the agent who was driving.

"I think she fits it like the clothes she's wearing," said the other.

The driver hit the brakes expertly, sending the car into a controlled slide that became a U-turn. In a moment they came within view of the other car and slowed, hanging back. At the outskirts of Harpers Ferry, the car ahead pulled off onto the dirt drive of an old white house with a sagging porch and vines entwined around its two front pillars. The agents passed by without pause but turned again and drove by once more, just as the woman was getting out. The man with her had a large plastic shopping bag, such as those used by liquor stores.

"She's not here for the quilting," said the agent who was driving.

"Not the usual kind, anyway."

"I'd better call in. I think we've found Senator Dubarry's country retreat."

Kreski had conversations with a number of other American officers at Barra Mono. They all said much the same thing. He learned that Jalisco's body had been shipped to his family in Veracruz. It was a favor provided in recognition of his service to the U.S. government. The many other bodies that turned up in the sector under mysterious circumstances usually were just buried on the spot, quickly. That night, Barren, the marine major, a Special Forces captain, and Kreski went drinking in the installation's makeshift officers' club. The other three became *baracco*—maximum drunk. Kreski worked very hard at not becoming so, but only half succeeded. The helicopter ride back to Tegucigalpa was an ordeal for him, but the night's drinking seemed not to bother Barren, unless these benders were the reason he always wore sunglasses.

They had radioed ahead, and Sandoval was waiting for them with a car and driver. Barren remained on the airfield, where he found friends.

"Well, señor?" Sandoval said, when they were beyond the airport gates. The day was very hot though it was not yet midmorning, and they had all the windows of the small car lowered. The wind blew bits of dust and dirt into Kreski's face.

"I'm satisfied," Kreski said. "About a lot of things."

"Yes?" The tall Latin smiled beneath his thick mustache. The more he was with him, the less Kreski thought of him as an American.

"I'm satisfied that La Puño is not an organization, but rather what Huerta called himself. I'm satisfied that Huerta was a fanatic bent on vengeance who was recruited for Gettysburg. I'm satisfied that the people behind it are likely not from here and that there's no reason to believe your group was involved. But then, that's what I thought before I came down here."

"But now you have seen things and talked to people. You believe them."

"Most of them. There were some contradictions, some evasiveness, some poor memories. But, yes, for the most part, I believe them. Certainly those who count."

"And you will make this known back in Washington? To the government? To the press?"

"I suppose, as best I can. You have more faith in my credibility than I do."

"Is there anywhere else you want to go? Anyone else you want to talk to?"

"Just one person. But he's dead."

"The unfortunate Jalisco."

"Yes."

"It is too bad, because we would have liked to have talked to him as well. Very much. He did some work for us, you know."

"I hadn't known."

"It's in the files of American military intelligence, but I'm sure they have it classified because of, what shall I call it?—our close association with the American government. Jalisco was able to bring one of our men out of El Salvador after he'd been captured by the Communists. He also made courier runs for us to units operating in Nicaragua. We paid him by the job. He cost a lot of money, but he was very good."

"Did you know anything about his association with Huerta?"

"Not until after the shooting at Gettysburg, when we made it our business to find out."

They passed by a row of houses set close to the road. A strong aroma of cooking smells assaulted Kreski's senses.

"Jalisco recruited Huerta for Gettysburg; there's no doubt of that," Kreski said. "For whom? Have you the slightest idea?"

Sandoval shrugged. "*Quien sabe*? He worked for so many."

"Could it possibly have been leftists? The Cubans? All the evidence points to the likes of all those dispossessed El Salvadoran landowners, but the evidence is too clear, too black and white."

"Again, señor, *quien sabe?* We have no way of knowing. I think the answer to your question lies in another country."

"The United States."

"Possibly. Certainly the ultimate answer to everything is there."

"Can you help me? In Florida, if need be?"

"*Lo siento*, señor, but I'm afraid not. When I return to the States it will be simply to run my hotel. I am not active in political matters there, and it would not be good for you and me to have any contact. Not for me, not for Mr. Brookes, not, I think, for you. Already we in the free Cuban community have had federal agents poking around. And reporters with them. It's not good."

The driver turned onto one of Tegucigalpa's major boulevards, still clogged with traffic.

"Is there anyone you might recommend I talk to about Jalisco?"

"In Florida? No, señor. To my knowledge, he was never in Florida. Never among us. A man like Jalisco. We would know."

"I'm not sure where to turn next."

"Stay here as long as you wish. We will help you however we can. Jalisco had a woman in Barra Mono. You could talk to her. But he had a woman here in Tegucigalpa. In many places. I don't know how much good it would do you to talk to them. They were simply his women, *comprende?* Here, we all . . ." He shrugged again, this time with a smile.

"*Comprendo.*"

"When do you want to go back?"

Kreski watched a line of Honduran army jeeps and trucks pass in the other direction. "I guess this afternoon, if possible. Tonight. As soon as I can."

"There is no direct flight to Miami anymore, because of the war, they say. You will have to change in Mexico City. From there, you can go almost anywhere in the States."

"I know."

"Where will you go?"

"Back to Washington."

"It will be very interesting to see what is happening now in Washington."

"I just want to go home. I'm a man who misses his wife."

Sandoval smiled once more. "*Comprendo.*"

When they pulled up in front of the high-rise Kreski reached for his bag on the floor.

"It was a tiring journey to Barra Mono," Sandoval said. "Would you like to rest awhile here today? Have dinner with us tonight? Return tomorrow?"

"No, *gracias*. I am ready to go home."

The other shook his hand with that same macho grasp. "It was a great pleasure, Señor Kreski. You are a good man. *Mucho hombre*."

"Thank you. Thank you for your hospitality." He handed Sandoval back the pistol the man had loaned him. "Thank you for this. I'm sorry I needed it."

"Everyone in Central America has such regrets. *Adios*, Señor Kreski."

"*Adios*."

Sandoval watched out his window until Kreski reached the glass doors at the high-rise entrance. He should not have. A car parked behind them down the street suddenly pulled out and roared by, at least two automatic weapons firing loudly. Kreski threw himself to the rough pavement of the sidewalk, head down, though no bullet came near him. He heard the car screech to a stop, and a man's voice shout, "*Da la Muerte a La Puño! Viva Ortega!*" Then, lifting his head, Kreski saw the auto speed off down the street, disappearing behind other parked cars. He could recall only that it was light blue. Slowly, glancing fearfully both ways down the street, he got to his feet.

Sandoval's driver, his pistol gripped uselessly in his dead hand, was lying half out of the car, his head in the gutter. Sandoval's big body had become wedged between the seats. The front windshield was shot out. Blood was spattered everywhere.

Kreski's shock turned to anger. He had lost or put aside all of his professional instincts. He should have taken note of the parked car the moment he saw it. He should have warned Sandoval the instant he heard its engine come to life. If he were still with the Secret Service and Sandoval had been the president, he would have been guilty of the worst possible dereliction of duty.

It was worse than that. Sandoval was his friend. Again he had lost a friend. Again he was at fault.

Assured the shooting was over, people began to crowd around, all of them much shorter than Kreski. He could hear police sirens, several of them all at once. He backed away, standing at the entrance to the building for a moment. Then, when he saw the first police Jeep round the corner, he retreated inside, as others from the high-rise pushed past him, seeking the street and the cause of the excitement. That death in Tegucigalpa could still occasion excited curiosity seemed almost amazing.

Kreski rode the elevator up to his floor all by himself, glad he had returned the pistol to Sandoval before leaving the car, then almost wishing he hadn't. He'd no idea what to do next, what would happen next. Once inside the apartment he bolted the door and poured himself a drink, mostly rum, remembering his first drink with Sandoval, saddened by the thought of it. He had really liked the man.

Using his less than perfect Spanish, he managed, finally, to get a call through to the Mexican airline and booked a seat to Mexico City on a seven-ten P.M. flight. He packed his other bag, checked through his small canvas one, and then went through the rooms in search of belongings he might have overlooked. He found none. He had nothing left to do, and hours to wait.

Feeling trapped by the apartment, he went out onto the balcony for the first time, into the heat and the city noise, the hazy brightness, the great sweep of space and rooftops extending into nothingness. But then fear of the unknown dangers of which Sandoval had warned him, which had just made themselves so violently manifest, drove him back into the living room.

He had never experienced this kind of fear. In all his career he had always been in control. Whenever something went wrong there were always established procedures to turn to, always a certain knowledge of what to do. This helplessness angered him.

He turned on the television set, finding only Spanish-language soap operas and variety shows, commercials for American cigarettes and whiskey, political messages from the government, but nothing that resembled a news broadcast. Leaving the set tuned to what seemed to be a principal channel, he turned down the volume slightly and sat upon the couch, alternately sipping his drink and looking at his watch, from time to time staring out the glass doors of the balcony.

"*Da la muerta a La Puño! Viva Ortega!*" The words had confounded him, defied all logic. La Puño was only Manuel Huerta, and he was already dead, a free-lance fanatic recruited by people who, for whatever reason, wanted Henry Hampton dead, people well enough placed to recruit at least one agent of the U.S. Secret Service as well, and to blow up the wife of the vice president of the United States. How was it death to Huerta to assassinate an anti-Castro

Miami Cuban, and in the name of the dictator of Nicaragua? Why would the Sandinistas be avenging the death of the president of the United States?

But logic was not an end. It was a direction. It led from where one began. Kreski was a religious man only in the most philosophical sense. The rituals and orthodoxies of organized religion offended all his sensibilities, all his logic. Yet in a long night's talk with a Jesuit, granting the priest the premise of an uncaused cause, an eternal deity, an unborn and undying God, the cleric had been able to argue all of literal Catholicism with compelling and irrefutable logic— given that premise.

What if Kreski granted his mind such a premise, assuming that the preponderance of evidence was wrong, that his witnesses had been mistaken, or deceitful? What if there were a secret, fanatical Central American right-wing organization called La Puño, one that reached across many borders and was allied with right-wing fanatics in the United States? One that had broken forth from its cover only to launch an all-out assault upon the leadership of the American government?

But why? Henry Hampton had been waging resolute counterinsurgency warfare in Central America, warfare that had taken American combat troops into Nicaragua and El Salvador, that had cost many American lives. And Hampton had been massing a force so formidable that, with a few words from Washington, he could instantly transform the conflict into another Vietnam, a Vietnam the United States, this time, would be prepared to win. Why would any right-wing organization interpose itself against that?

Unless the right-wing La Puño was in itself a creation of the left, a plot within a plot within a plot, a device of Nicaraguan and Cuban manufacture. Felix Dzerzhinsky, the brilliant and ruthless Polish revolutionary who had served as Lenin's first security chief and established the Bolshevik secret police—had he not created such an organization? It had been the most-powerful, best-financed, best-organized, and most-effective anti-Bolshevik, anti-Communist underground in Russia, effective but for one thing—Dzerzhinsky himself actually ran it. Were the Sandinistas that clever?

Sandoval's assassination might simply have been an attempt to reestablish their cover. How convenient that the assassins had waited so carefully for him to exit the car, to walk out of firing range, to be in position to witness the entire performance without suffering injury to himself, to return to Washington to affirm the existence of La Puño, enemy of Managua.

Kreski set down his glass and began walking about the room, finding it confining. Witness and fool, that was his role, a one-man conduit to the credulous of America, to an American people who had only the uninformed assertions of television networks and newspapers with which to grope their way out of their bewilderment. He was merely serving someone's interests, and he really hadn't the slightest idea whose.

Kreski supposed he had been a thoughtful and fairly able administrator, that he had a good sense about people, that in many ways he was an insightful and skillful detective. But his image as a genius policeman was a rotten myth. As the last six weeks had proved, his agency had failed more disastrously than any in the history of the federal government, save perhaps for the navy intelligence apparat that hadn't responded to the Japanese threat to Pearl Harbor. He had been precisely the wrong man for the job at a time when the right kind of man was most vital. He had, to quote the Lewis Carroll line, sat in uffish thought, when what had been needed was a mean, tough cop who would have clamped an iron lid on everything at the first shot, even a pretentious, class-conscious man like Steve Copley, who had known enough to turn over every rock in sight.

A key turned loudly in the lock at the apartment door. When it opened only an inch or so against the bolt there was a pause, and then a violent crash. The bolt came off, swinging on its chain, as the door swung, smashing against the wall. Kreski had seen a glimpse of a boot-clad, kicking foot. An instant later, pistol in hand, Mason Barren stood in the doorway, filling it. His eyes, dark with anger or hate, took in as much of the apartment as he could see, then he stepped inside, slamming the damaged door behind him, aiming his pistol at Kreski.

"They hit us," he said. "All over fucking Tegucigalpa!"

"I know. I was downstairs when they shot Sandoval."

"You don't have a scratch."

"I know. I . . ."

"They wasted Victores in his house, in front of his wife. They took out two of my boys sitting in a café. One of them came after me, but I blew his fucking brains out."

Kreski only stared. He supposed his face was drained of color. His fear was overwhelming him, enraging him.

"In every case they pulled this 'death to La Puño' shit," Barren said. "They made out like they were 'Nistas. It's all bullshit, Kreski. Fucking, lying, bare-ass bullshit. And I wouldn't be surprised if right now up in the States some asshole Fed has pulled Mr. Brookes over on a traffic stop and conveniently found some fucking phony 'La Puño' flag in the trunk of his car."

"I wouldn't be surprised, either," Kreski said.

Barren took a few quick steps forward and slammed Kreski back against the wall, shoving his pistol up against Kreski's sternum. Kreski knew many practiced ways to disarm a man. He had used them many times. But he would not have dared with this man, certainly not now.

"You're mixed up in this, Kreski," Barren said, his voice lowered, but more menacing. "I don't know if somebody's just using you or you're a willing agent or you're part of the brains behind the whole fucking thing. But you're a big part of the reason we got hit today and if it was up to me this wall would be a blood-covered lab display of your anatomy." He stepped back, lowering the pistol somewhat. "But my orders from Mr. Brookes were to protect your ass as long as you were in this country, and I follow orders. I'll deliver you to the airport and get you on your plane, but I don't ever want to see you again, mister."

"That will suit me fine, Mr. Barren."

"Colonel Barren to you, Mr. 'Director.'"

C. D. Bragg was the only senior staff person on duty at the Camp David command center. The phone call from Washington caught him yawning, but he snapped to upon hearing the caller's message. By the end of the conversation, however, he was smiling, a rare expression for him even in normal times.

The message was sufficient cause to wake Bushy Ambrose from his slumbers. Bragg hurried to his cabin.

"Is it war?" said Ambrose, sitting up in his bed.

"No, sir. There was some trouble in Harpers Ferry. You were right and Andy Rollins was wrong."

"What do you mean?"

"You were right that it was a bad place to stash Meathead. A bunch of FBI hit it tonight."

"And?" Ambrose rubbed his eyes and turned on the light on the night table.

"Fortunately, Andy and Meathead decided you were right. Dubarry moved from there this morning. The FBI got nothing but a bimbo and some hootch."

"Was anyone hurt?"

"The bimbo put up a fight and got knocked around a little. One of the agents shot himself in the leg."

"The vice president isn't going to like that."

"If he's even aware of it. Rollins says he's still pretty withdrawn from things."

"Where did Meathead go?"

"To a place where he'll be happy. Rollins said he should have thought of it in the first place."

The telephone on the night table rang. Ambrose had left instructions that only high-priority calls were to be cleared through to his cabin. He wondered if it was Rollins.

It wasn't. Ambrose listened somberly as the other party spoke, then said thank you and hung up, looking not at all happy.

"You look like there's a war on."

Ambrose stared vacantly a moment, then brought his attention back to C. D. Bragg.

"There was some gunplay in Tegucigalpa," he said. "A lot of Peter Ashley Brookes's people were hit."

"By whom?"

"No one knows. Walt Kreski was down there. He wasn't hurt, though."

"What does it mean?"

"No one knows that, either."

"Why don't you call up Admiral Elmore? The CIA takes night calls."

"That was Admiral Elmore."

When the wheels of the Mexicana Airlines 737 lifted from the tarmac of the Tegucigalpa airport Kreski swore the holiest oath of which he was capable that he would never, ever enter this country again or even look at it on a map. When the pilot informed them, in Spanish, that they had not only left Honduran air space but had crossed the border separating Guatemala from Mexico, Kreski's blood pressure probably lowered ten points. Landing in the night at the Mexico City airport, gliding into that enormous mountain-ringed valley so endlessly filled with glittering lights, his relief was such he felt almost happy. He stepped into the terminal like a rescued survivor of a shipwreck returned to civilization. He had nearly three hours to wait until his flight to Dallas, where he would transfer to a red-eye run that would get him into Washington's National Airport shortly after sunrise. It was the quickest way back, though far from quick enough.

Stretching his legs in a stroll through the international terminal area, he came upon a café, seated himself at an empty table, and ordered coffee. It was strong and hot. Rather than stimulating him, it relaxed him. He looked about. There was a middle-aged couple nearby who were obviously American, a dozen or so others who were obviously Latins, a man in a dark suit reading a newspaper who could have been either. In a waiting area not far from the café he could hear an infant crying. In Central American airports there was always a baby crying, no matter what the hour.

Finishing his coffee, Kreski looked at his watch, depressed at the hours still remaining. The area of the airport available to him without passing through customs was relatively small, containing only some duty-free shops, a restaurant and bar, a newsstand, and a waiting section encompassing several rows of uncomfortable leatherette seats. He made several circuits of it, then headed for the bar. The man who for most of his life had seldom taken more than a glass of wine or two in the evening was about to have another strong drink.

He took a seat at the end of the bar and ordered a rum and tonic. As soon as it was served, someone slipped onto the empty stool beside him. It was the man in the dark suit from the café, and he was definitely American. He ordered a beer.

"I haven't much time," he said softly, not looking at Kreski, after his beer had come. "Do you know me?"

Kreski glanced at him quickly, then stared at his glass. "No."

"We met. Five months ago. I worked with your people advancing Hampton's trip. Identifying locals." He took a large gulp of his beer, then refilled the glass from the bottle. "I work for the admiral."

"Admiral Elmore? You're with . . ."

"Just listen to me. Get it straight. The admiral wants to be perfectly neutral in this. No sides. We just do our job. By the book. Follow orders. By the book. No sides."

"What do you mean, sides?"

"Just listen." He drank again, seeming bent on consuming the beer as quickly as possible. "Get it straight. The admiral is going to be perfectly neutral, but the admiral knows we all work for the American people, and the American people have something coming."

He took another gulp. Kreski sipped his own drink again, pretending to be looking off in another direction.

"The admiral wants you to know this. Listen good. Juan Jalisco held three jobs."

"Jalisco had many jobs. He worked for almost every outfit down there."

"I'm not talking black job stuff. I mean civilian work. Before he got mixed up in the Central American war. The three jobs were all in Mexico, one in Tabasco, one in Veracruz, one in Tampico. The admiral thinks you should want to find out what they were."

The man drained his glass and stood.

"That's all?"

"The admiral has just done you a big favor. Be careful."

Kreski did not turn to see where the man went. He knew that when he finally did, he would have vanished. Tabasco. Veracruz. Tampico. He kept repeating the names to himself as he consumed the last of his rum and tonic. Tabasco. Veracruz. Tampico. Tabasco, the center of the off-shore oil drilling. Veracruz, Mexico's largest port. Tampico, the oil-refining center. Tabasco. Veracruz. Tampico. "The admiral has just done you a big favor."

Kreski paid his bill, then sought out a telephone booth where he could use his AT&T credit card. His line was undoubtedly tapped, but that couldn't be helped.

His wife answered before the phone had rung twice. "Hello?" Her voice was a little tremulous.

"It's Walt. I'm fine."

"Where are you?"

"Out of Honduras."

"Thank God. They said on the news there were all kinds of shootings there, that some leftist assassins had murdered some leaders of that La Puño organization."

Kreski swore to himself. There'd not been a word of it on Honduran television, but already the story was all over the American media, and all wrong.

Probably all wrong.

"I'm fine. I was hoping to get back by morning, but something important has come up. I've got to make a side trip. A long side trip."

"Walt. It's almost Christmas."

"We've missed Christmases before, Babs. This is just as important. Maybe more so."

"All right, Walt."

"We'll have a hell of a Valentine's Day."

"I love you so much."

"I'll keep those words with me. I have to go. Be careful."

"I am. I never go anywhere without friends. Just like you said."

Kreski wished he had some friends. "Good night, then, Babs. Everything will be fine." He hung up. He wished he were a better liar.

He looked at his watch. It had been one month, two days, and nine hours since the shooting of the president. He had to keep on.

Back in Washington, they stopped first to get Dresden another hotel room, this time in Arlington, just across the Potomac from Georgetown. He chose the Marriott, taking a room with views of the converging highways below and the high Key Bridge that led across the river. There was a Metro subway station a block distant that could take him anywhere he wished in the District of Columbia. The hotel was also not far from McLean.

He left his bag in his room, but kept the briefcase. Maddy drove, with no apparent nervousness, though each mile of the George Washington Parkway brought her closer to McLean and the dreaded confrontation with her husband. It was a day of intermittent clouds and sunshine. The river's surface kept performing a ritual light show—shifting gray-green shadows, followed by dappled wavelets and shimmering sweeps of brightness.

Holding the Mercedes at a steady speed, she reached and held his hand. It was a demonstration of affection, not a need for it. She was in full possession of herself. From this point on, it would be her show, her responsibility. Charley's fate was fully in her hands, and they both understood that.

"I keep wondering if I should have called him first," she said.

"No. I think you were right in the first place. It's important to take George by surprise."

"Nothing has ever taken George by surprise."

"Then it's damn well time."

"I have this fear he might not be home, that he might have gone off on some trip to the Far East, or Central America. But I know better. Our Christmas plans are always the same. Make all the Christmas parties in Washington during the week, then on Christmas Eve fly back to California to spend Christmas Day with his family. He wouldn't dare disappoint 'momma.'"

"Are they having Christmas parties in Washington this year? With everything that's happened?"

"Don't be ridiculous. They may shut down the Congress and turn the White House into a fortress, but if they cancel the Washington Christmas parties, then you know they've really brought the American government to a halt."

She barely slowed, turning into her cul-de-sac and her own drive, the garage door rising just in time to miss scraping the Mercedes' roof. It slid down again with a decisive slam, imprisoning them in the big garage as might the grate of a castle gate. Their only way forward now led up a flight of steps into the house. Parked next to them was a long gray BMW sedan. Calendiari was home.

Leading Charley past a huge kitchen, Maddy went in to the wide entrance hall, setting down her bag by the main staircase and matter-of-factly turning to the front closet as she took Dresden's coat and then hung up her own. As she shut the closet door, another one opened across the hall, revealing a large, sunken room with logs burning in an oversize fireplace, revealing also a perplexed and anxious George Calendiari.

"Madeleine, where have you been?" His large, dark eyes went from her to Dresden, and narrowed.

"Hello, George," she said, almost casually. "How is Europe coping with the American crisis?"

Calendiari stood staring at Charley, unspeaking.

"This is Charles Dresden, George. From California. I'm sure you remember. We were talking about him just the other day."

Madeleine's insouciance amazed Charley; it must have infuriated Calendiari.

Dresden nodded to the man he had cuckolded, for all practical purposes, twice, now, in a lifetime. "Senator."

"I remember too well," Calendiari said. "Where were you, Madeleine?"

"In New York. I'll explain it all in a moment, but now I think we could all use a drink. It's been a long drive."

"Goddamn it, Madeleine, you went to New York with Dresden? And you bring him back here? I've been waiting for you for two days! I had no idea where you were."

"I'm familiar with the experience, George. If I had had a staff aide with me I would have had him call you."

Fuming, shoulders hunched, Calendiari turned and started hurriedly toward another door that led to what Dresden presumed was a library or study.

"What are you doing, George?"

Calendiari halted, glaring at both of them. "I'm calling the police. The man's wanted for murder in California. I'm a member of the United States Senate, Madeleine. I'm not going to harbor a fugitive. Not even for a few minutes."

"George, by now I'm sure Charley and I are both wanted by police in New Jersey and New York. The charges include robbery and assault with a deadly weapon. If you're in a mood to call police, you'd better call them up there too."

"What are you talking about?"

"We're in trouble, George. And now you are too. As you said yourself, Charley didn't kill anyone in California. Those people were friends of his, murdered by someone else. Charley's stumbled onto something, something very important, about the president, about what's going on here in Washington. I went to New York to help him get more proof. Now, we need your help."

Calendiari was rapidly losing control. "You went to New York to shack up, you goddamn whore! I go to NATO on important government business and you can't wait to hop in the sack with your old lover! Bring him all the way out from California!"

Maddy's calm was icy. "George, you're acting like a child. Go back into the living room and we'll talk this out." She turned to Dresden, speaking more warmly. "There's a wet bar through there. Make yourself a drink and wait until I convince George of the seriousness of this."

Dresden did, turning on a light over the bar and selecting a bottle of expensive scotch. Behind him, he could hear the Calendiaris, speaking loudly.

"Time after time I've heard you complain how I've never been willing to put the interests of our country ahead of our marriage," Dresden heard Maddy say. "Well, now, for once, I'm asking the same of you."

Calendiari swore, and then a door slammed shut. Dresden took his drink to a nearby armchair and sat, nervous and uncomfortable. He studied the titles on a bookshelf next to him. They were all works on Italian Renaissance art.

He could hear Calendiari shouting now. There was a crash of breaking glass, and Dresden half rose from the chair, intent on intervening but uncertain. He had not known Calendiari to be a terribly passionate man, and did not know what to expect of him. At their first encounter years before violence had been the least of his concerns. But people changed. Still, Maddy had not cried out. Dresden eased back in his seat. At the first untoward sound from her he'd break in. Until then, he'd do as she said.

At length, the door opened and Madeleine emerged. Her face was flushed, but she still seemed completely in control. She put a hand on his shoulder.

"This is going to take some time, Charley," she said. "I'm going to call a cab for you. I want you to go back to your hotel and wait. I'll contact you as soon as I can."

"Are you sure you'll be safe?"

"Perfectly sure. Perfectly safe."

He set down his glass and rose. "All right. You know what's best."

"And leave the briefcase."

"Leave the briefcase? It has everything!"

"I know. I'm going to show him everything. But if you're here he's just going to keep losing his temper. I want him to calm down and pay attention. He's a very bright man, Charley. He'll understand what we have."

"What if he tries to destroy it? To get back at us that way? He might just throw it in the fire."

"He has a lot of flaws, Charley, but he's not irresponsible. Inconsiderate, yes. But not irresponsible."

"How can you be sure he won't just call the police and turn me in? Have them pick me up at my hotel?"

"Because I told him I'd leave him if he did that."

"But Maddy . . ."

"In its way, Charley, it is about the most honest thing I could say."

The cab ride to Arlington took too long, as did the elevator ride to his floor, as most certainly did the wait in his room. Removing the pistol from his belt, he checked the cylinder to see if it was still fully loaded, then clicked it closed, wondering if he still had any need for it, if he shouldn't just stick it in his bag. He decided to stay with the habit of the last several days. He'd not been ill-served by it, except once.

Walking about the room, he paused to draw the drapes open, exposing the entire panorama of river and city that included the Victorian building fronts of Georgetown across the river, the elaborate curves of the Watergate complex downstream, and the piercing spire of the Washington Monument rising beyond it. The day was fading, and the twin red lights at the monument's pinnacle came on and began to blink.

Dresden stared down into the now dark waters of the wide, flowing river. So many people dead and endangered, so many miles traveled, so much done, and now so much known and provable. Yet it was all in the hands of a woman who was now all that mattered in his life. Just a few short weeks before he'd forgotten she still existed. Now, he had relinquished everything to her, and to a man who hated him with a raging, violent passion.

It was time for the early-evening television news. He snapped on the set. The story on the air was about a rash of terrorist shootings in Honduras, nothing of moment to his own predicament.

The telephone on the night table rang. He snatched it up, hesitating before speaking. It was the clerk at the front desk.

"There's a party in the lobby to see you, sir."

"What name?"

"Calendiari, sir."

"I'll be right down."

He stepped quickly out of the elevator, but there was not a blond head to be seen anywhere, not in the lobby, not at the desk, not in any of the adjacent corridors. There was, however, a tall, bald-headed man in an expensive overcoat, standing by one of the pillars. Dresden approached him slowly, for a fearful moment wondering if Madeleine were still alive.

"Well, Senator," he said.

Calendiari had regained all of his composure. His eyes were very serious, but cleansed of their rage. His voice was very even.

"Madeleine showed me everything. The videotapes, the voice prints, the audio tape. Everything. It's very convincing. It's very disturbing."

"That's what I felt from the beginning."

"What's between us we can deal with later, and we will. Believe me, we will. But this is more important than all of us. In all sincerity, Dresden, I admire you for what you've done so far. I want to do everything I can to help."

He began pulling on his gloves.

"Get your bag and check out. We've decided that, under the circumstances, it would be much safer all around if you stayed with us."

21

Chief of Staff Ambrose had called an emergency meeting. As those summoned walked down the curving paths of Camp David to Ambrose's cabin in the surprisingly balmy weather, they assumed the subject would be the bad news David Callister had brought back from New York, but Ambrose deferred discussion of that—for the time being. His agenda was "prioritized," as he put it, and at the top of the list was national security. More specifically, war. Real war.

It was the largest single gathering Ambrose had convened since the night of the president's shooting. C. D. Bragg, Jerry Greene, and Peter Schlessler were there, as always. So were Senator Andrew Rollins and National Security Adviser James Malcom, and Callister, though he enjoyed no official status. General DeVore, the chairman of the Joint Chiefs of Staff, had pointedly not been invited, and no notice had been sent to Admiral Elmore.

Presidential press secretary Weigle had yet to be allowed an appearance at the compound. He was performing too important a role for Ambrose down at the White House, making a nuisance of himself with the vice president's people and confusing the press.

"Has everyone read the latest report out of Tegucigalpa?" Ambrose asked, as Schlessler poured coffee. All nodded except Rollins, who had arrived late, and Callister, who disdainfully yawned. Ambrose shoved Rollins a copy of the report, but ignored Callister.

"The situation there is getting out of hand," Ambrose continued. "As out of hand as it has been up here. Everything depends on our maintaining control over operations in Central America. I mean absolute control and I mean all operations. It's getting away from us and I want absolute control restored."

"The chain of command starts here," said Moran, the defense secretary.

"I know that," Ambrose said. "A presidential order to the National Military Command Center and the tanks roll across the Rio Coco. You don't have to familiarize me with standard operating procedures. What I'm interested in is nonregulation procedure. How do you control that? How would I start a war down there without presidential orders?"

"You couldn't," a general from the Joint Chiefs said. "Whatever you did you'd have to go through the defense secretary, the war room, the chairman of the JCS, me, CIC Southern Command, and the field commander, not to speak of the navy secretary and CIC Atlantic Command, Military Airlift Command, and anybody else involved in purple operations in the region."

"You're still talking orthodoxy," Ambrose said. "I'm not talking about ordering anyone into combat. I'm talking about spontaneous combustion. What set of circumstances could one create in which a war could begin all on its own?"

"An incident," said C. D. Bragg.

"The battleship *Maine*'s already been sunk," Rollins said.

"You could provoke the other side," Bragg said. "An assassination attempt on Ortega. A major bombing in Managua or San Salvador. A naval incident that would draw them into an attack on our shipping."

"The Congress and the public wouldn't stand for it," Ambrose said.

"We may have gotten rid of the No-More-Vietnams syndrome," Senator Rollins said, folding the Tegucigalpa report and putting it in his pocket, "but not the No-More-Gulfs-of-Tonkin syndrome."

"And our response would have to go back up the chain of command," said the general.

"So there isn't any way then," said Ambrose.

Everyone nodded agreement, except Malcom, who cleared his throat. A former Green Beret major and Rhodes scholar, the national security adviser was a taciturn, thoughtful man whose comments were so infrequent and circumspect that everyone always listened when he spoke.

"There is a way," he said. "World War I began not because anyone deliberately sought to start it but because the mobilization of troops by the major powers in response to perceived threat was so massive that a clash all along both fronts was inevitable. If you were to put the American military on a very high level of alert and then create an incident, there likely would not be time to involve the full chain of command in initiating a substantial response."

"All right," said Ambrose. "What are the options for putting the armed forces on a high state of alert?"

"I can with a simple order," the general said. "As we did after Gettysburg. The president can order any kind of alert condition he wishes."

"Right," said Ambrose. "So that option is absolutely under our control. What else?"

"The JCS chairman can order full-scale alerts," the general said.

"He's playing it perfectly straight," Ambrose said. "He wouldn't start anything without good, substantial reason."

"A false intelligence report," C. D. Bragg said.

"No one is playing it straighter than Admiral Elmore," Ambrose said. "No false NIE is going to get by him."

"What about the National Security Agency?"

"What about Wimex?" the general asked. "If you could access Wimex, you could call an alert. It's not hard to access Wimex."

"What the hell's Wimex?" Greene said.

"I sent everyone a memorandum when the emergency began," Ambrose said. "Wimex is the computer complex inside Cheyenne Mountain in Colorado. It's hooked up to our geosynchronous satellites over the Soviet Union. It's programmed to initiate our immediate response to apparent launches of Soviet ICBMs while the president and the Pentagon war room decide what to do next. Wimex is authorized to scramble tac air and B-1 flights, and order alerts up to Def Con Four—all on its own."

"In fact, it's done so several times by accident," the general said. "In one of those incidents, some fool colonel mistakenly put a war games tape into it."

"Def Con Four would not suffice," C. D. Bragg said. "You'd need a hair-trigger situation. Def Con Two or One."

Everyone sat in silence.

"Anyone holding a 'Gold Codes' card could create such a situation," Malcom said.

"'Gold Codes' card?" said Ambrose. "They're for use in nuclear war!"

"The 'Gold Codes' card accesses the command center," the national security adviser said. "Its code numbers authorize the caller to initiate a nuclear strike at his option. But they also authorize the caller simply to order a state of alert. The holder of a 'Gold Codes' card could put the nation on Def Con One."

"On Def Con One," the defense secretary said, "you could set off a firecracker on the Coco and all hell would break loose."

"All hell could include an accidental nuclear exchange," the general said.

"All right," Ambrose said. "Let's look at it the other way around. How would someone go about trying to stop such a war? How could someone prevent that kind of alert from being called?"

"There's the Watergate precedent," Rollins said.

"Watergate?" Ambrose asked. "What the hell does that have to do with anything?"

"When Nixon began to go funny Jim Schlesinger—remember he was defense secretary then—he and Jerry Ford and the others got together and worked it out with the war room that no White House 'Gold Codes' card calls were to be honored without their being consulted."

"That was four against one," Ambrose said, "and you had a president known to be off the deep end. What's our situation?"

"The president has a 'Gold Codes' card, meaning you in the present setup, Bushy," the defense secretary said. "I have one. My deputy has one, and he's completely reliable. With us all the way."

"The JCS chairman has one, and he'd use it only in the most extreme circumstance," the general said. "He would not take part in any effort to prevent another card bearer from carrying out his responsibilities."

"And the fifth and last card is held by Vice President Atherton," Ambrose said. "Three versus one versus one."

"But you'd only need minutes," Malcom said. "The force in Honduras is virtually on lock and load as it is."

"And mentally they've been on Def Con One since Gettysburg," the general said.

Ambrose chewed his lower lip. He looked at each of those present, and then down at the tabletop, drumming his fingers. "All right," he said. "I want the 'Gold Codes' cards changed."

"They will be, automatically," the defense secretary said. "In exactly twelve days."

"You're talking about all five cards," Ambrose said. "I'm talking about just two, yours and mine—I mean, yours and the president's. I want those codes changed and I want the new numbers the only ones authorized for war room access."

"You can't do that, Bushy," Rollins said, leaning back in his chair.

"We're in the middle of a national emergency. Why the hell not?"

"For one thing, it would require an action of the full National Security Council—the president, Atherton, Secretary of State Crosby, and the defense secretary here. I don't think Atherton and Crosby would be very compliant. You'd also be required to consult Admiral Elmore and the JCS in their advisory capacity. They wouldn't think it a very hot idea, either."

"We could just go ahead and do it."

"Bushy," Rollins said. "The American people know the president's been shot. They see him as completely isolated up here. They see Atherton in many ways as an acting president, especially since he moved into the White House. If you try to take away any of his powers to act in the president's absence in a military emergency, there could be hell to pay. You can't do that unless you've got the president back in the Oval Office."

"So we sit," Ambrose said.

"The timing could be better," C. D. Bragg said.

"This has not been a very useful discussion," said Ambrose.

"Hypothetical ones seldom are," the defense secretary said.

Some of those at the table began to stir, as though assuming the meeting was over. An arch clearing of the throat kept them in their chairs. Ambrose looked over at Callister.

"I forgot," Ambrose said. "We have this other problem, thanks to Mr. Callister here. What do we do? Those people who broke into his house have to be neutralized. Fast."

"Do you want to call in the FBI?" Rollins asked.

"We've got to notify them, at least. Callister, have one of your staff in New York do that. Just inform the field office up there that that couple forced their way into your house at gunpoint and asked questions about the president. Volunteer nothing beyond that, and don't bring the police into it."

"Your advice is sound," Callister said.

"It's not advice," Ambrose said. "Those are orders."

"If you want to neutralize those two," Bragg said. "You can't leave it at that."

"We can deal with them with the military," the defense secretary said. "We have a whole office full of Defense Intelligence Agency people at the Pentagon who were frozen out of the Gettysburg investigation by Kreski and Copley. They'll jump at something to do."

"I want that couple iced, before they stir up trouble for us." Ambrose turned to Bragg. "C. D., you and Schlessler serve as liaison on this. I want frequent reports."

People started to rise, but Ambrose's raised hand stayed them.

"One more thing," he said. "Christmas. I'm sorry, but it's no can do. I'll permit family visits at the Rustic Motel in Thurmont on the afternoon of Christmas Day, one P.M. to five P.M. Nothing more. We simply can't risk it." He moved his gaze to Callister. "As for you, sir. You don't leave Camp David. Not until this is over. Not until I give you permission. Am I making myself clear?"

"As usual, you are making yourself insufferable."

"Just don't get out of line, Callister. At this point you're making yourself very expendable."

The vice president readily agreed to meet with them, not at the White House, but at his official residence on Observatory Hill, and at night. George Calendiari drove them, with Maddy riding in the front seat beside him. It was a protocol, a matter of appearances. It was the unspoken sense of all three of them that her real place was in the back with Dresden. On the drive from McLean, she kept turning to talk to him, and on one dark stretch of Canal Road on the Maryland side of the Potomac, reached back and squeezed his hand.

This was the culmination of all their efforts, all they had endured, all they had set out to do. The two of them could do no more. The responsibility would now pass into the hands of people awesomely more powerful than themselves, the questions of resolution, justice, and ultimate restitution of authority to be taken up by the gigantic, inexorable workings of the government itself. This night would mean their freedom. They must conclude matters with George. They had not decided how they would go about this, but it was a necessity. When they left the Vice President's House it would be to begin their new lives.

Turning off Massachusetts Avenue, they were stopped at the entrance gate by a large number of security men, some in civilian clothes, others in police and military uniforms. But after a courteous examination of Calendiari's Senate ID and a quick look inside the BMW, they were waved on. A curving ascent of the long drive took them to the top of the hill, where they were greeted by yet more security personnel and guided politely to the entrance of the old Victorian mansion, where a butler opened the door for them. Their coats were taken, and they were conducted into a large, comfortable parlor with a cheery fire burning despite the outside warmth.

"George, Mrs. Calendiari," said the vice president, rising. Dresden was struck by how aged the man now looked. "You must be Charles Dresden."

"Yes, sir," said Charley, stepping forward and shaking Atherton's extended hand. There was a great deal of seriousness in the vice president's voice, and sadness. His eyes seemed somewhat vacant and staring.

He introduced the others in the room—his secretary, Mrs. Hildebrand; Chief of Staff Richard Shawcross; Secretary of State Merriman Crosby; Press Secretary Neil Howard; and Steven Copley, director of the Federal Bureau of Investigation.

"I'd offer you some refreshment," Atherton said, "But I think that, under the circumstance, it would be best if we got on with this as soon as possible. Our videotape equipment is in my study on the second floor. If you'll come this way, please."

The room was not an overly large one, but they all managed to crowd in and find seats, Dresden pulling up a chair next to the expensive VCR. With not a little nervousness, he explained the slow-motion and freeze-frame tapes of the shooting at Gettysburg as carefully and methodically as Tracy Bakersfield had explained them to him. He had tried four more times to reach her on the telephone. Without success. He could only hope she had gone into hiding as he had urged, but there was no certainty of that. Tracy could now be as dead as Charlene.

He was just as meticulous with the presidential radio recordings and the voice prints. The videotapes of the supposedly recovering president at Camp David, however, he let speak for themselves—showing his audience the president in his various poses speaking hoarsely. Then, using the tapes he had taken from the network archives in New Jersey, he showed the president in exactly the same poses, the same clothing and expressions, speaking in his normal voice and saying things that were not only completely different from those heard on the Camp David tapes but remarks most in the room remembered from past newscasts. Afterward, Dresden passed around the tape cassette cases from the archives, with the network slugs and file dates clearly visible and clearly authentic.

While these were being examined he played back the audio tape of Howie King's doorman and of David Callister. There were some frowns and dark glances at the sound of Dresden's threatening voice and that of the blows and pain suffered by Callister, but when the man's confession finally came, their apparent antagonism vanished.

Tapping his foot, Atherton asked to see everything again. Without hesitation or complaint, Dresden complied. When he clicked off the last of the audio tapes for the final time, the vice president turned to FBI Director Copley.

"It's been definitely established that the president was not wearing his Kevlar vest?" he said.

"Yes, sir. He disliked them. Walt Kreski noted that in his report."

Atherton stared at the empty video screen for a long moment, then looked to Dresden. His eyes had changed. They seemed aglow. "Is all of this for us to keep?"

"Yes, sir," Dresden said. "That's why I'm here."

"I'm very grateful. We'll place the material in the custody of Director Copley, if there's no objection."

No one spoke.

"Very well," said Atherton, "I think perhaps, now, that some refreshment is in order."

They all had drinks in the same downstairs parlor, but this time everyone stood, the vice president taking his whiskey to the fireplace and resting his arm on the mantel. "Mr. Dresden," said the vice president, carefully. "As much as I appreciate your bringing this material to us, indeed, all that you've done, there's a complicating factor. You are the subject of a murder warrant in Santa Linda County, California, technically, at least, and that puts us in something of an awkward position."

"My office has been asked to assist in your arrest," Copley said. "For breaking into Callister's house. So you also put us in a difficult position."

"Mr. Vice President, the victims of those murders were people very dear to me. If I hadn't been delayed in getting home that night, I probably would have been a victim myself. I think they, the killers, were after some of the things I've just shown you. They came after me after I appeared on a local television show in San Francisco. If I had anything to do with those murders I wouldn't be here now, I'd be in another country."

Copley cleared his throat politely. "I had the San Francisco field office make a few checks this afternoon, Mr. Vice President," he said. "The evidence against Mr. Dresden is strong, but it's entirely circumstantial. Mr. Dresden's side of it is not only plausible, a lot of it checks out."

"Very well," said Atherton, setting down his glass. "We'll let all that pass for the time being. Certainly there are more important matters before us now." He looked to Calendiari. "George. I don't know what our course of action is going to be, but I'd appreciate your continuing cooperation and discretion."

"Of course," George said.

"And I'd appreciate it if you'd remain where we can get a hold of you quickly. Mr. Dresden, you and Mrs. Calendiari are key witnesses in a matter of very grave concern. We may need you at any time. If you have any fears for your safety, Mr. Copley can make arrangements for your protection."

"Thank you, sir."

"I can be reached at our home in McLean or my office on the Hill," Calendiari said. "Your staff has all my numbers."

"Good. Mr. Dresden, just one more question. What prompted you to get so involved in this in the first place?"

"That's simple enough, sir. The truth. I just didn't want to let it pass. I've had, well, many years of experience in television, and the truth just seemed obvious to me from the beginning."

"As it did to no one else. Including me. As I said, we deeply appreciate what you've done. We'll be in touch with you again soon. Very soon." He shook Dresden's hand again, and then Maddy's, and then Calendiari's. As though on signal, the butler appeared with their coats. Calendiari nodded to the vice president one more time, and then led the others out.

When they were gone Atherton and his entourage seated themselves again. Neil Howard ordered another drink for himself from the butler. No one spoke until the servant had once more departed.

"First of all," said Atherton, stretching out his long legs. "Has anyone any doubts whatsoever about anything we've seen or heard?"

Shawcross, Howard, and Copley shook their heads. "We've won capital cases with less evidence than this," the attorney general said.

"Precisely," said Atherton. "We have Mr. Ambrose exactly where we want him. Exactly. Do you suppose this Dresden fellow made copies of these things?"

"Anyone smart enough to put together what he did is smart enough to make copies," Copley said.

"Yes, and presently you will have to deal with that matter, Steven. The question now is, what next?"

"I say we move at once," said Howard, "on all fronts."

"Maybe," said Shawcross, a shadow of uncertainty on his face. Mrs. Hildebrand, as always, simply kept her eyes on Atherton.

"No, not now. Certainly not," said the patrician Crosby, sipping from his brandy. "It's Christmas, don't you know. The American people would be totally unprepared for this kind of revelation, and certainly for any sort of national and international turmoil. No, we must bide our time. We must wait for public frustration over President Hampton's continued absence to build."

"He's right," Shawcross said. "The time will come for Bushy Ambrose to put up or shut up. Then we move."

"If you will observe your calendars," Crosby said, "you'll note that that time is not all that distant."

"The State of the Union address," said Shawcross.

Atherton glanced at his watch. "There are a number of matters to attend to," he said, rising. "A number of matters. Steven, we must talk about the elusive Senator Dubarry. The rest of you can go home. I'm returning to the White House. I can't stand to be in this house for any length of time. Not any length of time at all."

No one needed to ask why. He had complained of hearing his wife's voice here.

Returning to the Calendiari home in McLean, the three went from the garage to the front hall again. George opened the closet door and removed his coat, but Maddy did not.

"I don't want to stay here, George," she said.

"What do you mean? This is our home."

"I'm frightened. What we just gave the vice president is very important. It's going to cause a lot of trouble for some very important people. And now a lot of people know about it. I just don't feel safe here. We're on this hilltop just two miles from the CIA. Anyone in Washington can reach us in fifteen minutes on the parkway. I want to go somewhere else."

"Somewhere with Dresden."

Charley stepped back, leaning against a wall. He wanted no part in this discussion.

"I want you to come with us, George. You're not safe here, either."

"You're being ridiculous."

"I'm not being ridiculous, damn it! People have been killed. I don't want to get hurt. I don't want you to get hurt. I don't want Charley to get hurt. I don't want anyone else killed. As you said, the vice president will know what to do. Let him do it. In the meantime, I want to sit everything out. I want all three of us to sit it out."

"Madeleine, you know I can't do that. I have responsibilities, especially to the vice president."

"You can do it, George. You're not that indispensable, no matter what you've thought all these years."

He controlled his temper. "Madeleine, I simply can't."

"I mean it, George. I'm going to go, and Charley's coming with me."

"Very well. Go."

"I'll pack a bag." She hurried up the stairs. In a moment they heard her moving back and forth in a room on the floor above. Calendiari stared at Dresden a long time before speaking.

"I realize I can't ask anything of you," he said, finally. "I did that many years ago and ultimately it didn't do any good."

Charley remained silent.

"Anyway, you know how I feel."

"Yes."

"Take care of her, Dresden. Protect her."

"I will."

"I want her back."

"I'll take care of her."

She came down the stairs again, quickly, carrying a bag slightly larger than the one she had taken to New York. She set it down, and hugged Calendiari tightly. "Good-bye, George."

"Where will you go?"

"The beach house."

"The beach house? You think that's safe?"

"It's just down from the Rehoboth boardwalk. And no one would expect us to be there in December. You'll be able to reach us easily, and, if it's important, we can be back in Washington in three hours."

"There'll be hardly anyone in Rehoboth this time of year."

"That's the idea."

"I have a gun," Dresden said, reaching to take Maddy's bag for her. She had also brought his down. "We'll be all right."

"I'll worry."

"We'll all worry, George. I'd worry a lot less if you'd come with us."

"No, Madeleine. That's final."

"All right, George," she said, moving on down the hall. "We'll call when we get there."

Dresden did not speak until they were speeding down the parkway in her yellow Mercedes, heading toward the bridge and the thoroughfare that would take them to Highway 50, and then to Annapolis, the Chesapeake Bay Bridge, and the Eastern Shore beyond.

"You really wanted George to come with us?"

"Yes. I want him to stop being my husband, but I don't want him hurt. I don't want him to stay with us, but I wanted him to come."

"You've thought it over carefully, about leaving him?"

"Yes. For years."

"You've thought about me?"

"Yes. I've thought about you. At odd moments. Driving. Doing housework. Late at night. Sometimes after making love with George. You two really are the only men I've had. I married George, but as I told you, I never really married him completely. I'm going back to you, but there's something very incomplete about us, too. There may always be. I probably should leave the both of you and start a new life altogether. I've thought about doing that, too. I thought about it today."

"Why don't you? It would be the wisest thing to do."

A car had been following them closely, but it abruptly pulled out and passed, hurrying on with seemingly no further care of them.

"Because I'm pretty sure I love you. Just as crazily and dangerously as I did in the beginning."

"But you left me then. Why not now?"

She said nothing. They were nearly to the turnoff for the Interstate that would take them across the Potomac and away from Washington.

"I'm not sure you'll believe me if I tell you."

"Of course I'll believe you."

"All right. A very big reason for my wanting to stay with you is because of what you're doing, because of what we've just done."

"I don't understand."

"The country's in trouble. You're trying to help. It's very brave of you. Very foolish, too, I suppose, but very courageous. I feel very strongly about this country, about what this country stands for in this terrible world. That's one of the reasons I put up with so much from George. I couldn't stand his being so inconsiderate. I couldn't take being telephoned by one of his aides instead of him, but I never tried to stop him from going on his trips. He was trying to help. He did a lot of things he didn't need to do and got no thanks for. All I ever did was bear up under it all. The noble wife, dining alone. Now, thanks to you, and also thanks to George, I'm doing something more. You never paid any attention to my politics, but I'm very Republican that way."

"Democrats aren't patriotic?"

"Of course they are. But putting the country first, what it stands for, that's what being a Republican means to me. That's what I think it meant to Lincoln, when being a Republican meant supporting that awful war. I think that, in a way, the country is in the same kind of serious trouble. I was appalled by what you were saying at first. Now it has me scared. Not just for us, but for everyone in the country."

"Why don't you trust the vice president, and the other people we met tonight?"

"Right now, Charley. I only trust you and George."

He caught a glimpse of her face in the flare of the oncoming headlights.

"Are you sure about this beach house?"

"Yes. It's right on the ocean. I'm always happy when I'm there. It's like Great Falls. It's a place where I go to sort things out."

"Just you and I."

"Yes," she said, patting his knee, "just you and I."

The multitude of guards and sentries around Camp David did not interfere with those within the compound at night, as long as they did not go near the perimeter fence. There were lights along the paths, but Ambrose had ordered them extinguished for security reasons. He had ordered constant helicopter patrols maintained day and night around the mountain, but an aircraft bent on deadly mischief could penetrate them easily.

For the late-night stroller, who had now been out of his cabin for more than ten minutes, the pale moonlight sufficed. He quickened the pace of his walk. As it had for most there, Camp David had become a frustrating, suffocating prison. No amount of alcohol, no narcotic, no exotic woman or companionship of any kind, however agreeable, could substitute at that particular moment for an evening's expensive meal in one of New York's four-star restaurants, or even a walk along Central Park South or Broadway. Ambrose seemed almost gleefully malicious, outright mean, in issuing orders against any departure. Patriotism was becoming a burden increasingly difficult, if not impossible to bear.

The stroller followed a path into the shadows between two cabins. He sensed movement, but heard no sound, until a strong hand suddenly clamped itself over his mouth and another bent his body backward. Two other hands pulled his arms behind him and bound his wrists. A moment later his ankles were bound as well, and tape was pulled over his mouth. He was placed in some sort of plastic bag, and lifted. He panicked, thrashing about, terrified, until he realized they had cut holes in the material through which he could breathe. He was not being murdered, just taken somewhere. He ceased thrashing, and a small measure of calm returned to him. Wherever he was going, it would likely be outside of Camp David. There was that consolation, whatever else happened to him.

After a careful, quiet descent of a gentle slope, he felt himself being lifted and swung, perhaps over the tailgate of a truck or station wagon. He was set on a hard surface, but laid against some large, soft objects—other bags, he presumed. There was a peculiar, if not clearly discernible, smell. He lay back, relaxing, listening as he heard the two front doors of the vehicle open and shut, the engine starting shortly thereafter. He had to go to the bathroom, but that could wait—surely it could wait until they were out of Camp David. He would do nothing to interfere with that.

The two in the cab of the truck spoke little, at least until they had descended the mountain and were through the last checkpoint. Reaching Highway 15, instead of proceeding directly across it into Thurmont, they turned right and headed south toward the town of Catoctin. Several miles before it, the driver pulled off into the entrance of Cunningham Falls State Park, halting the truck behind some trees and killing the lights.

"He's been too quiet," the driver said. "You'd better go back and check on him."

"Shall I let him out of the bag? There's no need for it now, if we keep the canvas down."

"Okay. Might as well."

The other stepped out, his footfalls noisy on the gravel in the quietness of the woodland night. The driver could hear the sounds of heavy movement in the rear, and then swearing. After a moment his companion returned.

"No use taking him out of the bag," he said. "He's dead."

"Dead? How the hell could he be dead?"

"He must have rolled over some way, cutting off the air holes."

"I didn't hear him struggle. Hell, you'd think he'd kick a little."

"Well, he's just lying there."

"Go back and check again. With the flashlight. He may have just passed out or something."

This time, the other man was gone longer. But he returned with no different news.

"Dead. One hundred percent dead. No pulse. His eyes are blank. His skin looks like the inside of a fish."

"I sure as hell didn't plan on this."

"What'll we do, dump him?"

"Yeah, but no place around here. Get in. We've got some time to make, some miles to make."

"What a way to die. Who'd want to die in a garbage bag?"

"When you're dead, you're dead. It's all the same. All the dead are garbage."

When Bushy Ambrose was awakened to be given the news he allowed himself thirty seconds of profane outrage, then got down to business—all military commander again.

"Get Jerry Greene here at once, and that goddam Callister too," he said to the army colonel who had burst in on him. "And I want the name and 201 file of everyone on duty inside the perimeter tonight, including yourself."

"Yes, sir."

Ambrose paced the room.

"Don't call in C. D. Bragg or Schlessler, not yet, anyway. I want them to finish what they're doing."

"Yes, sir."

"But get another team of DIA agents up to New Jersey. They're beginning to get rough, and I don't want the same thing happening to Senator Dubarry."

22

No one had followed Charley and Maddy. They were not certain of that until across the mountainous span of the Bay Bridge and well along the four-lane Highway 50 that led into Maryland's Eastern Shore, but when they turned off onto the smaller, two-lane Route 404 that cut across the peninsula into Delaware, no lights came after. Not for miles. When a tiny pair finally did prick the darkness behind them it was not for long. They fell behind and faded, then were gone, leaving Dresden and Maddy to speed their course across the moonlit flatness of winter-fallow farmland alone.

Dresden had taken the wheel. He had put his arm around her and she had nestled her head against his shoulder and chest. He had long before turned off the radio. They were completely unto themselves.

"How different," he said, "and how much the same."

"Whatever are you talking about, Charley?"

"I was thinking about a night when we were almost killed."

"When on earth was that?"

"Years and years ago, a millennium ago. You were still in your last year of college. We went up to San Francisco for an evening that went on a bit too long."

"How long?"

"At three A.M. we were still necking at Coit Tower. It was a warm night."

"Oh, yes. I remember that night. I remember Coit Tower. How did we almost get killed?"

"Driving back to Santa Linda on the Bayshore Freeway. I couldn't stay awake. We were in your father's car. A big Fleetwood."

"That part I don't remember."

"You shouldn't. You slept the entire way back. I kept trying to wake you up, but you wouldn't."

"You tried to get me to sing. 'Yes, We Have No Bananas,' and 'Puff the Magic Dragon.'"

"You sang two words and went to sleep again. I had to do the whole stretch myself. I lost control twice."

"Oh, dear. Did we make it?"

"Yes."

"What happened when we got home?"

"We had a big fight, and you left me standing on the walk outside your father's house."

"What's different? And what's the same?"

"What's the same is that it's the two of us all alone rolling along the highway in the dark again. What's the same is that we're in love again. What's different is that everything is completely different. Everything's for keeps now."

She snuggled closer. "Let's not get killed. And when we get home let's not have a fight."

"Home."

"It's my house. George bought it for me. He almost never uses it. I consider it mine. Now it's ours."

A winter's owl, pursuing something in the fields, flew in a quick, darting swoop across the road, then vanished, a dark flicker in the moonlight.

"For now," Dresden said.

"Home" was a large, contemporary wooden house just behind the dune from the sea, raised on pylons, surrounded by deck and walled mostly with windows. It was a little way down the shore from the town of Rehoboth Beach, Delaware, near a neighborhood of substantial, year-round homes with lawns and hedges, streetlights and sidewalks. A private road led to the Calendiari home, and beyond it to other shore houses just as large. To the landward side of the road was the still, black, glimmering surface of a large lake. If they had to run, there was only one route out, except for the beach, but Dresden had no care for running again. As they stood in the darkness in the main floor living room, looking out large sliding glass doors past the grassy top of the dune toward the sea, it occurred to Charley they could go no farther in any event. He had traveled from one ocean to the other, had crossed three thousand miles of America from a cabin in an obscure canyon in California to the Washington residence of the vice president of the United States, in reality, the *president* of the United States. There was nowhere else he need go.

She turned on a bright light, and the ocean vanished. He looked about the room. It was simply but elegantly furnished, in California style.

"When we're in Washington I'm out here whenever I can get away, from May well into October. George comes out in late July and August, when the half of Washington that doesn't go to Martha's Vineyard or the Hamptons flees here to the shore. George does business down on the beach, standing in the water trading votes with sleazy, fat-bellied committee chairmen who have condominiums and bimbos down the coast in Ocean City. I pray for Labor Day then. After Labor Day, till the next August heat, this is mine. This is where I'm my own person."

He put his hand on her back. "A lonely person, out here."

"No more so than when I'm in Washington." She put her arm around him. "And I'm not lonely now."

They turned and kissed, gently, looking into each other's eyes for a long time afterward. Then she moved away, busying herself with preparing the place for their stay. There was a kitchen off the main room, beyond a long counter. Dresden noticed some liquor bottles.

"Would you like a drink?" he asked.

"I suppose. A scotch. You've only had two drinks today. I took careful notice. Are you improving?"

"I don't know if that's the word for it."

She set their bags by the stairs, straightened some chairs, then joined him, taking the cold glass he handed her. "We'll worry about that some other time. Not tonight."

"Not tonight. Let's go out on the deck."

The breeze greeted them at the opening of the door, coming at them obliquely from the south, a slight sting of sand in it. They went directly to the rail and leaned against it, standing close together, hip to hip. The moon was almost directly above them, brightening all the ocean before them except for the dark stretches at the horizon.

> *No ripples curl, alas!*
> *Along that wilderness of glass—*
> *No swelling tell that winds may be*
> *Upon some far-off happier sea—*
> *No heavings hint that winds have been*
> *On seas less hideously serene."*

She looked up at him, eyes widened, lips parted, half smiling. "What was that?"

"My favorite poet. Edgar Allan Poe."

"I'd forgotten. I remember you reciting Robert W. Service to me, and A. A. Milne. And singing some Civil War folk songs."

"It's from 'The City in the Sea.' Rather gloomy, I suppose. Among other things, it's about Hell."

"No, Hell, please. We've had enough of that."

> *By a route obscure and lonely,*
> *Haunted by ill angels only,*
> *Where an Eidolon, named Night,*
> *On a black throne reigns upright,*
> *I have reached these lands but newly*
> *From an ultimate dim Thule—*
> *From a wild weird clime that lieth, sublime*
> *Out of Space—out of Time . . ."*

"I like that better."

> *Bottomless vales and boundless floods,*
> *And chasms, and caves and Titan woods,*
> *With forms that no man can discover*
> *For the tears that drip all over;*
> *Mountains toppling evermore*
> *Into seas without a shore;*
> *Seas that relentlessly aspire,*
> *Surging into skies of fire . . ."*

He held her very close. "I've forgotten the rest."

"That's enough. It's a good place to stop."

"The poem's title is 'Dream Land.'"

"Dreamland. Dreamy dreamland."

"Many kinds of dreams."

"Let's go inside, Charley. The seas will be surging into skies of fire soon enough."

The sea was taken from them with the closing of the sliding glass door. She turned off the bright lamp and started toward the circular, wrought-iron staircase that led to the bedrooms, taking him by the hand, but he halted, holding her back.

"I'm sorry, Maddy. There's something I have to do."

"Something you have to do here?"

"I want to call California. I need to keep trying."

She turned on another lamp, irritated slightly at the interruption of her mood. "The phone's on the desk."

He nodded his thanks. It was not quite midnight on the West Coast. Tracy's phone never answered. Bill Jenks's phone rang many times. He was either in heavy sleep, or not home. Dresden was about to hang up when Jenks's groggy voice at last came on the line.

"Bill, it's Charley. Are you alone?"

"None of your business. Where are you, amigo?"

"Far, far away."

"Good. The police have come to see me twice about you."

"I'm sure they have. Is everyone all right?"

"'Everyone all right'? That's a hell of a question. Zack, Danny Hill . . ."

"I didn't kill them, Bill."

"Nobody thinks you did. None of your friends, anyway. But your taking off like that—it spooked a few people. Jim Ireland, I'm told, thinks you finally went off the deep end. He ordered special security guards at Channel Three."

"He would. Bill, no one else has been hurt—or killed? No one I knew, or worked with? Isabel? Anyone?"

"Everyone's fine. Even Jimmy Moon."

"I'm serious, Bill. Tracy. What about Tracy Bakersfield?"

"I haven't seen her."

"What do you mean?"

"I hadn't seen her for weeks before all this happened. I haven't seen her since."

"I told her to leave town for a while. Maybe she took my advice. If she shows up, look out for her, will you? I'm afraid I got her mixed up in my trouble."

"I'll do whatever I can. When will I hear from you again? Will we ever see you again?"

"Oh, yes. Sometime. Who knows when, but sometime. You're my best friend."

"Ain't that the unfortunate truth."

"Goodbye, amigo."

"*Adios*, best friend."

Dresden hung up slowly. Madeleine was leaning against the stair rail, not impatient, but weary.

"I was trying to reach Tracy Bakersfield. I told you about her. She didn't answer. I'm worried."

They started up the stairs. "I guess you have reason to be, but there's nothing you can do now, Charley. Not from here."

He rose early, washing and dressing quietly, leaving her to her sleep. Downstairs, the huge windows revealed a vast stretch of sea and shore, but no skies of fire for the sun to rise into. A striated overcast had drifted over the coast, the sun visible only as glimmers and flares amid the soft ribbons of cloud. Dresden found a plastic mug and poured some whiskey into it. Taking it out onto the deck, he lingered, alone and lonely, at the rail a moment, remembering with sweetness the night before. Then, beckoned by the shrill scree of gulls, he descended the wooden stairs to the sand. The wind had fallen, and the day seemed even warmer than the one previous. Only wavelets and the occasional shrug of a shallow, breaking swell disturbed the sea's calm. Conscious of his city shoes, he took them off and rolled up his trousers, walking north along the curving lines of wetness drawn and fading on the hard-packed sand, the water cold but tolerable against his bare ankles and feet.

In California the sea was a patient, if sometimes violent, sculptor, carving its rock faces and pinnacles and tunnels over the millennia from cliffs and mountains that were its equals. Here it was a thief, dragging back into its swirls and currents the endless tonnages of sand that were the work of its ceaseless labors, shifting and heaving the dunes and shoreline as pleased it, despite the feckless insistence of man on keeping everything where it was. Man's habitations—cabin, cottage, grand house, and concrete building—stretched in a crowded line to the hazy apex of a horizon's joining of land, sea, and sky. Each one doubtless gave its occupant the sense of permanence, of sameness, of the sea's eternity. But it was delusion. To watch the sea was to observe the constancy of change, the brevity of life. Whatever one put here, the sea would take back again. This was no place to plant a tree, or dig a grave; no place to build a house. If unknowingly, Maddy had chosen a fitting sanctuary. No surrounding spoke so much of the temporary.

Pausing as he passed the groins and sand-catching jetties to sip of the warm, scentful scotch, he moved on among the wheeling gulls and dark-windowed houses, passing only one other human being, an elderly man surf-casting in windproof clothing. He nodded a morning's greeting, but kept his eyes on his line out to sea. A few sips later and the old man was a dark dot far behind, and the wide wooden boardwalk of the town of Rehoboth Beach was just ahead. At a set of steps rising from the deep, soft sand, he set his cup where it would not be disturbed, and ascended, stopping to put on socks and shoes at the top.

The main street of the town, a broad resort boulevard of four lanes divided by a grassy esplanade and bordered by perpendicular parking places, was nearly as empty as the beach and boardwalk had been, with only a few cars parked here and there and no one visible on the sidewalks. It took some walking, but at length he found an open drugstore that sold Washington and Wilmington newspapers, and another with beach clothing among other general merchandise. There he bought some boating shoes, a pair of khaki slacks, and a red Windbreaker. He would once again look like he belonged, though he didn't. This was George Calendiari's place, a Washington place.

The plastic mug of whiskey was still where he had left it, unmolested, the alcohol's warmth gladdening him as he started back along the sands to the house. The wind had begun to rise and was blowing full in his face.

She was still asleep on his return, and he slid the door closed quietly. Changing into his new clothes, he sat down at a long wooden table in a dining alcove that also possessed a sea view, spreading the newspapers in front of him. They took only about forty minutes to get through, and he had pushed them aside by the time he heard her come down the circular staircase.

Maddy came up behind him and put her arms around him, lowering her head until her warm cheek was against his. She sniffed the mug.

"Our morning coffee smells strangely of fermented grain," she said.

"Stirrup cup."

"You've been to town, I see. New duds."

"I thought a three-piece suit was a little conspicuous for the beach."

"Only when you go clamming. No one ever goes clamming in three-piece suits around here." She kissed the top of his head and stood up. "I'll make breakfast. I don't know what we'll have, but whatever it will be, it will come out of a can, at least until we can get to a grocery."

"There was nothing in the papers."

"Nothing?"

"The *Washington Post* is full of stories about the Gettysburg investigation, just as it has been for weeks, but there's nothing really new. Nothing at all concerning the vice president."

"We get the early edition out here. It probably went to press before we even saw Atherton."

"There's a story that things are getting worse in Central America. Russian ships are in the Caribbean—freighters escorted by naval vessels."

"What are we doing about it?"

"Apparently nothing. We are 'concerned.'"

She brought plates of corned beef hash, with artichoke hearts on the side. "We must get to the grocery."

"This will do," he said. "My friend Danny Hill used to eat meals like this all the time."

She sat down opposite him. She was wearing running shoes, white duck pants, and a white sweater. Her blond hair was carefully brushed, held back with one of her ubiquitous powder-blue hair ribbons. She still was not wearing any ring. He smiled, then looked back to the sea.

"The waves are breaking twice," he said. "A hundred feet out, and then again at the shoreline."

"Sandbar. They're frequent along this stretch. You can probably see it at low tide."

She went to do the dishes. He followed to help her, and she kissed him for that.

When they were done she put on a navy blue sailing jacket. "Did you enjoy your walk?"

"Yes, very much."

"Good. Because we're going to go on another one, a long one. It's the major part of my day out here."

They headed south, into the wind, hand in hand. Glimpses of

blue appeared from time to time in the clouds, but there was no sign of clearing. Farther to the south, the horizon was darkening.

"I've been thinking about us," he said. "About the future."

"Me too. Not happy thoughts."

"I'm down to about twenty-four hundred dollars of Charlene's money. Whatever happens in Washington, I'm wanted for murder in California. You're very much married to the very much Catholic George Calendiari."

"That's not what's troubling me."

"Why not?"

"Money is the least of my worries. If Laurence Atherton is able to prove that the president's dead, that *he's* president now, he can order an FBI investigation into what happened to your friends in California—show that they were killed as part of this assassination cover-up. God knows, enough people have been killed because of it. As for George, an annulment is within the realm of possibility. Given the fact of our adultery and the lack of children, it's quite possible. The alternative would be a messy California divorce. I'd automatically come in for a great deal of community property I'm not even interested in, and the public aspects of it all would be something neither the Calendiari family or George's political mentors would appreciate."

A long freighter was steaming north along the coast, high in the water. Dresden stopped to watch it.

"Cape Henlopen's just north of Rehoboth. It's the entrance to Delaware Bay," Maddy said. "That ship could be going to Wilmington or all the way up to Philadelphia. They go by all the time. We can watch them tonight."

They moved on, still without another human in view.

"So you see," she continued, "all those things can be managed. I'm troubled by something else."

He didn't let her finish. He wasn't sure she was ready to.

"What if things didn't work out so neatly?" he asked. "What if we just had to cut and run?"

"We'd manage. I'd find a way to get some money from Daddy and . . ."

"No money. No daddies. Just us. I once knew some people who lived way back up in the Carmel Valley, so far back there were wild boar in their woods. They had a cabin without glass windows. Just some books and musical instruments and a well and a garden—everything those people needed. Could we hole up in a place like that?"

"There's no place in the Carmel Valley anymore without glass windows, or a swimming pool."

"Up in the Sierras then. Or in Brooklyn, or Jersey City. Some crummy walk-up apartment with cooking smells and people jabbering in Spanish or Haitian or Russian. You and I working under assumed names at wretched little jobs just to get by. Or living in some tank town in upstate New York or Ohio. Or out of the country, on the run in Canada or Mexico or God knows where. Maybe even stealing just to get by. Are we up to that, Maddy? Am I? Are you?"

"You've obviously already answered that question for yourself. My answer is simple. Yes. Of course. I'd do any of those things, whatever it took for as long as it took, and not a second longer. I'd hate it, but I'd do it. I will do it. If you feel otherwise, you don't understand what's been between us in these last few days."

"I don't misunderstand what's between us. It's the one thing in my life I understand perfectly."

The more substantial houses were behind them now. There was an interlude of dune, traversed by snow fences, and then a stretch of closely packed motels and bungalows, closed for the season, gaudy signs advertising soft drinks and souvenirs that were not for sale.

"What's troubling me, Charley, is something else. It's marriage."

"Your marriage to George?"

"No, damn it. My marriage to you! I'm the marrying kind, Charley. Present circumstances excepted, monogamous. A husband's loving wife, that's the essential me—the wife of a loving, giving husband. If we get out of this, in splendor or in squalor, I should become your wife."

"Or leave me."

She said nothing. They continued to hold hands, but walked a little further apart now. Finally, she dropped his and put both of hers in her jacket pockets.

"I made a rash mistake when I went off with George all those years ago. It took me a long time to pay for it. I don't have all that much time to pay for another mistake."

"I'm not George Calendiari."

"Of course you're not. But you're you."

"Are you afraid I'd be unfaithful?"

"Such a very male question. Of course you'd be unfaithful, on occasion. Rare occasion. It happens. You're going to be middle-aged in a few years. It's not a time of life conducive to saintliness. I can't guarantee that I'd be altogether perfect that way, either. But that's not my worry. What I'm afraid of is that you might not be my husband, in the way I want, that we might not be truly married in the sense that's most important to me."

"I'm not sure I understand."

"What I called your 'wildness,' Charley. It was a large part of what attracted me to you in the first place, and even now, a little. Maybe even a lot. You've always been the great free spirit—shooting off guns in your house, driving all the way up to the Sierras just for a date, tearing through forest fires, howling at the moon, quitting your jobs, making piles of money and losing it in poker games. Doing whatever came into your head.

"I've been married nearly all my adult life, Charley. You're going to be forty in a few years and you've never married. Your relationship with Charlene Zack—if none of this had happened, where do you think you two would have been, say, a year from now?"

"I don't know. I'd still be in Tiburcio probably. She might be back up at Tahoe, or down in L.A. or San Diego, or possibly a very successful business woman in Santa Linda. There's no telling. That's the way it's been—the way it was."

"But your little house, it would still be part hers, always, whenever she came by."

"Yes. That was our understanding."

"Charley, do you realize that arrangement is as close as you ever got to a serious, meaningful relationship with a woman in your entire life? And, from what you said, I don't think that was enough for Charlene, not toward the end, not when she came back the last time." Maddy halted, looking up at him. "But that wildness—freedom, self-indulgence, immaturity, rugged individualism—whatever you want to call it, it got in the way."

She stepped closer, her blue eyes troubled, fiercely serious, hypnotic in their perfection.

"I have to be married, Charley. I'm not a possessive woman. I'm not domineering. I'm not a clinger or a whiner or a shrew. I'm so grateful that we found each other again, that we're in love again, but I can't settle for an 'arrangement.' That wildness in you. I don't think it's run its course. I'm very much afraid that it would get in the way."

They moved on, in silence. Occasionally, she'd kick at little fragments of shell upon the sand. The dark hull of another ship was visible in the murky gray of the southerly horizon.

"That life I led, Maddy. My coming out to California in the first place, the magic of it was that it let me escape from what I feared most, and that was failure, the kind of failure that destroyed my father. With my kind of life, I couldn't fail, because I've never really tried to succeed."

The approaching ship shifted course slightly, seeking the channel. The breeze had become a gusting wind.

"Are you telling me you're afraid you're like your father?"

"No. I'm just telling you I've spent my whole life avoiding having to find out."

"Well, just let me lay a few things on the table, Charles August Dresden. I saw some of your television work. It was brilliant."

"My father was brilliant. No one doubted that."

"Be quiet. Your friend, Tracy Butterfield . . ."

"Bakersfield."

"Bakersfield. When she told you you could do whatever you wanted to do she was quite right. Your problem is you never stopped to give any thought to what you really wanted to do, what you should do." She stopped. "End of lecture. Anyway, this is as far as we go. This is where I turn back. At the towers."

There were two of them, one near, the other perhaps a mile farther down the beach, stark, forbidding sentinels of pitted concrete, as high as lighthouses, and shaped somewhat like them, but without their life-saving purpose. The role of these structures, dark, gaping slits cut curving around their tops, facing out to sea, had not to do with life, but death.

"They're from World War II," Maddy said. "They used to have them all up and down the coast. There were machine guns in them, and I think some small cannons. George told me all about them once. I don't know what happened to all the others. There's been a movement to have these preserved as historical landmarks. They're on state park property, but the kids have gotten into them."

She took his arm, and started them back toward the house, this time walking closest to the sea herself.

"We shouldn't be permitting ourselves troubling thoughts," he said.

"We can't afford them yet, can we? We're still trapped in the present. The past's been taken from us. We don't yet have a future."

He took her hand. "We'll have one."

"I feel quite happy now, sadly happy sometimes, but sometimes giddy too. Like a little girl."

Facing the north, the wind behind them now, they found the horizon much brighter. The peeking sun had already reached its zenith and was easing west.

"I'm happy," he said.

"Let me ask you one troubling question, then. Just one more," she said.

"All right."

Her eyes were playful now. "Would you like to have a baby?"

"What?"

"A baby, that would grow up to be a child, and an adult, and all the rest."

"That's a question that never occurred to me before."

"And?"

"It's a question I'd have to think about a lot, but I can in all honesty say this to you."

"Yes?"

"It's not a troubling question."

They kept on past the house on their return, going on up the boardwalk and into Rehoboth, Maddy to do some odd shopping, Dresden to buy some later newspapers.

Once back—for good for the day—Maddy turned on the gas flames in the living room's free-standing fireplace. Without being asked for it, she poured him a glass of scotch with ice as he settled into a nearby chair and began to look through the papers—the morning's *Philadelphia Inquirer* and an afternoon edition of the *Baltimore Sun*. It was in the latter that he saw it, an article at the top of page 3.

"Nothing in there?" She was in the kitchen, making a drink for herself.

"No, not nothing. Something."

"The vice president's done something?"

"Not him. More likely the other fellows. Howie King is dead."

"Dead?"

"Yes, ma'am. They found his body in a Baltimore garbage dump this morning."

"What happened? Was he shot?"

"They don't know what killed him. He was in a green plastic bag. Some dogs were trying to tear it open."

She stood beside him, putting one hand on his shoulder. The ice in the glass she held in the other rattled slightly.

"My God, Charley, did we cause this?"

"No, we didn't. They've caused this, all of this. We're just honest citizens. I wonder how far it is from Camp David to Baltimore. It can't be far. Fifty miles or so."

"But why would they do it? Don't they need him? How can they put a President Hampton on television without King?"

He went over to the television set. "Can this get Washington? On cable or something?"

"No, just Wilmington and Dover. Baltimore and Philadelphia, if the weather's right."

He clicked the dial through its full rotation, but it was too early for any newscast. Leaving the set on, with the volume low, he resumed his seat by the fire, drinking and thinking. Madeleine took the newspapers, reading through them carefully, then sat staring out the window, at the darkening skies and sea.

"Maybe I'd better call George," she said.

"No, I don't think so. Let's leave well enough alone. If George needs us, if he has something to tell us, he'll call."

"He may have tried to. We've been out."

"We've been back for nearly an hour. If something's up, he'd keep trying. Please, Maddy. I know this must be hell on your nerves, but be patient. Let George handle his end of things."

The news came on and Dresden increased the volume. It was one of the local stations in Wilmington and the lead story was of a trailer-truck auto accident on Interstate 495. After that was a piece on a warehouse fire the night before. The rest of the news was as insignificant. Even the sports managed to be dull. The weatherman said the unusually warm temperatures would continue, but skies would be cloudy and intermittent rain and thunderstorms were predicted.

Finally, as though it had been added at the last moment, there was a brief item on the finding of Howie King's body, but the newswriter had bent the story to the fact that a neighborhood of sleazy bars, nightclubs, and massage parlors was not far from the garbage dump. They closed with a feature piece, about a Christmas party for handicapped children.

The network news began more consequentially, with a press conference at the temporary center set up in the Rustic Motel in Thurmont. National Security Adviser James Malcom, White House Chief of Staff Irving Ambrose, and Defense Secretary George Moran presided at a table crowded with microphones. They said additional warships had been dispatched from Galveston, Texas, to augment the task force on station off Honduras and that they understood Secretary of State Crosby had sent a warning to the Soviet Union that the intrusion of Soviet vessels in Honduran waters would be considered a hostile act. The three, with the defense secretary as spokesman, said that American troops in Central America had not been placed on a higher level of alert, despite earlier reports to the contrary, and that they did not consider the situation critical. The president had developed a slight case of bronchitis and was resting, they said. Otherwise, he would have made a statement himself from Camp David. His condition was not now serious, they said.

The network switched to correspondents in the field, a blond woman in Tegucigalpa and a dark-haired man in Managua, who both wore khaki safari shirts and both said tensions were high. In another story the chairman of the Senate Foreign Relations Committee said he had left a meeting of the Latin American Contadora nations on the Central American crisis and was en route to one with NATO leaders. The secretary-general of the United Nations said the Security Council had met but had taken no conclusive action.

The newscast did not get to Howie King for another four stories. It was a brief report. The sound bite was of an off-camera reporter noting that King had been a habitué of gambling casinos in Atlantic City as footage was shown of his covered body being wheeled to a police van.

The newscast concluded with footage of First Lady Daisy Hampton waving briefly from some distance at Camp David, then some of an army choral group singing carols in the White House with Vice President Atherton and some other dignitaries looking on, and finally a shot of the White House Christmas tree on the Ellipse.

"George and I used to go to the vice president's Christmas parties," Maddy said. "Every year. I half expected to see George on the screen."

"He may have been there," Dresden said, turning off the set. "They're obviously keeping up appearances."

"I wish George's appearance had been one of them."

He got up and put his arms around her. "We'll call George, before the night is out."

"I really want to, Charley."

"But not now. Let's go into town for dinner. I'm not up for another bout with canned hash."

They drove, a patter of rain spotting the windshield by the time they arrived. Charley missed the turning and so parked on the main street, leaving them a half block to walk around the corner. They didn't mind. In their beach clothes, in the sea air, a touch of rain in their faces seemed a pleasure, almost obligatory. The restaurant was small and warm and cheery, with red tablecloths.

"Do you realize it's Christmas Eve?" she said, reaching into her purse. "I bought you a little present." She set down a small, thin cardboard box, tied with a tiny ribbon. "If you don't remember about this, you'll think I'm just being silly, or very cheap."

She watched, chin resting on folded hands as he opened it. He smiled, holding it up to the light. It was an inexpensive gold wedding band, the kind one might find in a better grade of discount store or a beach shop that sold jewelry among its souvenirs. On their second date in California, on an impulse, feeling a little crazy about each other, they had dashed into a five and ten in Santa Linda and bought each other such rings—to wear forever.

"I remember," he said. "I more than remember."

He reached in his jacket pocket and took out a small packet of tissue paper. Inside was a similar ring, inexpensive and very plain. She smiled, slipping his onto his finger, then put on her own.

He raised his glass. "Merry Christmas, Madeleine Margrit Anderson."

Hers touched his. "Merry, Merry Christmas. And all good things."

When they left, arm in arm, a light rain was still falling, but they paid it absolutely no mind. A man was at the corner, leaning against the brick wall of a building. The very last thing there should have been in Rehoboth Beach, Delaware, on Christmas Eve was a man standing at the corner, in the rain.

Instead of crossing the street to the car, Charley pulled them the other way, down the empty main boulevard, toward the boardwalk.

"Are we going for a walk on the beach, Charley? Can't we wait until the rain stops?"

Not speaking, he kept them moving, glancing back over his shoulder. The man had left the corner and was following them. Across the way, on the other side of the grassy median strip, two other dark figures stepped from behind a parked car.

Charley Dresden was the stupidest man who ever lived, the most arrogant, cocky, egomaniacal, unthinking, thick-headed fool there could be. He had flamboyantly signed his name all over Washington, paraded all over New York, beat up David Callister in his own house, appeared at the vice president's mansion, and had gone off for a little seaside idyll at the Calendiaris' well-known beach retreat. They had tracked him down to his canyon house in California and murdered his friends, yet he had had the appalling presumptuousness to think they could not possibly find him on their own territory. Now he might die for his stupidity. And so might she.

"We've got to run, Maddy! There are men behind us! Both sides of the street!"

She turned for a frantic look over her shoulder, but did as bidden, holding onto his hand.

"Run where, Charley?"

"I don't know! Just keep going!"

Their beach shoes gave them an advantage with their good traction on the wet pavement, allowing them to keep ahead of the three men, who were obviously in streetwear. But there was no sanctuary. There were many storefronts, but they were closed and locked and dark. The glistening wooden planking of the boardwalk was in sight, and nearing.

"Where, Charley? Where do we go?"

Their pursuers had made a mistake. Not knowing which way Dresden and Maddy were going to turn, the two from the parked car had crossed to join the third man, and they were lunging after them in a pack. If one of them had stayed on the opposite side of the boulevard, he would have been in a position to cut them off.

"Turn right at the boardwalk!" Charley said. "We'll try to get to the house!"

They might never make it. There might be more men waiting for them there. But it was a chance, and Charley could think of no other. It would give them an opportunity to lock a door behind them, to make a quick, frantic call to police, to shoot whoever came in after them. If they could make it.

Hastening on, his injured leg paining him now, Charley pulled Maddy along with him. She ran with head high, her hair streaming wet. Rounding the corner, the three men came relentlessly after, gaining ground, till one of them slipped and fell. The other two paused only an instant.

"Keep up, Maddy! Run as hard as you can! I swear they mean to kill us, Maddy!"

"I'm running. Oh God, I'm running."

There were more storefronts, dark and locked, lightless signs in the windows. One of the men was pulling ahead of the others. In a quick glance, Charley saw a dark object in his right hand.

Hearts thumping, they pounded over the wooden planks, passing the opening of the end of a street, the large green enclosure of a public toilet at the curb. Just ahead was an enormous two- or three-story structure, the sides of its ground floor all open to the street, but enclosed with chicken-wire netting.

Maddy now pulled ahead. In the shadows within, Charley saw odd objects. Video game machines, the stilled, circular procession of painted horses—a carousel. There was an opening in the wire netting, a sort of gate, standing ajar.

"In here, Charley! I know this place! It's an amusement arcade. Quick!"

Ducking, they slipped into the darkness. With Maddy leading him by the hand, they darted and scurried around and among the rides and devices. There were dozens of places to hide, but she kept on, pulling him past the carousel and the bumper car track toward the rear. There the roof gave way to sky again in a vast open space that allowed room for the Ferris wheel and the major thrill rides. The rain was heavy now, falling in thuds.

"Damn!" she said. "I thought there'd be a way out back here. That wire's everywhere!"

They looked desperately around them. Over by a high wall he saw a spinning teacup ride, now motionless. He pulled her over to it, pushing her into one of the cups and clambering in after her, pulling out his pistol. Two of their pursuers had found the same gate they had, and had entered. They were soon joined by the third. The men fanned out, but it could take them an hour to search the entire arcade. Dresden allowed himself the luxurious thought that, with care, moving quietly in the shadows, he and Maddy might still have a chance to break free.

But one of the men now embarked on another, more pragmatic search, apparently with a fair idea of where to look. He disappeared behind some machinery for a moment, and then at once all the shadows, all the darkness harbored by that cavernous enclosure utterly vanished in the glare of hundreds of lights. The three moved forward now with deliberation, methodically, as hunters, seeking paths through the rides and amusements as they might work their way through heavy brush. All three had drawn weapons.

The one who'd been bright enough to seek out the main power switch moved to the center. He stopped, calling out: "We mean no harm! We just want to talk to you! That's all! Just talk to you! Come out!"

Maddy was almost panting in fear. His own breathing was so heavy he could scarcely hear hers. He held his revolver aimed loosely at the man coming nearest them, but to little point. The distance was too great for even as good a pistol shot as Dresden. And if he hit his mark, what then? The Magnum held only six rounds. They were cornered. His first shot would give their location away.

But then the men made another mistake. To aid in their search, like beaters flushing game in a medieval hunt, they began throwing the switches, pushing the buttons, and pulling the levers that turned on the rides. At once children's rocketships began their mindless, orbital flights; shooting gallery devices began to buzz and beep; the carousel started to revolve, the brightly painted horses whirling into their lifting, falling dance. Music played amidst a dozen grinds and rattles and roars. The noise grew to a din, eerily so in the vast emptiness of the place.

Maddy pulled Dresden close. "Charley. The fun house. If we can make it, there's a way out through the fun house."

Its garish facade was nearby, fifty feet from the edge of the teacup ride. A narrow track emerged from one set of black-painted double doors, ran along the facade, and then disappeared into another set. Hanging suspended above the track were a number of black-painted, two-seat chairs, looking like something miners might ride into their shafts.

The noise was increasing. The man nearest them came nearer still, reaching the place where the teacup ride's attendant would stand, the place with the "on" button.

"Now," said Charley.

They hurled themselves forward, out of the teacup, sprawling onto the platform, just as the machinery began its movement. Hurrying on hands and knees, slipping and sliding, they avoided an oncoming teacup beginning to spin in its track. The man saw them and shouted. Gun in hand, he leaped up on the platform, just as they rolled off its edge, and just as one of the wildly spinning teacups came round and knocked him sprawling, his weapon flying from his hand.

Running at a crouch, Dresden and Maddy fled for the fun house doors, breaking one of them off its hinges as they smashed their way into the blackness. Here there would be no glaring lights.

Maddy took the lead again, holding tightly to his hand, groping forward. There was enough pale glow of light in the chamber to see by as their eyes became adjusted to it, some of it reddish in hue, other corners a ghoulish gray-green. Spooks and skeletons, fiends and horrid heads, odd lights and disorienting devices, all hung loose and lifeless, staring, looking more frightening than they likely did in their customary motion.

Through the thin walls behind them they could hear shouting again, running footsteps, and a crash. Maddy kept on, finding her way, pausing as she lost it, then remembering, moving slowly forward. Suddenly there was the sound of a lurching grind. Another switch had been thrown. The empty chairs were beginning their swinging procession through the house of horrors. With the slam of doors, one banged its way into the chamber where they stood. Another followed.

"Get in the next one!" Maddy shouted. "It will take us where we need to go!"

"But they'll only be waiting for us when we come out!"

"No! There's another way! Do as I say!"

At the next slam and bang they both leaped at the approaching car from either side, almost in unison, causing it to sway violently as they fell back against the seat. The monster creatures were in full function now, jangling and hooting and screeching, leaping out and back. Charley, gun poised, kept looking beyond them for a face that wasn't painted, for a figure of menace that only stood still. The seat cranked and jerked, banging through another set of doors, and then abruptly rising.

"Get ready!" Maddy said. "Jump when I say!"

"But where?"

"Just jump! When I say!"

They rattled up the incline in pitch blackness, reached its summit, then slammed through more doors. Instantly, Charley glimpsed sea, dark sand, the moist wood of the boardwalk below.

"Now!" shouted Maddy. She disappeared to his left. He flung himself to the right, smashing into a wooden wall, his knee hurting.

The little car, swaying and empty, proceeded on without them, disappearing into the cavernous fun house again with a snap of metal hinge and wood. Maddy was back against the railing. They were on a small open place on the structure's second floor.

"A little added attraction," she said, trying to catch her breath. "A little look at the real world again before you're plunged back into hell."

He waited for the next chair to emerge and rattle past, then leaped to her side.

"We have to climb down," she said, peering down at the wooden framework supporting the structure. "We'll have to jump to the boardwalk. It's the only way."

"Okay."

He helped her over the rail, then lifted himself onto it as she began to lower herself with careful grip on the slippery uprights. He was crouched when the fun house doors banged open yet once more, this time revealing a chair that was not empty.

Charley had only an instant's look at the man's startled, angry face. The recognition that would come later would be that of a vague figure in the background at the press conference he had just seen on the network newscast. But Dresden had time only for impulse. His first was to shoot the man, point blank. His next, coming just a millisecond later, coming just as the chair rumbled directly past him, was kinder, but not much. He brought the sharp, heavy butt of his pistol grip down on the man's head. His victim cried out and sprawled forward, hanging over the safety bar.

With that, Charley stuck the revolver back in his belt and hastened over the side, quickly reaching Maddy. She clung to a beam, swaying and looking down, then dropped, legs giving way as she hit, but rising quickly to her feet. She looked up. He dropped as resolutely, but landed not as well. His knee went from pain to agony, but he fought it, rising.

"I'm okay," he said. Their faces glistened in the drenching rain. "Let's go!"

He wasn't okay, but he forced his leg to work. They stayed close to the shadows of the empty storefronts, Maddy in front, moving farther into darkness, at last finding the stairs that led down to the soft and silent sand.

They tottered more than ran, feet sliding and slipping, breaths coming in spasms. Ahead Charley could see the dim flickering of what must be the lights of their house, but he could not gauge its distance. The measurement did not matter. All that counted was to run, run as he had always run, as life had made him run from the very beginning. Run for life. Run for Maddy. Run.

But it wasn't fast or far enough. A loud crack sounded in the downpour and a whining, whizzing object burned through the air beside him. Then another. He looked back, faltering as he did so. Two figures were behind them. Silhouetted farther back against the glowing lights of the town, he could see a third.

Another gunshot. The damned, wet sand was slowing both of them, but especially Charley. If they had stuck to the pavement, found some sidestreet off the boardwalk, they might have escaped. They might have.

There was another exploding crackle, but instead of a bullet singing past, he heard Maddy shriek. She lurched, spinning around, and fell to her back.

He had an instant's examination of his soul to make, an instant's search of his entire being for some shred of honor and purpose, of decision. They had taken everything from him now. They had taken her. All he had left to him, all that could drive him now, was that urge to run, to flee, to keep alive whatever small particle of himself yet remained, to resist to the very last what his father had found so easy: to die.

She arched her back, writhing, crying out in pain. He dropped to his knee, his good knee, and reached to hold her shoulder, just to touch her, reassure her. With his other hand he brought up the big Magnum and fired off a bellowing round at their pursuers. In that faint light, in the rain and distance, the bullet missed, rocketing on into nothingness. But it had effect. One of the men darted sideways, toward the houses lining the beach. The other moved closer to the shore, moving forward at a crouch. Charley fired at him, missing again, cursing the rain in his eyes. Maddy was clinging tightly to his arm.

This was it then. Death in the rain by the sea. His mind had emptied of Poe. He could think only of a snatch of remembered words, the last words of an aged actress. Someone his grandfather had known. Ethel Barrymore. "That's all there is. There isn't anymore."

That's all. Two figures, three. Advancing relentlessly, sent by the gods. The Valkyries had made their choice.

Or had they? The rain was thickening with another sound, a droning, chattering sound. As it increased, a huge cone of light poked through the darkness at the boardwalk, slanting down from the sky.

As it came closer the light switched back and forth, sweeping the beach from side to side, searching. The three men halted, standing and looking back, looking up, their weapons lowered.

The helicopter clattered on until it was directly over them, hovering, its light searingly bright. They kept looking up expectantly, when suddenly the machine slid to the side and two quick rattling bursts of gunfire dropped one of the men into a crumpled mound, then another. The third, the farthest distant, started a limping retreat back toward the boardwalk, but he was cut down in a few seconds.

Now the machine, seeming to be a living creature itself, came on slowly toward Charley, its light piercing the way ahead. Dresden rose to his full height, waving his arm, his hand still holding his gun, joyful at their rescue.

The gunner, perhaps impatient, began firing before the helicopter was directly overhead. Though Charley and Maddy were fully bathed in the searchlight, the bullets missed, slashing only into sand.

Charley flung himself to the side, rolling, drawing the helicopter away from the sobbing Maddy. Rolling again, turning onto his belly, he lifted himself onto his elbows, raising the pistol with both hands. He had only the tiniest fraction of a hope of a chance. A thousand fears and angers pounded through his head, but so did one great, enraging, inescapable truth. He took his particle of chance, firing the big revolver once, and then again.

The searchlight went out with an explosive, hissing burst of smoke and falling glass. The helicopter, enveloped in darkness, skittered to the side. Above its chattering roar Charley could still hear the surf.

Lurching, he dragged Maddy up into a sitting position, then lifted her until she was draped across his shoulder, his own leg feeling pain so sharply he feared it would collapse beneath him. But he staggered on, driven to his very last snatch at life, wondering if the gods would even deny him that.

23

Maddy staggered and fell as they plunged into the icy sea, bitter waves rising against them. She fell again several times as he pushed on into the deeper water, half swimming, half lunging. Once she slipped from his tired grasp and fell completely beneath the water. But at last they reached the sandbar, nearer to the shore now than it had been that afternoon. Apparently the tide had fallen, for the breaking water once they were atop the sandy mound came only to their knees. Dresden crouched down, pulling Maddy with him and against him, enfolding her protectively with his arms, taking the brunt of the thudding, chilling waves with his back. He had never been so cold, so wet, so furious, helpless and terrified in his life. He had no idea of what the survival time was at this time of year in these waters; there was no measuring of it or of the temperature save by the continuing ticking fact of their being alive. If they slipped blue and frozen and unconscious now into the bone-cold ocean, then their survival time had elapsed. If they still lived, then it had not. All he could do was hold this injured, dying, lovely woman to his chest and wait and hope and pray and hate.

They had not yet got him. The helicopter had quickly settled to the sand, its rotors still turning as two of its occupants, both armed, one holding a flashlight, leaped out and made a hurried search of the beach. They looked up and down, flashed their light at the darkened houses along the dune, but they failed to turn in the one direction in which it would make no sense to them to turn—toward the sea, where the dark figures of Dresden and Maddy huddled in the flowing heaps of wave.

They were making haste, these men. There were winter residents in Rehoboth, as well as streetlights and police cars. Despite the deadening effects of the rain, there had been too much shooting, too much noise and light from the helicopter. The intruders each took one last look about them, then went to work, dragging the fallen bodies of their victims to the aircraft and hefting them within. Three times they performed this struggling chore, then clambered into the machine themselves. It lifted at once, leaving the beach beneath it clean of any sign of their coming, rose high above the rooftops, then climbed further, turning toward the west.

Dresden's limbs, his toes and fingers, had no feeling, but he could move them. He rose and pulled Maddy to her feet, heaving her and himself forward despite the drag of the water-laden clothing, helped by the push of waves behind them. Floundering, they reached shallow shore water again, and the scrape of stones and shell and sand against their knees. He pulled her up full upon the beach, leaning down to make certain she was still breathing, then rose, tottering, to bring himself to some sane decision.

An idiotic notion struck his numbed mind. He would get them both back to her warm, waiting house, pull off her soaked, cold clothing, and tend to her wound, get her in bed and telephone for help. Simple as that.

He cursed himself for this mindless indulgence, this waste of time. He had no idea who or what might be waiting by those beckoning lights of the Calendiari home, what helicopters might still swoop out of darkness, how many pieces Death still had on the gameboard. What he needed now was haste, frantic haste, the maximum use of time.

Lifting her, stumbling, he moved down the row of darkened houses till he came to one holding the best promise of usefulness and easy entrance. Dragging Maddy up to its deck, he kicked until he had broken open a window by a door. Once inside, he found a lamp and turned the switch. It came on.

Maddy was conscious, shivering and trembling, muttering, but her face was the blue of a dead woman. Stretching her out on the floor,

Dresden rolled her over and methodically pulled back and lowered her crimson-soaked white duck pants. The bullet had struck at the line where the upper reach of thigh joined buttock. It seemed not to have touched bone, but had burrowed through the skin, breaking out through a tear of muscle a few inches further. The salty sea had cleaned the wound, but there had been much bleeding, and the blood was flowing again.

He bent over, leaning close to her face. "Hold on, Maddy. Hold on. I've got to get some things. Got to stop your bleeding. Hold on. Be right back."

Turning on only the few lights needed to find his way, he hurried through the house, searching. He found bandages and gauze, and some sort of disinfectant, in a bathroom. He found sheets. He'd need strips from them to bind her leg tight. He found blankets. He'd need them to warm her in her shock. There was no time to change her clothes. There were no clothes. He found tape. He found many useless things. He found a bottle of whiskey. Swearing, he repeated his climb up the stairs to where he'd located the blankets. He needed pillows. She'd need pillows to sit on, or she'd ride screaming in pain.

Ride where? Ride how? He'd have to get back their car. There was no other. They must flee this erstwhile perfect refuge, this place of talk of love and babies. There'd be risk in running back to town, if he could still run—risk in darting across the broad, open, empty street. There might be some bomb attached to the floorboard by now, some waiting gunman. But the risk from doing nothing else was infinitely greater.

He turned out all the lights in the house they'd invaded but the one beside her. He poured disinfectant onto her wound, gripping her arm as she cried out, then piled on the gauze, ripping the sheeting into strips and winding it about her leg, firm and tight, over and over again. Then he made one last binding with adhesive tape. He pulled up her still wet underwear and trousers, securing them as best he could. Whimpering, she lay face down on the hard wooden floor, not moving.

"Be right back, my darling. Be back. Have to get the car. Just wait. Be right back. Got to get the car. Got to get out of here. Just wait. Just stay alive my darling darling."

Nothing moved in the slick wet street but him. His leg dragging, he followed an endless course, over more sand, stumbling past garbage cans, reaching the long black leeward lake, finally reaching its end, emerging into streetlights, heaving and wheezing until he finally came to the wide main street again. A car was moving on it, many blocks distant, moving away, inland. The yellow Mercedes sat all by itself at its curbside, the streetlight a bright glare on its windows.

Death or no, he had no choice, nothing else to do. Pulling out the keys, dropping and retrieving them, he hobbled to it, opened the door, and, without hesitation, turned on the ignition. There was no explosion. No one yanked open the opposite door. No one rose from the backseat behind him. He slammed shut the door and, with a snarling squeal of tires that gave voice to his torment, sped the car skidding back to the house.

He made a bundle of the injured woman, wrapping her thickly in blankets, arranging the pillows under and around her as best he could to ease the pain, limit the discomfort, positioning her so that she would face him, so that he could glance and take a measure of the ebb of life. He ran back into the stranger's house and took a blanket for himself, for he was now shaking violently. He pulled it full around his shoulders, restarted the engine, and roared off down the street. He knew no other way to go but the way they had come, the way that led back to the monumental bridge and the nation's capital. That was likely wrong, but his mind produced no other useful idea.

Finally, Rehoboth far behind them, he reached and shook her. She made a weak sound, but did not stir. He tried again, with the same result. His teeth were rattling, his shivers now tremors. He had brought the whiskey, throwing it, his gun, and the house's first-aid kit onto the Mercedes' floor. He reached and took a long swallow. It helped. He turned up the car's heater to high and clicked on the radio, wincing at the loudness. This was truly like the long-ago late night ride down the Bayshore from San Francisco, but Death was now closer than he ever could have imagined, rode with them right in the car, watching them, waiting. It was hours to Washington, but what else to do?

Dresden shook her again, hard. "Maddy. Listen to me. Please, Maddy, wake up!"

She murmured again. He heard the word *wake*.

"Are you awake? Can you hear me?"

"Can hear you. Yes, hear you, Charley. Love you, Charley."

"Maddy. I'm heading back for the bridge. Heading back to the city. Don't know where else to go. Maddy, where should I go? Where do I go? Do you have any friends?"

"No friends now. No friends to trust." He could glimpse her eyes upon him. There was life in them—pain and love. A purpose. He reached and touched her cheek. It was so cold.

"We've got to find friends, Maddy. Someone, anyone who can get us a doctor."

"Friends. Yes. One friend. I trust him. A good friend. George's. Mine. A British friend. He'll help us. No part of this."

She began breathing heavily, without words, then quieted, and resumed what she was saying.

"British friend, Charley. No stake in this. Journalist. British TV. Spy too. He'll help. We've helped him. Good man."

"Who is he, Maddy?" Dresden was tearing down the open, rain-slick road near eighty miles an hour. He drank whiskey, keeping going. He had to do it. He had to do all the things he had to do. "Who is he? Where do we go?"

"Back to the city. Up Massachusetts Avenue. Just past the bridge. The bombed bridge. Mrs. Atherton bombed there. That bridge. First left. Take first left. Up Whitehaven Street. Big white house up long drive. Big house on right. Picket fence. Graham Thompson. He's a good man. Good friend . . ."

She trailed off. Her eyes closed. Death was riding with them, riding, watching. Waiting.

The Bay Bridge toll collector looked at Dresden strangely, but did not halt him or summon police. Little other traffic moved on the highway. He rumbled along at high speed, tires thumping, drinking, alternately sweating and freezing, not understanding any of the words spoken on the radio, concentrating everything on aligning the car with the road, on willing Maddy alive.

He swerved badly on the streets of Washington, taking turns clumsily, becoming hopelessly lost several times. But it was Christmas Eve, and there were cars being driven that way all over the city. Once a policeman pulled up close behind him, following, but abruptly pulled away, turning with a sudden display of flashing lights and siren in pursuit of a problem more serious.

Dresden found his way to the bridge—the GLOVER BRIDGE, a small green sign proclaimed. The rain had long since ceased and the pavement was drying. A large, glass-walled, modern building, held erect on its hillside by an architect's huge freeform pedestal, loomed ahead. Just before it was a tree-lined street leading diagonally off to the left. A sign said WHITEHAVEN.

Christmas Eve. There'd be many, many parties. But the British journalist was a family man, a Christmas-keeping man. A tall, thin, Dickensian character with bony face, long gray hair, dark-rimmed glasses, and a rosy flush to his skin, he opened his door with curiosity, but no alarm. A fire burned brightly behind him.

"Charles Dresden," Charley said, his voice hoarse and barely above a whisper. "Friend of Madeleine Calendiari. She's in the car. She's shot. She may be dead. We're in trouble, terrible trouble, and we need your help. It involves the president, the Gettysburg shooting. Got to help. Got to help Maddy. Need a doctor."

With that, he fell forward. He remembered the warmth of the room and his head striking the sharpness of the doorframe.

He awoke to daylight and an utterly strange room, yet one that gave him the vague impression that he had awakened in it before. He recognized no single object in it, but it seemed somehow familiar, high-ceilinged and expensively furnished, a large fireplace at one end with a marble mantelpiece. The bed was large and high off the floor, with ample covers and soft pillows all about his head. He had experienced few things so comfortable in his life, but when he moved it caused great discomfort, a sting and ache in his hand, sharp pain in his knee, and an awful sensation between his legs. He lifted his head, then fell back, blinking. His vision was not quite clear. He could see that the room's door was open. He sensed some human presence just beyond it, hushed voices or movement.

"Hello," he said. Immediately, the door opened and a woman all in white stepped in, a nurse. She was blond, somewhere between young and middle-aged, with a pinched and narrow but quite friendly face.

"There's what we've been waiting for," she said, her accent working-class British. "A word from you."

"Hello," he said again. "Where am I?"

"The important question, love, is how are you?" she said. She put a thermometer in his mouth, then reached to take his pulse. She waited a moment, then smiled. "Well, your heartbeat's right enough." A brief wait later she retrieved the thermometer, and studied it with satisfaction. "Can you sit up?"

"I think so." He did slowly, feeling at once stiff and woozy, but after a minute his brain cleared. He could see everything quite sharply.

She plumped pillows up behind him, then came around again and looked carefully into his face. "You do look much better, love. A nice bit of sleep you've had."

"Yes. Very nice."

"Do you want to try standing? Moving about? You'll need crutches. I've a pair in the corner for you."

"Yes, I think so. After a minute."

"In that case we'd best dispense with these inconveniences." Moving quickly and cheerily, she removed an IV taped to his left hand, dangling from a bottle suspended above him, and then, tossing back the covers, a catheter and a curved metal pan. The discomfort there increased sharply, then was gone.

"Here's the rest of your pajamas, love. I expect you'll be grateful for them."

He quickly, if painfully, got them on, then slid to the edge of the bed, gingerly putting his feet to the floor as she handed him the crutches.

"Have a go for the chair by the window," she said. "If you've a need for it and are up to it, the loo's through there. If you've a problem, just call. Mr. Thompson's been waiting downstairs. I'll let him know you've come round."

Dresden tried a few steps around the room. His knee, heavily bandaged, hurt dreadfully. He couldn't imagine what he'd done to it.

He paused at the window. The house or building he was in was immense, a huge brick structure of Georgian architecture. He was on a high upper floor, but his view, but for a formal garden, was obscured by trees. There was a great deal of snow on the ground. He judged he'd been there, sedated or unconscious, for several days.

Turning about, he lowered himself onto the soft armchair, resting his leg on a footstool and laying the crutches on the floor. The paintings on the wall, landscapes and still lifes of flowers, were originals, very old, and expensively framed. He had not been in so richly furnished a room, that he could remember, certainly not since his Westchester years.

Quick footsteps ringing on marble or parquet flooring approached. They stopped, and the lanky face of Graham Thompson peered round the door, his long gray hair hanging over his brow and right eye. He smiled a quick, British smile and stepped inside, closing the door behind him. There was a companion armchair across from Dresden's and he took it, crossing his long legs and putting hand to bony chin.

"Damn good to see you coming round, Dresden. It was a close-run thing for both of you."

"Maddy's alive? She's all right?"

"Oh, quite alive, thank God. But I'm afraid not so ambulatory as you. She lost a tremendous amount of blood, and was in terrible shock when you got here. So were you, for that matter. Someone gave you whiskey. Who on earth did that?"

"I gave me whiskey. It's what kept me going."

"Extraordinary. I can't believe you drove all the way here from the shore. You had a bullet in the back of your leg, did you know? Can't believe you drove that distance in that condition. You're quite a re-markable fellow."

"A bullet? I was in an automobile accident a few weeks ago. I thought my leg had just gone out."

"No. One of those bastards shot you. Three of them, I believe you said. Damn near did for good. But the bullet was quite small—a .22 caliber, I think. I'm told that's what professional assassins are using in your country these days, the mafioso types, but these chaps seemed to be aiming for your legs. Could have been an awfully lot worse. Especially for Madeleine. She lost alot of blood. Our doctor did a bang-up job. Not much of an operating theater on the premises. It's good to see you both so much on the mend."

"Speaking of premises, where am I?"

"Why, the British embassy, of course. The ambassador's residence, actually. You're quite safe. Under the protection of His Majesty's Government."

"How did we get here from your house?"

"A simple stroll. My garden gate virtually opens onto the embassy grounds. It's been a convenient arrangement for American guests of mine over the years who feel a need for a discreet conversation with someone from HMG, and vice versa. Your good Dr. Kissinger was a frequent guest for that reason. And the prime minister popped over for a private chat with Secretary Crosby on her last visit. The proximity was certainly a blessing in your case. I'm not sure Madelaine would have made it all the way to hospital at that point."

"You say she's all right?"

"Yes. Much on the mend. But they have her rather heavily sedated. And on some medication for her heart. None of this was exactly a tonic for her, you know, with her heart condition."

"What heart condition?"

"You didn't know? I've forgotten the clinical term for it, but it has to do with an extra, erratic heartbeat. She developed it some years ago. I should have thought you'd known. It's not usually fatal, but it can be dangerous, certainly for someone who's been through what she just has. Never told you?"

"No. Never mentioned it."

"And went through all this nasty business with you? A most courageous woman."

"I'm fortunate."

"Yes." Thompson looked away, somewhat somberly, and a silence fell between them. Dresden sought to divine from it what the Britisher had on his mind, and at once it became obvious.

"George Calendiari," Charley said. "Does he know?"

"I'm afraid not."

"Mr. Thompson . . ."

"Call me Graham, please. We've already had several conversations, though you probably don't remember. You were in a rather bad state."

"Well, I don't remember, and I don't know what Maddy might have told you, but if you're presuming there's something going on between us . . ."

"You needn't . . ."

"It's more than just an affair. Our relationship goes back many years. I don't know why I'm telling you this, but she said you were an old friend and I want to clear the air. Anyway, George should know. That we're here. That Maddy's all right."

"Yes, of course. Unfortunately, Charles, if I may call you Charles, he can't. I'm afraid George Calendiari is dead."

"Dead?"

"Yes, poor devil. Blew his brains out. At his home across the river in McLean. It happened the night you showed up on my doorstep. For a bit we thought the events were all mixed up together."

"I don't believe it. George Calendiari wouldn't commit suicide."

"I knew him quite well myself, old man, and I'd be inclined to agree with you. But he wrote this mournful letter, about Madeleine leaving him for you. It was quite mordant . . ."

"That I'd believe. Last time, years ago, he wrote a number of such letters. To himself, to Madeleine, to me. The one to Maddy worked, that time. But shoot himself? The man was devoutly Catholic, and he hated guns. Couldn't stand them in the house. It was one of the things he disliked about me."

Thompson moved forward in his chair, as though to rise. "Yes, quite. Well, we've not said anything to her about it. I'm afraid I'm going to leave that task to you, when she's better up to it, which I think may take several more days."

"What day is it?"

Thompson smiled. "Wednesday, old man. You've missed Christmas." Now he did get to his feet. "We've retrieved everything from the beach house. If you do feel up to getting dressed, you'll find all your things in the closet. If these crutches become a nuisance, we can fetch you a cane. Dr. FitzGerald will look in from time to time. I believe he has you on some antibiotics."

He turned, glancing at his watch. He had a very proprietary air for someone who was merely a neighbor of the embassy. A very Oxonian air as well. This was no mere Fleet Street newsy, Charley concluded.

"There's a sitting room down the hall to your right," he said, "and a smallish study just beyond with a television. We'd appreciate it if you'd confine yourself to this floor. The residence is much in use this time of year, and we'd rather keep your presence our little secret."

"Certainly."

"The ambassador looked in on both of you after we brought you in. I daresay you were quite talkative, but not at all lucid. He'll be wanting to chat with you now that you've recovered some. And to make a better showing of British hospitality. But he's on rather a busy schedule the next few days, socially and otherwise. He begs your forgiveness."

"Of course. I'm very grateful to him. To all of you. We'd no idea where to turn."

"I'm afraid you'll have to be the guests of His Majesty for the indefinite future. There's no guaranteeing your safety otherwise. To employ our traditional British understatement, you don't seem to have a great many friends out there."

"Have there been any developments? Anything new about the president."

"Nothing beyond this continuing epidemic of sudden fatalities. We're told they're bringing in an entire army division to protect the Capitol for the opening of Congress next week."

"Nothing from Camp David?"

"Utter silence, except for the daily medical reports. And routine written statements."

"And the White House? The vice president?"

"A sympathetic statement concerning Senator Calendiari's death, otherwise silence. Everyone seems to be waiting for something,

something soon. That's among the many things the ambassador would like to talk to you about. I'll have the back newspapers sent up, so you can catch up with the lack of news." Thompson paused at the door. "You went on some about copies of videotapes and the like, having to do with the president's shooting. We went all through the beach house and Madeleine's car, but found nothing. Did someone get to them before us?"

"No. I'm sure not. They wouldn't have had time." Charley was beginning to feel woozy again.

"We looked everywhere. Inside the door paneling. Under the floorboards. Under the spare tire. Everywhere."

"It's inside the spare tire. Just pry it off the rim."

Thompson grinned. "The ambassador will be delighted to hear." He started out the door.

"Mr. Thompson."

"Please, 'Graham.'" The Britisher was in an obvious hurry now, probably to secure the tapes.

"You're a journalist?" Dresden said. "With British television?"

"That's right. I've been here nearly twenty years. I've known the Calendiaris for almost half that long."

"When Maddy told me about you, she used the word, *spy*."

"An indelicate term, though not altogether accurate. Let us just say that we in the British press tend to be far more supportive of our government than you American chaps. When we can be useful we are."

"I was a journalist myself, for a time. I was news director of a TV station in San Francisco."

"Jolly good. But now you're quite something else, aren't you? Cheery-bye, Charles. Keep on with the recovery."

It was three more days before they let Dresden see Maddy. He had to content himself with visits from the nurse, Dr. FitzGerald, Thompson, and a few very circumspect servants. FitzGerald rather surprised him, for he seemed an unusually young physician to have as consequential a charge as the British legation. He also bore a striking resemblance to D. H. Lawrence. Dresden mentioned this, and FitzGerald appeared flattered by the comparison, but was in no ways more helpful. Maddy was apparently in a very bad way. Dresden wondered where they were keeping her. If on the same floor, she could be just a few feet away.

Bored with the repetitious lack of news on television and in the newspapers, Charley took to exercising his injured leg with pacings up and down the full length of the wide upstairs corridor. Twice he poked into some of the other rooms, on both occasions startling and irritating the servants. After that an embassy security guard, dressed in a somewhat ill-fitting black civilian suit, was stationed in the hallway by the main staircase. They gave the man a straight-backed chair to sit in, and also, apparently, instructions not to converse with Dresden. His only words were greetings and idle discourses on the odd winter weather. Dresden took to spending most of his time in the little study, reading. Most of the volumes there, curiously, were about American history. He was halfway through the second volume of Samuel Eliot Morrison's *Oxford History of the American People* when Dr. FitzGerald finally summoned him to Maddy's room.

They had her seated in a chair, in nightgown, robe, and slippers, the latter peeking out from beneath a comforter. The chair was by a large window, and its bright light accentuated the paleness of her skin. She was quite drawn and thin, only her animated eyes reminding him of all the health and beauty with which she had greeted him at their first reunion that bright California afternoon a few weeks before. Her voice had a slight slur to it. He wondered how much medication they were giving her, and why.

Looking up at him, she took his hand. He kissed hers. He waited for the doctor and nurse to leave. Then he pulled up a side chair from her fireplace.

"You saved my life, Charley. I'm told you almost died yourself."

"I almost got you killed, Maddy, is what I did. I've no thanks coming. I deserve your everlasting condemnation for what I've done to your life."

"Please don't say that, Charley," she said, softly, weakly. "All I've had these last blurry days are thoughts of you and love for you."

He took both her hands, leaning closer. "The doctor says you're regaining your strength. Your wound is healing. I hadn't known about the trouble with your heart."

She shrugged, with a faint smile.

"You had enough worries. And it's not all that serious. Really."

He looked down. "Maddy, there's something you have to know."

"You're going to tell me that George is dead. I already know that. I could tell from their silence, their evasiveness when I asked about him. I knew that George was probably dead when those horrible men came after us in Rehoboth, that they would have come after him, too, probably before they did us."

"The official word is that George committed suicide, because of you and me. That can't possibly be true."

"No." She dabbed at her eyes. "Will there be a funeral, in the church?"

"There'll be some sort of service; I don't know if it will be in a church. I suppose that's between his family and the priests. Maddy, there's no way we, you . . ."

"I understand. No one is supposed to know where we are. George is dead and I'll never see him again. Someday, I suppose, I can go to his grave, and look at that."

"I'm sorry."

"I want to talk about it, Charley. It's better than lying there just thinking about it, about everything."

"We're all right, Maddy. We're safe, as long as we stay here. The trouble is, they're not giving us much choice."

"The ambassador's out of the country. In the Caribbean or some-where. I overheard them saying that. When he gets back our situation will change."

"I hope so."

"I'm tired, Charley. I just got out of bed and now I want to go to sleep again."

"No more Rehoboth midnight swims," he said. She could barely smile in reply. Not bothering to summon the nurse, he lifted her and set her on her bed, gently arranging the covers around her. The room's windows were admitting a bright winter's sunlight, but she paid it no mind. She was already asleep.

Stepping into the corridor, fully dressed to the extent of jacket and tie, he took his cane firmly in hand and, moving quietly down a turning of the hall that took him out of the security man's view, found a servants' back stairs and descended it two floors below. Moving along as though he belonged on that level and had some purpose, he found a door leading outside and made quick use of it. The air was cold despite the sunlight, with a brisk wind. The snow on the ground had melted and shallowed, but had refrozen now into a crust. He crunched over it, following the garden hedges around behind the immense house. Thompson had told him it had not been an old American mansion originally, like so many Washington diplomatic establishments, but had been constructed specifically as a British embassy. Moving on beside it, his cane making odd marks in the old snow, he wondered what the building contained. The ambassador's residence itself was easily three times the size of the Soviet embassy on 16th Street, and there were adjoining Georgian brick outbuildings as well, not to speak of the gigantic modern office building that housed the chancery.

Dresden moved on unmolested, following the succession of snow-covered lawns and gardens that separated the embassy from the high wall and fence behind it that were its protection against the outside world. He could find no sign of the gate or doorway through which Thompson must have brought them. Finally, passing along one side of a long parking lot bordering the chancery, he came to the end of the compound, standing at the wrought-iron bars of the fence. Like the prisoner he supposed he was, he gripped their coldness with his bare hands. There was a roadway just beyond, jammed with cars parked perpendicularly along its wide dirt shoulder. On the other side, a chain-link fence followed the circumference of a high wooded hill, an armed guard with a dog walking the perimeter. Though he had only seen it at night, the hill was quite familiar to Dresden, as was the high Victorian house on its summit. It was the residence of the vice president of the United States.

A few days before that house had been their ultimate refuge, his ultimate goal in his effort to get the country to pay attention to his truth. Now it was nothing but mystery, holding perhaps the answer to all the mysteries. Dresden stared at its windows as he had at the darkened windows of the White House from the Willard Hotel, seeing menace, remembering the helicopter that had come out of the night at the beach.

There was a crunching in the snow behind him. "Excuse me, sir."

It was a security man, wearing a macintosh, a cockney gentleman.

"Excuse me. They'd like you to come back now, sir, and to stay inside if you would. This cold can't do you much good, now can it, sir?"

He led Charley to the nearest door of the huge residence. Dresden wondered if it would be spring before he experienced the out-of-doors again.

Charley and Maddy finally got to meet Sir Guy Hyde-Milne a few days later. An immensely tall and imposing man, with dark, flashing eyes, bristling dark brows, and blackish hair gone to gray at the sides, he'd been ambassador to the United States for more than a year, having served previously as ambassador to Bonn. He had had two postings to the United States in lesser capacities in the 1970s. Given to typical diplomatic dress—dark blue striped suit, blue shirt with white collar, and the idiosyncrasy of a large bow tie—he was a cheery, bluff, impeccably upper-class man with a commanding presence and the air of having many important things on his mind.

He greeted Dresden and Madeleine in the downstairs drawing room, ushering them to chairs with effusive friendliness and apologies for his long absence. A servant was instantly summoned and brought refreshments, a small sherry for Maddy, who was somewhat stronger now, and a whiskey for Charley, who was not, but felt the need of one nonetheless. The ambassador, who remained standing, had a whiskey as well.

"I'm just this afternoon back from Bermuda, and Belize before that," he said, "which accounts for my swarthy hue. Had to confer with some of our military gentlemen and they have this penchant for the out-of-doors." He raised his glass. "To your health, dear lady." He turned. "And to yours, sir. I'm so delighted you're coming along so well."

"Thank you, Mr. Ambassador," said Maddy, in a quiet voice. She had known him slightly in the past, and seemed quite at home in this enormous establishment that still somewhat intimidated Charley.

"Well now, it's New Year's Eve, a holiday this capital of yours treats with great exuberance. I'm afraid my wife and I have a number of parties to drop by as a consequence, but we intend to keep an early evening nevertheless. If it's not an inconvenience, and you're not too tired, I should appreciate our having a bit of a chat later tonight. There's such an awfully lot about all this I don't understand, and I should greatly like your help. I've asked Mr. Thompson, and a Mr. Llewellyn from, well, from our office. In the meantime, do make yourselves at home, and I don't mean simply those confining quarters upstairs."

He paused, lifting his glass, but using it to gesture at the chamber around him. "This is the main drawing room. A bit larger than most, I daresay. It's where we keep our Rembrandts and Turners. Do have a look at them before dinner. I'm afraid I must dash off now. In the event we've not returned before midnight, may I wish you a happy New Year."

They all raised their glasses. The ambassador emptied his decorously but thoroughly, set it down among a forest of framed photographs on a side table, and was gone, the room a much emptier place in his absence.

"All very charming," Dresden said.

"Yes," said Maddy. "The British are always very charming, especially this ambassador. But they always want something. I just wonder what he wants from us. Graham's been a good friend, but the ambassador doesn't owe us anything, certainly not all this."

"You're making me feel vaguely unpatriotic."

"That's all right. George felt very patriotic. Now George is dead."

Their meal was served in the main dining room, with Dresden and Maddy seated opposite each other at the middle of the long table, rather than at the distant ends. A fire burned in the hearth and the multitude of candles made the room quite cheery, though Maddy was not.

"When I started down through the mesquite of that mountainside that last night in Tiburcio," Charley said, "I never would have thought I'd end up here."

"We never know where we're going to end up, do we? Our trouble, Charley, is that we haven't yet ended up."

"Soon enough."

"Perhaps too soon."

The meal was of several courses, but she only picked and dabbled at each. Afterward, they returned to the drawing room.

"I know coming to Graham Thompson was my idea," she said. "But I'd like to leave this place. As soon as we can."

"Would you like to leave me, also?"

Her voice was very weary. "No, Charley. I don't suppose that's ever going to be an option, is it? I'm just so tired, tired of what's going on, tired of being used, tired of hiding and being hidden."

"Do you think I've used you, Maddy?"

"Charley, if you don't mind, I think I'd like to go upstairs and lie down for a while. I'm so very sleepy."

And sad, he thought. "Do you want me to awaken you, just before midnight?"

"No, Charley. Let's just let the new year happen all by itself, and hope it's better than this one."

As it turned out, the ambassador was back before eleven-thirty P.M. His wife looked a woman quite full of her class, but spoke very pleasantly, excusing herself shortly after being introduced.

"Mrs. Calendiari's already gone to bed," Charley said. "I'm afraid she hasn't quite fully recovered yet."

"Terribly sorry to hear," the ambassador said. "We'll have Dr. FitzGerald take a more attentive look at her tomorrow. You're the one I need most to talk to, if you're not too tired yourself?"

He spoke the last words while leading Dresden down the main

downstairs hall, and eventually into his library. Graham Thompson was there, and a man with a clipped British military mustache and tweed suit introduced as Llewellyn. It didn't take much imagination to guess in what branch of British government service he was employed.

Thompson had had servants wheel in a television set with a videotape unit beneath. Llewellyn pulled up a chair close by, preparing to take notes. There was some brandy on the sideboard. The ambassador served it himself, a glass for everyone all around, then pulled up his own chair.

"First, I want you to know that you and Mrs. Calendiari may count on our assistance from now henceforth," he said, lowering his voice somewhat. "I've arranged for what amounts to political asylum status for you both, and can assure you of the Crown's protection— or at least as much protection as the Crown can provide here in Washington."

"Why?" said Dresden. "Not that I'm not grateful, but what's your interest in helping us this way?"

The ambassador smiled, glancing down at his large hands. "We have a personal interest," he said, raising his eyes to Charley's again. "Graham Thompson and I do. You are two people who, acting with the most patriotic of intentions, have gotten themselves into dreadful trouble and great danger. You came to us for succor and sanctuary, and we shan't deny it. Senator and Mrs. Calendiari were very good friends of the U.K. here in Washington and Graham and I aren't going to let that be forgotten."

He cleared his throat. "There is, of course, a British interest in this," he said. "As there is in most everything I do. Principally, it's one of adding to the intelligence we've already gathered about this astounding and most appalling situation. It's no exaggeration to say that the security of the Western alliance and perhaps the entire world is caught up in this. The power of the United States is simply too immense for a crisis of this magnitude in its leadership not to carry great hazard."

The ambassador looked to Thompson, who nodded. "We think there is a possibility that His Majesty's government may be able to help effect an early resolution of this crisis," the diplomat continued. "We're not quite sure how yet, but we think it's likely you could be of considerable assistance to us—if you choose to be. We'll take all that up later. For the moment, I'd like to deal with these videotapes and that other material of yours. I've had a cursory look at it all, but I'd appreciate it if we could go over everything you've brought together, very carefully. And I'd appreciate it very much, Mr. Dresden, if you'd explain in the greatest detail possible what we're seeing every step of the way."

By the end, the ambassador had taken off his suit coat. He sat back, glancing at his colleagues.

"Damn conclusive, wouldn't you say, Graham? Incontrovertible."

"Certainly the videotapes, Sir Guy."

"Mr. Dresden, that footage of the shooting is most graphic. You say the president was definitely not wearing a protective vest?"

"I don't know that for certain. I only know that the director of the FBI—Copley—stated that in front of the vice president. He cited a report from the director of the Secret Service."

"So there we are. Henry Hampton is dead. Incontrovertible. It confirms what our own intelligence branch has only been able to guess." He looked over to Llewellyn. "I shall want some hint of this communicated to the Foreign Office and 10 Downing by telex. Nothing coded or in the diplomatic pouch, mind. Just a few appropriately ambiguous lines in a routine telex. Within the hour. They'll know what we're about."

"Yes, Sir Guy."

"Now, Mr. Dresden." The ambassador leaned forward in great earnest, his huge eyebrows bunching, his white cuffs and collar still perfectly crisp. "I'm rather curious as to Vice President Atherton's response to your presentation of all this. Did he seem taken aback? Was he much surprised?"

"He reacted much like you did, Mr. Ambassador. It seemed to confirm his own suspicions, or findings. He was very interested in detail."

"Did he keep your material?"

"Yes. You've been looking at a set of copies. I've another set as well. Hidden."

The ambassador stroked his chin, which was beginning to darken with the need for a shave. "Yes. Very prudent. Now, Mr. Dresden. Did he mention anything with a time element in it? Something that must happen or might happen within the next few weeks—within the month of January?"

"No, sir. There was some talk among others in the room about the Twenty-fifth Amendment, but he hushed that up."

"The transfer of presidential powers amendment. Yes. We've been studying that. But he made no specific reference to any forthcoming event within the next thirty days or so?"

"No."

"Did he ask you any more technical questions?"

"Yes. He wanted to know if it was possible to reproduce the president's voice without using a mimic—if one could lift words and phrases from the president's past recorded remarks and speeches and dub them onto videotape footage of him speaking. I told him it could certainly be done but that to do it properly was a very elaborate procedure."

"Did he ask how long it might take?"

"Yes. I said a television network would have the resources to put together something airable within a few days, but that it would take longer for anyone else, even a fair-sized production company."

"A matter of weeks."

"A few weeks. Maybe two."

"Hmmmm." The ambassador rose and poured brandy for everyone, though not for himself. "I should explain to you our most immediate concerns, Mr. Dresden. They're of some significance. The first, of course, is NATO. The first is always NATO."

He seated himself again, looking into the fire. "There really isn't any danger of war, I shouldn't think. There can't be that, because the instant you have shooting on the Rhine you have theater nuclear conflict, and then there is no Europe, no NATO, no Warsaw Pact. But there's always nervousness, nevertheless. And the discovery that the United States has no president is not going to help.

"Our more immediate concern is Central America and the Caribbean. As you know, we have military forces in Belize and are extremely concerned about the stability of the region, particularly vis à vis Guatemala. His Majesty's Government has been a strong supporter of the Contadora process and, until a few weeks ago, thought we'd brought your administration around on that question. Now we're told—by every intelligence source we have in the region, mind—including your good friends in Costa Rica and Panama—to expect an outbreak of all-out war there by the end of January.

"By 'war,' Charles," said Thompson, pushing his glasses back up the bridge of his long, elfin nose, "the ambassador isn't referring to this tit-for-tat cross border stuff you chaps have been engaging in the last several years. We're talking about total engagement, with fighting from the Gulf of Panama all the way to bloody Chiapas—U.S. forces certainly engaged and likely Soviet personnel involved as well."

"Our third concern is the most essential," the ambassador continued. "You are our closest ally, after all, and we're jolly well interested in who is, or will be, president. If, as you seem to have established, Hampton is dead, Atherton's succession would have been quite satisfactory. He's a reasonable sort of chap, well educated, has quite the global view, and has certainly got on well with our people. But from what you tell us of your misadventures out at the beach, directly after your audience with the good Mr. Atherton, well, we'd have to consider the vice president's role in this under a cloud at the moment, wouldn't you say, Graham?"

"A deuced murky black cloud."

"Hardly His Majesty's favorite candidate in the next election, at any rate. That leaves us with the septuagenarian speaker of the House, a New York Irishman whose idea of Anglo-American relations is Brits out of Northern Ireland, and after him, presuming next week's ceremonial vote seating the new Congress remains pro forma, we have this warhawk philanderer from the South—what's his name, Graham? Maitland Dubarry?"

"In the local lingo, 'Meathead' Dubarry. Bright but besotted."

The man named Llewellyn continued taking rapid notes, though he had likely heard the ambassador run through all this before. Dresden had contributed little to the conversation.

"So from our point of view," the ambassador resumed, "your Constitution isn't working very well at all. If this appalling killing goes on, the succession goes from bad to worse . . ."

"To unthinkable," said Thompson.

". . . unless someone intervenes with a military coup, which may well be what those chaps up at Camp David have in mind."

"But the opposite is just as possible," Thompson said. Dresden wondered how closely he ranked to the ambassador in his unspoken government role. "The Camp David chaps may be trying to prevent a military action."

"Quite so," added the ambassador. "A dust-up in the Caribbean could be used by the vice president and his people to force the imposition of the Twenty-fifth Amendment. Certainly if there was no president about to come forward and deal with it."

"'Whenever the vice president and a majority of either the principal officers of the executive departments or of such other body as Congress may by law provide, transmit to the president pro tempore of the Senate and the speaker of the House,'" Thompson read, from a small copy of the U.S. Constitution taken from his pocket, "'their written declaration that the president is unable to discharge the powers and duties of his office, the vice president shall immediately assume the powers and duties of the office as acting president.'"

"I'm not exactly a constitutional scholar," Dresden said. "And neither is Maddy. You should be discussing all this with someone else."

This was not exactly true. He had been thinking many of these same things himself, in the long hours of his enforced detainment, though he had not articulated them so clearly.

"And so we have," said Thompson.

"Discreetly," said the ambassador. "We just want you to understand the exact nature of our concern, and what we might be up against if we choose to act in this situation. And by 'we' I include other members of the alliance."

"That's not to be repeated, Charles," said Thompson.

"The only other person I get to talk to is Dr. FitzGerald," Dresden said, somewhat sarcastically.

"Yes, of course. But you see why we're so interested in these reports—and they've been numerous and from many quarters—that it's all to happen in January," the ambassador said. "Unless they've just arbitrarily picked some date, there are only three events of consequence in the month. The first is the opening of the Congress and the election of new officers."

"And that doesn't involve the presidency at all," Thompson said, "Except that the vice president administers the oath of office to the new senators. Usually in the Old Senate Chambers that they've preserved on the Capitol's ground floor."

"Which have always struck me as an ideal setting for an assassination, as a matter of fact," said the ambassador. "Or some such melodramatic occurrence. But that is to digress. The second consequential event is the formal submission of the president's budget, but that's not done in person, and we're given to understand that this year's will be largely the same as last year's, with only a minor change or two."

"We're told there won't even be a fight over farm price supports."

Dresden was tiring of this British loquacity. He thought of asking for another brandy, if only to provide a break in the conversation, if not an end to it.

"So there's just one event left," said the ambassador. "The State of the Union message. No president fails to appear for that. Franklin

Roosevelt made his last one in person, and he was virtually on his deathbed."

"Woodrow Wilson was the last American president not to make an appearance for that speech," Thompson said, "having been totally incapacitated by a stroke. That incident was in part the inspiration for the Twenty-fifth Amendment."

"So you see how our interest rather focuses on this event," said the ambassador.

Dresden drained his glass and sat silently, staring at it pointedly. This time it was Thompson who went to refill it.

"How may I help you gentlemen?" Charley said, after a sip.

"As this proceeds, I'm sure in a great many ways," the ambassador said. "But right now, I'd like you to search your memory very carefully. Was there anything the vice president or any of his people said concerning the State of the Union, in any context?"

"Not that I can remember. Just that background talk about the Twenty-fifth Amendment."

"Do you suppose someone might have said something about it to Mrs. Calendiari?"

"Possibly, but she was with me throughout the entire visit, as far as I can remember."

"Her husband doubtless talked to the vice president, though, out of your earshot."

"Yes. I'm sure he did when he arranged our appointment. Perhaps on a number of occasions."

"And he might have discussed some of what was said with Mrs. Calendiari?" Thompson looked at his watch.

"Gentlemen," Dresden said. "Maddy is not feeling at all well. She went to bed early, long before midnight. She's certainly more than a little depressed. I would strongly suggest that a chat tonight is not in order." He was beginning to talk like a Britisher himself. Worse, like a diplomat.

The ambassador sat back in his chair, allowing his massive body to relax into a disorderly slump, his bristly brow sliding over his eyes like a coverlet. His repose was that of a man acting as though he had completed a great job of work.

"Graham," he said, without looking at Thompson. "I fear you've neglected our guests during my absence. This place is mournful enough to rattle about in at the best of times. Perhaps your dear Pamela could find the time to drop round and cheer up Mrs. Calendiari a little."

"They're old chums, Sir Guy, I'm sure they can find something to do."

"We're having the German ambassador and his wife over for dinner Friday," the ambassador said, directly to Dresden. "I hope you'll both be up to joining us. He's quite an agreeable chap. Spent quite a bit of time in the States; last time as military attaché. You're of German ancestory yourself, aren't you?"

"Prussian," Dresden said, as the ambassador rose and the others followed suit on cue. "My grandfather was in the German Air Service in the first war. As I fear some of your people had occasion to regret."

"Old war, long ago," said the ambassador, with a pat on Dresden's back. He paused as they reached the door. "I just want to reiterate, Mr. Dresden, how grateful we are for your help, for this material, for all that you've done. We consider you our friend and hope the feeling's mutual. I'd also like to emphasize that, at the moment, I fear we're your only friends. It's really quite dangerous out there for you, for both of you."

"So I've seen."

"By the by, were you able to watch the television tonight? No? Well, there's been quite a spot of news. The FBI has arrestd Peter Ashley Brookes for complicity in the president's shooting."

"The one who bankrolls all those right-wing causes?"

"That's the chap. Charged him with accessory to murder and conspiracy to cross state lines to assault a federal officer—by that, meaning the president."

"Did they arrest anyone else?"

"Not yet. But they've identified the ringleader of this right-wing terrorist group La Puño. He's an American, a mercenary chap called Colonel Barren, Colonel Mason Barren, a protégé of Brookes's. His name's been in our files a bit, hasn't it, Graham? Helped stir up a bit of trouble in Rhodesia during the transition to Mugabe's Zimbabwe. I gather they're searching to the ends of the earth for him."

24

Atherton was in the library of the Vice President's House. As usual, he had told the servants he had reading to do, but they knew that now to be a euphemism for drinking. He sat before the fire, staring with melancholy eyes into the flames, a whiskey in hand, his government papers untouched on a table beside him. He had come back to this house on Christmas night with his daughter, and now spent much of his time here. That he heard his wife's voice calling to him no longer disturbed him. According to the servants, he sometimes talked back to her.

"Daddy?" His daughter stood in the doorway.

"What?"

"Mr. Shawcross is here, with Mr. Howard and Mr. Copley. Do you want to see them?"

"No."

"Shall I send them away?"

"No." He coughed. His health had fallen with his broken spirit. "Give me a few minutes. Then send them in."

When she did they entered and stood in a row before him. He waved them to chairs, chiefly to get them out of the way of the fire.

"Well it's done," Shawcross said. "Meathead Dubarry is now officially president pro tem of the Senate. He even got votes from across the aisle. Some people like to rub it in."

"Was he there? At the Capitol?"

"Yes," said Howard. "But he left immediately after. By helicopter. There was talk about your not being there, especially for the swearing in of the new senators."

"Let them talk."

"We told them you were ill."

Atherton coughed again, and took a draught of whiskey as medicine. "Precisely."

"We think we know where they're keeping Meathead," Copley said. "Should have looked there in the first place."

"Where? Back in Louisiana?"

"Atlantic City. Close to Camp David. Close to here. Bushy Ambrose has another helicopter war going. We've tracked three chopper flights to the Jersey Shore. I don't think they're taking blackjack breaks."

"You find Dubarry. Find him fast. It's almost time for the State of the Union."

"We'll find him. But then what?"

"We can't have any more public trouble, Larry. We just can't."

"You just find him. Find him fast. Then we'll decide what to do next."

Bushy Ambrose stepped from his Camp David cabin accompanied by White House Communications Director Jerry Greene and two black beret sergeants from the Special Functions Force, armed with fully automatic M-16s with the safeties off. It was a cold day, a fully January day, and all were dressed for the weather, Ambrose even wearing a rabbit fur shapka he had bought in Moscow on a presidential trip. But, at Ambrose's insistence, the meeting was held outside, standing.

"I just want to be absolutely, positively sure we're not overheard or recorded," Ambrose said.

Waiting for them, dressed in overcoats, hats, and gloves, were the rest of what remained of the Camp David team: Senator Rollins, the defense secretary, the National Security Adviser, David Callister, Surgeon General Potter, Jerry Greene, and Press Secretary Weigle, whom attrition had elevated to a more respected role in the group's affairs. They were grumpy at what they uniformly viewed as an idiotic winter outdoors session, but were more attuned and responsive to Ambrose's wishes than ever.

"I know it's colder than hell," said Ambrose, rubbing his gloved hands together, "but this won't take long, and most of you will be glad to hear what I have to say." He turned to Jerry Greene. "First, I want to hear everything on C. D. and Schlessler."

Greene, still troubled by the loss of his friends, coughed before speaking. "The bodies were dropped in regulation body bags in a wooded section within the perimeter here by an unmarked Hughes Five Hundred helicopter, the same kind we've been routinely using for the Special Functions Force. They had one of Peter Brookes's men with them. His body was dropped, too."

"The drop mashed up C. D.'s face," said the defense secretary. "And Schlessler broke open like a watermelon. It was like that on the low paratroop drops at Normandy."

"It was goddamn murder," Ambrose said. "They weren't out to hurt those people. They were just going to put them on ice."

"They weren't out to hurt them *yet*," said Callister. "The conditional tense is applicable. That man Dresden is a violence-prone, gun-loving psychopath, genius that he may be."

"Well, C. D. and Pete and the other guy will be buried with full military honors—after this is over. In the meantime . . ." Ambrose looked hard at everyone there, "not the slightest intimation this happened. Expropriate some morgue or funeral parlor in West Virginia. Give the undertakers a lot of money up-front, and not another word."

The others were unsure to whom these orders were addressed. Ambrose sensed that, and turned to Defense Secretary Moran. "Have your Special Functions Force attend to it. No questions, and sure as hell no answers."

"No problem."

"All right," said Ambrose. "The good news. We're going to move. For all practical purposes, the Camp David operation is going to be shut down. Countdown is to the State of the Union address."

"Just a moment," said Callister. "There's a matter of justice here. At least one of honor. You can't let those men just be dropped in the trees like so much garbage. Let's be biblical about this. I wouldn't mind seeing a dawn drop of the corpus delecti of Shawcross and Neil Howard."

"You don't know Atherton had anything to do with this," said Moran. "All we know is that Atherton wants to be president."

"There can't be any more killings," Rollins said. "One more casualty and there'll be demands for full-blown congressional hearings, impeachments, martial law, who knows what. We won't be able to wait until the State of the Union. We won't be able to do anything."

"Well, we will do something," said Ambrose. "Starting now. George," he said to Moran, "I want you back at the Pentagon full-time. I want you sitting in the National Military Command Center at least four times a day. Including late-night visits. I want a service secretary, not deputy, in there at all times."

"Yes, sir."

"And I want General Houck, the army chief of staff, in operational charge of Southern Command, Panama to the Rio Grande, including both Pacific and Atlantic naval battle groups. He's to operate not from Panama City but Tegucigalpa."

"The navy secretary will bitch. General DeVore will bitch."

"This will be by order of the president. Everything in Central America will be purple. He'll be completely in charge. And I want lots of press with him. I want them watching this thing from the very beginning, and first hand."

"Yes, sir."

"Jim," he said to National Security Adviser Malcom. "You're going to have the biggest load. I want you or your deputy in the White House morning, noon, and night, in full charge of the NSC. If Atherton calls an NSC meeting, I want you to make sure nothing proceeds unless Defense Secretary Moran, one of the Joint Chiefs, and Admiral Elmore are present. I want you to pick your reliables from the NSC staff and have them sack out on the White House basement floor if necessary. At the same time, I want you to get down to Mexico whenever it's at all possible. You'll be needed."

"I've already attended to that, Mr. Ambrose."

Ambrose looked to Weigle, who was almost embarrassingly over-joyed that he had at last been invited to Camp David.

"Surgeon General Potter is going to remain here and issue medical reports and bulletins every day from Thurmont. You're to assist him in these daily briefings. The president's condition will improve daily."

"Who will brief me?"

"I will. Every day. I'm the poor son of a bitch who's going to have to stay up here, until the State of the Union."

He looked to Jerry Greene. "How soon can we get on the air again?"

"A week, at best. Probably two. I'll figure out an appropriate occasion."

"Just one. We'll save everything else for the State of the Union. Callister. All right, damn it all, I'll call you David, we've been in this all together long enough. David, I want you back in Washington. That's Washington, not New York or Bermuda. If you can stop thinking—and acting—like a Harvard-educated Mafia hit man, I want you and your wife all over the capital social scene, at your most affable. You *can* be affable?"

"Magnificently affable."

"Good." Ambrose turned to Rollins. "Andy, the same goes for you. Full-scale normality. The president is on the mend. There *will* be a State of the Union address. If you don't show up for lunch three days a week at the Monocle I'll consider it an act of treason."

"Thanks."

"All right. Is there anyone here who has never leaked anything to the press?" The only person to raise his hand was Press Secretary Weigle. Ambrose shook his head. "Okay, excepting for Weigle, you all know how it's done. I want the other side on the defensive. I want you guys to pull every trick that Sun-tzu and Dr. Goebbels ever dreamed of. I want a torrent of leaks—the president's pissed because he's heard that Atherton's been using the Oval Office, and sitting in his chair! I want to hear rumors that Washington is crawling with Russian agents. That the speaker wants to become president. That the Special Functions Force is preparing for a military coup. That the Israelis have readied a nuclear weapon. That the vice president is cracking up."

"That's no rumor," said Rollins.

"You know, Admiral Elmore has a file of highly compromising photographs taken of Atherton with a Brazilian lady at the conference at Cancun last winter," Moran said. "But he wouldn't release them to us without an order under presidential signature."

"Why did we ever let Central Intelligence stay in the hands of God?"

"No vice presidential nudies," said Ambrose. "But everything else you guys can throw at the press, and I mean most of all the TV types, stuff they can chew on from now to the State of the Union. Andy, what can we do about Peter Brookes?"

"Absolutely nothing. Even if he weren't being railroaded, he's been into enough squirrelly stuff to keep him in the slammer on a ten to twenty."

"All right. Top priority, when this is over, is getting him out. He's the best friend the president ever had and we've left him out to dry. Now, most important of all, what's your best cabinet nose count on the Twenty-fifth Amendment?"

"In the cabinet, we lose," said Moran. "You gave them too many cabinet jobs at the convention."

"Except for State and Justice, we gave them shit."

"When shit votes, shit counts."

"We can stop them in the Congress. The Constitution allows a body designated by Congress to rule on the Twenty-fifth. The applicable resolution requires a two-thirds vote of Congress to approve the body's recommendations."

"You can't stop them in Congress if they move first in the cabinet," Malcom said.

"Then we'll move first," said Ambrose. "I want our people—that means you, Andy—introducing a Twenty-fifth Amendment measure tomorrow. A blue-ribbon commission to clear the air, but it's not to meet before the State of the Union."

"It'll be too obvious if my name's on it," said Rollins. "I'll get one of the moderates. Two of them have been after me on this ever since Gettysburg anyway. Especially Larson."

"Just make sure they get moving before Atherton does."

"What about this Dresden and his, uh, doxy?" said Callister.

"He sure punched out your ego, didn't he?" Ambrose said.

"Maddy Calendiari is no doxy," said Rollins.

"I'll leave such assessments to your well-researched expertise," Callister said. "But you can't just leave those people walking about. They are entirely too well informed, and too damn dangerous."

"I don't want to mess with them until after the State of the Union," said Ambrose. "Then I want to mess with them a lot. I want to know everything there is to know about how C. D. and Pete got it."

"They know everything," Jerry Greene said.

"Quite possibly," said Callister, "they did everything. That maniac was carrying a gun that looked like one of those ceremonial Gettysburg cannons. And we have no idea where the Calendiari woman and Dresden are."

"After the State of the Union we'll find out," said Ambrose. "No more trouble now. No more bodies. This is the United States of America. This is its government."

They all started to leave, but were premature. "One last thing," said Ambrose. "Daisy Hampton."

"Up to two fifths a day," said Rollins, sadly. "If we try to stop it, it'll all get worse."

"Two fifths?" said Greene. "Three days ago I logged two liters. Jack Daniels Black. What's a liter? More than a quart."

"It's time for a dryer. Detox," said Rollins. "She could kill herself. Talk about problems."

"Not in Washington," Ambrose said.

"You're right," said Rollins. "Go into any first-class detox and you'll find some House committee chairman and a Pulitzer Prize winner. No place for any First Lady. Especially this First Lady."

"Not Virginia," said Callister. "No Virginia gentleman puts a Virginia lady in detox."

The vice president's session was billed as a full-fledged cabinet meeting, though it was far from that. The full-fledged cabinet members included only Secretary of State Merriman Crosby, the attorney general, and the commerce secretary. The others at the long table in the Roosevelt Room included the navy secretary, a Princeton classmate of the vice president's; FBI Director Steven Copley; and the triumvirate of chief aide Richard Shawcross, Press Secretary Neil Howard, and the ubiquitous Mrs. Hildebrand. The chairman of the Joint Chiefs of Staff had perfunctorily been invited, but to everyone's relief, had sent regrets, pleading the exigencies of the Central American situation. The treasury secretary, at Atherton's request, had been sent to Brussels for a GATT meeting.

"The military's ready to pop a Def Con Two at the first shot of a BB gun," said the navy secretary, "and by God do we have BB guns."

"Not to be used until the State of the Union," said Atherton. He was more serious than anyone in the room could remember. The vagueness and melancholy had gone.

"*D'accord.*"

Everyone else at the table nodded.

"What's the latest on Camp David?" the vice president asked.

"They're moving," said Shawcross. "Interestingly, their D-Day is the same as ours—the State of the Union."

"I'm sure for the same reason," Atherton said. "They can't afford to wait a moment longer. Precisely. Have we any reading on what they're up to?"

"They're planning to bring in a lot of heavy audiovisual aids into the House chambers," Shawcross said.

"Which smacks of more videotaped president," said Howard. "They're also leaking every wild rumor imaginable as hot official stuff, just to keep the newspapers full and the nightly news jam-packed with garbage."

"*Comme toujours*," said the secretary of state.

"Very well, Merriman," said Atherton. "What can you report of Central America that is nongarbage?" He used the French pronunciation.

"It's all proceeding as we've been informed and have expected," Crosby said. "Almost anything can make a shambles of it, and almost anything is likely to happen."

"Though not until the State of the Union!" Atherton snapped.

"Indeed. But you could almost go out and tell the press in all honesty that the diplomatic situation is rapidly deteriorating. The Nicaraguans are holding out for everything they can get."

"As the late Mayor Daley of Chicago once said, they smell the meat a'cookin'," said Neil Howard.

"The quote is actually attributable to an Illinois politician named Paul Powell, who was found to have eight hundred thousand dollars in small bills stashed away in shoeboxes in his closet when he expired."

"Nowadays, a pittance," said Copley.

"Let us not wallow in the esoteric sleaze of the past," said Atherton, looking most directly at Copley. "What is the status of this Charles Dresden and Senator Calendiari's wife?"

"There've been several hundred APBs issued and a manhunt ordered such as you haven't seen since the days of Melvin Purvis."

"They are to be apprehended and interrogated," said Atherton. "Not massacred. Did I send flowers to Calendiari's funeral?"

"Yes," said Mrs. Hildebrand.

"David Callister has a column today blaming the Central American situation on your, in his words, interference and incompetence," Neil Howard said. "I can get a reply onto the op-ed page of the *Post*."

"No," said Atherton. "Nothing until the State of the Union." He looked darkly around the table. "Is that absolutely understood?"

"*Entendu*," said Crosby, speaking for all.

*   *   *

Kreski was at a sidewalk café's table on Mexico City's Paseo de la Reforma. On the table in front of him was a pile of official papers in Spanish that had cost Kreski $4234.26. They were Juan Jalisco's resume, compiled by Kreski during his visits to Tabasco, Tampico, and Veracruz.

In Tabasco, many years before, Jalisco had worked as a deck hand and general roustabout on an off-shore oil-drilling rig, eventually getting promoted to crew chief. The drilling company was a privately owned firm under contract to Pemex, the Mexican state oil monopoly. An affiliated firm, also under contract to Pemex, ran a refinery operation in Tampico. Jalisco had moved there to take a better-paying foreman's job, and subsequently was promoted to supervisor. According to Kreski's generously bribed informants, the promotion had come as much from his outspoken right-wing politics as from his abilities, though these were considerable.

Then, mystifyingly, Jalisco had moved back to his native Veracruz to take a position little better than a clerk's with a shipping line, becoming as politically active as he had been outspoken. It was shortly after that that he became an operative in the battle zones of Central America.

The shipping line, though operating under Panamanian registry, was owned by the same family that owned the drilling subcontractor in Tabasco and the refinery operation in Tampico. The family was large, with several branches and many different names, though all of them very old and high-bred Spanish, some of them dating back to the days of the dons and the conquistadores. It was nevertheless a very close-knit family, almost Sicilian in its traditions and loyalties. The drilling and refinery businesses and the shipping line were minor subsidiaries. Most of its vast and immeasurably wealthy holdings were agricultural, extending throughout Central America, including Honduras and Guatemala. Until expropriated by the leftist governments there, they had been amply manifest in El Salvador and Nicaragua.

The family had an American branch, whose roots north of the border had predated the conquests of President Polk's Mexican War. The name of this American branch was one extremely familiar to Kreski. It had chilled him to the marrow when he had come across it. He had stared at it for long minutes in disbelief. He had looked at it upon his papers several times, as though he had made some mistake, as though he could make it disappear. It had not. It remained boldly visible on the top of the pile of papers before him.

He returned them to their folder, wound the fastenings tightly, and placed and locked them in the nondescript briefcase he had bought. His job, as the cliché went, was done there. Now his chief task was to get out of Mexico—and into the United States—alive. Into the United States and the city of Washington.

Dresden supposed they could call their continuing January stay in the British Embassy comfortable. There were cheery blazes kept on every hearth. The ambassador, Graham Thompson, and the occasional extra guests were as friendly and convivial as the circumstances allowed. Books, music, and other entertainments provided made the passage of time tolerable. Dresden found at length that he was getting used to the place, and not a little fond of it. It was a healthy attitude, as the ambassador and Thompson remained firm in their refusal to allow either Dresden or Maddy off the premises. "Your lives couldn't be more in jeopardy, old boy," he was reminded. "The book of the dead since Gettysburg is a most ample volume. It needs no appendix."

So they made do, Dresden perhaps better than Maddy, who seemed to grow more morose. She had days that, if not happy, at least were marked by participation in conversation and the occasional wan smile. Most days, especially the gray, gloomy, rain-wet ones, were marked by long silences, and often tears, though not outright sobbing.

Dresden had not expected the same forthright courage with which she had surprised him so often in previous weeks. Indeed, he had anticipated just the opposite—a complete, if temporary, emotional collapse. That she persisted in this unresponsive and often sullen state perplexed and frustrated him. He tried every imaginable means of penetrating her wall of implacable sadness—laughter, jokes, nostalgia, recitations of the dangers that surrounded them, discussions of the unfolding events reported in the newspapers and on television. He sought her sympathy for his own anger, fear, and sadness. He even lost his temper with her. Nothing worked.

Attempts at lovemaking, especially, did not work, even after she had recovered from her wound. Sometimes she would allow him into her room, even to sit on her bed in conversation. But when he tried to climb into it, or simply to hold her protectively and caress her affectionately, she always turned away. She never struggled. She would curl up like some creature retreating into its shell, or just lie limp and staring.

One night, however, she suddenly reached for him, clutching his arm with a hard, pinching hand and pulling him over and onto her. He caught just a glimpse of her face in the pale light. There was no passion in her fierce expression, just urgency, need, and pain. She was full of anguish. When after a few frantic moments they were done, it was not diminished.

"There is a rat in the house that Maddy built," she said.

They were lying side by side, very still. He took her hand, holding it very lightly between both of his.

"What did you say?"

"That poem I wrote you once:

> This is the house that Maddy built.
> Over a river, surrounded by trees, with sun
> on the pool behind it.
> This is the wine that lay in the house that Maddy built.
> Champagne, Mumm's '59.
> This is the rat who drank the champagne that
> lay in the house that Maddy built."

"Do you mean me?"

"No. You are 'the friend who chased the rat who drank the champagne that lay in the house that Maddy built.' You are 'Handsome Lancelot Charles D.' Except you haven't chased the rat. This place, this is the house that Maddy built, and Maddy has come to loathe and despise it. This is the house of the rat."

He turned his head to look upon her face in profile. Her eyes were fixed on the ceiling. There seemed no madness in them.

"I feel dead, Charley. I feel that I have died and this great endless house is my grave and I shall never ever leave it."

"They're very civil about it, but we are their prisoners here, aren't we?"

"No. We're prisoners of ourselves, of what we've done, of what we are. If they let us walk out that huge iron gate tomorrow, we wouldn't do it, would we? We'd be afraid. We'd come scurrying back. There is no other place for us now, except this house."

"We'll get out of here. Trust me."

She said nothing, blue eyes staring.

"Please trust me," he said. "I love you. You have my love. You'll always have that. Don't you love me?"

"Do I love you, Charley? Somewhere inside, in some old part of

me, I love you. Somewhere inside I love George. I am a little girl
again, loving my father, clinging to him. But it is the love of the
dead for the living, the dead for the dead. I thought that making love
might somehow miraculously revive me, shake me from this, but I
still feel cold as stone, more so because making love made no difference."

"Did I hurt you? Your wound . . ."

"No. There isn't anything."

He lifted himself on his elbow and reached to touch her brow with
his fingers, and then her lips, which were cold and trembling. He
brushed her cool cheek.

"I'll get us out of here," he said.

"It wouldn't make any difference."

He tried one more idea.

"You've made a difference. We both have. You said you wanted to
help the country get out of its trouble and you have, very bravely.
Thanks to these British, there's a chance now to stop these terrible
people for good. We can make this end happily."

"Not for us, Charley."

He sat up.

"Go away now, Charley."

"I love you."

"Go. Don't make love to me again. Don't make love to the dead."

The next afternoon, the ambassador summoned him to his private
study. President Hampton, back in his bathrobe, was on the television screen.

"He's come out again," Hyde-Milne said, gesturing Dresden to a
nearby chair. "Like the French fleet at Trafalgar. Yet he's rambling
on about the civil rights movement."

Dresden made a quick search of his memory. "It's Martin Luther
King's birthday."

"A national holiday," the ever-present Thompson reminded. "The
only individual in this country honored with his own day."

"Hampton always waxed very eloquent on this occasion," Dresden
said. "It was his substitute for dealing very actively with race problems."

"Yes," said the ambassador. "But listen to his voice. It's clear as
Waterford crystal. The hoarseness has utterly gone. Listen, it's his old
self."

"Very old self," said Dresden. "I'd guess most of what you're hearing is from last year's speech."

Suddenly, Hampton switched the subject to Central America, making another, somewhat jarring appeal for national calm and unity in dealing with this time of crisis.

"Bloody marvelous," said Thompson.

"And you're going to tell us that he's still quite dead," said Hyde-Milne, "and that these words have all been ingeniously edited together and dubbed onto a videotape that itself has been ingeniously edited together."

"Of course. If you took voice prints, the trick would show up immediately."

"It looks as realistic as anything I've ever seen on television," said Thompson.

"It's supposed to," said Dresden.

F.B.I. Director Steven Copley was driving down the Atlantic City Expressway from a heliport at Camden, New Jersey. He was past McKee City and almost to the Garden State Turnpike when the patch call he'd been trying to complete finally came through over his car phone.

"Before going any farther, sir," he said, "I must tell you we're speaking over a very open line."

"Understood," said Vice President Atherton. "Precisely."

Copley gestured to his driver to slow down. He didn't know what his instructions might be. "We have located the subject," he said. "In a hotel on the boardwalk. He's been in there for hours. He's had the room for weeks."

"You've made a positive identification?"

"Yes, sir. The subject and a lady friend were observed in the hotel casino and they subsequently returned to their room. My men on the scene say they are there now."

They were very near the sea, and wide patches of mist hung shroudlike over the road.

"Have they any protection?"

"There's one man in the lobby. I think they may have another one roving. They're trying to keep a low profile this time."

There was silence on the line. His driver was staring hard at the road. Copley glanced back at the chase car he had following. It was keeping very close.

"All right," said Atherton at length. "Go get them. Bring him back to Washington by the quickest means possible. Be careful. I don't want the sen—the subject hurt. I only want to talk to him. I simply must talk to him. We can bring him to our side. Then all will be well."

"I should perhaps remind you, sir, that the involuntary transport of a person across a state line is a federal offense."

"You're just doing your duty. Damn it, get him!"

"Yes, sir."

He nodded to his driver to increase their speed, then replaced the phone set and picked up his radio microphone.

"All units," he said. "Execute, execute."

What followed was audible to him only as confusion. Finally, one of his agents came on the air to announce that the subject was not to be found on the premises. When Copley pulled up in the hotel parking lot he came up to explain. Copley lowered the window, glowering at the man.

"I'm sorry, sir," said the agent. "They took a whole row of connecting rooms. Dubarry came in one and went out another around the corner. It's just like his Senate offices."

"Your men in the corridor missed him?"

"They all rushed the room he went in."

"And your men in the lobby?"

"He didn't come out through the lobby."

Copley ran his hand wearily over his eyes.

"They knew we were coming, sir," said the agent. "This was all a setup to draw us in. They left this."

He handed Copley a business card with "United States Senate" printed on it. The card was one of Dubarry's. On the back were written just two words: "You lose."

"We have a lot of mobile units in the area, sir. Do you want to try an intercept?"

"No," said Copley. "If we tried, they'd just pull this stunt all over again. We'll let them win this one. We'll see Senator Dubarry again at the State of the Union."

As they drove back across the state, Copley tore the card into tiny pieces, then tossed them out the open window into the car's slipstream and the mist.

25

For the week preceding the scheduled date of the State of the Union address, the news reports had been vague and confusing, but generally in agreement that the president would deliver his speech via television from Camp David, as he had been speaking to the nation since the Gettysburg shooting. On the morning of the speech, however, the "Today Show" interrupted the first segment of its morning broadcast with a report from unnamed sources that the president would actually be making the address in public, a symbolic declaration that the national crisis was at last over. In the next hour's segment, the report was simply repeated. By then, ABC's "Good Morning America" had one of its own, more excited in tone, but more restrained in wording, to the same effect. "CBS Morning News" ignored the story entirely, but the network broke into a following soap opera with a bulletin citing unconfirmed reports that the president might actually appear in person.

Subsequent radio news reports were a babble of confusion, with not a few radio preachers hastening onto the airwaves with sermons evoking Moses's descent from the Mount. The headlines on extra editions of afternoon newspapers rushed onto the street hours ahead of press time all ended in question marks.

In the White House, Vice President Atherton called an emergency meeting in the Roosevelt Room, made more comfortable in doing so because of National Security Adviser Malcom's absence from the capital, reportedly for another unpublicized trip out of the country.

For all its urgency, the meeting began with everyone around the table sitting in stunned or cautious silence. Finally, Atherton broke it.

"All right," he said. "If I didn't want your opinion, I wouldn't have asked for it. Just what the hell is going on?"

After a moment's additional silence, Press Secretary Neil Howard became the first to respond.

"I think it's more of the same. The rumors, leaks, and lies they've spread around this town are deeper now than the snow in the winter of '79."

"Begging pardon," said Merriman Crosby, "but that particularly harsh winter was 1976–1977."

"I recall there was a hell of a lot of snow in February or March of '79."

"Damn it!" said Atherton, snapping forward in his chair. "We all know what's at stake here! Let's get damned serious."

"I tend to agree with Neil," said the attorney general. "More deliberate confusion and obfuscation, designed to keep us off balance, prevent us from doing or saying anything before the president, or his facsimile, makes tonight's speech."

"But our press conference isn't scheduled until tomorrow morning," said Atherton. "They know that."

"Should I call it off?" Howard asked.

"They could have some bombshell planned for tonight," said Shawcross. "Something calculated to render our press conference moot."

"Begging pardon," said Crosby, "but it's we who have the bombshell planned for tonight."

"Except it's designed for late tonight and after the speech," Wilson said. "And they may still know nothing about it."

"Just a minute, just a minute," Atherton said. "Let's back up here and return to our basic premise. I'll ask the question again I've asked a hundred times. Is there anyone here who doubts the evidence that Dresden and Mrs. Calendiari brought us?"

There was a universal shaking of heads.

"Haven't we checked it out that many times?"

The shakes became nods. Atherton turned to Howard. "And you had the president's Martin Luther King birthday tape analyzed?"

"As I told you, in every way possible. Including voice prints. It was a complete phony."

"Precisely," said Atherton, leaning back in his chair and swiveling back and forth. "So then. There can be no doubt that President Henry Hampton is dead. Long dead."

Everyone nodded.

"Therefore," Atherton continued, "how can they possibly stop us? How can they resist the obvious, the truth? How can they obstruct the irrevocable processes of the Constitution and the Twenty-fifth Amendment? By God, they have to produce a president, and they can't! Rollins himself has had to sit on his hands while that Larson resolution rolled through committee."

"There are things they can do outside the Constitution," Shawcross said.

"Damn it, Dick! I'm tired of hearing that. This is, may I remind you yet again, the United States of America!"

"Wasn't it," said Merriman Crosby, wearily.

"Just the same," said Howard, "it might be smart to consider not showing up tonight."

"That may be exactly what they're trying to scare us into," said Shawcross.

"Precisely," said Atherton. "They're the ones who are going to have a glaring absence to explain. It's our whole purpose to be gloriously manifest." His dark, shining eyes darted around the table. "Can any of you really offer a logical, plausible, and damned convincing reason why I should not appear? Why we should change our plans in any way whatsoever?"

Once again, no one spoke. Shawcross scratched his balding head and Crosby drummed nervously on the table with his perfectly manicured fingers.

Atherton studied his watch a moment. "All right. Here's what I want you to do. Go back to your offices and do absolutely nothing else until twelve noon but strain your brains trying to think of such a reason. If you can, report to me at once. Otherwise, we proceed as planned."

The ambassador joined Maddy and Dresden for breakfast, which he had never before done. His conversation was brisk and amiable, but a diplomatic device. As he spoke, deftly weaving the morning's news into practiced and disarming chatter, he was measuring them, assessing their moods, preparing them for something. His gentlemanly banter was lost on Maddy, who ate listlessly and mostly stared at her plate. Dresden engaged in the game, doing his part to help get them through the meal without tacit recognition of the stark realities he had no doubt would shortly confront them. As Maddy finished with a last sip of tea and set down her empty cup with a nervous rattle, Dresden decided that the ambassador was at last about to set them free.

Hyde-Milne asked if they might join him in the drawing room, as he had an important matter to discuss. He put a solicitous hand to Maddy's elbow as they proceeded down the great hall, but the chatter thereafter ceased. Dresden followed quietly after, his glance lingering on the paintings they passed in growing wonder if he would ever have opportunity to look upon them again. Graham Thompson, bony face flushed and not a little excitement in his eyes, was waiting. So was the man Llewellyn, though there was no discernible change in his demeanor.

"Well, then," said Hyde-Milne, when all were seated comfortably. "Today, as they say, is the day."

Maddy stared at him coldly, though with some curiosity. Dresden merely listened as casually as possible, which was difficult, as Thompson was staring at him.

"As I said earlier, we've been keeping you here for your own safety," the ambassador continued. "Under the circumstances, I can't possibly think of another place safer in Washington for you to be."

"Maybe the Russian Embassy," Dresden said. He had blurted that out, and it sounded churlishly ungrateful. Whatever the British might have in mind for them, they had without question saved Maddy's life. "I'm sorry, Mr. Ambassador. One can go stir crazy even among Turners and Rembrandts."

"Stir crazy. Yes, of course." The great eyebrows compressed for a moment, his only sign of irritation. "We would have arranged a more secure sanctuary for you outside of Washington, quite far out of Washington. It's always been our intention to do so, at the appropriate time, which I have every expectation will be rather soon. But in the meantime, it's always been our hope, if not expectation, that this nasty situation would be resolved by now. We were convinced that the several parties to this ghastly mystery would have moved against one other by this late date. It's been two long months. This is the United States, not the Soviet Union."

"All the parties to this ghastly mystery are aware that you two know exactly what they've been up to," Thompson said.

"And they're also aware that you've disappeared, that you've gone to ground completely out of their reach," said Hyde-Milne. "Your escape should have provoked them into some rash or hasty act, but there's been nothing. It's been a *sitzkrieg*."

"Not quite, Ambassador," said Llewellyn, with deferential tone if not language. "We had another telex from Tegucigalpa this morning."

He held a small notebook and gold pen at the ready, but had not yet written a word. Maddy was beginning to fidget.

"We'll discuss Tegucigalpa in a moment," said Hyde-Milne. He rose, went to the fireplace, and stood facing away from it, hands clasped behind his back, feet tight together. He looked like a man standing on a gallows. "Now, we must act."

Llewellyn at last began to write. Dresden looked to Thompson, who turned away.

"We thought that, at the end of the day, as the Irish say," said the ambassador, "that if matters weren't satisfactorily resolved, you might be of some help to us, and of course to your own nation. Inestimable help. To the entire free world, I daresay. What we have in mind involves considerable risk—I mean physical risk—to the both of you."

Dresden had never seen Maddy's face so hard and grim. Only the wide blue eyes and golden hair remained of the woman he loved.

"Perhaps you could be more precise about what it is you want us to do," Charley said.

The eyebrows compressed again, then shot up. "Whoever 'they' are," Hyde-Milne said, "'they' shall likely all be in attendance at the Capitol for tonight's speech, notwithstanding the president's probable absence."

"Everyone of consequence in Washington will be there," said Thompson. "Including the ambassador."

"And, we hope, including yourselves," Hyde-Milne added. "We want you to serve as a provocation, a catalyst, to stir them to action—with luck, before they're quite ready for it. We want you to be there for the State of the Union address."

"To do what?" Dresden demanded.

"Merely to be present, to be visible, to be seen by one and all." The ambassador smiled cheerily. "It should more than suffice."

*   *   *

Kreski had traveled under a fictitious name and used feeder airlines to fly in short hops across the Gulf states and up the coastal Atlantic states of the South. He had overflown Washington on a Piedmont Airlines flight to New York, taken the Eastern Airlines shuttle to Boston, and returned to Washington via an Air Canada jet landing at Dulles. Despite all this, as he exited the terminal at the taxi loading area, Steve Copley suddenly appeared at his side. Kreski sighed.

"Good evening, Steven."

"Hello, Walt. I trust you had a good flight. Or should I say flights?"

"I hadn't counted on being met."

"We've had agents at all the major airports ever since Gettysburg, and you, as they say, are a well-known figure. You're out of practice, Walter. A good policeman wouldn't let something like that slip his mind, and you're about the best cop I know."

"Not good enough, it seems."

Copley waved the taxi attendant away. "On the contrary. If anything, too good."

"I suppose it would be discourteous to decline your generous offer of a ride."

"It would be pointless, at any rate, as my car's just over there." He nodded toward a black, nondescript but highly polished sedan parked at the opposite curb. There was no one in it or around it.

"We can have a little private chat," Kreski said. "I was meaning to do that sooner or later after I got back. Though not in these circumstances."

Copley started them across the cab lane. "Oh, sooner is best. I'm anxious to learn all that you were able to find out."

He held open the door on the passenger side, waiting until Kreski had put his luggage into the rear and seated himself, briefcase on his lap. Then he shut the door firmly and hurried to his own side. Neither of them spoke again until they were pulling away from the terminal.

"Steven," said Kreski. "I think you already know all the things I was able to find out."

"More than that, as a matter of fact. Having been out of the country, you couldn't possibly know about all the evidence we've been able to produce against Peter Ashley Brookes. You're aware, I'm sure, that Juan Jalisco did work for Brookes's guerrilla outfit in Central

America. We've come up with actual correspondence between the two."

"Doubtless with little yellow La Puño flags on the letterhead."

"Something like that. The judge was quite impressed. Brookes's bond was set at one million dollars. He made it, of course, but it shows how seriously the courts are taking our case. I haven't the slightest doubt we'll get a conviction."

"Steven, I've just come from Mexico."

"Yes. I know."

"My itinerary included Tabasco, Tampico, and Veracruz. I have Jalisco's complete employment record. I know everything there is to know about the companies, including the family that owns them, and the family's most illustrious member." He tapped his briefcase. "It's all in here."

"So I presumed."

They had been following the exit road around the shore of a mir-rorlike lagoon. Abruptly, Copley steered the car onto a long drive that led around to the airline services area of the airport. There was a wide expanse of parking lot, most of it completely empty. The FBI director pulled to a stop at the edge, at least a football field from the nearest vehicle.

"Don't get strange ideas, Walt. Your door is securely locked and I'm holding a PK Walther on you. It will ruin a rather nice Brooks Brothers jacket, but I'll pull the trigger at the slightest move. You'll lose much of your digestive system in the process. Not that you're going to be much in the mood for food."

"I don't understand how you think you can get away with shooting me in the middle of Dulles Airport in broad daylight."

"Simple. I'm going to shoot you in the line of duty. You're a key part of the Brookes assassination conspiracy, Walter. I met you at the airport to question and detain you if necessary. You, unfortunately, pulled a gun on me—a standard Secret Service–issue revolver. I have it under my seat. I also have some interesting correspondence between you and Brookes and a La Puño artifact or two. Combined with the indisputable fact of your travels and activities in Honduras, agent Perkins involvement, and the large cash sum you accepted from Brookes, it ought to be enough to convince any jury—or investigating committee—of your treason and deep involvement in the murder plot. How about that?"

He killed the car's engine and turned in his seat to face Kreski, pulling the Walther out from under his coat as he did so.

"What's ironic," he continued, "is that we never intended for things to get this far. All it was supposed to take was a single, well-placed rifle shot. Just one shot, Walt."

"In the manner of Sarajevo."

"As far as Central America is concerned, yes. But all that's happened in this country since the assassination, none of it was planned. That bloodbath in the press pool at Gettysburg was your people's doing."

"I accepted the responsibility for it. I had nothing to do with blowing up Mrs. Atherton's car, or gunning down those people in Tegucigalpa, or all those other endless murders."

"Yes, you did, Walt. You wouldn't give up. You kept at it, day after day, week after week, on and on, ever the good cop. You gave us no damn choice, Walt, for anything we did. In the end, nothing we did worked. You were never put off the trail, but as I say, there's an irony here. Our cover-up didn't fool you, but it developed the existence of a La Puño in the public mind as nothing else could. And that's made everything we have to do now very easy."

"You owe me something."

"And how is that?"

"You're an honorable man."

Copley laughed, shaking his head. "You're the honorable man, Walt. That's what got you into so much trouble."

"I just want to know how far this conspiracy goes, how many people are involved."

"All told, in one way or another, I suppose it involved hundreds. But most of those people were just doing their jobs, doing their duty as they saw it, doing what they were told. Unquestioning patriots. Only a very, very few had any idea of what was really going on. It's amazing how government bureaucracies work that way."

"Perkins knew what was going on."

"Yes, sir, he surely did."

"How did you acquire him?"

"That asset was bought and paid for. The neat and tidy sum of five hundred thousand dollars. He was quite the cynic, your Mr. Perkins. He had no compunctions except those having to do with his own welfare. He had no objection to the killing. I suppose you should expect that from a former army sniper."

An airline truck drove slowly by. The driver glanced once in their direction, but continued on.

"Who else were you able to turn?" Kreski said. "Just how dirty did you get my agency?"

"There was no one else. Except for Perkins, the Secret Service was squeaky clean, especially the White House detail. You chose your people well."

"You were able to shoot the president of the United States by bribing just one agent?"

"It's amazing what you can do if you put your mind to it. Now Walt, it's getting late."

"Just one more thing. You said only a very, very few knew what was really going on. How many was that?"

"Very, very few."

"How many were in on everything?"

"Everything? Why, just the vice president and myself. As I said, this was supposed to have been a neat, simple, garden-variety presidential assassination. The kind they have in the Third World all the time."

"The evidence concerning his mother's family, the Hidalgos, is overwhelming. But I still can't believe he was involved in this—not this far."

"Why not? He had more reason for wanting to see Hampton shot than anyone did the Kennedys, unless you're prepared to think that Lyndon Johnson was behind those."

Kreski was beginning to itch again, but for all the wrong reasons. The end of his life could be just a few words away.

"But it's hard to think of Atherton being that homicidal. The casualties in this have been horrible. My God, he blew up his own wife."

"He didn't do that. We agreed to have Perkins eliminated, but it was supposed to happen after she was taken home. The car bomb's timing was off."

"Steven. It wasn't off. That bomb was detonated by remote control. You had a car in Rock Creek Drive."

"All right. That's true. Taking out Mrs. Atherton was my idea. He knew nothing about it. I thought it would throw suspicion the other way—shut the investigation down as far as our side was concerned."

"You were wrong."

"Those will have to serve as your last words, Walt. I don't want to miss the State of the Union."

The gunshot reached Kreski's ears as a shattering roar.

The British had unearthed Maddy's yellow Mercedes from its embassy hiding place and, nervous, she was driving it rather erratically down Massachusetts Avenue toward the Capitol, Dresden at her side and Graham Thompson in the rear. Dresden shared her anxiety. Released from their confinement at last, he found himself experiencing less a feeling of freedom than dread. Thompson had assured them that the car following so closely behind was also from the embassy, but Charley sensed menace in all the headlights around them. The image kept returning to his mind of their being cut down by government bullets before they even reached the Capitol. He kept seeing Maddy lying stricken in his arms, as on that rainy Delaware beach.

He had come very close to flatly turning the ambassador down. He had already accomplished what he had set out to do, and paid a terrible price. Maddy had suffered similar deprivation. They had disclosed all they knew, turned over all their evidence, fulfilled all their obligations. However grateful he was to the British for their succor, he did not feel they had thereby incurred any new obligation. Nothing warranted their being sacrificed as pawns in a very British form of end game. Dresden had not turned coward, but he could not tolerate the powerlessness of his position. If he was again to put his and her life at risk, it should be on his own terms, by his own rules, in a game of his own choosing.

But Maddy gave him no choice. She wanted out of this situation, wanted escape, and she had accepted the British's terms. For all the excesses of her driving, her eyes were hard and steady on the road ahead, the goal ahead. Her grip on the steering wheel was just as hard, and her features were locked into a fierce expression. She was no less the beauty—if anything, her allure was all the more compelling. But she was so strange, so foreign to him. She was no longer someone he knew. In all those years of separation she had changed not at all, but in the space of a few weeks she had been transformed utterly. She was completely beyond his control.

She had lived a life absolutely free of violence and unexpected trouble, but for two months she had been assaulted daily by little else. She had been painfully wounded and almost killed. She had seen so many others, indeed, so many long-established institutions of her nation, treated with similar brutality.

The ambassador had explained the international concerns at issue that night in only the vaguest terms. He said there was intense military activity on both sides of the borders that joined Honduras to Nicaragua, El Salvador, and Guatemala. Soviet ships were swarming all over the Caribbean, even as more American vessels poured in. At the same time, there was an ongoing secret if highly volatile and ill-tempered diplomatic exchange taking place in Mexico—conducted by unknown Latin American parties and the American Defense Department, not the Department of State. Hyde-Milne said he need not discuss these matters any more deeply as there was little, if anything, they or the British government could do about it.

Left unsaid was how unfamiliar with the subject Dresden was anyway. He might be able to quote exhaustively from the works of Poe and the philosophical self-dialogues of Albert Camus, but in the matter of his country's foreign problems he was as untutored as any bus driver or fast-food waitress. As with millions of Americans, his knowledge of these matters came only from what he occasionally saw on the network news. If there was to be a major war, he would be just as confused as they as to what it was all about.

If the British ambassador was correct, however, that war's opening battle would be in Washington that night, beneath the floodlit dome of the Capitol that now beckoned as they turned onto Pennsylvania Avenue. It could be decisive, the ambassador had said, and Dresden and Maddy were to have a major role in it.

Charley the pawn. He took a deep breath to calm his unhappy nerves. It was one thing to stalk his enemies from the sanctuary of seedy bus stations and nondescript hotel rooms, even to confront them unexpectedly in their homes. It was quite another to stride into their collective midst and stand before them, vulnerable to their wrathful retaliation—indeed, demanding it.

Hyde-Milne had promised all manner of protection. Though without explanation, he guaranteed the presence of British operatives and agents, and the help of those from two or three other NATO countries' embassies. Graham Thompson had foreseen no difficulty in their gaining admittance to the House chambers. Maddy still had the ticket to the upper gallery she had been entitled to as Senator Calendiari's wife. The British had quietly fetched it for her along with some fresh clothing from her locked and deserted house in McLean. For Dresden, they had produced a forged congressional press pass, the laminated plastic card bearing his photograph but issued in the fictitious name of Ian McLennan, identified as a correspondent with Thompson's broadcast service. He had also been given the ticket numerically assigned to Thompson for a seat in the press gallery above and behind the House speaker's rostrum. Dresden was to explain that Thompson had been sent on another assignment and he was a last-minute substitute. He had to somehow pass himself off as British. They had tried to assure him that the difficulty would be minimal.

Though there would be some Secret Service and FBI agents about, the security would be handled principally by the Capitol police force, a notoriously unprofessional organization whose ranks were in large part filled with congressional patronage workers.

Dresden was little mollified. The whole purpose of their getting past the Capitol's security checkpoints was to expose themselves to people far more dangerous than political minions in badges.

For all her nervousness, Maddy was showing no signs of fear. She reminded Dresden uncomfortably of some radical underground member preparing a clandestine bombing attack. He wished desperately that she might just once reach and take his hand, or share an intimate glance, or even say some kind word. But there had been no real gesture of affection from her for days.

Coming to the end of Pennsylvania Avenue near the foot of the hill beneath the Capitol, Maddy turned left into Constitution Avenue, heading toward the ascending file of Senate office buildings that lined the thoroughfare on the left.

"Just drive right in," said Thompson. "There's a major gap in the security defenses of this complex, and its bloody name is garage."

It was true. Those in charge of Capitol security had not exactly been far-sighted or swift thinkers. According to Maddy, they had responded to one attempted bombing by installing speed bumps at the entrances to the House and Senate office building garages, to foil terrorists in speeding cars. They had put the obstructions only in the entrance lanes, however, leaving the exit lanes clear, as though presuming terrorists obeyed all Capitol Hill traffic regulations. Now they had speed bumps in place in the exit lanes as well, but they still required only a cursory look at a congressional pass or windshield sticker to allow a car to enter, no matter what it might be carrying. Once inside one of the garages, a person had access to nearly all of the Capitol complex.

Maddy's pass and car sticker were valid until the end of next month. The two guards at the entrance door recognized her, in fact, and offered condolences for her husband's passing. She thanked them sadly, but sweetly, then introduced Dresden and Thompson as security men assigned to her for her protection that night. The guards nodded and waved her on, half saluting.

"That was uncalled for," Thompson said, as she drove into the garage's vast interior. "We're both newsmen with valid credentials, may I remind you. If one of those miscreants had asked to examine them and noticed the discrepancy with your story, you might have blown the whole show."

"I'm sorry," she said, the sweetness gone from her voice. "I wasn't thinking. It won't happen again."

"Please. Everything has to be all tickety-boo."

She pulled into Calendiari's official parking space, between a Cadillac Fleetwood with Arizona plates and a Toyota from Connecticut with a teddy bear in the rear window. After turning off the engine, she took a deep breath, and then just sat there.

"Second thoughts, Maddy?" Thompson asked.

"No," she said, decisively, and snapped open the door.

"Just remember," Thompson said, after he had gotten out. "When this is over go to the fountain at the bottom of the hill. Look for a British car with the lights off and the engine running. I don't know what make or model it will be or who will be in it, but go to the British car. If there's any trouble and you're able to run for it, go directly to the fountain. Remember the British car."

"I think we get the idea, Mr. Thompson," Dresden said.

"I'm not trying to patronize you. This will be your only means of escape. We've deployed everyone we have available in Washington, but the other side has thousands."

"We understand," said Maddy.

With her leading, they passed through some doors and a short corridor, emerging at one of the platforms of the little subway line that connected the office buildings with the Capitol building proper. Maddy was expensively dressed in a Valentino beige coat and a bright, light blue Dior sheath that matched her eyes. She was quite definitely recognizable as a senator's wife. Both Thompson and Dresden were wearing dark, vested suits and passed for important officials themselves.

The subway cars were open and seated just twelve people. Waiting their turn, they took three seats together in the rear of one, trying to look as disinterested as possible.

"We're going to be early," said Thompson somewhat loudly, looking at his watch with a frown.

"Yes," said Dresden. He could think of nothing else to say.

Reversing its electrical motor, the motorman urged the car back into the curving tunnel from which it had come, its rubber tires gliding it along with a gentle whoosh. As the tunnel straightened, disclosing the lights of their destination in the far distance, a terrible realization came over Dresden. He put his hand inside his coat, and swore.

"Damn it all," he said, whispering to Maddy beside him. "I stupidly brought along my gun."

"Drop it over the side," she replied, not looking at him.

"It might go off."

"Get rid of it!" she hissed. "They have metal detectors in there."

Glancing at their fellow passengers opposite, who were talking excitedly among themselves, Charley turned halfway around in his seat and cleared his throat as though to spit, counting on that to induce people to look away. He did spit, noisily, and then coughed loudly, dropping the pistol butt-first between the rails as he did so. The sound was detectable, but no one seemed to notice. As he turned back around, he coughed again.

"I must do something about this throat," he said with raised voice.

"You certainly must," she said with some disgust. He presumed little of it was feigned, but then she did something unexpected. She took his hand, and held it tightly against her leg, not far, as it happened, from where the bullet had struck her. They were rapidly approaching the platform at the other end.

"We're actually going to do it," she said, her voice returned to a whisper. "Right now."

"Yes," said Charley, "there's no getting out of it."

But there was. Thompson would not be with them in the House chambers. He would have no ticket and would have to wait in the corridors outside. At any time they wished, they could find another exit and flee the building. The elaborate security was for people seeking entry, not escape. They could make their way out into the night to some future other than that the British had designed for them—if the British intended them to have a future at all.

She squeezed his hand hard, then lifted her face to kiss his cheek.

"What does that mean?" he said.

"I'm not sure yet. I suppose that I need you very much."

He squeezed her hand back. He wondered if she realized that there was an opportunity for her to escape, to walk out a door and away from this nightmare. But for all their idle, empty, unhappy hours in the embassy, they had never discussed this. They could not talk about it now with Graham Thompson near. If they were to choose that course, it would have to be a matter of spontaneous initiative. As they would be seated on opposite sides of the chamber, it would mean not simply escape but abandoning each other. They had no rendezvous point except the British car that was to be waiting by the fountain. They might never see each other again.

Dresden had never considered anything other than a resolute conclusion to this. To walk away now would be to depart the path he'd been following for two months and three thousand miles, to walk away from his revenge, discarding his pride and courage. It would mean a denial of his manhood, of what he had taken on the entire world to prove.

What would Maddy do?

The subway car was coming to a stop. "Charing Cross Station," said Thompson, rising. The doors slid open. Thompson and Maddy moved into the crowd, leaving Dresden, as planned, to make his way to the third-floor press gallery, alone.

Walt Kreski stood watching the unmarked van carrying Copley's body as it drove away, not moving until it had disappeared around a distant curve. He shook his head—in remorse and disgust. There was still some shattered window glass and a spattering of blood on the shoulder and sleeve of his suit coat. Kreski brushed at them ineffectively, then picked up his bags and walked to where Special Agent Hammond stood by the open door of a dark sedan. He paused, then dropped his luggage in the rear and eased into the seat, not speaking until Hammond had shut the door and come around to the driver's side.

"The last time I got into a car this way, I wished I hadn't."

"Don't worry, Director," said Hammond, as he turned the ignition key. "I guarantee an uneventful trip, at least until we get to Washington. No telling what's going on there just now."

He backed up smoothly, then turned and headed for the access road that led out of the airport to the expressway.

"I wish Copley hadn't been killed," Kreski said. "And not just for professional reasons."

"He didn't give us much choice. We hadn't expected him to try to take you out here at the airport. It didn't give us much chance to set up."

"That was a damn good shot."

"Behind left eye, through and through, from a hundred yards. Piece of cake. It helped that I used a scope."

"Judging from your records, you didn't need one. You're a better shot than Perkins was."

"I was afraid that when you noticed that and my proficiency in Spanish, you'd put me at the top of your suspect list."

"No way, Dick. You were too much in the line of fire at Gettysburg. What I was thinking of doing was putting you up for a commendation."

"You deserve one yourself for dragging Copley out to the bitter end that way."

"He could have told us a lot more."

"He wouldn't have. You were two seconds away from finito, Director."

"Did you get it all on tape?"

Hammond pointed to the rearview mirror, indicating an unmarked Secret Service van that was following close behind.

"Every syllable," he said. "They're making copies in our little mobile recording studio right now."

"I don't want too many of those things around. Tell them to stop."

"You just did." Hammond smiled.

Kreski swore, then pulled his tie aside and unbuttoned his shirt. In a moment he had pulled free the flat microphone pack that had been taped to his side. He clicked off the switch and set the device gently on the console between them.

"I'm tired of being listened to," he said.

Hammond slipped the microphone pack into his pocket. "I'll make sure there are no more than three copies of the tape. That's all we had official requests for anyway."

"I'm not even sure any of them will ever be used."

"I think they will be in part, Director. It only seems fair that Copley be used the way he was going to use you."

"What do you mean?"

"They did such a good job of creating this mythical La Puño outfit, why not leave it in place? Only instead of portraying you and Peter Ashley Brookes as the leaders, produce evidence that puts the mantle on Steve Copley instead. The public is convinced someone high up was involved in the assassination plot, and all the other killings. Why not Copley? He's perfect for the role, especially because he actually was involved, and most especially because he's dead."

"Only Copley. No one else?"

"I was just thinking out loud, Director."

They rode along in silence for a mile or so, passing a lonely airport bus in the darkness, and nothing else. The lights of some of Washington's outer suburbs glowed against the reflecting overcast in the distance.

"I wonder why they picked January for these ceremonial occasions," Kreski said. "It's the gloomiest time of the year."

"The state of the Union is usually gloomy."

"The speeches never are. All right, what's on the immediate agenda?"

Hammond pulled a folded piece of paper from the breast pocket of his jacket. "This restores you to the post of director of the Secret Service, effective immediately. Jelicoe goes back to Los Angeles and I'm to resume charge of the White House detail. By order of the president."

"I approve," said Kreski, glancing quickly over the paper. "What else?"

The other man handed over another document. "Here's a copy of another White House directive, also bearing the president's signature, that's being put out all over town. It orders all FBI personnel within the jurisdiction of the Washington field office to report to the J. Edgar Hoover Building auditorium at once for further instructions."

"To be given by whom?"

"The president's old friend, the solicitor general. But it doesn't matter who. The main thing is to get the feebees far away from the Capitol and some other key places, just in case."

"That's all you have for me?"

"It's enough. Your call from New York only came this afternoon, after all, and it kept us pretty busy. Our principal mission tonight is to make sure no one else gets killed, or even hurt. Those on high want very much for Copley to be the last victim of the assassination plot."

"That suits me fine."

"Me too. Real fine."

"I have just one lingering problem, Dick, and that's you."

"How so, Director?"

"You haven't been playing straight with me. You've done a wonderful job for the Service, but it's clear to me you've also been working for someone else."

"I think you'd better explain that, sir."

"You were a thousand times overqualified when you joined the Service in the first place and you've been overqualified for every post you've held since, including your present one. Your life-style has been just the slightest bit more extravagant than your financial records would indicate you can afford, even with big debts, of which you've had none. I've thought for some time that you've had a source of extra income—cash income. Besides, you've been far too knowledgeable about a lot of governmental matters than anyone in the Service has a right to be, including me. You've done a lot of 'thinking out loud.'"

"Thinking out loud can be a useful procedure, sir."

"Who's your patron, Dick? Bushy Ambrose? Senator Rollins? Peter Ashley Brookes? Or is it Vice President Atherton?"

"That makes no sense whatsoever, sir."

"Who's it been, Dick? If we're going to have a future relationship, professionally or otherwise, you've got to tell me."

Hammond tapped the steering wheel for a moment. "I can tell you this, Director. Any outside involvement I may have had was with a disinterested party—disinterested, that is, except for the national interest."

"Who, Dick? Not our warm, loving, jovial friend Admiral Elmore? Not the gray ghost of Langley?"

Hammond said nothing—and everything.

As a young congressman, following the advice of a wheezing old veteran of more than twenty years on Capitol Hill, Atherton had developed the habit of arriving extremely early for State of the Union addresses, assuring himself a seat on the aisle and, consequently, his appearance on national television when the president entered the chamber and made his slow, handshaking way to the rostrum. If things were going well for the nation and the administration, Atherton could make a highly visible point of greeting the chief executive warmly. If the White House was in trouble, he could evidence a certain diffidence. In either case, he had never failed to gain at least a few seconds of network exposure.

Once he'd been elected vice president, of course, he'd stopped the practice as one far beneath his dignity, and had been careful to enter the House chambers on these occasions just before Hampton himself made his appearance.

This night, despite his best intentions to maintain the aloof demeanor required by his high office and somber new responsibilities, he had been among the first to enter. Wild rumors about the presidential address to come had been rampant in the city all day. The vice president had believed none of them. His certainty as to what would actually occur had in no way diminished, or so he told himself. Over and over. Yet there was so much excitement in the capital, and the situation was so unprecedentedly bizarre, that he could not resist the compulsion to be where everyone else of consequence was or would soon be. This was the only night of the year when virtually the entire American government could be found under one roof. Despite fears of a terrorist attack, no one was staying away that evening. Congressmen, senators, cabinet officers, foreign ambassadors, Supreme Court justices, the wives of ranking members, and even a few astronauts and military figures, all kept coming in a steady stream. Their entrances were nearly all the same. They stepped through the doors with practiced smiles, making their way through the cordon of security men and waving or nodding to familiar faces. Then at once they stopped short, transfixed by the huge screen that hung behind the speaker's rostrum in place of the customary American flag. It was similar to those used at the convention that had nominated Hampton three summers before, in Philadelphia. Improving upon a visual-aid technique first perfected by Ronald Reagan at his last nominating convention, Hampton and his communications gurus had used the system to magnify his presence when he was speaking and to generally dominate the convention with his persona by running silent videotape footage over it of Hampton and his family in an assortment of views and poses while the convention was concerned with other business and speeches.

The Philadelphia system had employed three of these outsize screens. The House chamber, much smaller than a convention hall, would accommodate only this one. As he watched workmen and electricians move about it, completing some last-minute labors, Atherton found himself unsure as to what purpose it would be put. A living president would not need to resort to such dramatic effects addressing the full Congress in the House of Representatives of the United States of America. And the television cameras would magnify his persona for the benefit of the home viewers without the need of screens, as they magnified everyone's. Atherton told himself that the installation of this system was simply confirmation that Hampton would not and could not appear to make the address in person. The members of his apparat would use the device for yet another—and it would have to be the very best—spurious videotape presentation. The dead president would speak to the Congress and nation again from his mountaintop retreat. Atherton was convinced of this. The great blank screen might well serve as a grave marker, so starkly did it proclaim the president's demise. Henry Hampton was dead. And after that night, anyone who would insist otherwise would be compelled to prove it.

Yet, for the first time in weeks—since those first unsettling days immediately after the Gettysburg shooting—Laurence Atherton was beginning to feel vague, unsettling tremors of doubt.

No. It was his mind, his nerves. From the very instant things had gone wrong at Gettysburg, he had had to cope with an unfolding madness, the nightmare of a lunatic. It was beginning to wear on him, with increasing severity. He really *was* convinced of Hampton's death. He truly did believe that in a matter of hours he would be installed as acting president of the United States at the very least. His problem was whether he could handle it. Atherton was having very serious trouble sleeping at night. Long periods sometimes passed now without his remembering them. Every so often he sensed his wife near him, following him.

The vice president was claustrophobic, and the press of people around him was beginning to be an irritant. With a faint smile of apology, he edged to the side, then made his way up to the speaker's rostrum, a throne representing much more majesty and power than the chair he himself occupied as presiding officer of the Senate.

His own chair had been brought from the Senate for the occasion. He seated himself carefully, well aware of how many eyes must be upon him.

The speaker was over at a doorway, conferring with an aide. Seeing the vice president, he gave a friendly wave, but continued his conversation where he stood. Atherton found himself joined on the dais instead by a man wearing what looked to be electrician's clothes. The fellow made some adjustments on a contraption that had been mounted on the lectern below, where the president would stand if he actually were to make his address in person. It was an odd device, one Atherton could not recall seeing before.

Whistling, the man followed a cable line that led from the lectern up to the rostrum, where Atherton was sitting. It connected with a small metal box, from which a thicker cable ran to a quite large metal case, which in turn had several electrical lines leading in a jumble from its interior. Atherton had very definitely never seen anything like that case before. The man opened the case's lid, and was doing something with a screwdriver and a meter.

"What's that?" Atherton said.

"It's a voltmeter," said the man, with a grunt.

"No, I mean the metal case."

"It's like a junction box. I'm checking the power level."

"What's that on the lectern down there? It looks like a photograph enlarger."

"It isn't."

"Well, what is it?"

"It projects things on the screen. Look, I'm kinda busy."

"Well, look yourself. I happen to be the vice president of the United States."

"Yeah, well, I work for Mr. Padua."

"Yeah? Well, Mr. Padua might soon find himself out of work, and you with him."

The man stared at him for a moment, then lowered the lid of the case and walked away without another word. Atherton turned back toward the House floor, squinting against the television lights. He should not have been so childishly short with the man. There were reporters around who might construe the incident to mean he had gotten so power mad he was abusing mere workmen. There were others who would simply say he was losing his grip. He was not. He was perfectly in control. If he was nervous, it was just that there had been something odd about the fellow. The man had lowered the lid of that case with entirely too much gentleness. The vice president pondered the possible reason for such excessive caution, then turned and leaned closely over the lid, peering at it intently, as though able to see through it. Finally, he reached with trembling fingers and slowly opened the case, finding only a metal facing and sockets into which the cable ends were plugged. Gripping the lid tightly he tried moving the box and found it heavy, perhaps excessively heavy.

"Are you all right, Mr. Vice President?"

He looked up to see the great bulk of the speaker towering over him. They had known each other for some years. On the odd occasion when they had a drink or two together, the speaker would call him Larry. But once the bottles were put away, it was back to "Mr. Vice President."

"I'm fine, Pete. Just fine."

"You're sweating like a navvy. You better towel off with your hankie. They'll be turning on the TV cameras in a couple of minutes."

Atherton did as suggested, hurriedly. The speaker lowered himself into his chair and picked up his outsize gavel, fondling its handle as a professional golfer might the grip of a favorite and lucky club. A congressman approached, the speaker's majority leader, and the two spoke quietly with heads close together. Unable to follow any of the conversation, the vice president sat stiffly in his seat, mustering dignity and control as best he could. He knew exactly how they must appear to those on the floor below, how in a few minutes they would appear to the many millions watching on television at home. He had studied the tapes of Hampton's previous two State of the Union addresses carefully. It was very difficult to maintain poise—to avoid the odd scratch of the nose or unthinkingly slack facial expression— while sitting directly behind the president of the United States for the duration of a long and important speech. He supposed few professional actors could manage it. He closed his eyes and saw himself again as he had been a year before, he, the speaker, and the president—the three most important men in the United States.

But there would be no president in front of him this night. There would only be himself on the rostrum, along with the speaker, and the big metal box.

The year before, the president pro tem and next in succession had been Senator Moses Goode, one of the most popular and capable men on the Hill. Now it was Maitland Dubarry. Atherton glanced about the chamber, back and forth, several times, but saw nothing of Dubarry. Meathead was somewhere else, somewhere safe.

Atherton looked at the big box again. He leaned over it again, this time listening. If there was anything to hear, it was lost in the general din. The chamber was filled to overflowing now. The doorkeeper and his staff would shortly have to clear the aisles and get everyone to his or her proper seat.

"Mr. Vice President," said the speaker once more. "You gotta do something about that sweat."

Atherton took out his damp handkerchief and again mopped his brow and cheeks.

"Sorry," he said. "I must be coming down with something."

"It's the season," said the speaker, and turned to talk to someone else.

Narrowing his eyes, Atherton made another visual sweep of the chamber. Senator Rollins was in a far corner, engaged in earnest conversation with a younger man Atherton recognized as Rollins's press secretary. Otherwise, none of the president's men were to be seen. Like Meathead Dubarry, they were somewhere else.

And Rollins was standing right by a door.

The vice president lifted his gaze to the galleries, looking to where the First Lady usually sat. Daisy Hampton was not there, nor were Hampton's two grown children. He saw them rarely, but they were always present on State of the Union night. Daisy might well be so tanked to the gills they dared not let her come, but it could be for another reason.

He could feel the sweat returning. The president's entrance was due a scant few minutes away, yet there had been no word beyond the terse statement from Camp David that Hampton would make the speech as scheduled. If only Bushy Ambrose or David Callister or one of the others would make an appearance. Then Atherton might feel reasonably reassured.

He sat on his perspiring hands to keep them from shaking, hoping the speaker would not notice. He again gazed along the front rows of the gallery, but there was no one who even remotely resembled Daisy Hampton. Something, someone, caught his eye in a seat higher up. A bright blue dress. Blond hair.

He stared, puzzled, then sat back with a painful start. Madness was indeed upon him. He seemed to be seeing Madeleine Calendiari, as real as life.

No. He would not let this happen. The woman there was nothing to him, nothing to this event, only a hallucination. She did not exist. He existed. He was vice president of the United States. He would soon be president of the United States. It was all arranged.

Indeed, the woman in blue was leaving. Her back was to him, and she was climbing the steps to the exit. It could not be Madeleine Calendiari. It was someone else and if he did not get better control of his mind he was going to ruin the entire magnificent and unstoppable plan.

She was almost through the door now. In a moment she would be gone and he could rein back his fears and wild thoughts and concentrate on the scheduled events before him, concentrate on the plan, on his presidency to come.

But she stopped. Her head hung down a moment, as though in contemplation or some sudden remembrance. At once she turned around, looking at him. She came down the stairs, slowly, deliberately, with such purpose it seemed she might step out of the galleries and continue on toward him through the air. She didn't. She stopped at the railing and leaned forward, her eyes fixed on him. Her face seemed close, magnified a hundred times, those large blue eyes, now all cold and hard and angry, looking into his. Directly.

All those around her appeared blurred and unfocused, but the clarity of her image was crystalline. He could see the sparkle of diamonds at her throat. He could look into those haunting blue eyes and see her mind. For the first time since the first body had fallen, Atherton felt accused. He felt guilt. He felt an all-consuming fear. She knew.

The door. Exit. Escape. Atherton looked once more to the large metal case, then lurched to his feet, shoving back his chair, pushing past the speaker, tripping over a cable, rising, plunging on toward the back of the chamber and the speaker's offices. There was a corridor. He followed it, his shoulder bumping against the wall, knocking the paintings of past speakers askew.

Dresden was sitting in the press gallery seat assigned to him, amazed that he was there, from time to time snatching nervous glimpses of the two Secret Service men at the top of the steps behind him, fearful they might realize their mistake in letting him past. His seat was at one end of the chamber's upper deck, giving a view of the speaker's rostrum, but not a close one.

His attention was very much elsewhere in any event, devoted to the gallery across the way, where Maddy was sitting quietly and stiffly. Suddenly she was standing. She moved down the aisle and up the stairs. She was leaving the chambers, leaving his life. He rose from his chair. He wanted to call out to her. But it was not necessary. She came back. She stood at the railing and looked down. She was the most visible person in the whole enormous room.

The vice president abandoned his chair and was fleeing from the hall, out the back. Dresden did the same, taking up pursuit, ignoring the two security men as he hurried between them.

One grabbed his upper arm, so firmly the grip brought pain.

"Come on, man," said Dresden, with feigned indignation but genuine anger. "I gotta keep a phone line open!"

There was a milling confusion of reporters behind him, pressing forward to see where the vice president was going. The Secret Service man gave him a quick, nasty last look and then released him, having other things to do. Dresden stumbled on, slowing to a fast walk as he went through the press working area, which was crowded with reporters watching the House's closed-circuit television monitors.

He kept to his rapid walk, going out the door to the hallway and through the security checkpoint beyond. At the stairs, however, he broke into a run.

Though far behind, it was easy for him to follow Atherton. The man was the vice president and he was running, his passage leaving a wake of babbling excitement among the bystanders in the corridors, his forward progress marked by the first exclamations of recognition.

There were security agents and Capitol police throughout the crowd. Dresden got past them by pretending to be running with, rather than after, the vice president. "Get help!" he shouted to one agent. "Get some men!" he called to another, squeezing by. He saw the man stare at him blankly, then reach for his two-way radio microphone.

Atherton was sticking to the main corridor, hurrying along the length of the Capitol toward the Senate end, his running footsteps echoing from the stonework as he clattered across the sudden open space that was the Rotunda and pressed himself through the phalanx of people massed in the hallway beyond, hesitating for just one quick look behind him.

It was enough. He saw Dresden. The recognition was instantaneous.

Unused to such exertion after his long confinement in the British embassy, Charley was losing ground, but salvation was in view ahead. The entrances to the Capitol were heavily guarded and barricaded. Anyone entering or leaving had to pass through metal detectors and revolving doors. The vice president would have to slow, probably enough for Dresden to catch up.

Atherton realized this. Drawing near the end of the corridor, he quickly darted into a side passage. With Dresden huffing behind, he followed it to another, and ultimately to a spiral stone staircase, which brought him down to the Capitol's labyrinthine basement. Wheezing himself now, the vice president resumed his pell mell retreat, dodging around pillars and ducking through archways. There were few people down on this level, and no sudden shouts of recognition to guide Dresden's way. He could only follow his prey by tracking the sound of Atherton's leather heels striking against the stone floor. There were pipes overhead, leading in every direction. Black arrows painted on the yellow brick walls pointed to a confusion of possible destinations. Occasionally he caught a glimpse of Atherton, but the fading sound of the footfalls indicated the vice president was once again getting away from him.

All at once there was silence. The maze confronted Dresden with a cul-de-sac that had three narrower passages leading from it. He stood a moment, the sound of his own frantic breathing heavy in his ears. He had no choice. He had to keep moving. He took the passageway immediately to the left.

It proved a dead end. Retracing his steps, he tried the next. It continued on, making a sharp left-hand turn. Abruptly, it opened onto the wide main corridor again, by a sign with an arrow that said

SENATE OFFICE BUILDINGS. Still, Dresden heard nothing. Groping along, he suddenly took a whacking blow to his shoulder and side and was sent sprawling. It was Atherton, come upon him from another passageway.

The vice president kicked at Dresden's side, hard, then clattered on. "Stop, you son of a bitch!" Dresden shouted, pointlessly, then he pulled himself painfully to his feet and lunged after.

He knew only vaguely where he was. Judging by the signs and arrows, Atherton was making for the basement of one of the Senate office buildings. There were garages there. Maddy's car was in one.

Dresden moved by dead reckoning, following in the direction marked by a sign that proclaimed RUSSELL SENATE OFFICE BUILD-ING. He made as much noise as possible, shouting and bellowing, hoping to harry the vice president toward the huge garage from which he and Maddy and Graham Thompson had come.

It was working. There was a silence, and then running footsteps, moving the way Charley wanted to go. Pursuing, Dresden at length ducked under an archway on which had been painted SUBWAY TO RUSSELL BUILDING.

Elation increased his speed. He reached the subway platform just as the train carrying Atherton was pulling away. There was no one else on it except the motorman and a man and a woman sitting in a forward seat. Atherton was in the rear.

Pounding along the track, Dresden caught hold of the back of the car and jumped onto it, clinging to the metal, just as it began accelerating into the tunnel. Atherton, a terrified look in his eyes, shrank back and started climbing toward the front, then reversed himself and came at him, fist swinging, hammering down at Charley's arm. The woman began to scream. The motorman ground the car to a shuddering halt. Atherton struck at Dresden one more time, slashing Charley's cheek with a fingernail, then clambered into the driver's cubicle, shoving the man out and slamming the speed control forward.

As they shot along far faster than the subway normally traveled, Dresden started to climb into the car, then halted. Atherton had abandoned the motorman's compartment and was coming toward him with a large tool in his hand. Charley hung back, just inches above the track. He had no desire to be in the subway car. Unless someone took the controls, it was shortly going to crash into the Russell Building platform. Charley wanted to be on the tracks, here on this end of the tunnel. It was here, somewhere in the darkness, that he had dropped his gun, the .357 Magnum revolver that had caused him so much trouble and that now, if he was able to find it, he could at last put to good purpose.

He lowered himself as far as he could and then dropped, rolling. His shoulder cracked painfully against the concrete and his still healing knee was twisted wrenchingly. He rolled over one more time, coming to rest stomach-down on the opposite set of tracks. Looking their length, he could see nothing, only the distant movement of several men running toward them. Turning on his side, he looked the other way and saw a glint of metal on the otherwise smooth surface not many feet away. He rose just as the subway piled with a great crash into the bumper emplaced to stop it. Limping, his ears full of the woman's renewed screaming, Dresden reached the pistol just in time to see Atherton drop from the side of the car and drag himself up the platform to the building escalator. Charley fired once, using both hands. He hit nothing, but the report filled the tunnel with the thunder of a cannon shot.

He hurried past the tilted subway vehicle, mindful of the woman's crying but unwilling to stop. With his knee reinjured, he ran awkwardly, but Atherton, limping badly, was moving even more slowly.

The vice president vanished around a corner. When Dresden reached the spot he found a bank of gray-painted elevators and, across from it, two swinging doors with round, porthole windows. Their telltale residual movement showed which way Atherton had gone.

Beyond the doors, a corridor led to the garage. Charley stepped out into its flourescent lamp–lit vastness and stood and listened. He heard a grunt and caught a flicker of something moving off to the side. He pursued it, raising his pistol. At the sight of another quick blur in the opening between two cars, he fired an echoing shot that thunked into one of the automobiles but struck no flesh. Atherton skittered away, at length appearing at two swinging doors in the opposite wall and vanishing through them. As Dresden approached in a painful trot, he heard a muffled slam.

His pistol held before him, he pushed open one of the doors, finding himself in a stairwell. Nothing could be heard on the staircase. In front of him was a painted metal door with a brass knob. It was locked and would not yield. Dresden, longtime hunter in the California hills, was sure of his quarry. Aiming the Magnum just below the knob, he fired, the mushrooming bullet pulverizing the metal. The door opened to darkness. Groping for the light switch, he found it, illuminating a small storeroom. Atherton was hunched, cowering, in a corner beside a stack of folding chairs. His eyes were quite mad.

Dresden pulled him forward and threw him roughly onto the concrete floor. He jammed the pistol barrel into the man's neck just beneath his chin and began cursing, spewing the vilest words he could bring to mind into the man's whimpering face. The mad eyes became ghastly, frightened ones, peering down at the huge gun as Dresden hissed the names of Charlene Zack and Danny Hill and Atherton's own wife.

Charley's sense of power both frightened and thrilled him. A few weeks before he'd been just an oddball in a bar, talking back to a television screen and retreating before the threats of a man whose only claim to significance was that he owned a small television station in a small city in a far-off state. Now Charley stood before the ultimate authority of the United States government, and stood as master. His power was absolute, for it was the power of life and death. One small muscular contraction against a curved piece of steel and this flawed, evil mistake of creation would be erased. The vulgar whining would cease. The vice president would die as wretchedly as his victims. Charley would be a willing executioner, a fulfilled man. One shot and he could slip off into the darkness from which he had come—with justice done and no price to be paid beyond what he'd already paid.

Or was this gross vanity? If he shot the vice president now, would it not be just another sordid cruel killing in a chain of murders started by someone else? There'd be no guarantee that they would stop, that any of it would stop. He and Maddy would continue their flight and the long, dreadful nightmare would go on.

This was no fit retribution anyway. The vice president would pay no great price by dying now, dying as one day all men die. He must pay a public price. He must suffer, atone, and do painful penance. He must grovel and be smeared with his guilt. His obligation was not simply to Charley; it was to the law he had so arrogantly defied. The fit retribution must come from the law. Charley's power was that he could see to that. Anyone could kill a man, but Charley would bring Laurence Atherton to judgment.

But first he would indulge himself. First Atherton had to suffer. Dresden dug the pistol barrel deeper into his flesh.

"You have no idea how much I hate you," he said. "You have no idea how much I want to blow your brain into a sticky mess . . ."

But now he was sent reeling, a sharp blow to the side of his head numbing him. A big man he recognized from television as Senator Andrew Rollins grabbed hold of his coat and slammed him back against the wall.

"That is the vice president of the United States, sir!" Rollins said. "He is not to be harmed!"

Dresden edged back, noting two other men in the room. One, tall and bearded, was Walter Kreski, the Secret Service chief. The other was younger, neatly dressed and wearing a small Secret Service earphone in his ear. Charley could not recall having seen him before.

Retreating further, Dresden watched as Kreski opened one of the folding chairs and Rollins lifted Atherton to his feet and eased him into it. He put his face close to Atherton's and set a hand hard on the man's shoulder.

"This is how it's going to be, Larry," Rollins said, his voice so full of menace it caused even Kreski to look over at him. "You are vice president of the United States. You hold the second highest office in the land. You are going to go back in there and be there when the president makes his speech. You are going to serve your president and help keep this government and this country together. You are going to do everything you're told."

"As long as you do," said Kreski, "no harm will come to you."

"But he's a goddamn murderer!" Dresden said.

The younger Secret Service man stepped in front of Charley.

"Give me that pistol," he said. "Give it to me. You have no use for it now."

Dresden did so, watching as the man slipped it carefully into his belt. The man then began pushing Charley sideways, toward the slightly open door.

"Listen to me," he said, in a lowered voice. "There's only time to say this once. Go now. You have only a moment. I know who you are. You're in great danger. You were in hiding. Go back into it. Disappear. Now. Forever. Your life depends on it."

Dresden stared into the man's steady eyes. The face was expressionless, but he perceived the truth therein. Charley turned and walked away, through the doors and into the garage, limping past the many cars, past Maddy's yellow Mercedes, past the people who were beginning to gather at the garage's entrance, on into the dark and cold of the Washington winter night.

The ambassador was waiting beneath the porte cochere on the front step of his residence when Dresden arrived in "the British car"—a Land Rover with two embassy security men in it. They had driven, careening in zigzag fashion through side streets in a frantic effort to get clear of the area, reaching the embassy in twice the normal time. Maddy had not been with them. The men had no idea what had happened to her and refused Dresden's demands to find out.

"Where's Maddy?" he said to Hyde-Milne as he thrust himself out of the car. "These two bastards don't seem to know."

The ambassador put his arm around him, as though shielding him from some danger, and they started up the stairs. "Don't be so harsh on these chaps. They know only what they've been told. She's in her room, packing, which you'll have to do yourself, and soon. Thompson managed to get her out of the Capitol, but only just. It took some doing."

"I couldn't follow the State of the Union address. The car radio wasn't working right. There was static and some confusion, and then the speaker of the House came on, rambling about Nicaragua and Central America."

"That *was* the State of the Union address, dear boy. Rather than attempt to explain it all, I'll put you in front of a television set. Llewellyn's taped everything. I'll also get you a drink. Then you have to pack. We must get you out of the country tonight. I don't know where yet. It doesn't matter. The important thing is to get you under the permanent protection of the British Crown. It's likely you're going to have to become His Majesty's subjects, I think."

"I don't understand. They have the vice president in custody. What more do they want?"

"You'll understand better once you've seen the tape. There's Llewellyn now. He probably has it all set up for you."

The tape began with the usual wide shot of the House chambers. Except for the huge screen, everything looked perfectly normal, like a dozen State of the Union addresses before it, until one noticed that the vice president was missing. The speaker was standing and looking off in the direction in which Atherton had fled. The broadcast had apparently begun just after Maddy's appearance at the railing.

Finally, Tom Brokaw appeared on the screen, with the House floor projected in the background behind him. After describing the incident of the vice president's panic in detail, including a reference to a mysterious "lady in blue," he began talking with White House reporter Chris Wallace about that afternoon's developments in the La Puño investigation, asking if Wallace thought all the events were related. Their conversation was scarcely underway when it was interrupted by a flurry of activity on the House floor that soon developed into confusion so noisy that the speaker was compelled to pound his gavel with great violence. The vice president was returning. He entered from the rear corridor behind the speaker's rostrum, Senator Rollins and Walter Kreski to either side of him. They put him in his seat beside the speaker as they might a child and then walked away. He sat without looking after them, without moving at all. His eyes stared straight ahead. He seemed in a trance, almost mindless.

A hesitant silence followed, enforced by stern looks from the speaker. Then chaos abruptly returned, with everyone rising and straining to see the House doorkeeper. The camera zoomed in on the man as he leaned over his microphone and announced: "Mr. Speaker, the president of the United States!"

There was more silence, a general reaction of shock and stunned surprise, and then there was a great shouting and an explosion of applause and cheers as Henry Hampton, escorted by his chief of staff, Irving Ambrose; his wife, Daisy; Surgeon General Potter; and a number of senators, congressmen, and Secret Service agents, came slowly down the aisle in a wheelchair. He gave a few weak smiles and raised his right hand slightly once or twice in recognition of friends, but mostly the president looked ahead to the rostrum.

Dresden was on his feet himself, standing close to the television screen and gulping his whiskey as he watched them lift the president into an elevated chair rigged behind the lectern. Hampton waited for the applause and cheering to abate. When it didn't after several minutes he looked back, with some difficulty, at the speaker, who brought his gavel crashing down.

After that, the mewing of a cat could have been heard in the great hall. So might the scratch of a pen, but Hampton's was not audible as he began to write on a large, brightly lit pad of paper before him. Each word was magnified by lenses and projected hugely on the great screen above the rostrum. If oversized, it was a simple device, that magnifier, one used in high school and college classes every day.

"Ladies and gentlemen," the president wrote, with some difficulty. "Thank you for your warm welcome. I am very glad to be alive."

The quiet was interrupted by more thunderous applause, which he halted with a strained gesture of his hand. His left arm hung limply at his side.

"I was badly wounded in the attack at Gettysburg," his pen continued. "One bullet caused damage to my spine, and my legs and left arm are paralyzed. The other bullet has temporarily deprived me of my voice."

The pages of writing paper fell to the floor as he finished with them, Senator Rollins reaching to recover them.

"I am sorry it was necessary to keep these facts from you until certain important negotiations were concluded," the president wrote. "I am thankful to Vice President Atherton and so many others for keeping the government going in my absence."

There was a brief scattering of talking, but it trailed off. Most of his audience was rapt, intent on his next written word.

"I have prepared a speech. I am going to ask the speaker of the House to read each page to you, so that all of my remarks will be perfectly understood."

"Ladies and gentlemen," the speaker began after the first page was handed to him. "The conflict in Central America is over. . . ."

Dresden sank back in a chair, his mind swimming with the magnitude of his defeat. When the president had been wheeled into the House chamber, Charley had actually felt elation, the same spiritual lift doubtless shared by everyone there in the Congress and in homes throughout the country. The president lived. The United States of America continued, its institutions and foundations essentially intact and unaltered. Those who had attempted such wrenching, catastrophic damage to the American system had failed utterly and awesomely. They had rendered themselves broken, pitiful remnants of their grandiose ambitions, to be remembered by history only as fools and madmen, if at all.

But Charley Dresden would have to be numbered among them. He had been propelled by as monumental an ego into as great a folly. He had been colossally sure of himself and he had been colossally wrong.

He had *believed* what he and Tracy Bakersfield had seen on the television screen. He had woven of that electronic woof and warp an image of his own making—not a reflection of the stark reality comprehended by millions but of the truth as he had wished to see it. Charles August Dresden, a man so full of himself he would stand up to all the world to prove himself right, had been spectacularly in error. He had played Jesuit scholar to an incorrect premise. The pulsing globules of bright color that he and Tracy had made dance slowly across his videotape projection had indeed been blood, certifiable blood, but they had not been death. They were evidence only of Charley's monstrous arrogance.

How could he have been so wrong? He couldn't blame Tracy. He had bullied her with his insistence, exploited her reflexive and long-standing indulgence of him. He had dominated their lonely little investigation as he had tried to dominate every aspect of their relationship, of all his relationships. Tracy had not wanted to doubt him.

Because she had not doubted him, she had disappeared. She was now in hiding or held prisoner or dead, just as Charlene and Danny Hill and George Calendiari were dead. Just as he and Maddy were as good as dead, two lost and redundant beings with no place left to them on the planet, left to them in life. Because of him, the president's desperate, dangerous gambit had almost been thwarted. He was no help to Hampton's people now. He was a hindrance, a threat to the new deceit they had arranged in the name of the country's security and stability. He knew all. He knew what the vice president had done. A word from him in the right place, to the right person in the news media—another clumsy, manic crusade for public attention—could undo everything the president's men had done, could throw the country into a turmoil from which it might not this time recover.

He had brought all this on for no reason but his own vanity—a barroom crank who would not leave well enough alone, who would now pay the inexorably demanded price. They would have to remove every trace of themselves, for no trace of them was now desired—or to be permitted.

The ambassador appeared at the door.

"I'm not sure I want to go," Charley said.

"Mr. Dresden. The time has come for you to do what you're told."

EPILOGUE

The reward for submission, no matter how much it might represent defeat and failure, can be bountiful. That truth is the basis of many religions, and all governments.

His work for the day done, Charley met Maddy for dinner at a favorite restaurant, a small, second-story place just up from Trimingham's department store on Front Street, Hamilton's principal thoroughfare. The menu was limited, but the pepper-pot soup was famous throughout Bermuda and the tables on the veranda overlooked the harbor and the ferry dock. It was May, and the daylight now lingered brightly into the evening. The afternoon showers had cleared the skies, and they were much the color of Maddy's eyes. The waters of the Great Sound and Granaway Deep beyond were almost the same blue. It had been a cool day, but the wind had shifted to the south and the breeze was warm, bringing the hint and scent of the approaching summer.

The waiters hovered attentively nearby, having little to do. Tourist travel had not quite recovered from the terrorism scares of the winter and customers were few. The restaurant staff would have lingered near Maddy in any case, as she had become a great favorite in Hamilton. Even Charley found himself treated as a personage.

Maddy was dressed for the season, in a soft white dress with matching shoes and hair ribbon, an unbroken habit. In local fashion, Dresden wore shorts and knee socks with jacket and tie. Both he and Maddy were very tan, though they had been there just four months and the weather that spring had been somewhat rainy. Dresden was now managing director of the company that ran both of Bermuda's small television stations, but he had not yet adjusted to the slow pace of island life. Often, he had entire afternoons free, which he spent in the sun with Maddy, or indulging his new-found passion for small boat sailing.

He looked down at his bare knees and highly polished loafers. A year before, the hour would have found him in the Tiburcio Saloon and Grocery, rolling dice with men in plaid work shirts for drinks.

"You're lost in the past again," she said, idly stirring her drink with a straw.

"Yes. You've caught me."

"You promised not to do that."

"I try, but sometimes it's unavoidable."

She paused, staring past his shoulder. "I won't quarrel with you on that point," she said, finally. "Guess who's coming up the street, having just parked his Cadillac Cimmaron?"

"Not King Charles."

"Definitely *not* King Charles. Though he tries."

"Perhaps he won't see us."

"He sees us all right. The way he's hurrying this way, I think he knew we were here."

"Well, Maddy, it had to happen sooner or later."

"The same can be said about death."

They had seen David Callister several times on Bermuda, the occasions including a large reception at Government House the week before, but had each time avoided an encounter. Now the man seemed bent on one. They had only themselves to blame. Hyde-Milne had offered them any place in what remained of the British Empire, though suggesting they decline the Falkland Islands. They had chosen Bermuda, despite knowing full well that Callister had a house there. As the ambassador had said, it didn't really matter where they went, as long as it was British. Their safety, such as it was, lay in nationality, not geography. Through a discreet act of Parliament, both had become British subjects.

Callister had seemed to respect that; there'd been no harassment. But now he was upon them.

"Good evening," he said, striding briskly onto the veranda. "Please pardon the intrusion, but I wonder if I might join you."

There were at least eight empty tables on the veranda. Dresden glanced at them. "It must be nice having your own network of informants," he said, finally. "You don't have to telephone around to find out where people are."

"Do be civil, Dresden," said Callister, pulling up a chair. "I'm trying to be, and it isn't easy for a man so traduced. I had to have plastic surgery done on my lip after you attacked me. Not to dwell prosily on the subject, but I think I owe you a punch in the nose."

"Not here, please. Someone might fall over the railing, and I've developed an aversion to corpses."

Maddy turned away.

"So have I, Dresden," said Callister. "Try to get along, will you? We're going to have to, you know. I'm going to be American consul here."

"Oh, goody."

Maddy stood up. "I'm not really hungry, Charley. I'm going to go on home. Good night, Mr. Callister. Perhaps we shall meet again sometime."

He started to rise, but by the time he was on his feet, she was gone. Seating himself again, he looked solemnly at Charley.

"I bring you news, Dresden. Important news."

"The president's disappeared again."

Callister hesitated. "Not quite. We'll discuss that in a moment. This concerns you, Mr. Dresden."

He'd been carrying a rolled-up newspaper. He unfurled it, straightened the creases, then passed it to Charley. It was a very recent issue of the Santa Linda *Press-Journal*.

"Page three, upper right-hand corner. This just came in. Washington sent it on an afternoon plane."

Dresden opened the paper to the page indicated and was startled by the headline. He gazed at it for a long moment, then began to read. He read the story twice.

"This clears up some misunderstandings we may have had about you," Callister said. "I hope it clears up whatever misunderstandings you may have had about us. To further that end, I jotted a little something in the margin there."

Dresden turned the paper slightly sideways, and held it close. There was a name and telephone number. He recognized the area code. It was for Vancouver, British Columbia.

"Thank you," he said.

"She's been perfectly safe, and so have you. We could have had you extradited, you know, on the murder charges. But it never entered our minds."

"I won't ask what did enter your minds."

"You're not going to be civil after all."

"Of course I am. One Westchester man to another. What other news do you bring? All I know is what I hear on my television, and I try to make them keep Washington news to a minimum."

"I'll give you an exclusive, knowing I can trust your discretion. You asked if President Hampton had disappeared. He's going to retire. He's not going to seek election to another term."

"That will put an end to all the wheelchair jokes."

"Vice President Rollins is going to seek the presidential nomination."

"Who's going to be his running mate? Laurence Atherton again? Or are you going to make him ambassador to the United Nations?"

"Mr. Atherton is still in St. Elizabeth's Hospital. I'm afraid the commitment remains indefinite. He doesn't recognize anyone anymore."

"Really? I must try to visit him sometime. Who's it going to be then, Senator Dubarry?"

"Mr. Rollins's choice, presuming he gets the nomination, is his friend Senator Moses Goode."

"Serendipity."

"What's depressing is that the public seems so indifferent. We took a rather comprehensive poll—nationwide sample, more than five thousand people interviewed. Andrew Rollins was by far the favored candidate, but he trailed 'no opinion' by almost twenty percentage points."

"The public is tired of having to learn new names."

"Stop it, Dresden. All that is over. Attorney General Kreski has declared the case closed. Everything's been laid to rest with Steven Copley's body."

"What about the others in the plot?"

"Except for the vice president, they're all believed to be dead."

"'Known to be dead.' I note some awful misfortunes have befallen some people on the vice president's staff, and in the FBI. Car crashes, boating accidents, a couple of suicides."

"Fate is often just, Mr. Dresden. Learn to be satisfied with that." He paused. "I thought you didn't follow the Washington news."

"A joke. We also follow the international news. Shooting has broken out in Central America again, I see. It's our lead story tonight."

"It's under control. The Russians are staying out of it, and we've kept American troop involvement to a minimum."

"Admirable restraint."

"I trust we can count on the same from you."

"I'm a British subject, sir, running a couple of small-time television stations on a faraway island."

Neither said anything for a while. There was a great deal of bustling and noise down by the quay, where one of the cruise liners was preparing to get underway. Dresden watched it, or pretended to.

"What will you do?" Callister asked. "Do you want to go back to California?"

"At the moment, that's not exactly for me to decide."

"British citizenship agrees with you."

"Quite."

"Mrs. Calendiari is now quite wealthy."

"'There is no wealth but life,'" Charley said.

The cruise liner was a beautiful ship, all white except for its raked, blue and red funnel. After the cruise season was over it would be sailing around the world, to so many places Dresden had not been, to other islands.

"Callister, I'm not exactly one of your greatest admirers, but I've finally learned to take life as I find it." He signaled to a waiter. "I'm going to make a long-distance telephone call now. In the meantime, let me buy you a drink."

It was nearly dark when Callister dropped Dresden off at his place on South Road on the other side of the island from Hamilton. The house, which they rented from the British government, was on a slope of Cobbs Hill, overlooking the sea. He guessed that he would not find Maddy inside, and was correct. She was seated on their favorite rock, beside the path that led from their terrace to a little beach.

She had changed into shorts and a crisp white shirt, but still had on the hair ribbon. She was barefoot, and her long legs were dark in the twilight.

"Are you still angry?" he said, standing beside her.

"I wasn't angry," she replied, without looking up. "Things were getting unpleasant, that's all. I wasn't in much of a mood for a scene."

Bermuda was essentially extinct volcano and coral reef, and there was a scarcity of pebbles. Dresden yearned for one to toss into the light surf below. He sat down on the rock, but kept his distance from her.

"Callister brought some news," he said.

"Good news or bad?"

"You'll have to tell me. The police in Santa Linda have arrested the people who murdered Charlene and Danny Hill. There were two of them, the brothers of Danny's ex-wife. They'd gotten drunk and into some bad drugs and came down to beat him up. They followed him to my house and apparently went out of control. When Zack woke up and tried to fight them off they panicked and shot her. Anyway, that's what the police are saying. They even held a press conference. The sister turned them in. They confessed. The case is closed."

"Do you believe them?"

He waited until a wave had broken against the shoreline below before answering.

"Yes, though I've good reason for not wanting to."

"You think that if you had called the police in the first place as an ordinary person would have, everything would have been cleared up and you would never have had to leave Tiburcio."

"Yes."

"And you would never have come to me in Washington and none of what came afterward would have happened."

"Yes. And George Calendiari would still be alive. A lot of people would still be alive."

She moved closer to him, their shoulders touching as she reached out and took his hand.

"You mustn't think that, Charley. We don't know what would have happened."

"Callister gave me a number where I could reach Tracy Bakersfield. They made a point of finding her for me."

"Why?"

"Ostensibly to show that all is forgiven. Also, I think, to remind me of the things they can do if they put their minds to it, if I give them cause."

"Where is she?"

"In Canada. She took me at my word, like she always has. To her regret, sometimes. She took a leave from the college the day after I called and went up to British Columbia. She has a friend up there.

She's been there ever since, waiting for me to tell her it's all right. Her husband must really hate my guts."

"Did you call her?"

"Yes. We had a long talk."

"And?"

"I told her how much she was loved and that she was foolish to ever listen to me about anything and to go home. At once."

"Now you can go home."

"I'm not sure. The British seem to consider us substantial diplomatic assets, what with all we could help them prove, if need be." He put his arm around her, drawing her near. He could feel the warmth of her flesh beneath the thin material of her shirt. "Maddy, do you want to go home? Back to California? To Washington?"

"No. Not now. I've thought about it. I was scared to discover how much George meant to me. How much he still means. How much hatred and sadness I still feel, all mixed up together. No, I couldn't go back there, to the surviving ruins, to the things we had together."

There were the lights of a ship visible beyond the reef, riding high near the horizon. If it was the one from the quay, it had left the Great Sound and had rounded Commissioner's Point and Ireland Island and now was making for the south, probably Puerto Rico.

"Charley?"

"Yes?"

"Do you want to go back, back to your canyon and your saloon and your house on the mountainside?"

"I've thought about it too. I can't travel through time, Maddy." She shifted herself so her head rested in his lap.

"You want to stay here then, on this little island?"

"Tiburcio was an island. The Washington you lived in was an island. I'm content here. In a way, it's the sort of life I felt I might have had if all those miserable things hadn't happened to my father."

"You're much at peace. It becomes you."

"Anyway, we're shortly to have company. Our friend Hyde-Milne is to be the new governor here. Callister told me. I think it has something to do with his being made American consul. Or vice versa. Nations send messages to each other this way. They speak in gestures. Words mean nothing."

"I lie here, looking up at the stars, and wonder if there's some satellite camera looking back. I hear the waves, and wonder if someone's listening along with me, through some hidden microphone."

"We're just two little people, Maddy. If we're careful, they'll leave us alone, by and by."

"Do you really believe that?"

"Yes. I believe that." He wondered if he really did.

"When I used to think back on our first times together," she said, "I always remembered you driving off in a small, open car, alone in the night. Into mournful nights of mordant truths, you used to say. You used to write me about the bleak, stark beauty of our mortality. 'Beauty is the scent of roses, and the death of roses.'"

"The mournful nights are all out there," he said, nodding to the far, dark line of sea. "Not here."

"I love you, Charles Dresden. That much has survived what we went through. Maybe it's all that has."

"Is that why you didn't run away that night during the State of the Union address? You've never really told me."

"I'm still not sure why. You were part of it. George was part. The country's troubles were part. Mostly I wanted to move on to the rest of my life, my next life. It seemed the only way. I wasn't being brave. I was just desperate."

He stroked her cheek gently with his fingertips. Her heart was beating quite calmly. He would keep it so.

"I once sat on a little cliff like this one night in California with Tracy Bakersfield," he said. "It was near Capitola. A warm night like this, with a breeze blowing. I fetched a wild flower for her from a crevice. I remember it all exactly."

"But all you did was bring her a flower."

"That's all."

"There should be more to such a night than a little flower."

"I've thought that for many a night now."

"I'm the marrying kind, Charley. If you're to have your way with me again, it will have to be as man and wife."

They gazed into each other's eyes awhile, then he kissed her. When he looked out to sea again the ship was gone. She sat up, and leaned against his chest, her head on his shoulder.

"I don't know how the British get married," he said.

"I'm sure it's quite romantic. A little piety, a little poetry."

He cleared his throat, and recited:

She tenderly kissed me,
She fondly caressed,
And then I fell gently

To sleep on her breast—
From the heaven of her breast.

When the light was extinguished,
She covered me warm,
And she prayed to the angels
To keep me from harm—
To the queen of the angels
To shield me from harm.

"And what English poet is that?" she asked.
"Not English, but the best I know."
"The gloomy Mr. Poe again."
"Oh, not so gloomy."

But my heart it is brighter,
Than all of the many
Stars of the sky,
For it sparkles with Annie—
It glows with the light
Of the love of my Annie—

She pulled away from him in mock anger, a sweet laughter in her eyes. "But my name isn't Annie."

It glows with the light
Of the love of my Maddy—
With the thought of the light
Of the eyes of my Maddy.

Maddy had been wrong. Happy endings were not all to be asked of life. He rose and pulled her up after him. Arm in arm, they started up to the house, and to all that was yet to be.

About the Author

Michael Kilian was born in 1939 and grew up in the Midwest and in New York's Westchester County. He is a Washington columnist for the *Chicago Tribune*, and the author of seven other books. He, his wife, Pamela, and their two sons, Eric and Colin, live in McLean, Virginia.